# THE HAVOC

# OF CHOICE

## WANJIRU KOINANGE

**JACARANDA**

First published in Great Britain 2019 by
Jacaranda Books Art Music Ltd
27 Old Gloucester Street,
London WC1N 3AX
www.jacarandabooksartmusic.co.uk

The right of Wanjiru Koinange to be identified as the author of
this work has been asserted by her in accordance with the
Copyright, Designs and Patents Act 1988.

A CIP catalogue record for this book is available from the
British Library

ISBN: 9781909762831
eISBN: 9781909762848

Cover Design: Christina Schweighardt
Typeset by Kamillah Brandes
Printed and bound by CPI Group (UK) Ltd, Croydon CR0 4YY

*For my father who made me start this book,*
*For my mother who made sure I finished it,*
*And for Christine who named it.*

We fail to trust that we knew ourselves to be possible from the very beginning.

—Binyavanga Wainaina
(1971-2019)

# 1

# VANILLA ICE CREAM

## 23 DECEMBER 2007

Kavata had trouble focusing on the sermon that Sunday. She kept reminding herself she was doing the right thing. Each time she felt doubt, she would slide her fingers into her handbag, feeling the side-pocket to ensure the envelope was still there. Her mind went over every detail, then, satisfied she had seen to every aspect of her plan, forced herself to pay attention to Pastor Simon. She would need something to talk about over lunch.

'Pastor Simon, what a powerful sermon, and so well researched,' Ngugi said. 'Thank you.'

The two men shook hands as their wives embraced.

'Yes, pastor! Truly *truly* inspiring.' Kavata kissed the air around Grace's cheeks and complimented her on her lovely hat. They seemed to get larger each Sunday.

'Ngugi! Kavata! Thank you! From your lips to the Lord's ears.' When the pastor spoke, he often chuckled as if he had cracked a joke only he heard.

'Please join us for lunch today. We won't accept no for an answer. Besides, it's the least we can do after those wonderful words. Isn't it darling?' Kavata channelled her most dazzling smile and glanced over at Ngugi who caught her eye with a flash of irritation before turning back to the pastor with a smile out-dazzling Kavata's by far. She knew he intended to play golf, but this was important and he had to make sacrifices. She also knew Ngugi would never say no to Pastor Simon.

Ngugi didn't miss a beat. 'Yes, do come over. I want to hear how those plans for the new sanctuary in Westlands are going. I've been meaning to make an anonymous donation, but have been too busy to go over the paperwork.'

'That's understandable. Things must be quite crazy at the moment. How is the campaign going? *Si*, these are the final days?' Grace said, pretending to be the only person in the country who was not keeping up with the coming election on a minute to minute basis. She had a reputation for weaselling her way into the congregants' homes. This was something she justified to those who dared to ask by saying that for years she had given up the luxury of sleeping in on Sunday mornings—this was payback. When the church elders proposed the pastoral teams only visit the homes of congregants who formally registered as members of the church, Grace was the first to oppose it. Less than a third of the congregation were registered members. And most of them went to the first service! But the law passed and now lunch invitations were a rarity. So Grace praisefully accepted Kavata's invitation.

Kavata spotted her daughter Wanja guiding her brother Amani towards them. She took in her daughter's appearance. It still shocked her that she raised such a stunning daughter. People often said Wanja had taken after her mother completely, but Kavata couldn't remember ever being as poised and graceful as Wanja was. Sometimes, she caught herself copying Wanja's mannerisms or wondering what her daughter would think of the shade of polish on her toenails. She was grateful Wanja still joined them for Sunday service. They saw less and less of Wanja since she had gotten into university and realised she could have an entire life of her own. Wanja greeted the pastor and his wife dispassionately and waited for the attention to move on to her little brother before she could ask her father for the car keys and escape the religious small talk.

'Actually, let's all just go. We can continue this conversation at home.' Ngugi reached into his pocket for the car keys and tossed them to Wanja. He liked to make a spectacle of these moments when he showed off his daughter. When she was younger, he would insist their dinner guests listen to her read the newspaper instead of watching the 7 PM news. He would beam and raise his whisky glass to her when she floated over words like *constituency* and *parliamentary*. When she turned twelve, he looked forward to their trips to the gun range because she would be the only child there. He taught her to drive well before she was old enough to attend driving school, and when she did eventually enrol, she was the only girl who signed up for the defensive driving classes.

'*Heh*, you are so blessed to have someone take the burden of the roads off your hands,' Grace chirped as Wanja caught the keys and smiled at her dad.

'They say if you can drive in Nairobi, you can drive anywhere in the world.' Kavata smiled and stroked Wanja's arm.

'*Ala*, is this my blouse?' Kavata asked, pretending that she hadn't noticed her *ankara* piece earlier that morning. She just wanted Grace to know she owned garments that appealed to twenty-somethings.

Wanja rolled her eyes. 'You don't wear it, and it looks better on me.'

'How would you know if I wear it, and when did you even take it?'

'If you wore it often, you'd have noticed it missing sooner,' Wanja said before she excused herself and sauntered away, no stranger to her mother's antics but happy to play her role in the performance.

'Let me ever catch you wearing my clothes?' Ngugi said to Amani as he lifted him up and threw him over his shoulder to the little boy's extreme delight.

'Ok then, we will head home and get lunch started,' Kavata said.

'Good, we will be there in about half an hour.' Pastor Simon rubbed his belly and scanned the crowd for his next conversation.

Kavata followed her family out of the church gates. The pieces of her plan were falling into place.

Nairobi on that Sunday was an experience best savoured with all senses.

It was an explosion of colour as families clad in their bright Sunday best rode in polished cars and buffed *matatus,* making their way out of their respective sanctuaries or to their relatives' residences. Hawkers who didn't care for the Sabbath stood at the traffic lights displaying their attractive treats: sugar cane, groundnuts, fruits, and newspapers to hungry commuters.

It was the smell of fresh laundry, talcum powder and whatever *Eau de Toilette* was on offer at Tuskys Supermarket.

It was the taste of quarter chicken and chips, roasted maize, stale alcohol and the bad decisions of the previous night.

It was the sound of children splashing away at the public swimming pools; excited parents rowing boats at Uhuru Park; live jam sessions on lawns, parks, secret gardens and forests; gospel music in the morning, jazz at brunch, reggae in the afternoon and golden oldies that matched the sunset. It felt like the gods had rewarded hard-working Nairobians with a few extra stress-free hours on Sunday as a respite from city-living the other six days of the week.

Ngugi's car, however, was a silent war zone. He was swollen with irritation and Kavata could feel it in the space between them, pushing against her as Wanja navigated through the light traffic. Amani's high-pitched voice offered an animated recap of what he learned at Sunday school. He studied the picture of Jesus feeding the five thousand that he was given in class and wondered out loud how long it must have taken him to divide two fish and five loaves amongst all those people. Amani's declaration that his Sunday school teacher must have been lying to them broke the tension in the car and they all broke into laughter.

'This lunch must be a brief affair. I tee off at three,' Ngugi sulked, and Kavata felt a tiny bit bad for him. She knew he needed to let loose after the pressures of the last few months, but he had left her little choice. She reached out and patted him on the thigh. It was a distant yet familiar gesture, reminding them both how long it had been since they shared any kind of intimate contact.

Kavata loved their home in Nyari, especially the way the house emerged almost out of thin air at the sharp turn to Red Hill Road. Their neighbours' well-manicured live fences offered a lush green boulevard on each side of the tarmac as they continued up the road to their house. Greenery was under threat in Nairobi until Wangari Maathai encouraged people to plant trees wherever they could. With time, the air in the cities and the suburbs became a few degrees cooler. When the family got home, Thuo opened the gate and let them in, waving as they drove past him.

'I didn't know Thuo would be working today,' Ngugi said. Kavata gasped silently. She hadn't counted on Thuo being early.

'Neither did I,' she said, grateful Ngugi wasn't looking at her. 'It's just as well—he can drive you to the club later.' Ngugi was out of the car before she finished her sentence.

The air was light and lovely, as was the conversation. Kavata served passion juice, cold mango and watermelon slices on the balcony before announcing lunch would be served in under an hour. She worked swiftly in the kitchen. In the oven, potatoes were roasting in garlic and rosemary on a cooking tray above a leg of *mbuzi* that had been cooking since the previous night and was now so tender a spoon could slice through it.

She stared at Ngugi through the kitchen hatch while she stirred some *dhania* into the *kachumbari*. He had changed out of a stiff African shirt into a pastel yellow polo she bought him years ago when he'd started playing golf. He'd been hesitant about the soft colour at first, but all the compliments from his fellow golfer mates changed that. Now he wore it so often, she sometimes hid it away for its own sake. He looked so frustrated, she thought and wondered if their guests could also see how much Ngugi longed to be elsewhere.

Her resolve weakened, but she reminded herself, for the hundredth time, that she had thought about this too long and hard to abandon ship now.

She drizzled lemon juice on the *kachumbari*, dried her

hands, dabbed the corner of her left eye with a kitchen towel and strode back out to the balcony.

As she replenished the tray of fruit on the table next to her guests, Kavata announced, 'Please excuse me. I need to make a quick trip to the supermarket. We need something cold to go with the lovely lemon sponge cake Schola baked yesterday. I'll be back just now.' Her voice quivered a tad.

Grace lodged a half-hearted protest. 'Oh, I hope we are not *too* much trouble Kavata. Don't let us inconvenience you too much. But ice cream and lemon sponge cake does sound absolutely lovely.'

'Not at all, I am happy to. I will be back in no time and then we can eat!'

'I come with you?' The pastor's wife mumbled as she dramatically scanned the ground around her feet for her handbag. Kavata panicked and was just about to object when both their husbands stepped in.

'Ah ah, please no,' Ngugi's hand shot up.

'If the two of you go into a supermarket, it will be midnight before we see our meal, and me I can smell some *mbuzi bwana*,' the pastor interjected and everyone laughed. Kavata smiled, turned around and walked away before another word was spoken.

'*Twende*!' Outside, her voice shook as she barked the order at Thuo who sprung off his seat and folded up the newspaper he was reading. She spotted Amani running after her and cursed under her breath.

'Mummy, where are you going?'

'To Nakumatt.'

'Can I come?'

'No, I'm coming back just now. Go entertain the visitors.'

'But those are your friends. Not mine.'

'Amani! Go back inside.'

'Pleeeaase. What are you going to buy?'

'No baba, I'm only going for some ice-cream and if you keep fussing I will come back with *maziwa mala* instead. I'll be back just now.' Kavata slammed the door shut and watched him sulk as he retreated into the house.

*Just like his father,* she thought.

It was only when the car came to a halt at the entrance of the supermarket that Kavata realised she didn't tell Thuo of their actual destination. She decided to go into the supermarket anyway. She had a few minutes to spare and was grateful for the time alone to catch her breath and think things over one last time. The busy supermarket aisles gave Kavata a good distraction from her overcrowded thoughts. Something about watching shoppers go on with their normal lives, negotiating with their children over chocolate bars as husbands decided which beers to spend their afternoon with, gave Kavata the emotional distance to carry on with her plan. She emerged a few moments later, raspberry ice cream in hand, got back into the car and instructed Thuo to take her to the airport.

'Which airport, madam?'

'JKIA.'

'Madam, are we going to the JKIA *now*? *Si una wageni nyumbani?*'

'My visitors are none of your business, Thuo—just drive.' She immediately wished she could take her words back. She always liked Thuo, even if Ngugi insisted his reckless driving was the reason the cars always needed repairs. He was a kind and trustworthy man. The kind of person who would shift his personality to accommodate anything you needed him to be. It was all Kavata needed at the moment.

Thuo filled the awkward silence with updates about his family.

'Cheptoo has started a new job as a catering assistant at the secondary school in Kangemi. She is already complaining about her boss. Knowing her it is only a matter of time before she either gets promoted to head cateress or gets fired.' When he spoke of his wife, it was often with a mixture of bewilderment and admiration. Cheptoo was not one to keep her opinions to herself and this often landed her in gauche situations Thuo loved to talk about. In fact, the only thing he liked to discuss more than his wife was the upcoming election.

'And did you see the election news this morning, Mama Wanja? This one looks like it will be a hot one. *Heh*, no one can predict...'

'Thuo, seriously. How many times must I say I don't discuss these politics?'

'Sorry.' Thuo was deflated.

'And the children? How are they?' She felt bad again.

'They are well, madam.' He remained silent for the rest of the trip.

They arrived at the Jommo Kenyatta International Airport in record time. Kavata expected to see the long line of cars waiting to be checked by the police at the toll booths as was characteristic of the airport which was quickly becoming too small to handle the increasing volume of traffic it received. As they drove past the check point the policemen waved them through without stopping to search the car. *Must be a sign,* she thought.

'Aah, we are lucky today. There are not many cars.' Thuo eased the car into a parking spot right in front of the arrivals terminal.

'Yes, we are. Please move the car and park near departures,' Kavata instructed. Deep creases appeared on Thuo's forehead, but he asked no questions. Kavata took a deep breath, stepped out of the car and walked round to Thuo's window.

'So now. Take the car back home. When *Mzee* asks you where I am, tell him you took me to Mrs. Agallo's house and waited for me for a few minutes, before I asked you to go back home. Mrs. Agallo will bring me home later.'

'*Ala*! Mama Wanja, *kwani kuna nini*?' Thuo asked. Kavata had never heard him be more sincere and she knew the only way to protect the kind man was to lie to him.

'I am expecting an important package for *Mzee*. It is a surprise so he mustn't know I am here. Please take the car back home and then you may take the rest of the day off.' She slipped five hundred shillings into his hand, '*Shika* bus fare.'

'Madam, I can wait for you, I don't need my off day. This is a short week anyway.'

'Thuo, please do as I say. Hurry back before *Mzee* starts calling. I will see you tomorrow.' Kavata spun around and marched towards the terminal. She felt his gaze on her back and hoped her legs didn't look as wobbly as they felt. When she was at a safe distance, she looked back to check if he was gone and then she leaned against a wall and allowed herself to unravel a little. She let out a sigh so full and desperate it left her a little light-headed.

The terminals were busier than the roads suggested they would be. Vans, filled with relatives who travelled for hours to escort their loved ones, dropped passengers off at the terminals. Parking marshals patrolled the area looking for drivers who were hovering around, trying to avoid paying the exorbitant parking fees. A young couple engaged in a teary embrace until an unconcerned security official asked them why they were crying as if someone was going off to war.

'You should be celebrating when they are going and crying when they come back,' the guard said as she shoved family members out of the queue intended for travellers only.

Inside the terminal, Kavata got to the front of the line, pulled the envelope out of her bag and handed her ticket over. The uniformed woman at the counter didn't bother to look up from her screen.

'How many bags are you checking in?'

'None.' The woman looked up, her pencilled-in eyebrows raised.

'Passport.' Kavata threw the booklet onto the counter. Nothing irritated her more than poor service. The only thing saving this woman from a serious tongue lashing was the fact that Kavata was hoping to slide out of the country as discreetly as possible.

The woman sneered as she flipped through the pages of Kavata's passport.

'Where is your visa?'

Kavata remained silent, determined not to lose her cool. She was suddenly exhausted; the farce she put on all morning had left her drained so she stood there with her eyes fixed on the woman's thick eyebrows as her eyes searched the page with the visa. Yvonne, her name tag gleaming in the light, looked at Kavata and then back to her screen. When she reached out for the phone on the counter and whispered something into the handset about a VIP, Kavata felt the dread she had only just gotten rid of seeping back into her gut.

'I'm sorry, Mrs. Ngugi. There are two issues with your ticket,' Yvonne said as she began to strike the keys on her keyboard frantically. Any trace of the disinterested person who served Kavata only seconds ago was gone and replaced by a humble version of the same woman.

'What?' Kavata's voice was barely audible.

'First, this is an economy ticket.'

Kavata stared back at her blankly, but inside her head, all manner of sirens were going off.

'Don't you want something... nicer?'

'No, I like my ticket as is,' she said and watched Yvonne's eyebrows again as they crept up and almost merged with her hairline.

'Is that it?'

'Um, no. The other thing is, Mrs. Ngugi, I can't check you in because you have a one-way ticket and a B1 visa.'

'I don't have a one-way ticket.'

'You have an open ticket.'

'Yes, an open ticket which I paid a full return fare to purchase. Your semantics mean nothing to me. Please check me in, it's been a long day already. Thanks.'

'You are welcome, but to the check-in system, an open ticket reads the same as a one way. I will need a return date, Mrs. Ngugi.'

'I don't have one.'

'Then I can't check you in. The system won't print your boarding pass without a return date. Immigration policy.'

'June 2nd.' It was the first date that came to mind. Ngugi's birthday.

'Next year?'

'Yes.' Yvonne's fingers assaulted the keyboard once again.

'Travelling to Atlanta, Georgia?'

'What does my ticket say, Yvonne?' Kavata leaned forward.

'My sincere apologies for the delay, Mrs. Ngugi. Your flight will be boarding from gate sixteen at 1525hrs. I have corrected it and upgraded you to business class.' She pointed to a man who Kavata hadn't noticed standing next to her. 'Simon here will escort you through immigration to the VIP lounge, and will come alert you when it is time to board. Thank you for choosing to fly Virgin Airways and enjoy your trip.' Yvonne stood cupping her elbow in the palm of her hand as she handed Kavata her passport and boarding pass.

'I don't want...' Kavata began to object to the upgrade until she realised she would probably be the only person in the history of this airport to reject an upgrade. And doing so would give Yvonne fodder for the rumour mill. So, she smiled her most tight-lipped smile and followed her guide to the front of the immigration line, ignoring the dirty looks from the disgruntled travellers who sneered at her preferential treatment.

She was, thankfully, the only passenger in the lounge. She sat in a corner on one of the dated leather armchairs and pulled out her cellphone. Thuo would be home soon so she expected Ngugi to call her at any moment. She scrolled through her phone book and dialled Anne, who answered the call on the first ring.

'Hey.'

'Hey.'

They shared a loaded silence. Both women understood this was Kavata's last opportunity to change her mind and go back home. They both secretly wished she would.

'Is it done?'

'Yeah. I'm at the airport now.'

'Jesus Christ, Kavata I have been so stressed. I've smoked two packs already.'

Kavata felt the sting of tears fighting to be free. She knew this was difficult for her dear friend, and was still at a loss for ways to express her gratitude to her.

'Did everything go ok?' Anne asked.

'Yes. All as planned. He hasn't tried to call me yet. But Thuo will be back home any minute now.'

'Ok, let me turn my phone off for the afternoon.'

'Thanks for everything. I will call you once I get there.'

Then, with trembling fingers, Kavata opened the back of her phone, took out the SIM card and tossed it into the bin.

As she waited for her boarding announcement, the only thing she could think was that she bought raspberry-flavoured ice-cream. Amani was expecting vanilla. He would never forgive her.

\*\*\*

'I can't imagine what could be taking so long. It's been almost an hour, right?'

'Yes, it has. Forty-nine minutes if I can be exact,' Pastor Simon offered, and Grace placed her hand on his lap. Her husband was the most irritable when he was hungry, and she could see his demon begin to emerge.

'Is her phone still off?' Grace asked. Ngugi tried her again and slid his phone back into his trouser pocket.

'Yes, it is. She must have forgotten to switch it on after church.'

'What did she say she was going to buy again?' Grace asked

'Dessert. Which is a shame—it's not even the most

important part of the meal.'

'Ah, this is a classic case similar to the one that is described in the parable about gluttony where...'

'Yes, I am sure it is, pastor, but we are yet to properly thank you for the sermon that you already blessed us with this morning. Let me get the children to set up the table for lunch. I'm sure Kavata would prefer to find things going so we can eat as soon as she comes. I don't think she will be much longer.'

The family had just sat down to a very silent lunch sans Kavata when Amani heard a car in the driveway.

'It's Mom!' He shot out of his seat towards the door.

'Be seated, Amani!' Ngugi snapped, then checked himself. 'I'm sure your mother can find her way to the table.'

Amani slunk back into his seat with his entire body still turned to face the direction his mother was poised to emerge from. But all that came was a timid knock on the door. Ngugi glanced over at Wanja.

'Excuse, I'll go check.'

'No. Me, I want to go check also.'

'Amani, sit.'

'Eat your food, little one. Or you will have to be tied to this chair until your plate is completely clear,' Grace said as her husband happily shoved a chunk of tender *mbuzi* into his mouth.

Wanja returned shortly with the keys to her mother's car in her hand. She placed them next to her father and sat down.

'Is everything alright?' Grace asked when it was clear that Wanja wasn't going to offer anything up.

'Yes—Mom is going to come later. Thuo says Auntie Anne will bring her home.' She avoided the puzzled look on her dad's face.

'What do you mean?' Ngugi asked.

'That Auntie Anne will bring Mom home later? Something must have happened. I don't know.' Wanja shrugged her shoulders.

'Is that all Thuo said? Has he left?' Ngugi didn't wait for Wanja's response. He rushed to catch up with Thuo before he left the compound. The table eavesdropped to hear if Ngugi's conversation would reveal more than Wanja had, but they didn't have to wait long for him to return.

'Well, he's said the same thing to me. It's quite odd but I'm sure she will explain everything when she eventually checks her phone. Please carry on—we've delayed you enough. I'm sure you'd like to get some rest.'

'Yes, yes, long day,' the pastor offered as he finished the food on his plate and glanced over at his wife's plate expectantly.

Minutes later, Ngugi and his family were waving the pastor and his wife goodbye. Ngugi stood at the door for a few moments longer, staring at his wife's car, trying to remember if she had mentioned anything to him that he might have missed. He strolled back into the house and mindlessly scanned the room for clues.

He thought back to the previous day—by the time he had joined her in their bedroom she was already pretending to be asleep.

'Are we going to church tomorrow?' he had asked.

'Yes,' she had responded immediately and Ngugi chuckled to himself.

She was awake and dressed by the time he woke up the next morning.

'*Kwani*, what time is it?'

Kavata rolled her eyes over at her stirring husband, lifted her handbag off the armchair next to the door, and said 'you have ten minutes—find us in the car.'

'*Ai*, why didn't you wake me?'

He couldn't remember what she had said in response. He was just about to call Wanja and ask her to clear the table when his eyes fell on the half eaten *mbuzi* leg that was still sitting at the centre of their dining table. He looked at it as if he'd never seen it before.

Kavata had served goat for lunch. Her grilled goat was a thing she took great pride in. It was a labour of love that she often started to cook for several hours, sometimes a whole day in advance. There may have been nothing impromptu about their last minute lunch guests. He began to wonder if something had actually 'come up' or if this was just another way Kavata had found to shame him. Like the way she would 'forget' that he had a campaign event at the house and give Schola the day off. Or how recently she had taken to hanging around the house longer than usual during these events, and then she'd pick the precise moment that guests began to arrive to make her exit so that it was just a little harder to justify her absence. He should have known that she was up to something the minute he smelled *mbuzi* that morning. He was seething.

Ngugi took his anger to the golf course as his children sat in front of the television trying to figure out the reason for their mother's odd behaviour.

# 2

# THE FALL GUY

## 24 DECEMBER 2007

Thuo had a confident spring in his step as he left his house the following day. He even made love to Cheptoo that morning, despite the argument they'd had about Ngugi winning the election.

'Who is going to vote for a man who can't seem to get his own wife to support him. *Aish*. And what is wrong with her anyway? How can she refuse to stand with her husband during the campaign? *Lazima kuna kitu alifanya* because if I were her I would become his second shadow.' Cheptoo glued her chest to Thuo who playfully peeled her off him and brushed her away. It had taken a few years for Thuo to assert his authority as man of the house. It didn't help that he had married a woman who was slightly larger than him, with a much bigger personality. It was the thing that he loved the most about his wife: that she was capable of taking care of herself. However, she was completely blind to situations in which she needed to let him roar. He had resorted to just telling her when to simmer down, and on most days it seemed to be work. Cheptoo's strong opinion about Kavata's choices was always the start of a fight and he wasn't going to fall for it. It was going to be a good day—he could feel it. And maybe whatever big, secret surprise Kavata had for Ngugi meant that she was finally coming around to the idea of the election. He was thinking about all the ways his life might change in just under a week, when Ngugi won.

*If Ngugi won.* Thuo reminded himself not to be too confident. Things could swing both ways—but Ngugi would win, he thought, and he made a mental note to check the final polls as soon as he got to work.

Each time he walked past a campaign poster that bore the smiling and reassuring face of his employer, he grew a little more joyful. He pictured himself wearing a nice grey suit and tie, driving a minister around as he had done several years ago when he had his short stint working for Kavata's father during his final term in office. It just so happened that Ngugi and Kavata were in need of a driver after Muli retired, and Thuo had accepted the job despite the slight pay cut. His sacrifice was finally paying off. He said a quick prayer of gratitude as he walked round the bend that led to Ngugi's residence.

'What did you do?' Schola, who was waiting for him at the gate, hissed the moment she saw his slender figure approaching the house with a blade of grass dangling from his lips. She shoved him behind a bush outside the residence gates. It took Thuo a moment to wrangle himself out of the older woman's grasp.

'Ah! *Ni nini wewe?*'

'There are police in there with *Mzee.*' She swiped the strand of grass out of his mouth and used it to point towards the house. 'Mama Wanja has not been home since yesterday and they are saying it's you who took her. What happened?

*Mama ako wapi?*'

'I don't know where she is!' Thuo raised his voice, but quickly checked himself. Although Schola wasn't old enough to be his mother, he always treated her with the same level of respect. She had worked for the Ngugis for much longer than he had, and it was mostly because of her that Thuo still had a job. Schola had witnessed several workers pass through the home but hadn't endorsed most of them. She had guided Thuo during his first months of working there and regarded him as a son. She often defended him whenever he would slip up and would convince their employers, particularly Ngugi, to give him a second chance. This was something Thuo never took for granted, despite the occasional disagreements they would have when Schola insisted on telling him how to do his job. Thuo was sure that she, of all people, would be able to see right through him if he attempted to lie to her. But he had given Kavata his word that he would not mention her whereabouts to anyone and that included Schola. His loyalties were slightly challenged, but he knew that once she was finished with whatever it was that she was planning for Ngugi, she would be back home with an explanation.

'I took her to Mrs. Agallo's house and brought the car back, then went for my off day,' he switched to Kiswahili. It was easier to tell a convincing lie in a local language. The look on her face said that he had failed to convince her. He tried again.

'They came home from church with visitors. I took her to Nakumatt then to Agallo's. She told me to bring the car back and go home and I did! If she didn't come back then me *sijui.*' The concern on his face was genuine, and Schola could see that. He started to walk towards the house when Schola held him back, grabbing the tail of his shirt and yanking it so hard that a button popped off and rolled away on the warm tarmac as if it was escaping the impending doom.

'Thuo, I hope you are speaking the truth because I have heard *Mzee* talking to the police and he is saying that you are to blame. I hope you have not put yourself in problems. I will not be able to fish you out of this one, Thuo.'

'Why would I come back here today if I had done something wrong?' he said, before he spun around and walked through the gates. Thuo didn't understand what was going on. He had done exactly as expected.

Schola followed him, watching him closely as he walked through the open gates. The sight of the Peugeot 504 with the government-issued number plates justified Schola's panic. He struggled to find his feet as he contemplated the situation and began to worry that something had actually happened to Kavata. He recalled her instructions. Had he misheard something? Schola walked past him.

'*Mzee* told me to call him when you arrive,' she said, as if she was betraying him.

Schola paused for a moment outside the living room to eavesdrop on the conversation. The man who she had earlier recognised as the Officer Commanding Police Station (OCS), of the Nyari police station, was instructing Ngugi to remain calm when Thuo arrived. The OCS was a short, stout man with a huge, bellowing voice, and a thick accent that made him mix up his L's and R's. He referred to Ngugi as *Mheshimiwa* even though he had not gotten into office yet.

Schola adjusted her blouse and straightened her skirt before she walked into the room. Two men sat opposite the OCS, digging their toes into the plush beige carpet to conceal the bare digits that popped out of their torn socks. The room was heavy with the stench of feet and bad breath and she wondered how the policemen could smell so bad so early in the morning. She usually got upset when guests failed to remove their shoes before they stepped on the carpet, but today she wished that they had kept their shoes on. It would take days to scrub that smell off the carpet.

'*Samahani. Mzee,* Thuo *ameingia.*'

Ngugi stood up before Schola finished speaking.

'And you, where were you yesterday?' Schola was staring so intently at the black toe nail protruding from one of the officer's socks that she didn't realise the OCS was speaking to her. 'Mama, I am talking to you. *Ulikuwa wapi jana?*'

'Leave her alone, she does not work on the weekends.' Ngugi was halfway out of the door.

'But *Mheshimiwa*, we must leave no stone unturned.'

'Don't waste time while the person you should be questioning is outside.' With that the three men leapt up and rushed out with their shoes barely on.

Thuo was on his feet when the four men met him outside.

'*Habari Mzee,*' he cupped his hands and bowed his head ever so slightly. 'Is there a problem?' Thuo turned towards the police car and then to the men behind Ngugi.

'Yes, Thuo, we have a big problem.' Ngugi's voice was hostile and tired. The OCS issued a silent instruction to one of his men who walked towards the gate before stepping forward to address Thuo.

'Yes, *kijana. Habari yako.*' Thuo nodded silently. He did not appreciate the OCS referring to him as a boy. He was a father of two.

'We have a small problem that we need you to help us solve,' the OCS continued, leaning his weight against the bonnet of the police car. 'But first, *jina?*'

'Joseph Thuo Maliti.' his gaze shifted from his interrogators' faces to the tyre of the car that seemed precariously close to bursting under the weight of the OCS.

'Where do you live?'

'Kangemi.'

'Are you married?'

'Yes.'

'*Na watoto*?'

'*Wawili*.'

'Inspector, how is any of this important?' Ngugi snapped before the OCS was able to ask his next question.

'Mr. Mwangi, we talked about this. Please allow us to do our jobs to the full extent of the law. We must know what kind of person we are dealing with.' As the OCS spoke, Thuo took this opportunity to look behind him, curious about where the other policeman had been sent to. He spotted him closing the gate and standing guard.

'Thuo, where were you yesterday?'

'I was here.'

'The whole day?'

'No. I was here in the morning, and then I went home in the afternoon.'

'Did you see Mrs. Mwangi when you were here?'

'Yes. I drove her.'

'Where did you take her?'

Thuo decided to stick to the script and reiterated the explanation he had just given to Schola and to Ngugi the previous day when he had brought the car back. Ngugi had already spoken to Mrs. Agallo who had offered him a similar explanation as Thuo, adding that Kavata had decided to take a taxi as they had both had too much wine and Kavata didn't want her friend to drive, even if it was a short distance between their homes.

'Where did you go when you left here?' The OCS continued with his questioning.

'I went home.'

'Were you at home alone?'

'Yes, but my wife came home from church after some time.'

The OCS pulled Ngugi aside. Thuo stood rooted, watching the two men talking in hushed tones. He thought about the last time he had been interrogated in a similar manner, nearly eighteen years ago.

\*\*\*

Thuo was born in Molo and had lived there until his family was forced to flee due to conflict around the Mau forest. He was ten years old at the time and still had a vivid memory of the day that they fled. His father had been planning their departure for weeks, but his mother, a staunch Christian, would hear nothing of it.

'This is our home,' she would say, 'and it is covered by the blood of Jesus.'

Thuo remembered his father scowling at her, asking her what blood would do for them in the face of machetes and *rungus*. They heard stories of people who had escaped from the north and ended up in Molo looking for temporary shelter before the conflict caught up with them again. Still Thuo's mother refused to leave. She would kneel down in a corner praying for hours until her legs were numb and the bottom of her feet turned dark from poor circulation. Then she would spend the rest of the day singing so loudly and joyfully that passersby would often stop by to ask how anyone could be so jubilant while they were surrounded by death.

The tension that night was so dense that it was hard to breath. Thuo's mother had been the first to hear the screams. She got up and knelt by her bed to pray. By the time Thuo's father woke up, the air was heavy with the smell of people's lives going up in flames. Thuo was frozen as he lay under the covers, waiting for the death he had heard his father predicting for them because they were still there. The door to his tiny bedroom flew open as his father burst in with instructions.

'Get dressed, put on your shoes and wait. I will come and get you.' There was fear in his voice.

Thuo did as he was told and stood by the door, looking across the corridor into his parents' bedroom where his father was trying to lift his wife off her knees. Thuo's mother remained completely tranquil, with a gentle smile on her lips. She didn't put up any kind of fight, but for some reason Thuo's father was completely unable to lift her. It was as if she was bolted to the ground. There were tears in his eyes as he begged her to go with them. The glow from their neighbour's burning house lit up the room, casting an ominous radiance on his mother's face. There was a loud continuous bang on the door. Thuo ran out of his room and picked up the polythene bags and sacks that had been sitting by the door for weeks in preparation for this moment. He called out for his father as he climbed out of a small window at the back of the house and began to run, afraid to look back in case his parents weren't there. He hadn't been running very long when he felt the bags he was carrying being snatched from his grip. He turned around, expecting to find death, but there was his father looking down at Thuo with immeasurable sadness as he led him to safety.

They arrived in Nakuru a week later and began their temporary life in an abandoned tin shack on the edge of the Lake Nakuru National Park, in the area that marked the border between the park and the airstrip. The shack was concealed by tall blades of grass. Inside, the corners of the shack had become habitat for all kinds of hibernating creatures and the large holes in the roof had ensured that the ground was damp enough for weeds to thrive. The windowless walls kept the shack moist during the rainy season and blistering in the dry season. It was the most decent place they had found to sleep in a week, so they did what they could to make it a provisional home using large polythene bags and other items they had found in the garbage bins outside the airstrip.

Thuo's father would sometimes leave him at home and walk to Nakuru town to work odd jobs. He would hurry home, relieved to find that they had not been discovered squatting on government property. Living at the edge of the National Park also meant that they were in danger of being attacked by wild animals. So they learned the airstrip routines and studied the patterns of the different animals in the park, ensuring that they kept no food in their shack when they spotted animal droppings close by. Months later, when Thuo's father found work, the pair were optimistic that life would change.

Earning commissions from the small petrol station outside Nakuru town didn't bring Thuo's father enough money to move. He often took Thuo to work with him, and on the days that he didn't Thuo spent his days indoors, reading old newspapers and magazines, and reminiscing about his short-lived school days. In the afternoons, when the house got too hot to bear, Thuo ventured out to the airstrip and sat hidden in the tall grass for hours, watching and waiting for small aircrafts to take off or land. He watched the people in the little tower beaming signals to each other and talking into their radios. He studied the drivers of the small cranes rushing from plane to plane. Before long he could tell when a plane needed to be refuelled and serviced based on how long it had been away from the airstrip. The pilots were the most fascinating to him. He wondered if the bands on their blazers were made from real gold. Sometimes he would imagine that he was a pilot, and would walk around the airstrip like he had seen them do, exuding confidence and commanding respect with their structured hats sitting atop their heads like halos.

*'Unafanya nini hapa?'* Two policemen grabbed him from behind one afternoon as he was daydreaming in his bower. The president was due to land at the airstrip in the next few days, so the Airports Authority had deployed extra security to patrol the airstrip. Thuo had noticed an unusual amount of activity, but it hadn't occurred to him to keep away. He had just been happy having more to observe.

'I was just looking,' he said, feeling a sudden, urgent pressure in his bladder.

'How did you enter the strip, you rat?'

The heat of the slap on his cheek and that of his urine on his inner thighs was almost simultaneous. Drops of urine trickled onto the policeman's boot. He cursed and threw Thuo onto the ground. He landed on an anthill in a lumbering heap, but quickly scampered onto his feet and tried to run away. The policemen took what seemed like two giant footsteps and caught up with Thuo, lifting his small body off the ground as if he was a paper-weight. They asked him the same question again, but Thuo didn't have an answer, unsure whether he should speak the truth or remain silent and hopefully save their home. He made a final attempt to slither out of the security guard's grip, but this only angered the guards more.

He raised his head and looked towards his home.

'Oh, so you are the one who lives in that *mabati* house, stealing from *serikali,* eh?' They made him watch as they demolished the shack, as best they could, with their *rungus* and boots. Then they frogmarched Thuo to the airstrip.

'What is your name?' asked a man in a ranger's uniform who sat in an office about twice the size of Thuo's now former home.

'Joseph Thuo Maliti.' Thuo was still terrified.

'How old are you?'

'Fourteen.' The man seemed shocked by Thuo's age; he looked much younger.

'Do you go to school?'

Thuo shook his head.

'Who do you live with?'

Silence. Thuo still hoped that he would be able to protect his father.

'*Kijana,* speak! Who do you live with?' The room vibrated as the man spoke.

'My father. He is in town.' Thuo surrendered and tears flooded his eyes. He was then taken to another room and told to wait for his father.

What seemed to Thuo like days later, his father came to get him. He was relieved to see that his son was well, but this was short-lived as he grabbed him by the arm and roughly led him out of the building. Thuo's father had explained the circumstances that had led them to Nakuru and begged for them to be allowed to stay for a few nights, just until he could find them a place to go. They had not caused anyone any harm; they had nowhere else to go. He begged and pleaded and grovelled like a man who had nothing, yet stood to lose everything.

Later that evening, Thuo and his father were escorted off the airstrip. Their slow pensive steps were covered in darkness and engulfed in the silence that now defined their relationship. Thuo's father, who was a few metres ahead, stopped suddenly and waited for his son to catch up with him before he spoke.

'We have no home now because of your foolishness.' The weight of this accusation hit Thuo harder than those blows he had received from the policemen. His father had addressed him in Kikuyu, which Thuo had not heard him speak since the night they left Molo.

'Since you think you are big enough to disobey me, you can go your own way.' Thuo's father dropped the bag he was carrying that contained their remaining possessions. He paused for a brief moment before he walked away from his son.

Thuo stood rooted and silent. He wanted to pick the bag off the ground and run after his father, but his feet wouldn't let him. He ached to call out and tell him that he was wrong, that it wasn't his fault that they had been kicked out of a home they hadn't had in years, but his voice, like the rest of his insides, was tied up in a petrified knot. So he stood there in silence, watching his father's fading frame disappear and accepting his fate as his mother had done.

\*\*\*

Thuo had since resigned himself to the fact that people like him did not have a decision about the course their lives took. Such privilege was reserved for those who could afford the price tag that accompanied choice. So he lived his life as a reaction to the blows that he was dealt. This is why he didn't put up a fight when the policemen stuffed him into the back of the Peugeot after Ngugi and the OCS had decided to detain him.

Thuo had always regarded the Ngugis as family. They invited each other to important family occasions, and though the Ngugis hardly attended the Thuo events, they always made sure they bought a goat or two to mark the occasion. When Cheptoo gave birth to their second child, Kavata had visited them at the local hospital and insisted on paying the hospital bill. Thuo's youngest daughter and Amani got on famously, and their parents had often joked that when the time came they would arrange for them to be married.

As he sat in the back of the police car, sandwiched between the two policemen, it occurred to him that while Kavata regarded him as family, her husband didn't. Recently, Thuo had begun to feel like, to Ngugi, he was merely an employee charged with the responsibility of making their lives a little more comfortable. He couldn't justify why he hid the truth about where he had taken Kavata, more so now that she was potentially missing and he was facing arrest. Still, he made the decision to stick with the story as she had asked him to.

He asked the policeman on his right if he could phone his wife before they got to the station. When he agreed, Thuo reached for his phone and dialled Kavata's number instead.

He ignored the logic that screamed at him that this was a waste of a privilege and was unsure of what he would do or say if she picked up. The policeman overheard the automated message informing Thuo that the number he had dialled was switched off. He began to dial his wife's number when the policeman on his left snatched the phone from him.

'*Wewe*, you are allowed only one call. Too bad the number is *mteja*.' The policeman confiscated the phone just as Thuo looked out the window and caught a glimpse of the same election poster of Ngugi that had filled him with such hope only a few minutes ago.

At the Nyari Police Station, Thuo was asked to sit on a bench at the reception that was directly opposite the holding cell. The policeman who had confiscated his phone went into a back room and re-emerged with handcuffs. He stood over Thuo and asked him to remove his shoes and belt, and then slapped one cuff onto Thuo's wrist and the other to the metal leg of the bench that he sat on.

'You can sit there and decide if you are going to talk, and if you don't, we can throw you in there with your friends.' He pointed to the large metal door behind the desk where the booking officer sat.

It was an unspoken rule that working on Friday was somewhat optional for most policemen. Those who had to work opted to do so on the roads, where they could earn some quick pocket money. This made it impossible for anything administrative to happen on Friday, so anyone arrested anytime after Thursday afternoon inevitably spent the weekend behind bars.

By Monday morning, these detainees were agitated, impatient and eager to be released. For this reason, Monday was the busiest day for most police stations in Nairobi. It was also the day on which the fewest arrests were made because it was assumed that holding cells would be at capacity. The queue of people waiting to bail out their errant spouses and rascal friends stretched out beyond the station doors.

From where Thuo sat leaning against the wall furthest away from the holding cell, he could smell the overwhelming stench of unwashed bodies that came from the cell. He wondered how the policeman who was right outside the cell was able to stop himself from vomiting.

The door to the cell was made of solid metal, with no bars or glass through which one could look into or out of the cell. Instead, there was a small peephole on the door, the size of a twenty-shilling coin. From outside the cell all one could see was an eyeball gazing back at them. Thuo stared at the cell door so long that he could tell when a different person was looking through the opening by the varying degrees of whiteness of their eyes. The eyeballs changed so frequently that Thuo imagined there must have been some kind of system where the inmates stood in a line with the front of their bodies pressed against the door, stepping sideways in order to take turns to see if someone had come for them.

Whenever a woman walked into the station, the prisoner at the eyehole began to bang on the door as a signal to his fellow inmates who started to whistle and call out 'Supuu! Sista smart! Msupa!' This went on for an amount of time that was determined by how beautiful the woman was to them.

One lady strutted into the station, completely ignorant of the queue of people waiting to be served.

She walked up to the desk, 'Excuse, boss. I need my license.'

The officer glanced up at her and chuckled, and then the catcalling began from the choir of suspects behind him.

She was rattled, but did an admirable job at hiding it. The booking officer asked her to get in line and wait her turn. She began to object in her polished English: she had very important places to be and she needed her license to get to them—it shouldn't even have been taken in the first place. This angered the detainees. Their affectionate calls had now mutated into thundering insults. She stepped back, terrified. The eyeballs at the peephole changed quicker than Thuo had ever seen. She was retreating faster than her high-heeled legs could carry her, and ended up tumbling into her place in the queue. The laughter from inside the cell was a hundred times louder than that of the people outside who had actually seen her fall down. She ran to her car, locked herself inside it and refused to leave until her license was brought to her.

It took a good ten minutes to restore the police station to some level of order. The catcalling ritual started again in no time, and it was only when some of the women hesitated to walk up to the desk that the booking officer would hit the door with his baton to silence the detainees. Thuo noticed that the officer didn't entirely object to this shared ritual. Every time the chanting started, he looked down the line to see which woman had caused it and then waited until the very last minute before he reassured the terrified woman that she was safe.

Several hours after Thuo had been cuffed to the bench, the booking officer stood by the cell door and began to call out the names of those who would be released, asking them to stand in the order that their names were called. When he was done, four other policemen joined him and stood behind the door, in case the detainees whose names had not been called decided to push the door open and try to escape. The booking officer opened the cell door and let them out one by one, ensuring that they had signed their discharge forms before they joined their families who had been sent outside to wait.

Thuo watched the men as they walked out into the bright mid-morning sun, testing himself to see if he could recognise them by their eyeballs.

There were only four men left in the cell by the time the exercise was over, and they could only be held for another forty-eight hours before they had to be released or handed over to the courts. Police stations all over the country were short staffed because officers had been deployed to the various polling stations in preparation for the election. Most stations would only have two or three officers on site on the polling day, so they were encouraged to minimise arrests over the course of the week.

Thuo's buttocks were numb and his wrist was sore from the handcuffs. The OCS had walked past him several times, but not once had he acknowledged Thuo who was still sitting there stoic and silent, certain that the less trouble he caused, the sooner he would be out of there. He began to panic and the gravity of his situation dawned on him. The fact that he was still here meant that Kavata had not returned home to clear up this mess. As the minutes passed his worry grew, and when he saw the OCS leaving the station, he decided to speak up.

'Sir, excuse me *Bwana* OCS. Please, I beg you to release me. I have done nothing wrong.' The OCS looked at Thuo, his face blank for a moment before he seemed to remember who Thuo was.

'*Kuna wangapi kwa cell?*' The OCS asked the booking

officer. The booking officer confirmed that there were four men in the cell. The OCS walked up to Thuo and stood over him so close that Thuo had to look down to avoid staring into the man's belly, which flowed over his belt like the top of a queen cake.

'Lock him up,' the OCS instructed, then made his exit.

Since the police station was located in the heart of an affluent suburb, it was better maintained than most in the country. The sign board at the police station gate was painted once a year and the base of the sign, like the path into the station, was decorated with white washed rocks that were so brilliant that it hurt the eye to look at them on a bright day. The Bougainvillea fence and all the bushes in the compound were kept symmetrically trimmed at all times. Members of the Nyari Residents' Association visited the station twice a year to review the needs of the station, and a few weeks later they would return, armed with reluctant spouses and unhappy children to paint the walls and sand the floors—this was their way of giving back to the people who had ensured that their bubble was kept afloat. So on his imagined scale, Thuo ranked the station pretty highly and assumed that the cell would be as well maintained as the rest of the station.

He was wrong. Nothing that Thuo had heard from people who had spent time inside police holding cells would have equipped him for this encounter. He had tried to prepare himself mentally for the worst during those hours he spent handcuffed to the bench, but even that had been futile.

The dank room had no windows. The only source of light once the door was shut was a single bulb, whose glow was inhibited by a brown substance that had caked on its surface over time. Along the dark walls of the cells were benches, similar to the one he had sat on outside, only these ones served as beds as well. The walls were filled with drawings of naked women and violent crimes where the victims were policemen. Some of the images were drawn in impeccable detail next to statements and declarations in various languages—none of which was English—all done in the only materials that were abundant in the room: faeces and blood. The only sections of the wall that were bare were those that had been eroded by constantly being urinated on. Thuo stood against the door, afraid to touch anything. The four men who were in there with him didn't bother to look up when the door slammed behind him. When he vomited over and over again, the men laughed, saying that it was just a matter of time before his body got used to the smell.

And it did. When there was nothing left inside him to heave, when he no longer sweat because of the lack of fresh air and his tear ducts dried up, he realised that his body had settled down onto the slimy floor and that he could finally breathe without gagging.

\*\*\*

It was noon on Christmas Eve when Kavata and Mutheu embraced at the airport. Kavata felt her current worries melt away only to be replaced with a wave of new emotions. She was grateful that the only thing Mutheu said when Kavata asked if she could visit was yes and regretted all the weddings, births, and deaths that they had experienced separately. But most of all she was happy that she could still feel joy at being reacquainted with the person who was her first friend.

There were still tears in Mutheu's eyes when she asked Kavata where her luggage was. Kavata planned to tell her that the airline lost it, but seeing Mutheu helped her realise that she had been telling so many little lies for so long that it was almost her default reaction. She didn't need to lie anymore.

'I don't have any. Decided to travel light,' she said.

Mutheu searched her cousin's face; she could still read Kavata well.

'And your flight? How was it?'

'It was long, but as pleasant as it could have been. Thanks for picking me up, and for hosting me—I know it has been a while...' Kavata said. She felt the sadness that she had temporarily forgotten wash over her again. She looked over at her cousin as she drove. She had put on some weight and her skin, which Kavata remembered was riddled with acne spots, was now clear and beautiful, bearing the paleness of too many winters.

'Are you hungry? Maybe we can get something to eat before we go home. I don't often have an excuse to leave Zack alone with the boys.' Mutheu hadn't picked up an accent in all those years. 'I'd like to take full advantage of it. Should we grab a bite?'

Kavata was eager to get out of the suit she'd worn since church on Sunday morning, but she sensed Mutheu's questions and obliged. She was grateful when they walked into a restaurant that wasn't too busy, and that they found a table in a corner that would conceal the tears that would surely come.

'So how long are you here?' Mutheu was never good at stalling.

'I don't know. A few weeks for now. Maybe months? I've applied for a few volunteer programmes to keep me busy while I figure things out. The Fullbright one looks promising.'

'I've heard about that programme. One of our neighbours

works for one of their funders. It's apparently very good...'

Kavata felt the tears coming on. 'I don't even know where to start.'

'What's going on, Kavi? Aunt Marge called me yesterday to ask if I'd heard from you. I got the sense that they didn't know you were coming?'

'No, I didn't tell her. I didn't tell anyone.'

'Anyone?' Mutheu was almost afraid of the coming news.

Kavata began at the place she thought was the logical beginning.

'It's been a difficult couple of years. Ngugi lost his job at the National Housing Commission and basically hasn't been able to find a new one, so we've been living on the peanuts that the school pays and my mother's help.'

'*Pole*. What happened, why did Ngugi lose his job?'

'He was implicated in some corruption that had nothing to do with him and everything to do with Dad. So once it was uncovered, no one would touch him.'

'Damn. Uncle Mutinda is still at it?' Mutheu knew full well the kind of man Hon. Muli was. He was the reason she moved to the US in the first place. Mutheu's father, Hon. Muli's half brother, was also in government. He was one of the only people to ever call Hon. Muli out on his corruption. He thought that Hon. Muli was a disgrace to the entire family's track record, which was spotless until Hon. Muli tainted it. Mutheu's father was involved in a car accident the day before a meeting with the Vice President, during which he intended to expose Hon. Muli. He survived the accident, but as soon as he was well enough, he moved himself and his family out of the country. Kavata only learned of the real reasons for Mutheu's sudden departure when Mutheu told her about it several years later, after her father passed away in Boston, and she returned home to lay his body to rest.

'About two years ago, my husband decided that he was going to represent my dad's party and run for the same office that Dad held. I was so mad. And hurt and betrayed. Since then, our marriage has gone to the dogs and I've been wondering if and how I can fix it. So I've left him. I just up and left.'

'Even the kids? They don't know?' Mutheu asked after several minutes of stunned silence.

Kavata shook her head.

'How old are they now?'

'Wanja just turned twenty. Amani is eight.' Kavata could still see the look on her son's face when she told him that he couldn't go to the supermarket with her.

'Jesus Christ, Kavi. That must have been hard to do.'

'I prayed so hard about it, Mutheu. For so many months.' Kavata couldn't blink fast enough to stop the tears. 'I don't know what else I could have done. I would have brought them with me. I still want to. But I needed to come first, and set things up—then maybe I can go back for them.'

'When is the election?' Mutheu asked, and Kavata immediately remembered that there were actually some people who were completely oblivious to the events that dominated her life for so long. She had also lost track of the days.

'On the 27th—Thursday?'

Mutheu nodded and beckoned for a waiter so she could order two beers.

'None for me,' Kavata interjected. 'I don't think I could handle a drink so early in the morning.'

'How couldn't you after all you've been through?'

Mutheu insisted.

'Ok then, but let me have some wine. Don't you remember your dad always telling us that women should never be seen drinking beer in public?' Kavata said, and instantly regretted bringing up her late uncle. She hadn't checked in with Mutheu as often as she should have after the funeral. They sat in silence until their beverages arrived.

'Then, what happens if Ngugi loses? Shouldn't you have waited until after the election to leave?'

Kavata shrugged her shoulders. 'There's no way he could lose with my dad's arsenal behind him.'

Mutheu agreed. As far as she could remember, her uncle never lost an election. They talked and drank for a little while longer. Mutheu informed Kavata that they had plans to travel later that night to spend Christmas morning with Zack's family in Florida. She invited Kavata to join them, though she suspected that her cousin would appreciate some time to herself.

The three glasses of wine allowed her to be cheerful enough to meet Mutheu's family, but it hurt to be around them and she was relieved when they left for the airport shortly after dinner and she was finally alone.

# 3
# MULI'S PLUNDER
## 1982 - 2005

**K**avata often tried to explain the complexities of growing up with a father like hers, but each time she only succeeded at sounding like an ungrateful brat. The Honourable Mutinda Muli was quite the politician in his day; the quintessential man of the people. Charming, generous and outrageously corrupt. Kavata suspected most, if not all, of his wealth was acquired from fleecing Kenyans faster than they could say *serikali*. For instance, the house she and her family lived in, a wedding gift from her father, was likely purchased with hard-earned tax-payers' shillings.

He spent his life paranoid someone wanted his blood. He was always ready to flee. He refused to open a bank account, or to carry a cell phone, or set up an email address. The phrase, *the guilty run when no one is chasing*, must have been inspired by Hon. Muli. His constituents loved him and those who didn't, respected him. He was the longest-serving Member of Parliament for Machakos constituency, a feat he took great pride in. His tenure in office turned him into a master crook—a corruption connoisseur.

Coming to terms with the fact her father was a

dishonest man was somewhat of a journey for Kavata. As a little girl, she knew it was wrong for him to send her to tell his visitors he was out while he was sat in his study, in his robe and slippers, reading the newspaper after his mandatory mid-morning nap. Too ashamed to play outside under the glare of her father's patient audience, Kavata would often stay indoors, daydreaming and counting the minutes until her father went to work. She would then put on her *sandaks* and run out to squeeze as much as she could out of the last few hours of the afternoon. Sometimes she would catch her father's guests' faces as he was speeding off in his chauffeur driven car, without a glance in their direction. She wondered how he had the heart to do it. On some days, she would only get to go outdoors for a couple of minutes before the national anthem played on the kitchen radio, telling her it was time for her evening bath.

In primary school, her classmates would often reiterate the things they would sometimes hear their parents say about Hon. Muli: that he was deceptive and unjust, that his generosity was steeped in greed, and he stood for everything wrong with Moi's government. She didn't understand these words at the time, but they still stung.

When Kavata was twelve years old, Hon. Muli orchestrated an elaborate scheme to redirect public resources intended to dig four hundred wells all over Machakos, one of the more arid areas south-east of Nairobi. Wells were indeed dug, twenty-five of them, scattered across the town. Then he selected a group of young community leaders and mobilisers and paid them well to organise events to open up the water sources and declare Machakos an oasis. He ensured the local newspapers printed photographs of women and children fetching water from the new taps and serving it to him to taste. They smiled for the cameras while pretending not to see the bottled mineral water he was actually drinking from. He 'encouraged' journalists to write articles about how much development he brought to Machakos, complete with statistics on how the region would gain economically from its new source of water. As a final precaution, he paid a surveyor to fabricate a detailed document claiming it was only those locations in the whole constituency that had water underground. This report recommended additional water be channelled from Nairobi so every house in his ancestral homeland had running water. To achieve this, more money would be needed. Finally, to expel any doubt, Hon. Muli commissioned a second analysis, which said the same thing and syphoned the remaining millions into bank accounts in Seychelles and Liberia.

In the mid 80's an investigation into the misuse of public funds began and Muli was implicated. So, he began to spread propaganda that the opposition was after his people's wells, and soon demonstrations started as people showed up to defend him. Only he could stop the unrest. He held an assembly and addressed his constituents, asking them to remain peaceful and promising them he would do everything in his power to protect their precious wells. Years later, Hon. Muli was accused of mismanaging money earmarked for repairing the roads, but this time he was prepared. When he sensed trouble coming, he renovated all the schools in the small town, repairing broken desks, replacing cracked windows and repainting the walls. He provided the latest textbooks and materials needed and paid bonuses of ten thousand shillings to be distributed to every teacher in the constituency. He organised a luncheon for them and they slaughtered so many animals for the event, for weeks after people still had smuggled meat in their homes. The teachers felt important and valued. At the event, Hon. Muli used words like 'pillars' and 'cornerstone' to describe the teachers. But later that evening, Kavata overheard him describe the head-teachers' event as a gathering of empty *debes*. For months after the luncheon, everyone sang Hon. Muli's praises. So when the interrogation into the road fund began, they gladly defended their minister as he obtained large tracts of land and properties with his new bounty.

The penny dropped for Kavata when she was in university. She was home for the weekend, paging through the photo albums filled with press clippings her father would insist be brought out every time they hosted parties.

The phone rang.

'*Wapi* Muli?'

'*Hayuko*. Can I take a message?'

'No, I know he is there. Call him. Don't waste my time.'

'He is not home—but if you tell me who you are I can-'

'No, I will keep calling until you give him the phone.'

The disgruntled caller hung up, but phoned again so consistently for the next six hours, Kavata eventually just stopped picking up the phone. He called again a few minutes after her parents walked in from their day trip to Kitui. Before Kavata could tell him her father was back, 'You self-important goats! You think you can just do what you want and take whatever you like. You make me sick. Tell Muli that. Tell him I pray he contracts an infection on his scrotum so bad, his penis drops off so he can never fuck another man's wife again. If he doesn't call me back in two hours I will go to the papers—all of them—even the gutter press—and tell them he impregnated my wife. Tell him he can come and collect his bastard son. Make sure you tell him.'

Kavata held the receiver to her ear long after the line went dead.

'Who's that?' her mother asked.

'I think it was a wrong number,' Kavata hung up and walked to her room, ignoring her mother's commentary about how fresh the *managu* was upcountry.

Discovering one's father had a mistress, a child, or a second and third family was nothing shocking for anyone Kavata's age. New siblings popped in and out of one's lives as regularly as the avocado season. It was almost a rite of passage. For all his faults, Kavata was thankful her father always honoured her mother, or so she thought.

Kavata paced around her bedroom, trying to figure out if and how she was going to walk back into the living room and repeat those words. She couldn't do it, especially not with her mother present. She started to write her father a note, but this news seemed even more damning when committed to paper. Then she realised she was being ridiculous. The man didn't leave his name or a phone number, like he assumed Muli would know who he was. She convinced herself the man would call again and this time, either Muli or her mother would pick up and speak to him and free her from being the messenger of doom. She hoped the mysterious caller was telling lies, but when she closed her eyes and replayed the conversation in her mind, she knew the pain and bitterness in his voice would be hard for anyone to conjure. She fell asleep waiting for the shrill ring of the phone to pierce through the large house, wondering what her alleged brother looked like and if her father would acknowledge him. But he didn't phone back and Kavata kept her lips zipped. Sweeping things under the carpet was the Muli way.

The next morning, she left home before sunrise. She

scanned the newspaper headlines expecting to see her father's shame splayed across the front page, but it wasn't there that day. Or the day after, or the week after, and soon Kavata began to wonder if she had imagined the entire thing. By the time she arrived on campus that morning, Kavata had made the decision to adopt the Muli way and act like nothing happened.

But she would soon learn that feigning oblivion would require a little more effort than she imagined. She was shopping around for university clubs to join when she walked past the classroom where Ngugi was addressing a small group of students seated on desks and chairs around the front of the room where he stood perched on a dark solid mahogany desk.

She noticed his crisp white shirt first, and liked that his ankles, exposed by a pair of navy cargo shorts, were well oiled. The first time she watched him speak, she saw his shyness and was drawn to the way he closed his eyes before he spoke. Almost as if imagining the words in his mind and only allowing them to roll off his tongue when he was sure they would carry his sentiments well. The first time they shook hands, she liked that he looked her straight in the eye and she believed him when he said he was glad to meet her. The first time they shared a meal, she thought it adorable that he wanted her to choose what he should order even if she threatened to go for the most expensive menu item. When she ordered the spiciest curry available, he insisted on eating every last bite because his incredibly low tolerance for West African pepper was worth powering through if it meant he could continue to watch her laugh. It didn't matter that she was laughing *at* him. The first time he spoke about his family, she was touched by the genuine love and fondness he possessed for them. It came from a place inside him so warm and earnest, she doubted she ever felt the same about her own family.

He spoke of his parents as though they were his peers. And would say things to her like, 'Kavi, our folks are raising us for the first time. They are allowed to mess up occasionally. And we must let them.'

The first time he asked about her family, she froze and struggled with what to say. Part of her was thrilled he genuinely appeared to not know who her father was. And the other part was shattered that he would soon find out her father was the infamous *father of corruption*. He saw her discomfort immediately and backed off, never asking about her family until that awkward event in May of their third year of university.

By now, Ngugi was a well-known and respected student leader. He was often invited to represent the university at student conferences and seminars, which required him to speak publicly. Kavata was surprised to learn that the thing which attracted her to him the most, was what he disliked the most. Ngugi was terrified of public speaking, but was so good at it, and under Kavata's watchful gaze, he got even better. She always marvelled at how well her father could charm a crowd. The way she saw it, it was the only reason he got away with the things he did. She inadvertently picked up public speaking tips and tricks from watching him over the years, and she was happy to put them to good use through Ngugi. Soon, he was serving at the helm of various campus groups with Kavata solidly supporting him, often as the secretary or treasurer. She didn't hesitate to take the work on when it was offered to her, but now she wished she had.

Student elections were around the corner and Ngugi

and his entire team were up for re-election. Theirs was a young campus with a small student body, so there was little opposition to them running things for another year. But it was the early 80's, people were growing weary of the current state of political affairs and were beginning to imagine what a multi-party government could even look like. So when a few of the major universities decided to join forces to put on a mock multi-party election, Ngugi and his team were more than happy to participate.

Ngugi had just finished addressing the crowd with what Kavata, beaming on stage behind him, and the rest of the team considered his best speech yet, when a tall, unreasonably handsome, bully from the University of Nairobi stood to speak.

'Thank you, honourable candidate, for that eloquent and incredibly passionate speech. I actually have nothing related to the topics your speech has addressed, but I would like to know one thing. How do you expect to get our votes when a senior member of your team is under the influence of one of the country's most corrupt individuals?'

The room erupted into a puzzled murmur. Ngugi began to turn around so he could see Kavata's reaction, but stopped himself as soon as he realised that glancing in her direction would answer the question many people were asking. Kavata's face was blank. She hadn't heard the question—Q&A was the section she disliked the most so she would often zone out. She was busy taking mental notes about Ngugi's delivery to share with him later when she felt the energy in the room shift from Ngugi and move on. To her.

'I think you are losing the point of this exercise,' she heard Ngugi's voice say, but Kavata's head was spinning.

'What did he ask?' she asked their deputy chair who was

standing next to her.

'You just ignore it. He's being petty. What a waste.'

'Petty about what?' Kavata thought to herself.

'Am I really missing the point? Isn't the person who is solely in charge of finances in your organisation the child of an MP who, only last week, was implicated in one of the worst corruption scandals since our independence? Apples and trees, my friend.'

This time Ngugi needed to look at her. He was shocked at the strength of his urge to protect her. Later, he would recognise this as the moment he knew he loved her. He mumbled an apology and turned back around to face their adversary. He took a deep breath and listened as the stranger listed, off the top of his head, all the things Muli was accused of over the span of the last couple of years. He revelled in the audience's delighted reactions to the specificity of his research. The audience stroked his ego and egged him on as he finished off the list with details of Muli's most recent scandal before he sat down, spent and basking in his audience's adoration.

Ngugi paused, eyes closed and face neutral, waiting for the inevitable moment when the room would get uncomfortable with silence and turn their attention back to him.

'Thank you, comrade. You are evidently, *very* well read.' Ngugi turned around again to inspect his team members whose faces, save for Kavata's, were an apt representation of the tension in the room. 'Just one question, if I may?' The handsome student nodded. *Always be polite*. Kavata's voice was in Ngugi's head. 'Thank you,' Ngugi said, and paused again. 'This corrupt individual you are speaking of, do you see him in the room today?' The handsome student shrugged his shoulders. 'I'd appreciate a response, please.'

'No,' his tenor boomed through the room.

'That's what I thought. So, if you would like to discuss all the reasons I or anyone else is not suited for this job, then I would be happy to. But that's a longer, more depressing conversation much better had over some beers and *nyama*. And while we were all obviously well impressed by your little—performance—I think a much better spend of our time here today would be to discuss why my team, and anyone else who will come up here today after us, *is* suited for the job. However, if you wish to use those excellent research skills of yours to unearth some reasons why anyone here,' he said pointing to his team, 'isn't the best person for the job based on their *own merit*—I will be the first to hear you out.'

Kavata's game face was a thing she took great pride in. It wasn't the first time she was being attacked for being her father's daughter. She was used to it. She'd learned long ago that if you play dead they will eventually move on to fresh meat. But she was feeling new feelings.

The first one was that she was surely going to reward Ngugi with a ravaging later. They hadn't gone there yet. Not for any particular reason—they just didn't want to rush into anything. But today she was particularly proud of him and grateful for his defence which, while endearing, was no match for the handsome stranger's attack. That handsome stranger was the reason Kavata was even thinking about a ravaging in the first place. It was the way he caught her gaze and held it for the last few moments of his performance before he sat down deliberately, taking up as much space as he could and slowly guiding her gaze to the bulging source of his bravado.

The second, less urgent feeling, was love. She, too, would recognise this as the moment she first considered spending her life with Ngugi. Some of the things the handsome stranger said about her father, particularly the most recent allegations, were news to Kavata, who usually kept very close tabs on her father's political life. Ngugi was the only person, in her whole entire life, who succeeded at getting her to forget about her father. She never considered a life where this was possible. Ngugi had made it a reality. Standing on stage that very awkward day, Kavata purposed to love him. That night, inside his hostel, she conjured all her new feelings and shared them with Ngugi via a series of very grateful thrusts of her hips as she straddled him and delivered a ravaging to erase all assumptions that she might be a virgin. He would never know she was indeed a virgin. She preferred to keep it that way because—while she was prepared to share many things with Ngugi over the course of their lives together—she was never prepared to give anyone the satisfaction of thinking they colonised her body.

A few days later, when they came up for air, and were growing used to all their new feelings, Ngugi finally found the courage to broach the subject.

'Kavi, tell me about your father?'

'Argh.'

'You knew it was coming.'

'What do you want to know?'

'Let's start with everything.'

And Kavata did. She started to describe their lives before politics and realised all that came to mind was the silence: the tone of her parent's hushed voices murmuring, the quiet meals for three around the dining table that, like everything else in their home, was intended for a much larger family. She remembered her father being very restless, only finding peace when the politics came and the silence started to dissipate. She talked about the hours she would spend reading about

Muli because she got tired of her mother telling her that what her father did for a living was not her concern. Kavata began to describe the feeling on the day when she found out about her alleged stepbrother, but held back. It was still too soon, and telling one more person, even one she felt so deeply connected to, would make it more of a reality than she was willing to face at the moment. When she was done speaking, Ngugi, speechless, held her long and snug until her shoulders began to inch further and further away from her ears, and she allowed herself to truly melt into him.

The next week, Ngugi dragged her to the library where he had gathered every article and piece he could find about Muli, along with some wine, beers, *mandazis* and sausages. He laid these out on a blanket in a corner of the reference section that should have been closed, and they sat there for hours. Ngugi would read an article and Kavata provided her version of the story—where she had one. He was impressed by how much she already knew, but he didn't want Kavata ever learning about her father from a stranger. This was his way of ensuring it never happened.

'So, are you still considering quitting the club?' Ngugi asked a few hours later, as they floated back to his room.

'I don't know. Maybe I'll join the Christian Union, or something less... hostile.' They laughed a carefree laugh.

'Maybe you wouldn't be such a hot target if you blended in more,' Ngugi said.

'What does that even mean? I can't help who my fath....'

'No. No. Wait, this has nothing to do with your dad!' Ngugi held his hands up to placate an already hissing Kavata. 'I mean, if you dressed different, you would fit in better.'

'What!' Kavata shrieked, and then giggled when she saw the panic spread on his face.

'Wait. Calm down. Let me explain.' Ngugi wondered why he'd gone there. He took a deep breath and did his eye-closing thing. 'How much was this jacket?' He tugged at the crisp navy embroidered jacket which sat on her like it was made for her.

'I don't know.'

'And why doesn't a fully grown woman know how much her clothes cost?'

'What's your point?'

'What about your shoes? Where did they come from?'

'A shop, you dummy.'

'And in which country was this shop located?'

Kavata mumbled.

'Excuse me?'

'Italy.'

'Yes. My point exactly.' He held her face in his hand, feeling her hot angry breath as it shot out of her, and kissed her on the forehead. This was the only way to calm her down. 'Baby, I like your nice clothes. To be honest, they are probably the thing I noticed first about you—well, after this incredible masterpiece,' his hands slipped from her face down to her hips before he gave her behind a gentle squeeze. Kavata yelped and quickly looked around. 'But the thing about leadership is, people need to be able to relate to you. It's hard to do when the value of the clothes on your back is equal to the GDP of a village in Northern Kenya.'

'Where was all this fire and wit when you were being thrashed by that handsome stranger?' Kavata retorted, and Ngugi was stunned.

'*Ati* handsome? He was a brute!'

Kavata laughed out loud. Ngugi was on to something, but she didn't know how to fix it—and she wasn't about to accept his help. She didn't need to though, because three weeks later, just as she was growing tired of the only campus appropriate clothes in her wardrobe, she met Anne.

Anne Agallo was a tall, fiery woman who spoke her mind and was impossible to impress. When Ngugi introduced them at a house party, the first thing Anne told Kavata was a hot comb would change her life. It did change Kavata's life because after Anne's second attempt to tame her hair using her hot comb, Kavata made an appointment with the only girl on campus who knew how to twist hair into locks. Anne gave Kavata's painfully coordinated outfits the street quality associated with shopping at second-hand markets. She walked her through her first pregnancy scare and told her about all the chemists in the city that sold condoms and birth control pills without batting an eyelid. They navigated their classes together and harboured a shared disdain at getting degrees in early education because their country had no imagination about the roles women could play. Teaching and nursing degrees were being shoved down the throats of female first years. They explored alcohol together and acquired a shared penchant for red wine and vodka. Anne would be the first to tell Kavata when her midsection looked a little fuller and would immediately dig up some diet they could both do. When Anne eventually met Mrs. Muli, they bonded immediately over their obsession with dieting.

'I don't know why you girls act like we never did these things in our day. How do you think we could fit into those little micro minis?' Mrs. Muli explained on the day she took Kavata and Anne for their first acupuncture slimming treatment. 'Africans are not naturally meant to be thin like white people. We need to work a little harder for those size 6's. Acupuncture, *ndimu na maji moto*, that's the only way to keep those stubborn kilos away.' At the time, Kavata didn't know what surprised her more. The idea of inserting needles into one's body to ward off fat, or that her mother had evidently been doing this for most of her life. It was more than Kavata could handle. She hated acupuncture and never went back for another session—happy to keep the few extra kilos around her hips. Anne, on the other hand, swore acupuncture made extra kilos a thing of the past.

Kavata often helped Anne deal with the drama that followed her when a bevy of her lovers' wives came hunting for her on campus.

'Anne, this love thing is making you reckless. You need to stop it with these married men. Is it really worth it?'

'Yes.' She flashed her new bracelet at Kavata. 'How many years do you think before Ngugi can afford this?'

'I don't want it.'

'Ha, spoken like a true *Babi*—'

'Anne—'

'—but, if I am honest, it's time to move on. These older men want to be given gold stars for keeping an affair. This one isn't even trying to be discreet. I think he must have told his wife where I live. I'm going to look for a younger man. One who is still in love with his wife and doesn't want to jeopardise the marriage. It's always easier when they feel like they have something to lose.'

Soon Anne started dating one of their professors. Kavata bit her tongue—but not for long as this was one of Anne's shortest affairs. Kavata held her sobbing friend when the professor told her he could not see her anymore because their affair had leaked to the faculty dean and his job was on the line. Months later, when Anne told Kavata her professor chose to quit his job and divorce his wife so they could be together, the two friends wept as they packed Anne's life up for her move to Kampala.

While Kavata was not in a hurry to replace her friend, any attempts at building kinship with Ngugi's sister Wairimu were unsuccessful. Kavata hated how badly she desired Wairimu's approval, and resented that Wairimu sometimes pretended to forget her name and acted startled to see her.

'Uhhm. Kavata, how nice to see you again,' she would say. 'You're still around, eh. So… sticky.'

'Sticky! What the hell does that even mean? She's making me out to be some needy child and she doesn't even know me,' Kavata once screamed at Ngugi as she told him of an earlier encounter with his sister.

Ngugi chuckled, 'I promise you my darling, Nimo knows exactly who you are. She's just doing that to get to you and because its fun. I've told you I can talk to her if you like. But then she's going to know that she's getting to you. So, I suggest you bite back or ignore her.'

Kavata opted to ignore her and did so successfully until the afternoon of Kavata and Ngugi's traditional wedding, which took place at the Muli family home. Wairimu was sent to sit-in-waiting with her new sister-to-be while the men negotiated the bride price. The whole affair was exhausting to Wairimu, but not nearly as much as it was for Kavata.

'I'm so sorry my parents are insisting on this whole thing,' Kavata said as soon as Wairimu settled into a chair across the room from the bed on which Kavata sat. It was quite the production. Extra hands were hired to scrub every nook and crevice in the house. There were gallons and gallons of *kaluvu* and *muratina* as well as more whisky and wine than was needed. Tents stood on the lawn, draped in a bright festive fabric Kavata abhorred. At least 600 seats, hired from a nearby school, were arranged in the tents and dressed in the same fabric. The dank smell of goat's blood hung in the air because the servants' quarters were converted into a temporary slaughterhouse. The ceremony had nothing to do with Kavata, or Ngugi for that matter. It irked her that her parents only adhered to traditions when it suited them, and in this case it did. The way she saw it, Kavata's impending nuptials provided the perfect avenue for Muli to show off and act like he was untouchable.

'It's a lot. But don't be fooled, my parents also love it. They've obviously made some questionable decisions to pull this thing off. It's not like you can exactly stick to budget when it comes to dowry.'

Kavata buried her head into her hands and shrugged, 'Oh no.'

Wairimu warmed, 'Don't worry it's not your fault.'

Kavata raised her head.

'It's Ngugi's fault.'

The two women laughed and settled into their new normal.

Wairimu snuck Ngugi onto the balcony and watched them share a forbidden embrace, after which Kavata launched into a series of rants about how her father had taken over the entire event even after he promised to keep things simple so as not to burden Ngugi's family. She completely forgot Wairimu was in the room.

'I can't wait to get out of here so he can stay away from my life and stop controlling everything.' Kavata's bottom lip trembled as she spoke, but Ngugi could only notice how stunning she looked as she sat perched on the balcony ledge like a damsel in distress, dressed in traditional regalia which she wore with an awkward elegance.

Kavata scarcely knew any of the people gathered at her home for the event, including the six girls who stormed into the room, startling Kavata and causing Ngugi to jump into a nearby bush. He sat there in the thicket for a short while, listening to the preparations for what would be the highlight of the ceremony: a ritual meant to test Ngugi's knowledge of the woman he claimed to love.

Earlier in the day, Kavata's aunties searched her bedroom for perfume, shoes and accessories Ngugi might recognise. Then they dressed each of the six girls in Kavata's clothes to throw him off. It was their duty to make it as hard as possible for the groom to identify the correct girl, as a way to express the sadness of losing a daughter. Shortly after Ngugi re-joined the ceremony, Kavata and her cousins emerged with every inch of their bodies covered in *khangas* to conceal their identities.

The groom got three chances to pick the correct woman. Ngugi failed to pick Kavata out of the lineup on his first try, so the girls went back into the house and would only come out when satisfied with the fine levied on Ngugi. They swapped clothes, making it more difficult for Ngugi to find Kavata. He began to realise the weight of this exercise. He walked past the girls, studying each of them closely, rejecting the ones with legs too long, hips too narrow, or breasts too large. When he'd narrowed it down to three girls, he called on two of his friends to help him. All this time Kavata stood in the lineup with her head lowered, trying to send Ngugi subliminal messages. Ngugi's friends were not much help, so he picked one of the girls purely by intuition. The gathering of over six hundred guests went silent, they too reckoning the importance of this moment. Ngugi felt more tested than ever. So when the girl he picked shook off the ladies who were helping to unveil her and threw her hands around him, he was filled with unimaginable relief, certain he wanted to spend the rest of his days with Kavata silently guiding him through life. Guests began to congratulate the new couple. Whether or not they decided on a church wedding, in the eyes of their parents and relatives, on that cool August afternoon in 1991, Ngugi and Kavata were married.

The first few years of their marriage were precious for Kavata and agonising for Ngugi. He began to feel completely inadequate the minute they stepped over the threshold into the house her parents gifted them. They'd received most of what they'd needed to start their home together, but this only served to make Ngugi a little more anxious. The disconnect between the quality of life he could offer her and what she was accustomed to became more and more apparent.

But Kavata assured him repeatedly that she wanted to build a life together as different as possible from anything she knew. Ngugi taught Kavata how to be more gentle in her approach to her father, and this enabled her to find the language to tell him she wanted to stand on her own feet and would not accept any more help from him. She got a job teaching Home Science at a public primary school, which angered Mrs. Muli. She couldn't understand why her daughter was choosing such a difficult life. For the first two years of marriage, Kavata's income was all they had because no one was hiring architects. Ngugi bounced from one hopeless attachment to the next.

When they announced they were expecting their first child, Muli, who was amused by their commitment to independence, pulled Ngugi aside and asked him what his plan was. Ngugi told him about a series of interviews he had lined up, but left out the part about none of them being with architectural firms.

On Wanja's first birthday, Ngugi received an out of the blue invitation to interview for a job at the National Housing Council. It was the kind of work he fantasised about all through his university days. The NHC was launching a project to construct hundreds of budget homes in low-income areas in a bid to decongest the slums quickly growing out of control. They needed an architect to manage the project and Ngugi was hired on the spot. Even if he sensed the opportunity wasn't as coincidental as it seemed, he kept his suspicions to himself and told Kavata he'd submitted his CV to so many people that one of them must have paid off. He knew Kavata would surely insist he quit his job if she suspected Muli had anything to do with him getting it. So he never asked how the NHC found him, and threw all his efforts into raising Wanja and proving he was the right man for both jobs.

He worked unstintingly on the NHC project; he spent days on the construction sites and nights going over the hundreds of applications from people living in Kibera and its environs who hoped to be granted new homes. He read each of the applications and savoured them as one would a good book. When he finished reading a batch of applications, it felt like he'd made a whole new set of friends.

Carol, the *chang'aa* brewer who needed a government house because she wanted to use her current home to expand her illicit business and needed to keep it away from her children. Euphestus, the primary school Business Education teacher who wanted to move houses because he grew tired of his reputation as being the man who got beaten up by his wife. Raha, the sex worker who wanted to upgrade her life after she earned a nice chunk of change blackmailing whichever customers proved unprofessional in their dealings with her. Ngugi was so pedantic in the manner in which he selected the successful applicants, it began to affect his core job, which was to build the actual homes. So when his boss suggested Ngugi delegate the allocation of units to the Ministry of Housing, Ngugi realised this would mean he could spend more time at home. Kavata, unaccustomed to the number of hours her husband now spent at work, agreed so Ngugi obliged. He handed over the administrative aspects of the project to the ministry and focused on what he loved.

The additional income was a huge relief. It came just in time to enable them to enrol Wanja into an international school, which she was especially thrilled about because the school uniform would be optional. They went on their first family holiday to Mombasa, and then Zanzibar, and South Africa the year after. Kavata was toying around with the idea of leaving her teaching job to do her own thing but, because she didn't know exactly what this thing would be, she kept her job for fear of boredom.

Ngugi built the houses quickly and efficiently and made sure they didn't possess the dull public housing façade. He was thoughtful in the design of the houses. The houses benefited from as much natural light as possible so the occupants could minimise their lighting bill. He built communal cooking areas because even if it was safer and more ideal to cook with gas, the cost of charcoal would be impossible to beat. Aware of the shortcomings of his middle class upbringing, he brought potential occupants in from the slums to look at the show flats and offer their suggestions, which he used to mould the houses into some of the most well considered, multi-purpose units the NHC had ever built.

On the day the houses opened, nine years after Ngugi

started at the NHC, his face featured on every newspaper in the country. The President called him a solution to post-colonial problems and encouraged young men to seek an education and follow in his footsteps. Online magazines based all over the continent profiled him. He was the man to watch, his name was on lists of influential Africans and he was a poster child for the future of African homegrown infrastructure. He received lots of glory as well as scrutiny which he welcomed for he had nothing to hide—or so he thought.

On the first anniversary of the opening of the NHC houses, which was also the day Ngugi broke ground on the second phase of the housing project, the *Daily Nation* published a huge three-page exposé on the housing project. The piece included a complete list of all the people who got homes, as well as their background. It was a stellar piece of journalism: complete with maps of the developments and flowcharts explaining the connection between everyone who got a house. More than half of the houses went to individuals related to Ngugi in one way or another, via Muli. Another dozen or so to Muli's buddies: old friends from his university days in London, cronies he met while in office and some of his former members of staff. And suddenly all those feelings he felt in his gut he learned to ignore so well came flooding back and settled on his shoulders like a massive bag of concrete.

Ngugi scanned the article over and over again, searching desperately for some of the names of people he selected to receive houses. The rightful owners of the houses indeed lived in the houses as tenants, but paid double or triple the amount of rent to the individuals on the list of shame. In addition to the increased rent, the cost of electricity, running water, garbage collection and security were too heavy a burden. So tenants began to sublet rooms and corners of their houses. A house intended for four people housed up to twelve. Some tenants, such as Raha, opted to move back into their former homes and rent out their NHC houses at massive profits.

Ngugi's suspicion Muli stole more than the twelve houses the journalist listed panned out. The entire family, including Wanja and Kavata, were listed as registered owners of homes, which in truth all belonged to Muli. Mrs. Muli was also listed, as was Ngugi's sister who had only ever interacted with Muli at their wedding. He bolted off his office chair and drove to Muli's house.

'*Haiya*, didn't you keep a few houses for yourself?' Muli thought Ngugi's outburst amusing. 'I thought you put a few houses in Kavata's name. Wanja should also have got a few more as well. Ngugi, we must eat *bwana*, you can't sleep on your ears like that. Next time you need to be *chonjo*.'

There was never a next time. Phase two of the project was paused temporarily. Ngugi was crushed and Kavata shared in his devastation. She called her father several times, each time finding herself at a loss for words. When she eventually managed to utter some words, it was when she heard her mother's voice on the other end of the line.

'Did you know?'

'Did I know what?'

'Did you know what Dad was up to at NHC?'

'Of course I did. Do you think your father does anything without me knowing?'

'Then why wouldn't you warn us?

'Kavata, you should be used to this sort of thing by now. Grow up,' Mrs. Muli said, and hung up.

It didn't matter that Ngugi knew nothing of the scandal, it was his name being dragged through the barely settled red dirt, not Muli's. They made him appear like an overzealous son-in-law who married all the way up and would now stop at nothing to please his wife's powerful father. No amount of explanations or PR distracted the public outrage surrounding the entire project.

A few months later, Ngugi lost his job and Kavata found out she was pregnant. Soon, white bread replaced the whole-wheat one with the roasted seeds baked into it that Wanja had grown used to. Concentrate replaced freshly squeezed fruit juice and laughter only rang through the house when Wanja had friends over. The comfortable lifestyle they had unconsciously grown to love now dangled on the single delicate strand of a spider's web.

Kavata didn't speak to her mother for months after their brief phone conversation. And when she did, it was because her mother called to tell her that Muli was retiring from office. It has been the Mwangis' most difficult year yet and it was extremely comforting to hear her mother's voice. Kavata was terribly lonely. They had thankfully put enough money away over the last few years to keep them going while Ngugi found new work, but it was becoming more and more evident that no one would touch him. Ngugi was a shell of the man he used to be. He had shrunk and aged and not even Wanja could lift him out of his funk. He was slipping further and further away from her and Kavata didn't know what to do. She told her mother just as much.

'You know there is nothing worse for a man than being unable to provide for his family.'

'And who do we have to blame for that, Mother?'

'Kavata, I didn't phone you so you can continue your

accusations.'

'What do I do?'

'Find him a job.'

'We've looked everywhere.'

'You haven't. Swallow your pride and speak to your father.'

When Kavata realised this would always be her mother's solution to her problem, she decided to steer the conversation elsewhere. She would need to go elsewhere for marriage counsel. They talked about the plans for her father's final rally and familiarity of the conversation offered her some respite from her current struggles.

'So will you come on Saturday?' Mrs. Muli asked.

'Mum, you know I don't like these *ma things*. It's such a waste of a Saturday.'

'Kavi, it is the last time. We stood with him in the beginning, we must stand with him at the end.'

'I wasn't there in the beginning.'

'You were.'

'Not consciously.'

'So what?'

'I'm so tired, this pregnancy is draining me. I'll die in the heat and all the dust.'

'*Kavi eka utumaanu*. Are you serious? *Basi*, let Ngugi *na* Wanja come if you will not. He will never go anywhere near Machakos without your blessing.'

'Does Dad even know I am pregnant?'

'Of course he does Kavata, don't be disrespectful.'

'Let me think about it.'

'What is there to think about Kavata? I am your mother requesting you do something for your father. When last did he need anything from you, eh? When? It doesn't matter what you think about your father and his work. You are not Jesus. It is not your job to pass judgment. You are his only child and will support him. I don't care if you are a grown woman. I am still your mother.' Mrs. Muli didn't speak to her daughter until the evening before the event, when she called to inform them their transport for the next day was sorted.

The sun was out with all its relatives and thousands of people came out to see Muli. The Mulis and the Ngugis sat on a tented wooden platform next to Hon. Muli. Behind them stood some people who worked with Muli over the course of his career, and the security personnel that he retained for years. Only the metal points of umbrellas hovering above them matched the shine from the crowd's foreheads as they stood in the harsh sunshine. '*Hamjamboni.*'

The crowd was rigid. Their collective murmur was a shallow boo. He began to talk about the things he accomplished over the years as minister of Machakos.

'What about all the money you have stolen?' A woman shouted from the front, inspiring others.

'Yes, are you going to give it back now that you have finished with us? Is it already with the Arabs?'

'Where is our tarmac?'

'And those pits you built were fake! They dried up! Take them back!'

Hon Muli gazed out with bewilderment moulded to his face like a father discovering that his children viewed him as anything beneath a god. He called for silence. They responded promptly.

'A true man's responsibility is to his *boma* first. I joined the government because I wanted a bigger *boma*. You are my extended family and I have served you in the best way I can.

*Lakini sasa nimekuwa Mzee sana,*' he paused and turned to look at his family. He captured the crowd's full attention.

'These are my people. My family.'

'But we don't know them,' they said.

He gazed out to the horde again and then he called his family up to the podium.

'You know *Mama.*' Mrs. Muli stepped up and waved. The women craned their necks. 'And my son, he is called Ngugi Mwangi from Central. The father of my *gacucu* who is not here today. I am told she is in school—these Nairobi children and their school on the weekends. Let me tell you, our Wanja reads the news better than Kasavuli. She will be on your TVs very soon.' At which point he stood next to Kavata who was restless and uncomfortable, melting in the intense heat. She accepted the handkerchief her father held out to her and tossed her flask of lemon water aside. 'As you can see, I am going to have a grandson soon. So I need to rest and repair my bones so I can take him around and show him his *munda,*' he pointed towards the hills. The crowd loved it. The energy shifted completely. Women applauded him the loudest and asked him to speak to their husbands so they too understood the value of family. They were still singing for him when Hon. Muli and his family were halfway back to Nairobi.

Each time Kavata thought back to this day, she wondered how her father could sense that she was carrying a son. She would also remember her and her mother sitting in the car for what felt like hours, waiting for their husbands. Kavata kept her eyes glued to Ngugi. Initially, he would squirm at the way Muli placed his arm on Ngugi's shoulder when he was introducing him to someone. But slowly by slowly he got into it and grew a little more comfortable, like a child warming up to an enchanting stranger. His demeanour transformed and by the time the two men were walking towards the car, they were chatting away like old friends. Kavata could swear she saw a glimmer of admiration on Ngugi's face and an intense feeling of dread seeped into her gut and settled in right there next to her unborn son and never left.

'What else did he say?' Kavata had asked Ngugi this over a dozen times in the week after her father's retirement rally.

'Nothing, Kavi, I've told you everything I can remember.'

'I know. But we just need to be sure. He's not being nice to you for nothing. He knows how angry you still are with him.' Kavata knew she should drop it, but these conversations were the most she'd gotten out of Ngugi in months. If Muli was all he wanted to talk about, then she'd take it.

'Yes, which is why he was trying to apologise to me,' Ngugi said, frustrated.

'Darling. My silly, adorable darling—Honourable Justus Mutinda Muli does not apologise to anyone. Least of all a disgruntled son in law.'

Ngugi shot her a wounded look.

'Sorry. I meant disappointed? Disillusioned?'

'Unemployed. And people change, Kavata,' Ngugi mumbled as he walked away.

'Not in their 70's,' she shouted back at him.

Slowly, Kavata's parents began to inch their way back into their lives and it seemed to do them all some good. Mrs. Muli absolutely loved helping her daughter get ready for Amani's arrival, and Kavata was really grateful to have more support this time around. Muli, already obsessed with his unborn grandchild, constantly sent Kavata and Ngugi heirlooms he claimed he had been saving for his grandson.

In the weeks before his birth, they were visiting each other weekly. Wanja had a connection with her grandfather Kavata would never have predicted. They spent most Sunday afternoons tucked away in his study. Occasionally, Hon. Muli's laughter would boom through the old house, and Mrs. Muli would stop what she was doing and follow the sound, with a reminiscent smile on her face as it travelled through the house. Ngugi was still worried, but seemed to hear her now when she reassured him that they would be just fine. He started exercising again which Kavata enjoyed immensely because in those final days, her hormones were out of control and the fitter Ngugi was, the longer he lasted in bed.

Thirteen hours into the new millennium, Amani was born in a luxury suite of the Aga Khan Hospital surrounded by his parents, grandmothers, big sister and a team of nurses and doctors who were paid well not to leave Kavata's side until Muli's grandson was born. Kavata didn't object to it because even if she was adamant in her quest for a simple life, she would not birth another child at a public hospital.

The weeks following Amani's birth were harder than she could recall them being with Wanja. She was emotional all the time, and constantly in doubt of her ability to raise a child. She spent half the time worried that she was starving him and the other half scared that he would drown at her breast. Her anxiety was draining and she was exhausted. Ngugi saw it, as did Wanja and Schola, the housekeeper Mrs. Muli insisted they hire. Ngugi was as supportive as he could be—but spending time with his new son only served to remind him that he was failing as his father. So he would find whatever excuse he could to get out of the house. He looked forward to trips to the supermarket and insisted on taking Wanja to school each morning even though she'd been taking the school bus since she was 6 years old. When he was out of options, he would go over to the Muli's because even if he could never have predicted it, Muli was the only person with whom Ngugi didn't feel like a complete waste of space. Muli, on the other hand, was so thrilled Ngugi gave him a grandson that he treated him like a prince.

Soon, mysterious envelopes branded confidential started to creep into Kavata's home like the stench of the sewer unclogged by the long rains. Followed closely by meetings with nameless strangers, that Ngugi would emerge from beaming as he had during the NHC days. Ngugi's new sunny disposition is what managed to lift Kavata out of her funk. Partly because she was so happy to be able to see parts of her husband return to her, but also because she was so curious about the source of his new joy. When she would ask him about his day, Ngugi would shrug and say that he'd spent the day chasing business leads. This week he was brokering a deal between foreign investors and local landowners. The next he was developing marketing plans for small businesses and considering chicken farming. He would bring home some money, but it was too irregular to rely on.

'Maybe you should spend a little more time with Amani and I can go back to work. We're going to need the income soon,' she offered.

'Yeah, maybe. But let's give it a little more time. Something is bound to come up,' he said, recycling the words she'd used to encourage him for the past several months. She immediately suspected an affair. But when she'd sent their driver Thuo to the post office to collect their mail and he came back bearing a letter from the golf club welcoming them as their newest members, Kavata confirmed the thing she was smelling on Ngugi was the scent of her father's influence. And this was worse than any affair he could have. Because while she was confident in her abilities to wrangle her husband back from whatever woman was nursing him out of his misery, she knew that no one took Muli on and won.

Over the next few years, Ngugi continued to spend more and more time with Muli. Wanja had just completed high school, Amani was starting kindergarten, and Kavata had long since resumed teaching although everyone, Ngugi included, insisted she didn't need to.

'Oh, so did you magically manage to conjure up a job?' she asked, with daggers in her voice.

'Kavi please, not again. You know I've been helping your father out.'

'Yes, I know it because that's all you keep saying, but unless you can show me a pay slip for all those mysterious deposits into our bank account, I don't want to hear it.'

'Everything we are doing is above board, Kavata. Please just trust me. Your dad is not as sinister as you think he is. We can actually achieve something great.'

'Are you mad?'

'Kavi, please...'

'No, don't *Kavi please* me...' and then the conversation would deteriorate into a series of quarrels and tears.

'You need to trust me.'

'I trust you completely. I don't trust that you are discerning enough to see him for the fox he is. What makes you think you know him better than I do?' And so it would go each time Muli's name was mentioned.

Then, on the afternoon of Amani's 5th birthday, Ngugi phoned Kavata more excited than he had been about any of the birthdays they'd celebrated in the past. He wanted to take the family out to the new restaurant in Gigiri.

'It's a school night. Plus, Amani had a party at school today. Can't we do this over the weekend?'

'No, I have some news that might kill me if I wait until then.' Ngugi sounded like the man she married.

'Then get some takeaways and we will eat here. We can lay the table and get the kids to dress up if you like.'

'Will you also? Dress up?'

'What for?'

'Because I asked nicely.'

'You didn't.'

'Kavi, please get fancy for me tonight? I think you will be grateful you did when you hear what I have to say. I know you think you know what this is about, but just keep an open mind.'

'Ngugi—'

'Kavata, just be patient. All will be revealed soon.'

She was offended that he didn't expect her to work out what he was up to. She'd suspected it for months and the only reason her suspicion hadn't yet morphed into full-blown knowledge was that a tiny part of her still prayed that the writing on the wall meant something else. Ngugi always underestimated how well Kavata knew him. She knew when to listen to the things he said and when to ignore him. She saw the way the muscles in his shoulders pulled him away from her when he lied and that he got a runny stomach when he was feeling guilty. Whenever their bathroom stunk of his runny bowels, she expected new shoes.

Either way, she relented and agreed to play along. She got dressed and managed to convince herself the love of her life would surprise her and prove her wrong. She hoped his big announcement was he'd secured a job far far away from her father. She would be so grateful if that was the case. She would give him whatever he wanted. Even the third child he'd been hinting about. Soon this possibility pushed all her anxieties out of her mind and she told herself if he delivered what she hoped for, she would break the long drought plaguing their sex life. She found herself reaching out for Ngugi's favourite scent and slipping on the fitted red dress that hugged her hips and made her irresistible to him. By the time she was dressed, Kavata's body wanted her to be wrong about Ngugi almost as much as her heart did.

The house was buzzing when Ngugi pulled into the driveway. Amani did his homework in record time when Schola told him the family was having dinner at the table. He insisted on helping to set the table even if he hadn't quite learned where to place what. The table was a bit of a maze, but he was so proud of his work that neither Kavata nor Wanja had the heart to correct it. Amani rushed to meet his father at the front door, more eager to explore the takeaways than to greet his father. Wanja emerged from her room moments later, having made the least effort of them all to dress up. Ngugi beamed when he saw Kavata sitting at the dining table with her legs crossed and her second glass of red dangling from her fingertips. She couldn't help but smile back and didn't protest when he placed a gentle kiss on her cheek and his hand on the small of her back, ensuring that his fingertips grazed her behind. She welcomed the sensations it sent the rest of her body.

'You look delicious,' he whispered, and sat across the table from her with his glazed eyes glued to her. Schola brought the food out.

'You might have guessed, I have a surprise,' Ngugi

announced.

'Is it my birthday present?' Amani squealed his eyes wide.

'Haha, no *baba*—that will have to wait until the weekend,' Ngugi said, and Kavata reached for her glass but put it back down because her hands were trembling. Wanja noticed this and kept her eyes on Kavata as her father spoke.

'I've put in a bid to run for office in the '07 election and it was successful! It is official, I am going to run for MP of Machakos. I've thought long and hard about it and I think I can win,' Ngugi hesitated and looked over at Kavata, 'with the right support.'

Wanja kept her eyes on her mother, searching for clues as to how she should react. Kavata felt her daughter's stare on her. She reached for her glass again and kept her eyes on Ngugi.

'*Ati* what does that mean?' Amani asked. Ngugi laughed—the silent women around the table made him nervous.

'It means that in the next election, I'm going to ask the people from Machakos to make me their leader...' Each time he checked, Kavata's eyes seemed to have hardened a little more. She'd never looked scarier.

'You mean like a school prefect?' Amani asked in between mouthfuls of honey and sesame-coated pork chops.

'Almost. More like a headmaster, but for adults.'

'You mean like a president?' The young boy's eyes widened with glee.

'Almost, but not for the whole of Kenya.' He was grateful for his son's inquisition. 'The president is in charge of the whole country—but Kenya is big, and he can't be everywhere at once. So, the country is divided into different parts called provinces. Kenya has eight of them. Each province has many constituencies and each constituency has its own boss called a Member of Parliament or MP for short. During an election like the one coming up in two years, people go to vote for whom they want to serve as the president and who they want to be their MP.'

'*Haiya, Si* Machakos is also mummy's shags?'

'Yes, it is!'

'How will you work for Machakos if you live here? Will we have to go live there?'

Ngugi laughed anxiously. 'No, I don't think so, but we can deal with that later. We have to win first.' Ngugi glanced over at Kavata, and then to Wanja who now looked down. Silence. 'Is Amani the only one with questions?'

'With which party?' Wanja wore a simper on her face her father mistook for joy. She braced herself for the hostilities she saw coming. She had never seen her mother drink so fast.

'With PNU. *Guka* Muli and I have already made some good headway.'

Silence.

'Anything else?' This time everyone around the table turned to Kavata who so badly wanted to say something but was sure that if she parted her lips for any reason than to pour wine into her mouth, she would explode. They didn't argue in front of their children and she wasn't going to start now. So she rose, lifted the bottle of wine off the table, went into their bedroom and locked the door behind her. At first, pacing back and forth at the foot of the bed was all she could do to release the tension. When that wasn't working quickly enough, she took long sips from the wine bottle but this was like bringing a match to a flame. It offered no relief. Her anger came fast—it grew and grew like a *mandazi* dipped in boiling oil. It washed over her as a demon would, and swallowed everything, including time.

Kavata wasn't sure how long she'd been swigging and seething, and she didn't remember leaving the room to go get more wine. But when she lifted another wine bottle to her lips and it was empty, she hurled it at the mirror. The sound of glass shattering rang through the house. Wanja and Ngugi were banging on the bedroom door in seconds, shouting for her to let them in. The sound of Wanja's voice released Kavata, albeit temporarily, from her angry trance. She lifted herself off the ground, walked to the door and unlocked it. Wanja gasped when she saw her mother's face and Kavata instantly regretted opening the door.

'Mom! What was that?' Wanja peered into the dark room behind her mother.

'Why are you awake?' Her voice was barely audible.

'Because we heard something break! Are you ok?' Ngugi said, and Kavata shot him a look so vicious he took a step back.

'Jaja. I'm ok—I just dropped a glass. Go back to bed.'

'Mom, its 6:30.' Kavata stared back blankly. 'In the morning,' Wanja added.

Kavata gasped and looked around the dark room again. Ngugi took a step forward again, this time to pull Wanja away from the door.

'Leave us, Wanja. Your mother and I need to talk,' he said, as he mustered all the bravery he could to attempt to step into their bedroom.

'Talk? Fuck off, its way too late for that!' she said, and slammed the door shut.

Later that morning, Ngugi took the kids to school and passed by Kavata's school to inform them she was unwell and would likely need the day off. Then he sent Schola and Thuo away and walked to their bedroom, determined to have a conversation with his wife. The door was unlocked and there she was. Asleep on the bed, curled up into a tight small ball. The room smelled of stale wine and the adjacent bathroom of vomit, which also made Ngugi wonder when she'd managed to go through three bottles of wine. He'd hardly slept the previous night—this being the first time he'd been banished from their bedroom—but he didn't hear her get into the liquor cabinet. He sat on the foot of the bed, his gaze shifting from his wife, to the broken glass on the carpet and the tissue strewn all over the room, back to his wife. He was unsure what to feel at the moment. The previous night was a mix of emotions, but the main one was annoyance that she was refusing to talk. He knew she would need some convincing, but hadn't expected her to be so volatile. This was unchartered territory. He nudged her gently again, determined to have the conversation while they were home alone. Her eyes flickered as he gave her a moment to wake up.

'We should talk before the kids come home,' he offered.

Kavata turned her back against him and didn't speak to him for weeks.

They settled into a wordless routine. She took the rest of the school term off and would only emerge from her room hours after Ngugi, growing more irritable by the day, nudged her when he woke up to ask if she was going to spend another day refusing to speak to him. She would pretend to be sleeping, although sleep was now a foreign concept. When Ngugi and the kids left in the mornings, she surrendered to the emotions that surged through her like a bull let loose to pursue its matador. On the sad days, she would stay in bed and cry until her eyes were swollen shut. When anger ruled, she would be a hurricane in search of someone or something to let her fury out on.

On the indifferent days, she flipped through magazines looking for pictures of politicians' wives and comparing their box skirts suits to the fitted trousers and sleeveless dresses that dominated her wardrobe. She tried to picture herself in a wig. No way her locks would be acceptable—she would need to chop them off and hide her bald head until she grew enough hair for a perm of a respectable length. She thought back to the conversation she and Ngugi had all those years ago when he'd encouraged her to change her wardrobe into something more relatable. *The idiot must have been planning this all along.* And on the days when she missed her husband and felt guilty at shutting him out, she would try to see things his way. She would make lists of the pros and cons of standing by Ngugi, each time praying the positives would outnumber the negatives. But they never did. Regardless of what kind of day she was having, noon found Kavata well through her second bottle of merlot.

Schola was the only person who witnessed Kavata's initial stages of grief. She would tidy up Ngugi's office after Kavata trashed it. She called Thuo to ask him not to bring Amani from his holiday classes just yet because Kavata was still in bed. Schola didn't want Amani to see his mother before she bathed. She made sure there was always food ready for Kavata even if she never ate it. She purposefully forgot to get more alcohol when Kavata would add it to her grocery list, but Kavata just resorted to sending Thuo to the liquor store. She had never seen Kavata like this.

One day, when Schola sensed Kavata was having one of her calmer days, Schola collected all the empty bottles she stored in the back for recycling and made sure they were in a spot where Kavata would see them. Kavata stopped in her tracks when her bare feet struck the basket. Schola was washing dishes with her back turned to Kavata.

'Mama Wanja, I don't know what has happened to you, *lakini wacha kuonyesha watoto hii tabia.*' Schola's lips pointed at the pile. Schola knew the exact cause of Kavata's pain. But she didn't understand her reaction, and thought it quite childish. But she was well aware of her place in this home so this was as much as she was going to say about the situation.

Kavata stared at Schola's back, catching her eye briefly when Schola turned around to confirm Kavata heard her. She searched for words and when she could find none, she spun on her heels and walked back to her room. Schola was right. In all her brooding, she momentarily forgot to consider her children. And when she tucked her pain away for a few moments and thought about what Ngugi's decision meant for them, things began to settle down and she gained some perspective. The truth was that she could probably live through five or ten years of being the first lady of Machakos. She was familiar enough with the life to perform the role on autopilot. What she wouldn't live with was her children living the life she endured while her own father revelled in the spotlight. The only way to get Ngugi to understand was to show him what his decision could potentially do to their children. Surely he could remember what it was like for her. He knew what life as Muli's daughter was like. She showed him all those years ago in the library. He must have just forgotten. This was it; she would just need to remind him.

She sent the children to Ngugi's sister's for the night and waited for him in the living room. He was shocked to see her out of bed and looking more like herself when he got home. And she was startled at how quickly his aura had changed. The idea of power was already finding a home in his bones and suddenly he seemed taller. Bigger even. She felt a sickness in her belly.

He walked right through the living room into the kitchen.

'We should talk,' she called after him. He stopped, his shoulders tensed.

'Not today—I don't have the energy for a fight, Kavata.' Kavata. He hadn't used her full name in years.

'Today, Ngugi. The kids are at Wairimu's and I need this war to end.'

'I am not at war with anyone. If you stopped acting so immature, you would see that.' His words cut like knives. There was absolutely no remorse in his voice. She didn't expect this.

'Please sit down.'

He did.

'Do you remember what Wanja said the day she saw her name listed in the newspapers when they published the story of the NHC scandal?'

Ngugi stared at her blankly.

'Oh, that's right, you were so pre-occupied with my father's betrayal of you that you probably missed it. I came home and Wanja was reading the paper as usual. Only this time she was reading about her father being in the middle of one of the biggest real estate scandals in our country's recent history. And because of this scandal, which you might recall was all my father's doing, Wanja's name was tainted in the national press. Do you know what she said?'

'Get to the point.'

'She said the next time her name was in the paper she

wanted it to be for something good.' Kavata waited a moment for that to sink in. 'Don't do this to our kids, Ngugi.'

'Don't do what? Provide for them? Teach them the value of public service? Damnit Kavi, the only reason I am doing this is for the kids.'

'We will find another way. There has to be another way. Trust me.'

'There isn't! No one will hire me!'

'And if they won't hire you what makes you think they will vote for you?'

'Kavata, I am not your father...'

'I know this, but you are becoming more and more like him. Every day I see more of him in you. And if this is something you really want, then let's do it together—just you and me. Elsewhere—far *far* away from his influence. We've done it before.'

'Do you know how long that will take! Do you think we have that kind of time? This is no longer uni—this is real politics! And why are you so selective about the help you will take from him? You didn't have any problems accepting his help when it took the form of this house or a luxury hospital room. You are being a fucking hypocrite.'

'How can you stand on his shoulders and expect him to not fling you over the mud and use you as a bridge? He is using you, Ngugi. How can you be so stupid!'

Ngugi took a deep breath and closed his eyes and Kavata knew she had lost this one.

'Kavata, I have a plan. I am not going into this blind. But you haven't heard this plan because you have been too stubborn to look past all your assumptions about this.'

'Ok, fine. Here I am! Tell me your grand plan. Explain to me, dear husband, how you plan to convince an entire constituency that you are not his protégé. Tell me how you will make them believe you didn't marry his daughter and steal a couple of houses for him so he would reward you with the keys to his kingdom. Because that's what everyone will be saying the minute you launch your campaign.'

'Is that what you really think?' Ngugi was broken. She had broken him. Kavata said nothing. 'You are unbelievable,' he said as he stood and walked to the front door.

'Ngugi, if you do this I will leave you. I swear to God I will.'

Ngugi chuckled. 'Leave and go where? But you know what, you do what you want to do.' The door slammed behind Ngugi.

*I will leave you...* the words repeated themselves in both their minds for the rest of the night, but at the time neither of them knew she'd meant it.

# 4

# FLY ON THE WALL

## JUNE 2005

Wanja believed her little brother was her superpower because the day Amani was born, she became invisible. She'd said this to her family often but they would simply brush it off, saying she was just bitter that she was no longer an only child. No-one paid mind to how true her statement was, so she embraced the new ability to vanish into thin air whenever her brother was around and got so good at it, she blended in even when her brother wasn't around to soak up whatever attention was up for grabs. Eventually, she became an expert at being inside rooms she didn't belong in. This is why she was in the room the day her grandfather planted the seed in her father's mind.

It was a Sunday, and one of those rare ones when her mother agreed to host her parents for lunch, which meant the house was noisier than usual. Wanja was sitting on the floor in Ngugi's office reading with her headphones on when Hon. Muli and Ngugi walked in. She muted her Mp3 player and began to guess how long it would be before they noticed her sitting there.

'Sawa, you are angry with me or whatever but we must talk these things over like men. How can you hold a grudge for so long, eh? Like a woman?' Muli said.

'You underestimate how impossible it has been for me to find work since my dismissal. With all due respect, this grudge is mine to do with as I please.'

'Kenyans are a people plagued with chronic amnesia—you should learn from them. You think they even remember what the NHC is? My son, I'll help you with everything. If we put together a good team we can easily win this election.'

'I could never spend all my days with dodgy politicians.' He realised the weight of his proclamation after it flew out of his mouth.

'So what's your plan then? How do you plan to provide for Kavi and the children?' Muli sat back and folded his arms across his chest.

'We will be fine.' Ngugi was adamant.

'On a public school salary, ha! Tell me another lie. And don't imagine I don't know Mama Kavata has been helping you out. Where do you think that money is coming from? Don't be a hypocrite,' Hon. Muli spat and Wanja suddenly felt uncomfortable being in a room where her father was basically being insulted. She raised her arm to scratch her scalp, hoping one of them would notice the sudden movement.

'Wanja, please leave,' Ngugi said, but she pretended not to hear them. 'Jaja!'

Now she faked a startled jump, pulled off her headphones and turned to face them.

'Yes, Dad?'

'Go read elsewhere, I need the room.'

'Ok.' She slid out of the office and shut the door behind her. When she was sent back into the office an hour later to call the men out for lunch, they were laughing and chatting like the best of friends.

Weeks later, Wanja received her admission papers into university and was celebrating the news with Ngugi when Muli popped in unannounced.

'What's the occasion? What did we miss?'

'This one got into university,' Ngugi said, with his hands on Wanja's shoulders.

'That's wonderful! Congratulations. What are you studying?'

'International Relations and Poli—'

'Very well done. Another political animal in the family. My blood truly runs thick in your veins. You should come with us. I'm taking your father on a small road trip. Then we can all celebrate after.'

'Ok, let me tell mum.' Wanja reached for her phone.

'No need to—I've already spoken to her,' Ngugi said, and Wanja knew he was lying, but she also knew her mother hated spontaneity so she put her phone away and followed her father.

Muli obviously sent word they were coming; by the time they got to his house in Machakos, there were thousands of people waiting. The entire town dropped everything to catch a glimpse of the great Muli. Even the young, jaded men couldn't feign disinterest for long as Ngugi's car inched closer to Muli's rural home. When Thuo finally got the car as close as possible to Muli's house, it took the three of them almost an hour to walk from the car to the front steps of the house. With each step, there was someone to greet and a child to bless and a moment to be photographed. By the time they got to the house, Wanja had eaten more sweet bananas and drank more cups of porridge than her tiny stomach could hold. A microphone materialised almost out of thin air connected to a bullhorn rigged to the roof of a green Toyota Corolla parked behind the crowd. Muli greeted the crowd and explained that this was a short informal visit to introduce Ngugi to the people who he hoped would vote for him. Then he invited the people to greet Ngugi and ask questions as he went into the house to sit with the *wazees*.

Wanja watched her father. He was nervous as people stood in line and waited for their turn to greet and grill him. Watching her father in action was intriguing. People's faces fell when they realised Ngugi didn't speak *kikamba* as well as they expected him to. Wanja found the women the most interesting to listen to. Ngugi struggled to find words for them when they said they were only there to meet Kavata; where was she? They were polite and reticent to his face, but then they turned around to share their doubts about him.

'Now, am I going to call him my MP or my child? He looks so young.'

'Does he even have a son?'

'He doesn't have a son.'

'He does. A small boy.'

'Where is his wife?'

'Why isn't she here?'

'Muli should run again—he is the one we know.'

These same women approached Ngugi with the important questions: 'Will you bring water?'

'Is it true Muli stole?'

'Will you also steal?'

'Why should we vote for a Kikuyu? Have your people rejected you?'

'But if you will have jobs for us, we will do them. Even in Central. *Kazi haina kabila.*'

'You must learn our language.'

The men just demanded the '*chai*' they assumed Ngugi would be dishing out, and when the word got around that Ngugi didn't come to line their pockets, the crowd thinned significantly.

'How dare he come empty-handed? Muli must train him well before he comes back here naked.'

The ride back home was peppered with excited chatter and all talk of celebrating Wanja's admission was forgotten. Like the women of Machakos, Wanja was unconvinced that her father would win this election. He lacked the seedy greed she saw in Muli. The way she saw it, Hon. Muli stood better chances of clinging to power if he grabbed one of those village women, put her in a suit, gave her a microphone and told her to assume the role of a politician.

'Wanja, and what do you think? Does your dad have a chance at winning this thing—if he decides to run?' The question drew her out of her thoughts. It surprised her that Hon. Muli would even ask for her opinion. He struggled to relate to her because she was at that awkward age, too old to sit in his lap and worship him, and too young to be fully significant to him because she hadn't had children. She considered his questions as she shifted in her seat so as to look at their faces as she spoke.

'Some people were saying he is too inexperienced to be an MP.' It wasn't what she planned to say, but courage slipped away at the very last moment.

'Did I ask you what uneducated women were saying? What do *you* think?' Hon. Muli prodded.

'I think educated or not, they might be right. Dad should sit out this election, and maybe run for the next one,' Wanja blurted out and Thuo, sitting in the driver's seat next to her, glared at her and mumbled something under his breath.

'I think...'

'It doesn't matter what she thinks, she's always agreed with her mother anyway,' Ngugi snapped and continued his conversation with Muli.

Wanja noticed something change in her father that day. He was excited again. He held a desire in his eye different to the one she remembered from the days he spent ensconced in building homes to change lives. It was a louder, more defensive passion, like the one she saw inhabit her grandfather anytime he was under scrutiny. Her relationship with him also changed. She didn't dislike him or respect him any less. Rather, she became aware that his spine turned to rubber around Muli.

She was watching an episode of Oprah one evening weeks later which featured a woman who was brutally abused by her husband and the love of her life. Oprah asked the woman what she thought transformed her husband from a man who kissed her feet on a daily basis to one who would only stop hitting her when he thought her unconscious.

'He lost his job and then lost his mind,' the woman said.

Those words stuck with Wanja. Maybe that was what was happening with her father. After much thought, she decided to speak to him, if for nothing else than to assure him that he was still a great father. On one of the evenings when Kavata was out late, Wanja cooked her father his favourite meal: spinach fried in salty *ndengu*, wrapped in *chapati*, and served with dry fried beef. She served the meal on his favourite plate when his car came up the driveway and met him at the door.

'Hi, Dad. Mom said she'll be home late. But I cooked!' She smiled and took his briefcase into his study so he could go straight to the table.

'Wonderful, I am ravenous. Have you guys eaten?'

'Yeah, Amani is in bed, but I'll come and sit with you.'

'How is school going?' Ngugi didn't look up from the meal.

'It's going well. I really like the campus, and I'm enjoying my classes. Actually, Dad, I wanted to talk to you about something.'

Ngugi looked up, his eyes searching hers, making her suddenly anxious.

'This whole...' she wished she had rehearsed this, '...MP thing.' He released his fork and the sound echoed throughout the large dining room. 'I'm just wondering why you are running? I know you might mean well, but I think it might be a good idea to listen to some of the things Mom is worried about?' The words ran out of her before she filtered them. Ngugi was now glaring at her. 'I know you mean well, Dad, and I know something changes for a man when he is unable to provide for his family, but maybe...'

'That is enough, Jaja.' Ngugi sat back. 'Since when have I been unable to provide for my family? Are those the lies your mother is feeding you?'

'No Baba, that's not what I meant. It's just—'

'I have told your mother many times not to poison your minds with her opinions of me, but she is too stubborn and proud to listen or to leave you out of this. Despite what you both think, I know what I am doing, and I am fully in control of this whole thing. I am making all the sacrifices and doing all the work while the two of you sit here sulking and gossiping. I have had enough,' Ngugi shouted.

'Dad, it's just that—' Wanja fought back tears.

'Enough! I am going ahead with the campaign whether or not I have your support and quite frankly, I don't need it. A few months at university doesn't make you an expert.'

Ngugi left his meal halfway eaten and walked away.

A stunned Wanja sat there with her mouth hanging open. It all happened so quickly. If he let her speak, Wanja would have been able to tell Ngugi her mother was more distraught about his decision than she let on. She would have confessed to listening in on his conversations with Kavata and shared that she didn't think either of them was wrong. This was just one of those situations where none of them could win. She would also have explained the reason she didn't want him to run this year was that they *all* were not ready but anyone who said as much could never be as loud as Hon. Muli. She'd have told him about all the hours Kavata was spending comparing the cost of living in various cities across the world. And it was a huge mistake to choose to listen to Muli when he said Kavata was just like her mother and that all would be well once there was a new office for her to decorate. That was the last time she mentioned the election to any of her parents.

\*\*\*

The United States International University was a secular institution that somehow managed to thrive in a fiercely religious country. Students were encouraged to shed their religious and political affiliations when they walked through the elaborate campus gates. Most students adhered to the rule, but it didn't stop them from having gatherings right outside the campus. Wanja signed up as a volunteer for the university's unofficial arm of the Party of Neverending Unity as soon as she learned of the underground gatherings. She submitted an application but only got accepted when whispers of her father's bid began to circulate. She was invited to join the Facebook group first. When she accepted, she received a message with directions to a series of hidden rooms at the back of Fifi's, the bar located outside the campus.

Fifi's was built as an afterthought. Legend had it that the quarter-acre piece of land it sat on belonged to a man who refused to sell his property decades ago when the government approved the construction of the private university. It was a long battle to get him to sell, but he would not budge. So the developers decided to build the university around him. When he died, the plot lay vacant for many years. A few of his relatives would come and check on the house regularly to ensure no students squatted on the deceased's property.

After a while, the property became bothersome and the family sold it to a local businessman who planned to build a block of affordable flats for off-campus housing. It cost more than he anticipated so the project stalled. Soon the construction site began to take on a life of its own. Every Thursday night, a few entrepreneurial students would fill the back of a pick-up truck with several crates of beer and park it at the construction site. They would sell up to two hundred crates of beer a night—more than most bars in the area managed to sell in a weekend. Another group of media students would smuggle a public address system out of the labs and set them up on the grounds. The Construction Site, as it came to be known, was the place to be on a Thursday night. Since the parties happened outside campus hours and on private property, the university could do little to stop them. But the new owner of the land inevitably found out about the parties and decided to reclaim his space along with the students' great business idea. Fifi's was born.

Fifi's owner anticipated that there would be resistance from the university against having a pub so close to the campus, so he didn't invest much into the structure. At first, it was a square room with narrow planks of wood as walls and a thatched roof. The floors were concrete and a few blue and green bulbs provided the only ambience needed. For tables, there were old oil barrels with a flat round piece of wood as the table top, and simple bar stools around each barrel. There was more seating for larger groups along the walls of the pub—long tables and simple wooden benches with nails sticking out that ripped many skirts. A radio by the bar played whatever local radio station the students wanted to listen to and, without a dance floor, people often danced by their tables. Fifi's was packed every night from the first night it opened. The university tried to shut it down several times, but the uproar from the students always prevailed. They claimed that Fifi's saved their lives. Now they didn't need to travel the few kilometres between the highway and the campus on foot, and then cross the busy highway (where a few students had died) to get to the closest bar. Fifi's was part of their community. When the need arose, he quickly constructed meeting rooms and encouraged students to hire them for activities banned on campus. So at any given point, some students would be at the bar in the front engaging in drunken debauchery, whilst others a few metres away would be engrossed in fiery Christian Union sessions.

The rooms were booked out by student politics groups for the duration of the election. The Kenya Patriots' Party occupied the first room along the corridor at the back of the bar. The sound of fevered praise and worship could be heard coming from the other side of the thin wooden walls. The Christian Union members were recruited as volunteers for KPP, led by a popular local pastor. During these meetings, the recruits would spend hours in prayer, after which they would sit and talk about the campaign strategies that God revealed to them. Next door, the Kenya National Democratic Association volunteers posted a guard outside their meeting room and hung a thick black curtain over the small window. The room was always eerily silent. Rumour had it the party members only communicated with each other via email, even when seated in the same room. Official Democratic Movement got the largest space, set up as elaborately as their head offices with the welcome addition of a snack table, well-stocked with *nyama choma*, potato wedges, *kachumbari,* as well as more soft drinks and beers than the people in the room knew what to do with.

The plain but functional PNU room became Wanja's second home. She often wanted to tell her father about her political affiliation, if for nothing else so he would understand that she could be useful to his campaign. Several of her colleagues didn't think he would win either and that his campaign was a colossal waste of resources. But she knew to keep her opinion to herself.

The Ngugi residence provided the venue for a series of fundraising dinners, parties and visits from supporters because Muli felt it necessary to show the public that Ngugi was accessible; an open house policy, he called it. Kavata's refusal to participate in the campaign extended to these events, so Wanja and Mrs. Muli often hosted them. When the guests began to arrive, Mrs. Muli would whisper to Wanja the detailed story they would use to explain Kavata's absence, then shuffle over to Ngugi and share the same message with him. There was a new story each time:

'Mum came down with such a horrible flu last night. She is resting. Will send her your regards.'

'Kavata has an emergency with one of her students. She

is visiting the child's family now.'

'Oh, my wife must be around here somewhere. I will ask her to come find you.'

Muli attended all these events, seizing every opportunity to tell anyone who would listen that he was the driving force behind Ngugi's political career. And while Wanja mastered the craft of masking her interest in the election, she would once in a while get caught up in an irresistible conversation. She was handing out donation envelopes when she met Tom for the first time. He stood in a small group of slightly younger guests—marketing execs and PhD students discussing the recent election in Ethiopia. He was handsome, with an understated charm and a beard she thought hideous. She stood with them long after she collected a total of one million shillings from three members of this group.

'It is so refreshing to hear a conversation that isn't about this election,' Wanja said when she began to receive curious looks from the group.

'There's really nothing left to say about this election— ODM are winning it—*kwisha maneno*.' The Ogilvy marketing exec studied her face for a reaction, surprised when she shrugged and nodded in agreement.

'For sure. People can rig all they want, but eventually they are going to give people what they want. Now is the time to get what we want,' the man standing next to Tom said. Tom nudged him in the ribs with his elbow. Wanja flipped through the donations in her hand.

'What's this for then? The cheque was for half a million shillings.'

'A little something to cushion the blow,' the Ogilvy man said.

'And to get us into this party, of course,' Tom added.

'Well then, I suppose I should hang on to these and buy Dad something nice. To lick the wounds of his loss, right?' Wanja relished the looks on their faces when they couldn't tell if she was joking. She excused herself and sauntered away. She and Tom exchanged numbers, and the following week they met for coffee at the university campus.

'So, you are with PNU?' Tom asked when they found a quiet corner at Fifi's. He ordered a Tusker Malt while she got a passion juice.

'I am. Have been for a few weeks now.'

'What year are you in?'

'Second. International....'

'IR, I know. I've done my homework.'

'Have you now?' She blushed. Wanja could never tell when a man was interested in her.

'I have.'

'Why?'

'Because I think you should stop wasting your time with these amateur politics and come work for us. There's real money to be made.'

'*Si* you've given me enough of your money already? Not that I need it.'

Tom laughed. 'Those cheques are no good. They are going to bounce. So hard. We do it all the time. The cheques get us into the parties—but no one says they have to be good cheques.'

He said he and his colleagues were sent to the fundraiser to scope out the level of support Ngugi garnered. This intrigued Wanja. These were the kind of tactics her father's issue-led campaign would always lose to.

'It's just another job—that's the way you must think about it,' Tom continued. 'We'll give you a contract for the remaining duration of the campaign. You will earn a bit over a hundred k—no taxes,' he paused, 'not that you need it or anything.' They both laughed.

'What's the job, though?' It didn't really matter to her. For one hundred thousand, she would happily serve as the errand girl. Tom paused.

'You'll work with my team—in communications.' Tom sounded like he just made up the position.

'We need a younger, more middle-class voice,' he sniggered.

'What are you giggling at? I'm as middle class as they come.'

'Of course you are. That's why I'm here. Then if—sorry—when we win, you can decide if you want to stay on. The position will still be available, since we're going digital and all.'

This was her first job interview—if she could even call it that. She couldn't think of a reason not to take the job. The pay was definitely more than any entry-level position paid, so she knew there was more to it than he let on. But she didn't care.

'Can I think about it?' She realised she would need to figure out what to tell her parents.

'We also offer benefits.'

'What kind?'

'The ones that come with working for the most heavily funded campaign in the country. Entertainment allowance, fuel, event invitations...'

'And aren't you worried I'll share your trade secrets with your competition?'

'No. Your father is no threat to us.'

'Ouch.'

'Sorry. Too far.'

'I still want to think about it.'

'What? You want more money?'

'Maybe.' Tom laughed, exposing a flawless set of teeth.

'You are nothing like your father, but you are certainly a Muli. I will not offer you any more money because as you said, you don't need it. We would like to have you, but we are not desperate. So, let me know by the end of the week. Job starts Monday.'

Wanja initially joined PNU because she genuinely wanted to work on an election campaign and here was the opportunity to work on the winning campaign. She thought about her family. Her mother was so steeped in her own worries that the only way she would find out was if Wanja told her. Her grandparents would probably never speak to her again. As for her father, she consoled herself with the fact that she offered herself to him first, and he turned her down.

The next day, Wanja called Tom to let him know she wanted the job.

'Great!' he said. 'Can you come in tomorrow?'

'You said Monday?'

'I did, but we're busy now. No point waiting.'

'Um, yeah. I guess I could. One thing, though...'

'Yes?' Tom seemed eager to get her off the phone.

'Why me?' She prodded for ulterior motives. Tom paused for a moment before he answered.

'Well, you obviously have a knack for this media thing—I've read your blog. But if I am being honest, I didn't think you would take the job.'

It wasn't the response she hoped for, but it would do.

# 5

# BEST LAID PLANS

## AUGUST 2005

Anne moved back to Nairobi in time to catch the pieces of Kavata's marriage.

'*Woi*, is it a *ndogo-ndogo*?' Anne asked nonchalantly when Kavata revealed she was thinking about leaving Ngugi.

'No, I wish,' Kavata said.

'Ah, money issues. You are tired of his unemployed behind.'

Kavata shook her head.

'Is he an alcoholic? Oh no, drugs? Aahh, he can't get it up?' Anne continued guessing to her own amusement and each time Kavata shook her head a little more aggressively. 'What did he do then?'

'He's decided to run for MP of Machakos.' Kavata heard the words as they left her mouth. She had to admit that this didn't sound as bad as all the other things that Anne had mentioned.

'And?' Anne watched her friend expectantly and Kavata realised that she would need to give Anne some more context.

'I told you about the NHC mess, right?'

Anne nodded.

'He never really bounced back. He would just walk around the house angry on most days and completely deflated on the others. Sometimes he would get so angry I worried that he would drive up to my dad's house and put a bullet in his head.'

'Wait, what did your father have to do with the housing scandal?'

'Everything. The only thing he didn't do was build those houses. But he was behind the entire scandal—somehow, and I don't know how yet—he found someone within the NHC to manipulate so that he could swindle some houses for himself.'

'And Ngugi didn't know?'

'He didn't. At least he says he didn't.'

'How did he get that job again?'

'He says he dropped his CV there and he got a call. But after we found out about the scandal, he suspected that Dad basically planted him there.'

'And how did he find out about the scandal?'

'In the newspapers—like everyone else.'

Anne burst out laughing but checked herself. 'Sorry. But someone needs to write about your father. He really should be immortalised in some way. Ok—so let me see if I understand this correctly. After he lost his job, Ngugi swore he would never look in your father's direction but has now decided to run for the same seat that your father held for years? I still don't see why this is such a horrible thing.'

'Then allow me to paint a clearer picture for you. Do you know what happens before a candidate is allowed to even submit a bid for a parliamentary seat?

'Have a whole lot of money and access so that anyone will even take you seriously. Two of the things my idiot husband lacks.'

'Ahh.'

'So how do you think said idiot was able to get this access?'

'I see.'

'Good, and knowing what you know of Honourable Muli, do you think he did this because he cares about my husband's budding political career?'

Anne shook her head. She was stunned. 'But have you said this to him? Or are you doing the thing women do where we expect our men to read our minds?'

'I've told him!'

'What exactly did you say to him?'

'I can't remember.'

'Yes you can. Kavata, you remember every fight you two have. What exactly did you say to him?'

'I said if he was all of a sudden so hell bent on a career in politics, he and I could do it together like we used to in university. And if he decided to run for office here, with my father, I would leave him.'

'Damn. And what did he say?'

'He laughed and asked where I would go.'

'Men are such fucking idiots. Does he really think you would struggle to find somewhere to go? The nerve!'

Kavata was silent. Tears rushed to her eyes. 'He is right. Where would I go? I haven't really invested in my friendships. Other than you, Ngugi is my only friend.'

'Then let's work on that first before we decide if you are leaving your husband.'

'I swear Anne, I know you are not one to pick a side just because, but if you take Ngugi's side this time you might as well go back to Uganda.'

Anne held up her hands. 'Calm down, mama. I'm not the enemy here. I'm just trying to make sure the punishment fits the crime.'

Kavata allowed her tears to fill the silence between them for a few moments.

'When did this conversation with him happen?'

'About two months ago.'

'And when is the election?'

'In 2007. Sometime in August or December. They haven't decided yet.'

'So what happens between now and then?'

'Campaigns basically?'

'Christ, two years of campaigning? No wonder Kenyan elections are so expensive. So does this mean you still have some time to convince him to withdraw his bid?'

'It does, but you should have seen his face when we fought. He had the determined look he has when he is absolutely set on something. I don't think he will hear anything I have to say.'

'That might be true, but if there is something I know about Ngugi it is that he lives for his kids. Maybe he will listen to them? You need to use them.'

'No. I will not drag them into this.'

'And how is leaving their father not dragging them through this? They're already involved. Let me guess, Ngugi said he is doing this for the kids, right?'

'Yup. How did you know?'

'You forget I have known Ngugi longer than you have. Let me see if I can get through to him. In the meantime, I need you to explore all your options. You have always been too quick to flee difficult situations. But you and Ngugi are really good together—you balance each other out well—and all good marriages deserve a fighting chance.'

Kavata nearly choked on her saliva. 'You are an imposter! What have you done with my friend? The Anne I know has no regard whatsoever for marriage.'

'Well, the Anne you knew woke up one morning and the man she stole from someone else's marriage had been stolen away from her.'

'What? When? How?'

'Yup. Three years ago. He wanted marriage, I didn't. So he found someone who did.'

'Three years, my God Anne, why didn't you ever say anything? What have you been doing in Kampala for three years?'

'I've been kicking myself for not fighting harder for him.'

'Why didn't you fight?'

'The short answer is I was too proud to.'

'And the long one?'

'The long one is too painful to get into now. Story for another day. But if you decide you want to leave Ngugi, then you are going to need to hear it all. For the last three years we've been trying to end our relationship. We got so involved in each other's lives, it was impossible to find the string which we could tug on to unravel everything. And we didn't even have kids. It has been the hardest thing I have ever done.'

'Do you wish you'd just married him?'

'No, I don't. But I wished we'd listened to each other sooner. He'd always been clear that he wanted to be married. I'd always been clear I didn't. But both of us assumed the other would change their mind. But anyway—back to you.'

It was like Anne had never left and the two friends continued where they left off. Kavata pulled strings to get

Anne a job teaching English and Religious Studies at her school, and Anne promised to speak to Ngugi. She was confident that she would be able to get through to him. She'd spent many years observing Kavata and Ngugi's relationship and it always fascinated her how two people from such different worlds could even find grounds for love. She watched them find a happy middle and it was a beautiful thing to see. But now, as she listened to her friend describe the reasons she felt such betrayal, a part of her heard her, while another wondered if this was one of those situations where they were speaking *at* each other in the languages from their past lives.

Two weeks later, the day after Anne and Ngugi met, she and Kavata were sitting in Anne's classroom over their lunch hour.

'So? I've been dying to hear. Ngugi came home stiff as a rock yesterday.'

'Argh, every time he spoke, I wanted to punch him in the groin. What has happened to that man?'

'You see what I mean? Tell me everything.' Both relief and sadness were present in Kavata's voice. Relief to have someone validate all the things she knew about Ngugi, and sadness that Anne had also failed to reach him. She described the night in detail.

He arrived an hour late with a fleeting apology about being held up at a meeting. She was shocked at how good he looked—he stood taller, and the hard years Kavata described didn't seem to have taken a toll on him at all. He was ageing well and confidence looked good on him.

However, his good looks didn't match his character. He seemed to forget he hadn't seen Anne in over a decade and she immediately felt like she was a needy cousin asking for a handout. He immediately assumed Anne sat with him to scold him on Kavata's behalf.

'Calm down. I'm not here as anyone's ally. I'm here to hear your side of this messy story.'

'This doesn't have to be messy. It's your stubborn friend who is making things difficult.'

'I'm not here to talk about Kavata. What's your plan, Ngugi?'

Ngugi mumbled and Anne suspected it was the first time anyone had asked him this question. 'My plan has never changed. I'm doing this because I need to work and this is the only thing on the table at the moment. And yes, I hear all the reasons this might not work but there are so many reasons why it could. Muli is problematic—I understand—but he is not all bad. Before I decided to do this, I spent more time talking to him than I believe Kavata ever has, and I did this because I suspect there must be some good in there. And I told myself that if I didn't find any, I would walk away. But he and I struck a chord when we discovered the thing most important to the both of us was family. Everything Muli has done has been for his family.'

'Ngugi—bullshit. You are talking about the same man who stole houses in his grandchild's name. How can you be so gullible?'

'I didn't say I approve of his methods.'

Anne sighed. She wasn't going to be able to turn this around. 'You still haven't told me what your plan is…'

'My plan is to run for election—whether or not I have Kavata's support.'

'And what if Muli screws you over, again?'

'He won't. That's why I'm keeping him so close. So I can

watch him. He's an old man. And he is tired. There are no more tricks left up his sleeve.'

Anne chuckled. 'Ngugi, I hope you know what you are doing because from where I sit, it doesn't look like you do. We've been friends for years, and I am not going to try and act like I understand all this, because I don't know what it was like to have been jobless for so long. But I do know what hopeless feels like. And I also know the reason your life felt so hopeless was because of the man whose ass you are now so well acquainted with. That's what I don't understand. *Bass*!'

Ngugi began to speak but Anne held up her hand.

'Ngugi, my friend, Kavata is broken. She is devastated and I hope that this thing you are doing is worth your marriage because I don't know how you guys can survive this.'

It was Ngugi's turn to chuckle. 'Since when did you begin to care about marriages?'

Anne stood. The conversation was over. She wished Ngugi well and left him seated there with a silly grin on his face.

'So, what do you want to do now?' Anne asked when she was finished telling Kavata the story.

'I want to leave him.'

'Fine, but what *exactly* is your plan?'

'I don't know.'

Anne rolled her eyes. 'What do you and Ngugi have against making plans? I need you to convince me that you have thought this thing through *sana*. Where will you go?'

Kavata glared at Anne.

'Weh! I'm asking a practical question. On the day you walk out of your home, to what physical place will you go?'

'I don't know.'

'Do you want to leave the country?'

'For sure—I can't imagine being here when he wins the election.'

'How sure are you he will win?'

'My father never loses. He will win. I have family in South Africa. Johannesburg is an option.'

'Ah ah, you know how xenophobic they can get over there. Perhaps somewhere a little less volatile?'

'I've been to Britain once. It was nice.'

'That grey weather will make you sadder! Pick somewhere sunny so I can come visit you.'

'I didn't realise we were picking out your holiday destinations…'

'Listen, things are about to get very real. If you are going to be all alone mourning your marriage, then pick somewhere that will make the pain a little more bearable. And maybe somewhere where you know at least one person. Do you know how hard it is to make friends at our age?'

'Remember my cousin Mutheu? In the US? She's been trying to get me to go visit her since she got her green card. I suppose this is as good a time as ever.'

'Ok. And the kids?'

'They come with me. I won't leave them here in this madness. Wanja is so angry at him.'

Anne shook her head.

'No. Leave them out of this. This is not their battle to fight. What happens when you leave and he changes his mind? Are you going to pack them up again and bring them back? Are you done with him for good? Or for as long as he is an MP? Because that's only five, maybe ten years. In any case, no embassy on the planet is going to grant a permit to a woman and her two kids without her husband's consent. Especially not the Americans.'

Kavata started to protest, but instead she started to unravel. Leaving Ngugi was one thing, but her children as well?

'Do you think it is all too drastic?' Kavata asked.

'What do you hope your fleeing will do? If it is time alone with your thoughts you need, then go to Zanzibar for a month and figure things out. Or go use my flat in Kampala.'

'When did you get a flat in Kampala?'

'I said I was heartbroken, not stupid. I wasn't going to walk away from all of that with nothing.'

Once again Kavata's bull-like pain came to the fore, this time loaded with exhaustion, despair and defeat. She shook and sobbed so hard the front of her dress was soaked in tears. Each time she tried to speak, her tears overpowered her. Anne walked over to the door and locked it, then sat and watched her until the sobs passed and made room for words. When Kavata was done crying, she looked smaller—as if she was carrying her sadness around like some extra kilos. When Anne was sure the tears were finished, she handed her friend a wet towel.

'So your eyes don't puff up. We are not the kind of women who display their woes at work.'

'Anne, I know it seems drastic. Even I can't believe I am considering this. But I can't do it. I can't see the man I love turn into a version of the man I have disliked for so long. I know what this will do to him, and to me, and to the kids. I've lived this! I can't do it again. I don't want to and I won't. I don't have it in me. I don't want to be asked to attend one more campaign event. I can't bare to see Amani become the face of Ngugi's campaign. I'm not sure what I want my leaving him to do. I'm leaving because I feel a pain and betrayal that is worse each time I see him, or hear him, or hear about this bloody election.'

'And you really think things won't be different when Ngugi's in there?'

'It's the only thing I am certain of. And it's sad because Ngugi would make such an incredible leader.'

'He really would. He was great at uni.'

'Yeah, it's why I fell in love with him in the first place. But each time I have thought that things would be different with my father, I have been wrong. Muli is as consistent as death.'

The two women sat in silence for several minutes until the school bell reminded them that there was life beyond their troubles.

'So now?'

'I'm not leaving my kids behind. So now—we make a plan. But not today and not here.' Kavata pressed the damp towel against her warm eyes for a few seconds and then left to prepare for her afternoon class.

It was several weeks before the two discussed Ngugi again. Anne didn't ask any questions. She realised her friend would need time to figure things out, and in the meantime the two worked on getting Anne settled back into Nairobi. When she wasn't doing that, Kavata was busy making lists, analysing her decision and exploring her options.

Mutheu was more than happy to have her visit, but also made the assumption Kavata was planning to travel with her entire family and Kavata didn't think she needed to correct her just yet. The more research she did, the more she realised it would be impossible to take the children with her. She decided she would go to whichever country allowed her to take her children with her without their father's consent, but was quickly learning that no such place existed. Even those that didn't require a visa from Kenyan passport holders insisted she would need consent from Ngugi to allow her to travel with Amani. Wanja would need to make her own decision about going with her mother and each time she considered this, she was sick with worry that her daughter would choose Ngugi. In any case, uprooting Wanja from university was unreasonable and she couldn't imagine separating her children. Planning to take her children was like trying to find her way out of a thick maze while balancing giant aeroplane wings on each shoulder. But, when she considered leaving them behind, the walls would simply fall away revealing a clear path ahead.

Then she would begin to rethink her decision. She started to pray to a God with whom she had a fleeting relationship. She even attended a meeting of Christian women, but politely excused herself when they began to talk about submission being the key to a happy marriage. She bought every book she could find that promised to teach her how to get through to her husband. Then she would test out the things that her books would prescribe: conversation starters and trust exercises. Each of them would fail miserably.

On a Sunday night, four and a half months after Anne's move back to Nairobi, Kavata spent most of the afternoon watching her husband spend time with his children. He asked them to help him select the portraits that would be used for his campaign. Wanja hesitated when asked and glanced over at her mother. Kavata watched relief spread over Wanja's face when she nodded her approval. Wanja got into it immediately—explaining in great detail that this photo was better than that one because the look in his eye was more sincere;

and that the one where he wore a blue tie was better than the red one because she'd read a study that said people were generally more receptive to hues of blue. Wanja had political potential; Kavata could recognise it. Amani was just elated at the celebrity that would follow his father's new job and for the first time in years, Kavata could recognise Ngugi. In all his morphing and changing, he was still the same father he'd always been. She also realised that her husband was spending no time at all questioning his decision to run for office. So why was she questioning her decision to leave him?

Later that day, Kavata put Amani to bed, grabbed two bottles of wine from her drinks cabinet and drove to Anne's house.

'The kids will be ok,' she said, when they settled down on the balcony. 'I'll leave them.'

'*Ala*? Tell me more.'

'I've been trying to figure this thing out for so long. I don't have a plan yet—but I know two things for sure: one is that I must leave him, and the other is that Ngugi is a good father and you were right. The kids don't need their lives disrupted. He hasn't done anything to them.'

Anne was surprised. She knew that her friend was hurting, but didn't actually expect her to follow through with her plan to leave. Kavata now possessed a resolve that wasn't there a few weeks ago and Anne started to worry that her friend didn't fully comprehend how much pain she was about to experience.

'Any ideas where you will go?'

'I think the US is my only option.'

'And when?'

'As soon as possible… in a few weeks.' Now that her mind was made up, there was no point delaying things.

'What? No that's too soon. I don't think you realise how much work goes into abandoning one's family,' Anne said, and was immediately transported to those months after she packed up and followed her lover without a word to anyone except Kavata. She painted Kavata a picture of what those months after she left were like. How she thought of calling her parents every single day and would daydream about the long distance conversations they would have on the phone when her mother finally forgave her. Her life had revolved around the professor and they both hated it. His family refused to acknowledge her—she was the reason their star professor walked away from the good Nairobi life. His friends treated her like an outsider and temporary fixture that would be replaced as soon as the professor got over whatever personal crisis he was going through. Thinking back now, Anne was sure that moving away was a mistake. 'You need to make the assumption Ngugi will abandon the kids completely once you leave. He probably won't—but you need to plan for it in case he does.'

'How do I plan for something that I can't even imagine happening?'

'Well—today is your lucky day, Mrs. Ngugi—or do we go back to calling you Ms. Muli?'

Kavata glared at Anne.

'Sorry, it's obviously too soon for that. So, what is the best possible outcome of you leaving?'

'That Ngugi realises what he has done, and stops this madness and crawls all the way to the US to beg me to come back. And then I will keep him there until I am sure that I have undone all of my father's brainwashing. And maybe we will stay there a few months until the election is behind us.'

Anne laughed. 'And you said you didn't have a plan. Ha!

And what's the worst case scenario?'

Kavata wasn't as swift with this answer. 'Worst case is nothing changes, he carries on campaigning, the children are dragged into the campaign and all this distance I have been trying to create between them and the politics is completely destroyed.'

'That's what you need to think about as we plan. When you plan for the worst, you take care of the best. Because if you leave in a few weeks like you plan, how will you be able to make sure he keeps the kids out of his campaign for the next year and a half?'

'You are right.' Kavata sank deeper into her seat. 'This is too hard.'

'It is going to be the most difficult thing you've ever done, Kavata, make no mistakes about that. Don't worry though. You are lucky to have me in your life. I may not have children, which I know makes this thing so much harder, but you have the benefit of all my poor decisions. Take my advice, I don't need it anymore.'

And she did. For the next few months, Anne continued to ask Kavata the questions that would help them map her exit. She would stay around for the duration of the campaign season because those were often the most gruelling bits and she needed to be sure that her children, Amani especially, did not get dragged into it. This would also buy her time to figure out her money. She had been insisting on running their home with her small salary, but eventually relented and agreed to let Ngugi provide for them as she saved all her shillings.

# 6
## DEAR NGUGI
### 24 DECEMBER 2007

The ODM campaign headquarters were based in a bright orange building in Kilimani. ODM made sure people were constantly reminded of their surrounding once they walked through the gates manned by a guard dressed in a bright orange uniform. Inside the building, the only thing not orange were the brilliant white walls fitted with several screens which continuously broadcasted ODM candidates' speeches. Each of them was programmed to switch to the news channels every hour. Framed campaign posters took up empty spaces between the screens. Save for the solid black desks, all furniture in the office bore the same orange shade. Her first day at work was daunting, but she was relieved to see everyone so busy doing their own thing that they didn't bother with her. Tom spent all of ten minutes introducing her to the people relevant to her role. Then he showed her to her desk, located right next to him, and put her to work. By the end of the week, she felt like she'd been there for months. She couldn't believe she was getting paid to do a job that she would have done for free.

Wanja walked into the headquarters that morning

a few minutes after the final Poll predicted that, in a few days, ODM's presidential candidate would win the election. The mood was celebratory as her workmates congratulated themselves on their virtual win.

'This is only a poll—the work ends when we've been inaugurated,' the campaign chairman announced, sending everyone back to work.

Wanja had worked there for a while and it still shocked her how dedicated her colleagues were to the campaign. It was impossible to figure out where the campaign ended and their lives began. One of her colleagues had sent his family upcountry so that he could dedicate all his time to the campaign. Everyone suspected that he lived at headquarters. She admired this—Ngugi's campaign was by no means as spirited as ODM's—but she still found it odd that her colleagues spoke about the presidency as though they would all be president when their candidate won. No one realised that, at the very best, they would remain nameless, faceless workers after the campaign ended.

She settled down at her desk, hoping that she could slip in without anyone noticing that she had missed the morning meeting. Their daily press meetings were getting shorter and shorter the closer the election got as most of the campaign team was out on the field. She grabbed a stack of newspapers and did a quick skim to check for any propaganda that the opposition had spread, so that she had an answer when Tom asked her how she thought they should respond. The opposition didn't give her much to work with—the media and bloggers were still spinning the propaganda that her team had fed them over the weekend. She was grateful for this because it had taken her forever to settle her mind—she kept looking over at her phone, checking for news from home.

'How are things at home?' Tom asked in lieu of a greeting, and Wanja looked at him, puzzled. 'After the recent prediction. Your dear Papa isn't doing so well. He should just quit now and walk away with his dignity, *ama*?'

'He has bigger things to deal with; I don't think he has even seen the polls,' Wanja said. On most days she could do with Tom's jabs at her father, but not today.

At first, no one at her office acknowledged that she was her father's child and she wondered if anyone other than Tom knew. But then the requests to confirm information about her father's campaign began to trickle in from senior campaign members.

'It's just a job,' Tom said when she looked over at him the first time the head of public relations asked her to confirm her father would be visiting the site of a building that collapsed and killed five people in his opponent's hometown. The requests became more frequent and more unabashed. Sometimes even from Tom, who would email his requests to her even though he sat right next to her. He would end his message with the words that now served as her mantra. It was just a job, and one she was good at.

Wanja carried on with her work that morning with her earphones tucked into her ears as she listened to a series of NGO-commissioned music.

Any singer-songwriter worth their name was approached to record a jingle that advocated for peaceful elections. She liked a few of them but thought most of them lacked the charm that was sacrificed for a script and a pay cheque. She kept listening to them because they provided catchy slogans for whatever speech or campaign she was working on. She was so caught up in the generic lyrics, she was oblivious to the fact that the attention of the entire office was directed at her. Sally, who ran the campaign rumour mill, tapped her on the shoulder and she looked up to a sea of faces staring at her.

*Argh, not today, Satan.* Wanja always sensed some hostility from Sally, so she made an effort to stay out of her way.

'We've just heard your mother has gone AWOL.'

'Is that a question?'

'Yes, has your mother gone missing?'

'No. I'm sure she'll show up. Eventually.'

Sally wasn't satisfied, so she didn't move—her perfume kept Wanja on the cusp of a sneeze. If anyone else asked, she probably would have told them the truth, but Sally's plastic concern irked her. Tom watched them, shocked that this was the first he was hearing of this.

'Oouuw daahling—you must be so worried. Where did she go? I do hope she shows up soon.' Sally perched on the edge of Wanja's desk.

'No wonder you look so...' Sally's acrylic nails adjusted Wanja's shirt collar, '...stressed today. When did you see her last?'

'Yesterday.' Wanja looked over at Tom, her eyes pleading for him to step in, but he seemed just as eager to hear what she would say. Just as Wanja decided to surrender and tell all, her phone rang.

'Uhmm, I need to take this.' She bolted out the door. It was her aunt Wairimu.

'Hi mama, are you ok?' her aunt asked.

'Yes. I'm just finishing up some work.'

'Work? Haven't you guys closed? It's Christmas Eve!'

'We have. I just came to campus to finish up some stuff I need to re-submit.' She was becoming such a good liar.

'And Amani?'

'He was fine when I left.'

'I think it's best that you go home. He might need you.'

'I will, I just needed a distraction for a few hours.'

'I can imagine your dad is quite preoccupied. Please go back home.'

'Ok, I'll go home soon. Thanks for calling, Auntie.'

Sally waited for her at the door when Wanja walked back into the office. The rest of the office's attention was on the screen where a reporter stood outside Wanja's house.

PNU CANDIDATE NGUGI MWANGI'S WIFE REPORTED MISSING.

The caption at the bottom of the screen screamed out for attention.

'Wanja, can you tell us what you know—this could be really useful to us.' Sally's plastic nails dug into Wanja's arm and she wanted to slap her hand away.

'Sally, *ebu* chill.' Tom walked towards them and Wanja walked back outside to phone home. The landline was engaged each time she tried it. She tried Schola's phone and when it rang unanswered, she could picture it on the kitchen counter where it sat connected to the charger all day while Schola went about her chores. Just as she was about to hang up and go home, Schola picked up.

'Wanja, *kwani uko wapi?*'

'What's going on over there?'

'Me, I don't know. The police arrested Thuo.'

'Arrested him? Why?'

'Ok, I don't know if they arrested him, but they went with him, and then the OCS came back and the news people came. Where are you?'

'Arrested him for what? He didn't do anything.'

'They said he was the last one with her. *Mama ako wapi?*

Do you know?'

As Schola spoke, Wanja looked through the reception window at the TV screen, recognising her house behind the OCS as he confirmed what Schola was saying. He was talking about a suspect, but the man he was talking about couldn't be Thuo. It sounded nothing like him. She hated the thought that Thuo was a suspect but not as much as the possibility of a complete stranger having a hand in her mother's disappearance.

'This doesn't make any sense. How is Amani?'

'*Ako Sawa.* He's still sleeping.'

'At this time? That doesn't sound like him. *Ebu* go check on him and then *uniflash* I call you back.'

'*Ako sawa.*'

'Schola, please,' Wanja insisted and then hung up.

Schola went to Amani's room and drew the curtains. He was still in bed but wide awake. He hissed when light poured into his room.

'I'm sick, I want to sleep.'

'Sick since when, Amani?' Schola sat on the foot of the bed and touched his forehead, but she already knew what was wrong. He had wet the bed and was upset.

'I'm tired,' he mumbled and turned his back to her.

'Ok, *basi pumzika.* I will bring you some cornflakes. But rest quickly, I need your help today. My hands are tired. I need you to soak everything that you need washed today so I don't have to scrub them too long. *Sawa?*'

Amani half turned towards her. 'Ok.'

'Good boy. I will put the bucket in the bathroom.' She stood and walked out, and Amani sighed as he sat up and cried.

He'd woken up upset about so many things. That Kavata

was still not back, and she couldn't even tell Thuo to bring the ice cream she promised him. The last time this happened, Kavata had told him that it was ok to pee the bed sometimes, and promised to always be there to help him with his bed before anyone else found out his secret. He woke up almost immediately after he wet the bed and went looking for Kavata, but she wasn't there. He knew that something was going on and no one was telling him what it was. Wanja was always busy somewhere, and he knew it wasn't school because she didn't always carry her books with her. And now Thuo had gone away with the police, and his dad was shouting to himself in the sitting room. What a mess. He found a dry spot on his bed, lay back down and went to sleep.

'Amani is *sawa*,' Schola said when she was back on the phone with Wanja. 'But you need to come back. What do I say when Mzee asks me where you are? *Na* your *cucu* and *guka* I'm sure *wanakuja*.' There was distress in Schola's voice.

'He won't ask. When are you travelling home?'

'I was supposed to go today, but how can I go now? I'm told fares to Kisumu have gone up *ati* because of the election. And now Thuo? I don't know if Cheptoo knows.'

'You should still go, we'll be alright. I'll be back in the afternoon, and I'll ask Dad about Thuo. But call me if anything happens.'

As soon as Wanja hung up, Sally bombarded her with questions.

'Where has she gone? For how long? What airline? We need to verify. Did she plan the trip or has she, like, left him?' Wanja shrugged her shoulders in response to all of them and each time, Sally's weaved head would twitch like her brain was short-circuiting.

'Sally, chill,' Tom said. She didn't.

'Please, we need this. We've had no new dirt for a while now, and this could be our final chance to swing things once and for all. I have my media guys on standby—just tell me.' Wanja said nothing but, after what seemed to her like ages, she could almost see the pieces fit together as Sally bolted to her desk to phone journalists. Wanja knew that there was no point stopping her. News always wrote itself. The knot that formed in her chest when her mother never returned got a little tighter.

An hour later, journalists could confirm from a source very close to the family that Mrs. Kavata Muli-Ngugi left the country without her family's knowledge. Tom sat staring at Wanja for moments after the news broke, his gaze a mixture of worry, shock and amusement.

'You can take the rest of the day off if you need to.'

'I don't. But thanks.' Wanja was touched by his concern. She slipped on her earphones but didn't turn on the music. She wanted to hear what her colleagues said about her and her family.

*It's just a job*, she told her knot and thought back to the only time she'd ever considered telling her mother about her job. She had braced herself for the conversation as she climbed into the car behind Thuo. Kavata's eyes were teary, her favourite Babyface CD was playing in the stereo, and Thuo was driving as if they were on a minefield. Wanja tried to be particularly kind to her mother on days like these—she'd been seeing them a lot recently and learned that sometimes the greatest kindness she could offer was oblivious silence. She watched Kavata twirl her wedding band around her finger, then her eyes fell upon an airline ticket, peeking out of her mother's open bag. She must have reacted subliminally because Kavata's eyes drifted away from the car window and followed Wanja's gaze. When Kavata realised Wanja saw the ticket, she looked her in the eye for a moment and then turned her teary attention back to the passing traffic. Wanja asked no questions, Kavata offered no answers and there was never any mention of Wanja's job.

Something told her that her mother had used that ticket—but something else told her that Kavata wouldn't leave just like that. It felt impossible. She regretted not checking the date on that ticket when she had the chance to. She was getting angry but then thought back to the misery that engulfed Kavata over the last few months and tears stung her eyes. She closed her eyes, then inhaled long and deep to send the tears back where they came from.

\*\*\*

'What is all this? Why did no one tell me Kavata was travelling? Are you people mad?' Muli barged into Ngugi's house where Ngugi sat in the sitting room, lost in thought since the OCS took Thuo hours ago. Ngugi looked up at his father-in-law. His cell phone rang incessantly for hours and when the battery gave in, the landline took over. He dismissed Schola's questions about what he wanted to eat for breakfast and brushed away Amani's series of gentle questions about where Kavata was and if she would be back in time for an event he started calling *the Christmaslection*. Ngugi needed a little more time to make sense of it all. He looked Hon. Muli in the eye and held his gaze for a moment before he shifted it to Mrs. Muli, who sat perched on the cushion next to him, rubbing her hands together, and bobbing back and forth like a pendulum. All he could see now was their resemblance. Mrs. Muli looked worried, but there was none of that concern on Muli's face; only accusation and lots of irritation.

'Let me get Schola to make some tea. Or do you want coffee? I need coffee.' Ngugi's tired voice was barely above a whisper. He stood before they could respond and made for the kitchen. He took a few steps, then Amani walked into the room to greet his grandparents; he stood on the tips of his toes to place three hesitant kisses on each of their cheeks, and then sat on the couch closest to the television with his left thumb in his mouth.

'Ngugi, sit down. Amani, go make us some tea,' Mrs. Muli instructed.

'I'm not allowed to touch the stove.' He didn't take his eyes off the screen.

'Then go find someone who is, boy,' Hon. Muli barked, and Amani leapt up and fled on the verge of tears.

'Ngugi, tell us what is going on. Where is she?'

Ngugi opened his mouth to repeat the account that he shared with the OCS, but then it hit him. 'Wait, how did you know?' he asked Muli.

'I know everything.'

'The OCS phoned me after you decided to inform him that you've misplaced our daughter before you thought to tell us,' Mrs. Muli offered.

'But you're not answering the question, Ngugi. Where did she go and for how long?' Hon. Muli was starting to tremble. Ngugi closed his eyes, sat back and prepared himself to tell his wife's parents that he had no idea where their only daughter was. Just then, Amani re-emerged from the kitchen triumphant, followed by Schola who balanced a teapot and cups on a wooden tray. She lowered the tray and began to pour when Mrs. Muli protested. 'Ah ah! Leave it. My husband isn't served by maids. I've told you a hundred times.' She waved Schola away and continued to bob. 'Amani, go call your sister to come and serve this tea.'

Amani shrugged. 'She's not here,' he said, his eyes already re-acquainted with the television.

'Aii, they've all gone?' Mrs. Muli muttered under her breath as she sat up to pour tea into her husband's cup first and then hers. They were so distracted by Mrs. Muli's tea pouring that they didn't notice Anne walk in. She cursed when she confirmed that Kavata's parents were indeed present. She almost turned around to leave when she saw Muli's car in the parking lot, but couldn't imagine having to muster the courage to come back to Ngugi's all over again. She hated the strain this whole thing caused on her and Ngugi's friendship and had been dreading this moment since Kavata asked her to deliver the letter.

'*Hodi.*'

'Hi *Tata*!' Amani leapt off the couch and ran into Anne's outstretched arms before he glanced over her shoulder.

'Is mum with you?'

'No, she's not, but you know what is?'

'What?' Anne pulled a Snickers out of her coat pocket and handed it to her godson.

'Go share this with Schola. I think she might also have something nice and frozen for you.'

Anne greeted Hon. Muli and then hugged Mrs. Muli, who held onto her a little longer.

'Where is she? Just tell me,' Mrs. Muli whispered to Anne.

'Good to see you, mum. You look so well,' Anne almost shouted. She wasn't about to discuss this now. She wasn't built to lie to Mrs. Muli. She glanced over at Ngugi who was looking back at her with a knowing suspicion.

'I can't stay long—I have some relatives waiting for me at home. I was just coming to check on these ones,' she looked at Ngugi.

'How nice of you,' Mrs. Muli's entire head moved when she rolled her eyes. Then she started bobbing again.

'Ngugi, will you walk me out?' Ngugi hesitated—his gaze still locked on Anne for a moment—before he stood.

'Um, yeah. I'll be right back,' he said to his in-laws, and followed Anne out of the living room.

'Can we chat a bit?' Anne led the way to Ngugi's office. The two friends stood in silence for a moment. Anne's hands were trembling inside her trouser pockets, and Ngugi was certain that the dread in his chest would suffocate him.

'Is she ok?'

'Yes, yes. Alive and well. Well....'

'Oh, thank God.' When he exhaled he looked instantly refreshed. 'Is she leaving me?'

'Umm. More like left? Look, I don't know if I'm the one to put labels on anything, but all I can tell you is that she got on a flight to the US yesterday. She was going to call you herself when she got there, but I hear the cops have been here already so I thought I would come and tell you before you bring in the flying squad as well.'

Ngugi stared at her wordlessly for several moments.

'Fuck,' he eventually muttered.

'Yeah. well.' Anne shrugged. She felt bad for her friend. For both of them.

'I was supposed to wait until she's called you to give this to you.' She handed him the envelope.

Ngugi held the blue and white envelope and stared at

his name, written in her old school cursive handwriting that reminded him now more than ever of the space in his world that Kavata occupied. He was scared of the letter and of the things it would release. And he was livid.

'She couldn't have picked a better time to do this?'

Anne gasped. 'Ngugi—seriously? Kavata has made what is easily the most difficult decision of her entire life, and you are concerned about the timing?'

'Yes! And why shouldn't I? How long has she been planning this anyway?'

'You are unbelievable.' She spun to leave. 'Let me know if you need any help with the kids. All the best with—everything.'

*Dear Ngugi,*

*You would be shocked how many drafts of this letter I've written. Teaching Home Science has ruined my writing skills. This is hard.*

*I am sorry to have left this way. I'd like to declare that from the onset because I know that from now onwards, it will not matter why or how I left. Only that I did. And that's ok. I am ok being the villain for a little while. Leaving this way, and the pain and inconvenience it will cause you and our children, is the only thing I will be apologising for in this letter.*

*You are probably wondering how long I've been planning this. I made the decision that I didn't want to be around you the day that you told us that you were running for office. I wanted to walk away on that day. But I stayed, for almost two years, because I realised this was the hardest thing I would ever have to do and I had to be sure it was the only way. Over these two years, Ngugi, I have prayed for our marriage harder and longer than I have for our children. I have looked for ways to explain and re-explain to you that this decision you made has broken us. I have also shifted and re-adjusted myself countless times, trying to find a version of myself that can continue to live by your side. I failed at this every time.*

*You are also probably wondering how you didn't see this coming... Yes, Ngugi, how could you not see this coming?*

*We've argued enough times about the havoc of this choice of yours—I'm not here to do anymore of that. I wrote this letter to you because I wanted to say something I only recently found words for. Over the past few weeks, Anne has been constantly asking me what I hope my leaving you will achieve. The hope is you will realise that you've made a mistake, but the reality is I'm leaving you because I am broken. You broke me Ngugi, and I need to heal. This choice you made succeeded in making me feel more abandoned and alone than I could ever have imagined possible.*

*I've spent my life doing this exhausting dance where I try to create as much distance from my father as possible, while still remaining respectful and present because he is my family, it is my duty to honour him, and for the longest time my parents were my only companions. Each time I created some distance from them, it felt as if I'd taken one step out of his shadow, then out the door, and then another out of the gate. Starting a family with you was like running into the house all the way across the country from him and learning that I could go back on my terms. You showed me that I could have all the distance*

*I needed from my father, without being alone. Ngugi, for that I will always love you. But when you decided to do this, with my father, knowing all you do, Ngugi, you packed up my entire heart and home—and moved it right back into his house.*

*So, I have gone to the US to stay with my cousin Mutheu. I don't know how long for and I don't know when I will come back. I will call you and the kids as soon as I have had time to settle down. Leaving you is painful—leaving them is excruciating. I thought long and hard about taking them with me but you have done nothing to wrong them and they don't deserve to be separated from you. Please protect them and please do not allow them to hate me—if you can. That is all I ask.*

*Your Wife,*
*Kavata.*

Ngugi read and re-read the letter. Some of the things she said sounded familiar, but he also felt as if he'd never heard them before. Not like this. Her pain was all that jumped out at him. Shock and regret and pain delivered a silent steady stream of tears to his eyes.

There was a gentle knock on the door.

'Daddy, *Guka* is calling you.'

Ngugi remained silent.

'He says you come now.'

'I'm taking a shower and coming. Ask them to give me a few minutes.' The boy hesitated at the door.

'I was told not to go back without you?'

Ngugi lifted himself off the ground and walked to the bathroom.

The pastor and his wife were sitting in his living room.

'Brother Ngugi, we heard it on the news and came right away. This is such a tragedy. Let us pray against this evil.'

'What. What news? You said you heard it on the news?'

'Yes, there was a brief story in the highlights at 10 am.,' Grace said.

'What happened. Didn't she return from the supermarket at all?' Pastor Simon asked.

'What of the driver? Where is he?'

'He showed up this morning like he knew nothing. At least Ngugi called the police by then, so they took him in for questioning. He will be kept in custody until I say otherwise,' Muli said.

'Were you here yesterday?' Mrs. Muli asked Grace.

'Yes, they invited us for lunch after the service. She made a lovely lunch, *mbuzi* and some wonderful *warus*. But she forgot dessert and went to Nakumatt to get some and that was it!' Grace clapped her hands for effect. 'We waited for almost an hour for her to come back, but Ngugi was getting late for his gam—uhm, appointment. So we just ate with the children and went home. Now I feel bad, I should have insisted on going with her. The driver must know something. *Ati* where is he from?'

Ngugi disconnected himself from the conversation. He scanned the room for the remote and flipped past Amani's Disney channels to find one that indeed carried news of Kavata's disappearance. They all stared at the screen.

'NTV have better coverage of it,' Grace offered. Ngugi chuckled. For months, they'd been paying heavily for media attention and now here they were on the morning news shows. Just then Amani burst back into the room, tickled.

'Dad, there are people with cameras at the gate. Schola is chasing them away with a broom! She wants to open for the dogs.'

'No! Tell her to stop. She shouldn't agitate the media,' Muli yelled, and was back on his phone barking orders.

'Ngugi, let's talk outside.' Muli didn't wait for him to respond before he led him to the balcony. Ngugi followed him to the last space in the house in which he had seen his wife and wondered how he failed to see this coming. He searched the air for a hint of her perfume and felt a tugging in his chest.

'Sit down.' Muli spoke gently and pulled his chair closer to Ngugi. 'I can see you are in shock about what is happening. *Pole*—I know these things can be difficult, so I will talk as your friend and not as your father in law. It's important that we keep things separate so I will not interfere with the matters of your marriage. But let me ask you one thing.' There was a new kindness in Muli's eyes. 'Do you know where she is?' Ngugi nodded. 'And she is safe?' Ngugi nodded again and Muli sighed with relief. 'I knew it. When I woke up this morning, it didn't feel like today would be the day that I lost my daughter. I knew she is ok. But you can't always be sure so I asked the OCS to just check.'

'She says she needs time to think. She's gone to stay with her cousin Mutheu in the US. She flew out yesterday.'

'What do you mean? And you didn't know?'

Ngugi didn't respond.

'Ok, then this is what we are going to do...'

Ngugi zoned out again as Hon. Muli spoke. He thought back to all their different arguments and wondered what made him doubt that she would follow through with her threat.

'...but here we are now, and we must finish what we started and work with what we've got. They don't always understand why we do things the way we do. Mama Kavata was also very angry about the politics when I first started, but now she cannot imagine a life without it. There are many people counting on you to win this election, so do not let her childish approach distract you.' Ngugi simply nodded, uncomfortable with this conversation, but grateful to be having it.

Muli continued speaking, going over the details of what needed to be done next, pausing often to shout into his phone whenever it was warranted. In order for Kavata's disappearance not to hurt the campaign, they would need to make it look like it was part of the plan. They would release a statement that a relative was very ill and Kavata travelled to support her family during this difficult time. Jane, Muli's former assistant whom he hired to run certain aspects of the campaign, arrived at the house a few hours later with a pack of volunteers.

'I know it looks like a lot, but we can get more done if we set up here,' Hon. Muli offered when Ngugi looked at him with questions in his eyes.

When the media confirmed that Kavata left un-announced, all the phones in the house rang simultaneously, Schola's included. Jane and her team used this opportunity to dispel the rumour and issue a rebuttal. It was less scandalous news to report, so within the hour the droves of journalists who camped outside the residence gates simmered away while the bustle inside the house grew steadily as the campaign team got back to work.

Ngugi found a moment to sneak away and phone his sister. Growing up, Wairimu was the glue that held their family together. She was everyone's little piece of joy. She cooked for her father, took her mother to church, covered for their other brother Dennis and defended Ngugi unconditionally. Later, she would introduce Ngugi to her single girlfriends. Their relationship suffered when Ngugi decided to marry Kavata.

'It's never a good idea for a man to marry up bro—it doesn't matter how mindblowing the sex is. She will never give you room to become your own man,' Wairimu often said, but Ngugi went ahead and married Kavata. Though angry about the seventy-five cows that the Mulis demanded for Kavata's hand, Wairimu showed up at the wedding, smiled as expected and delivered her speech expressing her joy at gaining a sister.

When it was her turn to get married, Ngugi also objected. He didn't trust Jommo and when he said this to her she was quick to remind him that she didn't trust Kavata either.

'That's different,' he snapped back, 'at least I married her because I love her; not because I'm afraid that no one else will have me,' He regretted the words as soon as he said them and Wairimu never forgave him

'You've really fucked up this time, eh,' Wairimu answered the phone. Ngugi chuckled. Wairimu always had a way with him.

'Wow, that feels great. But yeah, apparently she really doesn't want to be married to a politician.' Now Wairimu laughed.

'No surprises there; I mean, have you met her father?'

Ngugi remained silent. The tugging in his chest returned, and this time he gave into it fully, letting it lead him further away from the hive to seek counsel from the only person he hoped would know what he should do. Wairimu could feel her brother's pain. It reached past the strain of the last couple of years, and she genuinely empathised with him.

'How are you?'

Ngugi sighed. 'Angry. Confused. How didn't I see this coming?'

'What happened?'

'Short answer is that she's gone to the US because she needs time to think.'

'And you didn't know? At all?'

'Nope.'

'*Aish*. Have things been that thick?'

'Apparently.'

'Do you think she will come back?'

'I don't know. She hasn't decided. She bought a one-way ticket.'

'*Wololo*. And how are the kids?'

'They're ok, I suppose.' Another brief silence.

'She's quite the woman, that one,' Wairimu said, and could hear her brother smile.

'I'm sure she'd fly back asap if she heard you say that.'

'So now, what do you need?'

'I don't know.'

'Where are the kids now?'

'Amani is here, thankfully distracted. What am I supposed to even tell him?'

'Nothing. Send him here. He can stay for a few days. Maybe through Christmas as well.' Despite their tensions, Wairimu and Ngugi made sure their children remained friends.

'Good idea. The house has been converted into campaign central. The church is here as well, holding prayers for Kavata's imaginary sick relative.'

'And Wanja?'

'I'm not sure where she is. She seems happier when left alone.'

'I'll call her again, she must be shocked.'

'She's coming with me to Machaa so I'll have some time to chat with her.'

Wairimu hoped that Kavata's stunt would be successful, but obviously nothing was keeping Ngugi away from this election. She didn't say anything. She didn't need to.

'I must do this, Wairimu. I have a responsibility.'

'To whom?'

'To my family. To the people we've employed. To the voters. To those guys in Machakos. That place has such potential, Wairimu. I can do such important work there.'

'I don't doubt that, Ngugi. But dogs and fleas. I suspect that is also Kavata's problem with your approach to this thing.'

Ngugi said nothing.

'Need anything else?'

'Yeah. Actually, the analysts think it will help greatly if the family are present in Machaa on poll day. Do you think you can make it? I wasn't going to ask, but now that we're talking...' It was quite the ask, and he could feel the resistance when she responded.

'But we are already registered here in Thome.'

'Muli says he can fix that.'

Wairimu laughed.

'Oh, so he is your analyst now? It's amazing how many jars he has his fingers in.'

'You don't have to.'

'No, don't worry. We'll be there. I'll speak to Jommo now.' Ngugi didn't expect her to bring her husband.

'You don't have to bring him. I know he would rather

eat lice.'

'No, don't worry. He's in the doghouse at the moment; he will do whatever I tell him to.'

Ngugi didn't ask what Jommo did, and Wairimu didn't reveal that after many years of suspicion, she confirmed that he indeed had a side piece. And that the woman had even borne him a child. She collected evidence and confronted him about it a few nights ago after packing a few of his things into a suitcase. He cried at her feet and begged her to let him stay. She agreed, despite her looming fear that he had given her a disease. She was just waiting to feel something before she could decide what to do.

'So will we need to re-register when we get to Machaa?' Wairimu decided to push her problems aside. At least she could help fix her brother's since she was utterly hopeless when it came to her own.

'No need to. Muli will fix it so your cards don't get checked.' They both laughed.

'While he is at it, can he fix it so we can all go vote in the US next year? That Obama guy needs all the votes he can get,' Wairimu said.

'I need all the votes I can get.'

'Will Thuo bring Amani over today? I can arrange for Penina to stay while we are away and watch them all,' Wairimu asked.

Ngugi felt guilt at the mention of Thuo's name and recalled Muli's instructions to keep him detained. He looked over at the tree that Thuo often sat under in his free time. His stool was still in place with an old newspaper held down by a stone. The guilt was quickly replaced by anger. Ngugi decided that he would let Thuo sit in jail for a few more hours. He obviously lied about Kavata and this was his punishment for picking the wrong team. 'No, I'll bring Amani myself. Thuo is... not here.'

A volunteer came to reel Ngugi back in. As soon as he walked back into the house, all benefits of his conversation were replaced by anxious madness. Every flat surface of his previously orderly living room was covered in paperwork being spat out by printers networked to each other in no time at all. Jane and her minions whispered away efficiently as more and more faces Ngugi almost recognised walked into the room carrying boxes and files and laptops and printers which all served to make Ngugi a little wearier now that this operation was taking place in his home. Kavata would lose it if she saw the state of her house. Then again, these people were only here because of her actions.

'It's only for today and maybe tomorrow,' the omnipresent Muli said from behind him as if reading his mind.

'It is best you work from home. You do not want to appear unmoved by Mrs. Ngugi's sick cousin,' Jane added as she brought some paperwork for Muli to sign, approvals for outside furniture to be brought in to accommodate the prayers and well-wishers expected to visit Ngugi before his departure for Machakos. It didn't sit well with him that Muli controlled a large chunk of the campaign finances. He had been meaning to bring it up for a while, but it seemed too late in the day to start an awkward money conversation.

Ngugi searched the house for his little boy, expecting to find him curled up on his bed, where he had been the last time he checked. Instead, he found Amani milling about among the campaign staff, clutching his own makeshift clipboard to his chest, acting as busy and important as everyone else in the room. The staff humoured him, partly because they didn't want to offend Ngugi but mostly because Amani provided a brief and refreshing break from an otherwise draining atmosphere.

He'd woken up from his short nap feeling a little better, and helping with the laundry was more fun than he'd thought. So when Schola looked up and saw Muli's workers walking into the house with folders and boxers, she sent Amani off to see how else he could be useful and he joyfully obliged. Clipped to his board was a sheet of stickers with different coloured smiley faces, which he awarded to those who correctly answered his pertinent questions. His Spider-Man sneakers lit up and squeaked on the wooden floors as he scurried around the room. He had taken to wearing caps on his head to protect his thick unmanageable afro from Kavata, who often threatened to shave it while he slept. Today, the cap of choice was one that bore Ngugi's face printed on the front of it, and he wore it so low he tilted his head all the way back to look people in the eyes.

'Will you vote for my daddy to be MP?' Amani asked before he affixed a luminous smile on whichever part of their body he saw fit as a reward for a correct answer. Everyone walked around with stickers on their foreheads and cheeks. When Amani ran out of people, he rewarded the computers, phones, paperwork and pretty much anything he could reach for doing good work to ensure his daddy would be MP. Ngugi watched his son, briefly forgetting his troubles.

In the car, as they rode to Wairimu's house, Amani was full of encouragement for his father.

'Don't be sad because Mom won't be here for the election. And don't worry about the sick *cucu* in America. Mum really knows how to take care of the sick.' Ngugi listened in sheer admiration. 'But it's ok to be angry that she didn't say bye before she left. I am also angry. She could have at least brought my ice cream back before she left. Will she even come back before my birthday?' Amani checked the back seat as he said this, just in case. Then, moving on swiftly, he listed, with surprising detail, all the things Ngugi should do when he won, which included arresting all the teachers who pulled children's ears and making sure schools only served chips and sausage for lunch.

It didn't take them long to navigate their way to Wairimu's house in the light pre-holiday traffic, and when they arrived Ngugi wished that he could sit in the car with his son a little while longer and listen to his juvenile wisdom. He couldn't remember when he'd last spent time with Amani; when did his son grow into such a perceptive boy?

Amani leapt out of the car as soon as it came to a halt outside Wairimu's door. With his clipboard in hand, he continued his sticker rampage which was quickly forgotten once he was amongst his cousins and their video games.

That night, when he finally repossessed his home, Ngugi walked around his bedroom. He picked at her things, everything just the way it was the previous morning before they left for church. He ruffled through her underwear drawer, aching for her in a way he hadn't in months. When he heard a car drive in just before 10 PM, he thought for a moment his nightmare was over, and then he realised it was Wanja's car he heard. He debated over whether or not to go and speak to his estranged daughter, but he discarded the thought when he recalled the new resentment that almost always lived in her eyes. He sat on the bed, staring at the open chest of drawers, hoping another message from his wife would jump out at him. When he could ponder no longer, lack of sleep the previous night and fatigue from the day's activities took over and gifted him with sleep.

# 7

# HAPPY CHRISTMAS

## 25 DECEMBER 2007

When Kavata finally woke up, re-adjusted to her new surroundings and changed the time on her watch, she realised that she had not only slept through most of Christmas Day in Atlanta, she had completely missed it in Kenya. She felt instant guilt—calling home on Christmas morning had been a solid part of her plan and she was going to stick to it. She got out of bed, trying to remember where she'd seen the landline. Her hands trembled when she started to dial Ngugi's number. She stopped to go over what she would say to him. Then she changed her mind and decided to call the house phone, that way she could break the ice with someone else and could ask to speak to Ngugi when her nerves had settled. But then she realised that it was 11 PM at home. It would be unkind to wake everyone up, she reasoned. Tomorrow, she thought to herself, and her anxiety was instantly replaced by fatigue. The travel, wine and the weight of the last few months had left her completely spent. With her decision made, she floated back up the stairs and slept through the rest of Christmas.

***

Thuo did not think he would survive the whole night in that holding cell. He was stirred from his sleep by a familiar voice—Cheptoo. Yelling. At the booking officer. He stood, his trousers sticking to the floor like velcro strips, and began to step away from the door slowly. His cellmates stood to look through the hole, and Thuo watched and imagined Cheptoo on the other side, just as other women had been when they got catcalled. It was a lot less entertaining from this side of the door. He stepped back up to the door and nudged his cellmate to move out of the way. Thuo was relieved and slightly disappointed when the man shrugged disinterestedly and stepped away.

He peered through the peephole and spotted Cheptoo and felt the way he had the very first time he saw her: comforted, amused and intimidated. She never looked more beautiful or more livid. Her hands akimbo as she growled, demanding to be told why her husband was arrested and held for a whole day and night. The station was fairly empty from what Thuo could see, but the few who were milling about watched Cheptoo with great amusement. The officer didn't stand a chance—and Thuo almost wanted to warn him to just play dead. At first, he tried to calm Cheptoo down, explaining that only the OCS could answer her questions and he was away attending to election issues. Then he turned his attention back to his newspaper.

'What are you doing here if you can't answer my questions? Must I speak English so you can listen to me?' she yelled, confident in her broken English.

'Or is it because I am wearing a *khanga* that you think you are better than me? We are the same! Your uniform means you work for me. Tell me where my husband is!' Cheptoo grabbed the newspaper from his desk and slapped the table. The officer stood gobsmacked.

'*Mama, nimekuambia*. Wait for the OCS.'

'I don't need the OCS to tell me why my husband has been arrested. Open this big book of yours and tell me what he has done! Joseph Thuo Maliti—those are his names. I can even spell them for you. Or help you look *kama umechoka*.'

'*Wewe*! Mama! *Wacha siasa*. Go home. Your husband will be sent home when his fate has been decided.' As he spoke, Cheptoo tilted her head and squinted her eyes at him and the officer realised his accent betrayed him. Cheptoo found common ground.

'How can you be so unkind to your sister, eh? What is your name? Who is your mother?' She asked in their shared mother tongue. He wouldn't answer her and this only restored her anger. She reached over the counter for the Occurence Book, but the policeman grabbed her hand and shoved it away so hard that for a moment it seemed detached from its socket.

'*Wewe*!' Thuo slammed his fist against the metal door. The sound startled both Cheptoo and the policeman, who didn't bother stopping her from going round his desk to the cell.

'Thuo, come out. *Twende. Hawa wajinga*—they do not know what they are doing.' Cheptoo tugged at the door handle and then began to scope the area for keys to the cell.

'Chep, *kuwa mpole*! You are only making things worse,' Thuo spoke into the peep-hole. He stepped away from the cell door, ashamed that his wife was dealing with this situation. He searched his brain for an explanation to give her but came up short. 'Just go home, this is a small misunderstanding. *Mzee* will sort this out. You go home and make the arrangements to travel upcountry tomorrow. I will be home by the evening.'

'*Aki* Thuo, what will Ngugi do for you? Schola says he is the one who told them to lock you up.' Cheptoo was on her tiptoes as she spoke into the tiny hole.

'Tell them the truth and they will let you go. Where is Mama Wanja? *Ulimpeleka wapi*? And when they arrested you did they tell you exactly what you did? Did they even write your name in the book? *Juu kama hawakukuandikisha basi* they have no right to hold you. *Toka twende*.' She turned back to the officer, 'Eeh, even us we know the law. *Atakama tunavaa shuka*. We know Google.'

'*Wewe, nyamaza na hizi ma* questions.' Thuo grew defensive and instantly felt stupid for it.

Something on the radio caught Cheptoo's attention and she stepped back to the booking officer's desk, grabbed the small portable radio, and turned up the volume, placing the radio next to the peephole so that Thuo could listen in as well.

The lunchtime news bulletin started with unenthused reports of Christmas ceremonies and celebrations across the country before it segued into vibrant reports of preparations for elections all over the country. Then it zoned in on Machakos constituency and re-capped the rapidly decaying, short-lived rumour that Ngugi's wife left him and re-played the hilarious soundbites that the opposition, no doubt, spread to poke fun at an apparently abandoned Ngugi. While Thuo sat in jail, the man who'd put him there was the national laughing stock.

'Eh, Thuo. Can you hear? They are busy saying *amewachwa na bibi*. Do you think that man is thinking about you *ama ako busy na campaign*. Tell them what they want to know and we go. *Watoto wanangoja.*' Cheptoo's fire began to fade. Tears were her last resort. She conjured sobs, reticent at first but growing by the second until she was wailing, begging for nobody in particular to explain to her what was happening. Thuo tried to calm her down from the other side of the door, but this only served to upset her more.

'*Wewe* mama, this is a place of work! Control yourself,' the booking officer spoke as he reached into his drawer and pulled out a new armour of courage. 'You are not the first to have her husband locked up! Go home and stop embarrassing yourself.' Cheptoo, shocked at his authority, tried one last time to convince the policeman to release Thuo, if only for a few minutes so she may feed him and check that he was ok.

Thuo was a little relieved when the officer refused. He didn't want her to see him in this state. He couldn't bear to face her. He repeated his instructions to her, asking her to go home and prepare to travel as they intended to.

'Under the bed, on my side, is an envelope with some money. Take what you need to travel. And for a phone—buy a phone so I can call you when I come out,' Thuo whispered. She had been asking for a new phone since hers fell into a pit latrine months ago. She was a little glad that he couldn't see her chuckle. She had known about his secret envelope for a while. She had taken a look inside it a few times to check if he had managed to save as much as she had. She could have bought herself a new phone immediately after she'd lost her last one, but she knew it was only a matter of time before Thuo did something that warranted penance.

'Don't worry, Chep, I'll get out today. This is a mistake. You just tell Schola *bado niko hapa*. She'll talk to Ngugi,' Thuo called out. Cheptoo gathered her things off the floor to leave. She nodded and walked out just as the news bulletin was ending.

'*Afande*, haven't you heard she travelled,' Thuo called out to the officer. 'That woman *mwenye mnasema nilimchukua*—she travelled. Please release me *niende* home.'

The policeman shrugged his shoulders. That wasn't Thuo's decision to make, he said. Only the OCS could make the decision to release him and he was in his hometown to cast his vote—it was Christmas Day after all.

A few kilometres away, Ngugi stepped out of the front door to find his back yard set up for an event and wracked his mind for any mention of an event. He was beginning to suspect that Kavata, in all her planning, forgot to cancel their Christmas party when he spotted Hon. Muli making a bee-line towards him. He fought the urge to run back into his house.

'Ngugi, I just sent someone in to fetch you. This is not the time to be sleeping in. Oh, and Merry Christmas.' Hon. Muli led him towards the tented yard.

'Please give me a moment, I need to find Wanja,' Ngugi said, walking in the opposite direction.

'She just left. She said she is going to spend the day with your sister's family. Mama Kavata is with them. There are people here who need to see you before they can also go be with their families. Come.' Hon. Muli led him past a hoard of strangers. 'I may have forgotten to mention this to you yesterday—it was all rather last minute,' Hon. Muli said as they walked towards a smaller tent at the farthest end of the yard.

Hon. Muli entered the tent first, and Ngugi stopped dead in his tracks the minute he saw the men, about a dozen of them, who sat waiting for him. These were men Ngugi grew up watching in the news and reading about in the newspapers. Hon. Muli's cronies sat gathered at his house on precarious plastic chairs that often bent and snapped under too much weight. Ngugi tried to keep his shock concealed. This was not the kind of thing one 'forgot' to mention.

'Here is the man of the hour,' Hon. Muli announced. 'Now, I know you have all been waiting for some minutes and I know he is sorry to have kept you. I will get right to it.' He turned to Ngugi who still stood ponderously at the tent's entrance.

'Ngugi, sit. Sit here.' He lifted one of the chairs and placed it front and centre. 'I doubt there is anyone here that you do not know, but for the sake of formalities, I will introduce them. I am sure some have forgotten each other.' Hon. Muli chuckled.

'You know Okwanyo, former energy minister. Then there is Mukimbia who took over when Okwanyo was sacked.' A few of the men laughed at Hon. Muli's brazenness.

'*Wewe* Hon. Muli, I was not sacked,' Okwanyo said defensively. 'I was given a premature golden handshake.'

The men now began to loosen up. Hon. Muli continued.

'Then there's the Honourable C.K Mibei from—was it public works *ama* water?'

'*Wewe* Hon. Muli, there was no water ministry in our day. It looks like you are getting old faster than the rest of us, eh. I was in public works *bwana*,' said Mibei.

The introductions continued, the former ministers for foreign affairs, resource management, finance and education were present, as well as the former speaker and attorney general. Ngugi surprised himself by how much he knew about most of them. How long they held office and their most infamous scandal. He didn't follow politics avidly during his campus years when the men served, but even with his partial interest, some things stuck.

'*Heh*, Hon. Muli, can we get started. Ole Kataro must get back to his nursing home,' the resource minister said, sending the entire group into laughter for the next few moments.

'*Haya, tuendelee*,' Hon. Muli said, and the focus shifted to Ngugi who was nervously watching the legs of those plastic chairs wobble when the men laughed. 'Now, the reason for this gathering of old friends and colleagues is you, and your impending position in government. As I have been guiding you through your campaign over the past months, I have felt ill-equipped to offer you all the instruction you need in order to tackle this important task before you. So I called upon those who have served before you to help with a few tips, to ensure you do your job well and avoid shaming my, I mean, our legacy. Consider us your political fathers. Your council of elders as you initiate yourself into politics. And even after today, I am sure everyone here would be happy for you to knock on his door for some advice. Whether you will be knocking on the gate to a farm, or the door to a nursing home is another story.'

The men laughed as memories of their forgotten camaraderie were rekindled.

'*Na kweli* Hon. Muli has never stopped talking a lot; he has so many stories one would think he swallowed my wife.' The former minister for pan-African affairs interrupted Hon. Muli before he shared his wise words. 'Run that place with a solid hand. Your constituency is your house. Don't let anyone else come in and take over your home.'

'Yes, I keep telling him that his leadership begins now—with the campaign. His opponent at ODM is no joke—they are the most experienced opposition party the country has ever seen! I dare say the continent. *Chunga*! These people are organised. And totally aware of the issues their people care about,' Muli added.

'What is his name? Is it that Munyoka fellow?' a voice from the back asked.

'Munyaki. Victor Munyaki is my main opposition,' Ngugi offered.

'But who has ever won an election in this country because they focused on the issues? No one! People only care about corruption when they are not on the receiving end of it. If you want votes, buy them. You can talk about constitutional reform all day, but there is no issue that voters can't solve with cash!' Sitati said.

'And be careful who you hire,' the foreign affairs minister offered. 'Your employees are almost always the source of the most trouble. Don't trust anyone until they have given you a reason to.'

'Especially nowadays with that *bookface* thing that is such a nuisance. Everybody thinks they can do our jobs because the Internet told them so. Things were much easier in our day when people got sent to Nyayo House for running their mouths carelessly,' Mibei continued.

'Be careful, Mibei. You know, just because he is not in that chair doesn't mean he's not still signing cheques and death warrants. *Chunga!* The dungeons of Nyayo House are still alive.' Kataro was a little jumpy as he said this. He was the only one of them detained by the old regime.

'And your family, you must decide now if you are going to involve them, totally or not at all. This business of telling the media where your wife is pure rubbish. Those fools will begin to think you owe them an explanation every time you leave the room,' added Kenya's longest serving education minister.

'*Kwanza*, on the matter of wives, never be caught with your trousers down. If you decide to keep a *ndogo ndogo,* pick one from the university and pay them well enough to keep their lips and legs sealed. But you shouldn't keep one for too long. They usually become more demanding the older they get.' The room went stiff and silent and Mukimbia who sat next to the attorney general whispered to him that Ngugi married Hon. Muli's daughter.

'Oh, *pole*. I thought this was his actual son. Hon. Muli, you are investing this much in an in-law?'

'How can he be the son with a name like Ngugi, *na wewe*?' the education minister retorted.

'But anyway, I'm here to provide advice. Is it not the reality of being a leader? Even if he doesn't go to the women, they will come to him. You just wait.'

'No, we will not tolerate other women. Let's move on,' Hon. Muli said, shaking off the urge to kick the attorney general out.

And so it went for the better part of the morning. Ngugi's personal advisory panel only stopped imparting words of wisdom to him when their wives and children began calling them to find out where they wandered off to. Ngugi escorted each of them to their cars, as Hon. Muli kept the ones less eager to leave occupied, reminiscing about their days in government.

Ngugi then turned his attention to the men and women waiting for him. Most of them only wanted to wish him well. Others shared additional advice, varying from things as simple as which route would get him to Machakos fastest, to what his first order of business should be once he got into office. The majority of them just wanted to eat, drink and chat. After enduring more endless chatter than he had time for, Ngugi excused himself from the tent.

Ngugi searched the house for Hon. Muli, and when he was sure that he was nowhere in the vicinity, he grabbed the first volunteer he could find and firmly instructed him to empty his house in under an hour or less.

Then he drank all the whisky he could find in the house and allowed himself to weep as hard and as long as he needed to, and welcomed the relief that followed his release. And the clarity. A thousand and one words for Kavata burned through him. He allowed himself to admit that not having her around, glaring and sulking at him consistently was great, and when he dug deep though all things he was feeling, he found that he still didn't regret his decision to run for office.

He thought back to the meeting his father-in-law organised with the men who were likely the main funders of his campaign. He wondered what their expectations were—and what Hon. Muli promised them. He realised that he didn't know what Hon. Muli meant each time he said he would take care of this cost or throw money at that problem. Then he thought about Pastor Simon and how he rallied behind him without a second thought, going as far as hosting a prayer service specifically for Ngugi and his campaign team before flagging off their campaign convoy to Machakos.

He had God and old money behind him, he couldn't lose.

# 8
# ROAD TRIP
## 26 DECEMBER 2007

'**A**re you ready to go?' Ngugi asked Wanja as soon as she walked into the house the next day. He had been packed, ready to leave, and was irked that she kept him waiting.

Wanja jumped, startled by the unexpected confrontation.

'Go where?' Wanja anticipated this moment, deciding feigned ignorance would be her safest bet. She watched the irritation grow on her father's face and waited for it to reach his lips.

'Wanja, don't waste any more time. I expected you here earlier than this and I've been calling. Prayers begin at the church in twenty minutes, we leave for Machakos immediately afterwards. You can meet us at church since it looks like you are not ready to travel. I have to go now.' Ngugi picked up his suitcase by the door.

Wanja stepped aside to let him pass.

'Make sure you lock all the windows and doors. You can leave the car at the church. It should be safe.' He opened the door.

'I can come for the prayers if you like, but I'm staying here to vote.' She sounded much more defiant than she felt.

Ngugi froze. Even with his back turned she could see him trying to process what he just heard. He turned around slowly, his suitcase still in hand.

'What?'

'I registered to vote. Here. In Westlands.'

Ngugi searched his daughter's face, hoping for a sign that she was pranking him, but there was no such thing. She avoided his gaze, looking awkwardly at the floor, at his suitcase and at the wall behind him. He continued to look for the little girl who, only a few years ago, would gladly walk on broken glass to please him. When she did eventually look him in the eye, there was frost in her eyes.

'Why?' He struggled to keep his tone of voice.

'Because I decided to vote here where I live and where it counts.' The slogans she'd been churning out had stuck to her. 'Besides, you made it clear that you didn't want my help.'

'Why?' Ngugi could feel himself unravel. He couldn't stop it.

Wanja rolled her eyes, 'Because, Dad, it was also just more convenient for me—'

The chair he was leaning on for support was tossed aside when he launched forward at his daughter, raised his arm, and swung it to slap her. She jumped back, flattening herself against the wall quickly enough for only the tips of his fingers to graze her cheek. He stared at her, puzzled, with his nostrils flared. He closed his eyes and waited for the feeling that he was discombobulating to pass. When he opened them she was still standing there, looking at him, like he was a panther about to pounce on her again. Then, as if remembering that she was no longer a little girl, her manner changed. She stood tall and looked him straight in the eye.

'Where is your voter's card?' His voice was strained, barely audible.

She didn't speak.

'I want to see that card. Now.'

She still remained silent, but her eyes glanced towards her handbag, which she dropped in her flight to escape his fury. He followed her gaze and lifted the *ankara* tote bag off the ground and gave it to her. She retrieved her wallet and pulled out the small card and handed it to him. Her hands trembled a little bit.

She was not lying. Her voter's card was issued months ago in Westlands. All the while she sat with him, attending his fundraisers and showing feigned interest in his campaign, knowing that her vote would be going to someone else?

A dozen thoughts ran through his mind at once, and he struggled to select one that captured all his sentiments. He looked up at her. She stood defiantly with her arms across her chest, her eyes saying, 'So now?'

'If you are not going to vote in Machakos, you are not going to vote at all,' he said as he ripped through the card's protective plastic laminate. Before she could protest, her card was in pieces and Ngugi hoisted his suitcase off the ground and left. The entire house rattled when Ngugi slammed the door. On the floor, pieces of Wanja's voter's card stared back at her.

Wanja stood reeling, and then the sound of his car door shutting and the engine roaring to life awoke the sudden urge for her to have the final word. Effervescent rage coursed through her. With her chest heaving, she swung the front door open and prepared to shout over the revving engine, but she was a moment too late. Ngugi sped off, his car tyres releasing pellets of loose gravel that attacked her shins like hundreds of tiny bullets. She caught his eye in the rearview mirror as he drove through the gate, and thought she might have seen tears.

She resented the familiar sensation of teary tension at the back of her own throat and scolded herself for wanting to cry. Then she realised that she had the entire house to herself and relief washed over her. She locked the door, sank onto the floor and allowed the walls she had erected to protect her from the reality of the past few weeks to fall away. She gave in to the waves of sobs and they took over for long enough to allow darkness to creep into the house through the undrawn curtains.

She wandered through the silent house, locking windows and shutting doors to make the house feel smaller, before settling down to lick the wounds on her shins which hurt like several safari ants biting down at the exact same time.

She turned on the television for some company and tuned into the news out of habit. She caught a re-cap of the opinion polls from earlier in the week, which predicted Ngugi's loss. She giggled. Ngugi reclaimed his position as clueless father and fumbling politician. She floated over to the spot on the corridor floor where her torn voter's card still lay. She collected the pieces, determined to glue, tape, iron or do whatever it took to put them back together and play her role in driving his political aspirations as far away as he'd driven both her and Kavata.

Ngugi was still reeling from his argument with Wanja when he parked at the church lot, trying to recall the last time he drove himself here. Wanja had been driving them for as long as he could remember. Part of him wanted to go back home and beat Wanja into submission. But another part of him couldn't believe that he had almost hit her. It was all finally starting to take a toll on him. It was almost as though he had a body double that was acting, speaking, and living his life for him while he sat at the back of his mind watching his life unfold and struggling to catch up. He was becoming a weepy man who couldn't get the women in his life to do what he asked—so he hit them? *I'm losing it*, he thought to himself and began to feel his heart rate rise just as it used to during those campus days when he would be about to give a speech and would be paralysed with nerves. In those days, Kavata would slide her hand in between his and wouldn't let go until she felt his breath simmering down.

*What the hell am I doing? I can't do this without her.* Beads of sweat formed on his temple. Just then, someone knocked on his car window and he jumped, startled, and then turned to see Amani, his little hands frantically waving at him with Wairimu right behind with an awkward, exaggerated smile on her face.

He mentioned the service to Wairimu, but only in passing, knowing it would take a miracle to get her inside a church.

'We figured you need all the prayers you can get,' Wairimu said in response to Ngugi's questioning gaze. 'If I end up a pile of ashes, it's on you,' she added as she embraced her brother. Jommo stood a small distance away from them, looking uncomfortable and unhappy to be there. Ngugi thanked him and he shrugged like it wasn't a big deal.

'This is very special. Thanks.' He hugged Amani once again and felt his anxieties melt away. 'I hear singing. Let's go inside.'

'Wanja?' Wairimu asked, scanning the inside of the car that Ngugi was now locking. Ngugi shook his head.

'Don't get me started on that one,' he said, and led them towards the church.

What he imagined would have been a small intimate service was far from it. The church was filled to capacity. When he and Amani walked in hand in hand, the congregation cheered as he made his way to the front row. Pastor Simon stood at the dais, smiling down at Ngugi as they took their seats next to Kavata's parents. On the screens behind the pastor, a series of good luck messages played on a loop.

'Let us pray,' the pastor said into the microphone and the congregation fell silent. That set the pace for a two-hour service during which people referred to Ngugi as a God-ordained leader, the Chosen One, and the one who would lift Kenya out of her delicate state into a prosperity that would shock her neighbours. Ngugi listened intently, wondering if they were really referring to him and ultimately accepting the expectations set for him. He didn't receive the divine intervention he was hoping for, but the service was all the encouragement he needed. Regardless of the doubts his wife and daughter placed in his mind, it was unlikely that a church full of Christians could be wrong. He was doing the right thing.

After the service, he bid Amani, whose hand he held all evening, farewell; hugging so tight and for so long that the little boy complained and wiggled his way out of Ngugi's arms.

'Be good. Don't give Peninah and your cousins a hard time. Eat your veggies and wash behind your ears every day.' Ngugi tried to remember what else Kavata would say at such a time.

'Yes, Dad.'

'Do your reading.'

'Ok, Dad. I hope you win! Bye!' Amani said, and he was off.

An hour after the final 'Amen' ended, Ngugi's entourage of over two hundred were ushered into *City hoppas*, luxury buses and four-wheel drives. They drove out of the church gates in a convoy as the youth in the buses sang and cheered for most of the two-hour journey. Ngugi sat in one of the Prados with Muli, who chatted excitedly for some of the way but grew tired of Ngugi responding with distant hmm's and aah's so he fell asleep, snoring away for the rest of the journey.

This was it. He was launching himself into a life where he would always be open to harsh public scrutiny. Him, a middle-aged man with an enchanting son, a difficult daughter and an errant wife, who grew up in Nakuru dreaming about building skyscrapers, was going to become an MP. He turned back to look at the string of cars behind him. Their half beams shone through the back window as assurance that they were still there, following and watching him. He felt hugely responsible for the people in those cars. What if there was some kind of accident? He wanted to jump out of the car and flag the others down and then have a word with the drivers to warn them against reckless driving. But sense prevailed as they snaked closer and closer to the place where his life as he knew it would potentially end, and a new one would begin.

That evening, Ngugi sat in the living room of Muli's five-bedroom rural house, drinking whisky with Hon. Muli. Jommo sat with them. He had never met Kavata's parents, so his expression was an awkward combination of awe and discomfort. In the kitchen, Wairimu and Mrs. Muli chatted away like old friends as they put together a simple meal for their men. There was no radio or television switched on. It would have been pointless to do so because of the fervent prayer and worship taking place outside, where the church members decided to hold a *kesha* for election victory. When the *kesha* coordinator knocked on the door to ask them to join in, to Ngugi's relief Hon. Muli said, 'We will join the prayers from inside the house. Our old bones cannot withstand the wind's teeth.'

The election was undoubtedly on everyone's mind, but everything that could be done, had been done. They sat in silence realising the election was the only thing they shared, so unless they were discussing it, there was nothing to talk about. Jommo gave short anecdotes about his business but his simple talk only irritated Hon. Muli.

'Maybe while we are here we will go to Kyamwilu and see the wonders of water that flows uphill. There must be some crazy *juju* up there.'

'That place is only exciting to simpletons who don't understand gravity,' Hon. Muli said, silencing Jommo for the rest of the evening.

'Listen, this is how it will go tomorrow. I think the polling stations normally open at 6am but we don't need to be there until around 9 or 10. Jane will call us when things are ready over there. Ngugi, you can ride with Mama and I.'

'I think it would be best if I arrived alone,' Ngugi said, surprising himself as well.

'Why is that?' Hon. Muli eyes glared, but his tone remained steady.

'It's important that I am seen to be my own man, right? To be standing on my own?' It's the kind of thing Kavata would say.

'That's a good idea,' Wairimu chimed in, and Ngugi

could see that she was enjoying this moment. Mrs. Muli nodded.

'Fine, so be it. Mama and I will go in one car. And you can go in alone.' Hon. Muli turned to his wife, 'Or do you also want to be seen standing on your own?'

Mrs. Muli simply crossed her arms over her chest and shifted her body away from Hon. Muli.

'What about the registry? We're still registered in Thome,' Wairimu asked.

'You two will need to walk in with us. We don't get checked,' Hon. Muli instructed. 'Ngugi since you will not be with us, you should carry your voters card. They might not know who you are.'

Ngugi chuckled. He had obviously poked the bear and he was unhappy. 'What if we lose?' he asked the question on everyone's mind.

'That's impossible. My instinct tells me we will win and it has never failed me.' Hon. Muli's leg twitched.

'Don't worry about that, the Lord will deliver those votes to us. Like He said to Joshua, *'Do not be afraid of them; I have given them into your hand. Not one of them will be able to withstand you.'* Then if we lose we accept the Lord's will because, *'he knows the plans he has for us.'* But until that happens, remain faithful that the victory is ours.' Mrs. Muli seldom weighed in on conversations of this nature, but when she did, her gentle words were peppered with scripture.

'The only way we can lose is if they do some *magendo*. We need to make sure that our agents are alert throughout the counting process.' Hon. Muli picked up his wife's phone to call Jane to ensure they had enough agents at all the polling stations.

After a few more drawn out silences, everybody retired

to their bedrooms to prepare for the long day that was coming. None of them expected to get any sleep, not with the singing and praying going on a few metres away. When the town shut down and the night was still, the sound of voices worshipping served as a divine lullaby.

# 9
# ELECTION DAY
## 27 DECEMBER 2007

The Nyari Police Station was a ghost town on Election Day. Thuo's cellmates were long gone. The cell door opened and a man in rubber gloves and gumboots, carrying two large buckets of water, a shovel and a stiff bristled brush was let into the cell. The putrid smell of the cell was reawakened as the waste was disturbed and piled into one of the buckets. When he was done scooping, the man poured the second bucket of water on the ground and left the broom behind for Thuo to clean more thoroughly if he was so inclined. The cell smelled worse than before it had been 'cleaned'. Thuo's stomach prepared to turn itself inside out.

He and Kiprop, the booking officer, formed a slight friendship since they were the only people still at the station. Kiprop sympathised when Thuo eventually decided to explain exactly what happened on the day Kavata left. He figured that there was no use keeping it to himself anymore since he was already getting punished for his poor decision. Kiprop accused him of having an affair with Kavata. Surely that was the only reason why he would go to such lengths to protect her.

'*Heh*, these big women can put you in a box.' Kiprop laughed at Thuo and prodded him to divulge details of their clandestine affair. Thuo didn't confirm the affair, nor did he deny it. He liked that Kiprop thought a woman like Kavata would take interest in him. They continued chatting throughout the day, exchanging stories and commentary on the polls. When Kiprop was certain there would be no one else coming to the station, he let Thuo out of the cell for some fresh air.

'But if you try anything funny, I will shoot you in the back and let our dogs eat you for lunch,' Kiprop said as Thuo stepped out of the cell for the first time in four days.

Thuo was surprised to learn Kiprop was only twenty-one years old. He possessed the jaded authority of a man twice his age.

'It is because of the things they make you do when you are training at the National Youth Service,' Kiprop explained. 'They treat you like you are worthless—like you have Ebola or something. And they give you the worst jobs. We are the ones who collect the bodies of people who have been hit by cars on the highway. Sometimes they are so badly disfigured and have decomposed so much the hospitals and morgues won't take them. So we bury them ourselves—like animals— and wait for their ghosts to come for us. Then after you are trained and have gotten used to being treated like shit, they give you a uniform and tell you *ati* it is a symbol of power. And, *ati* we should use it to protect *wananchi*. But by this time you feel as if the people should be protected from you!' Kiprop's face twisted into an odious sneer. 'It doesn't stop when you get a job,' he went on. 'You will always be expected to bribe someone so that you can get a posting in a good police station, or so you can join the traffic department. I used to be in the army. You guys don't know what it takes to protect our borders. I didn't last two weeks. I'm lucky to be posted here; at least this station is quiet, but I really wanted to get into the traffic department. Most people make four times their salaries in traffic. The things I went through to get this job...' Kiprop trailed off and his mind appeared to have left the room and gone to a difficult place.

Thuo studied his expression, grateful that they made an unexpected connection, but uncomfortable with the details of the stories he told. They sat in silence, with the continuous drone of the portable radio filling the room with news of record numbers of voters showing up at polling stations all over the nation.

He asked Kiprop when the OCS would be back. Kiprop didn't know. The best he could do was grant Thuo a phone call to his wife.

'But don't bother calling your big woman. She has forgotten about you by now,' Kiprop joked and gave Thuo his phone. Three minutes,' he warned Thuo.

'Chep. *Ni* Thuo.' Cheptoo let out a joyous scream as soon as he spoke. Thuo was so happy to hear her voice.

'*Uko* Wapi?'

'*Bado kwa* station. But they are releasing me soon,' he lied. 'Did you travel well?'

'Yeah, we reached well. The house is so dusty we've been cleaning *tangu* we got here.'

'Did you go and vote?'

'Yes.' Cheptoo knew he was eager to know whom she voted for, but she preferred to tell him in person. 'When are you coming home?'

'Soon, I am just waiting to sign the papers.'

'We can come back and meet you in Nairobi. We don't

have to stay here. Things are tense over here.'

'Tense *aje*?'

'People are scared of the election. *Ati* since last month *kuna watu* going round saying that there will be problems if the right person doesn't win.'

'That's *kawaida*. People say that everytime. *Ni siasa tu*.'

'This time *ni* different. I'd be happier if we came back.'

'No. Don't. I will come there and we will stay until the new year like we planned. Tell me about the election. Did you wait long?'

Cheptoo shared the details of her day with him. About the long queues and hot sun and how their children gave her a hard time because she refused to leave them at home alone while she went to vote. She went on and on until Kiprop signalled to him his time was up. He re-assured them that he would be there with them soon and handed the phone back to Kiprop.

It had happened.

The election that Thuo anticipated would change his life had passed. Just like that. And it had left him behind. For the first time since being brought to the station, Thuo was enraged. The feeling built up inside him, swelling like a *mandazi* dipped in hot oil. He had been in jail for three nights for no reason at all. The only thing he was guilty of was doing what Kavata had asked him to. His anger coursed through his veins quicker than he could process it. His gaze was fixed on the Kenya Police logo painted on the front of Kiprop's desk. *'Utumishi Kwa Wote,'* he read the slogan that declared service to all, over and over. Each time becoming more aware of how untrue those words were. They were as untrue for him as they had been for Kiprop. With muscles tensed and fists clenched, unable to contain his anger any longer, Thuo sprung out of his seat and made to connect his balled fist with the offending logo. The metal links around his left wrist clang loudly, reminding Thuo that he was still cuffed to the bench on which he sat. His wrist snapped. Thuo fell to his knees; his rage was rapidly replaced by excruciating pain.

'Now you, what are you trying to do? I do you a favour and then you want to attack me?' Kiprop, his friend, was now gone and replaced by the man the police college trained him to become. He ridiculed Thuo as he writhed on the ground. His wrist was getting swollen so fast that soon the cuffs constricted it. Kiprop waited for Thuo to calm down before he walked over and slapped a new set of cuffs on to Thuo's right arm and then dropped a poorly stocked first aid kit by his feet and went back to his seat, turning up the volume on the radio.

'Hurry up and put a bandage on so you can go back inside,' Kiprop said.

'*Asante. Lakini* I need some help. I can't tie it with these on.' Thuo winced through the pain.

'That sounds like a personal problem,' Kiprop said. All signs of their new friendship disappeared.

\*\*\*

Before Wanja went to bed the previous night, she made peace with the fact that she wasn't going to vote. But now, on the morning of the poll, she could not imagine not having an inked finger to wave around for all to see. Surely everyone at the office would be sharing voting stories. How was she going to show up without a purple pinky? She switched on the news and checked her timelines to confirm that her polling station was open.

As she got dressed, she paid attention to the tips on how to avoid causing unrest at polling stations. Voters were encouraged to be patriotic in the way they dressed. Colours of the flag were encouraged. White was good. Colours that showed an obvious affiliation to any party were bad.

The Matatu Owners' Association announced that they would offer free services to those going to the polling stations. This decision did not sit well with the drivers and *makangas,* who worked on commission, so most of them kept off the roads. Those who did work made no effort to collect passengers and whizzed past silently. The roads were deserted, void of the street vendors, maize roasters or vegetable sellers who served as landmarks. Even if she hadn't been in a *matatu* in years, she decided it would be the most sensible way to get to the polling station. But after an hour of trying to flag down rogue *matatus,* she opted to walk.

She stood in line for hours waiting to vote, sending several prayers to the heavens that she would be served by a male voting official. She could play the damsel in distress as she explained why her voter's card was in its current state. She practised her story over and over again on the other officials who checked her card while she was in line to confirm she was standing in the correct line. Each of them assured her her tattered voter's card was still valid and they had seen some cards that were in much worse condition. But they were all men.

Wanja fingered the card in her back pocket, wishing that when she pulled it out it would be sans sellotape and magically restored. Her supplications went unheard when the voice that shouted 'Next,' signalling it was her turn to get her voter status verified, was of a woman.

The woman sneered as Wanja handed over her documents, holding the voter's card with the tips of her fingernails as if it was dripping with some highly contagious virus. The voting official raised her head to look up at Wanja, pausing momentarily to snigger at her white patriotic t-shirt that bore the image of a huge tick, beneath the declaration she voted.

'Are you sure?' she muttered under her breath.

'Sorry?' Wanja smiled and channelled her chirpiest voice.

'*Ulifanya nini na card yako*?' She showed the card to her colleague who glanced at Wanja and laughed before she called for the next voter.

Wanja said a final prayer for good measure.

'Our house girl washed it by mistake,' Wanja mustered in her most respectful tone.

'Oh, so it's also her job to look after your property, eh? And *kwani* she washed it with a stone?'

'It was an honest mistake—*niliwacha kwa pocket*, then she washed it.' Wanja wished she had gone with the truth.

Voters giggled as they walked past her to the ballot boxes, and she could no longer remember why she was so intent on voting. The room was dank and bore that government office smell despite the breeze coming in from the bare window panes.

'But I have registered to vote. If you just check the register, you will find my name,' Wanja whispered.

'And how will I find your name if I can't read your voter's card?' It was clear to Wanja that this woman was being difficult because, for a few hours, she possessed a tiny bit of power.

'Justine Wanja Ngugi. It's there. On my ID card.'

Wanja's black polished fingernail trembled as she pointed to her name, printed boldly on her intact ID card. The voting official flicked her hand away, and Wanja let out a surprised yelp.

'Madam, you do not tell me how to do my job.' Her voice raised an octave higher, drawing the attention of everyone in the room, including the armed policemen at the door. The stocks of their rifles hit each other as they turned around, and a few people jumped backwards, afraid that the guns would go off.

'The ID is used to verify the voter's card, and the voter's card verifies the register. If I can not verify your voter's card, you will not vote *sawa*?' The voting official was enjoying this.

Wanja couldn't decide if she should grovel, or be defiant. 'I know my rights,' is what she went with.

'Good for you,' the voting official didn't miss a beat. 'Now step aside with those rights of yours.'

Wanja wanted to scream and slap this woman in the mouth while explaining to her in detail how much she went through to vote at this polling station. How long the walk to the polling station was and how many hours she stood in the sun while the woman was seated in that smelly room nurturing her distended ego. Then Wanja would explain to her who she was and how easy it would be to get her released from her duties. Instead, she firmly and politely requested her documents back. The voting official shook her head, eager to derive her day's laughs from Wanja as she signalled for her supervisor. The younger man, who seemed terrified of her, went towards them and asked Wanja to stand aside while they deliberated.

'Justine Ngugi,' the supervisor called out loudly into the room even though Wanja was standing two feet away from him. The voting official sat back, arms folded across her chest and stifling a triumphant grin as her supervisor addressed Wanja. 'I am afraid we cannot verify your registration due to the poor nature of your voter's card. You should have visited the IEBC office to request a replacement card when this one was defaced.'

'Yes, but—'

'Also,' his demeanour changed and he suddenly seemed to be towering over Wanja, 'be knowing that your voter's registration card is property of the government, and defacing government property is a criminal offense punishable by law. You are now required to leave the polling station. If you do not leave at your own individual will, you will be escorted out by an officer from the Kenya Police.' He gestured towards the two policemen who looked desperate for a chance to exercise authority. 'If you have any questions, you can refer to the election guidelines or visit the IEBC offices with your query after a period of less than fourteen days after the election.' The supervisor completed his recitation and stood tall, proud of his work.

Wanja didn't dare speak. She simply held out her hand and the supervisor, confusing her request for her documents for camaraderie, took her hand in his sweaty palms.

'No,' she swiped her hand back. 'Bring my ID back.' She removed her hand from his moist grip and made sure he saw her wipe it on her jeans. He handed both documents back to her and she bolted out of the room, tossing her useless voter's card behind her in a final dramatic exit.

'*Ai.* Madam—*eish*!' the supervisor called behind her, and she ignored him as she took the final steps towards the door, satisfied with the flair of her performance.

'Can you come back here? *Askari, hebu shika huyo.*' She

forgot about the policemen in her moment of mini protest. The two men stepped in front of her.

'*Madam wacha siasa mingi*,' the younger looking of the two policemen said as his colleague looked on smiling and gestured for her to do as she was told. She turned around, with her head held high and her insides trembling. All activity in the room halted.

'What?' She intended for the words to come out sounding more hostile than they did.

'Pick it up.'

She only noticed now how tall the supervisor was. She didn't move.

'*Msichana, kwani hujamskia*. Are you deaf? You are interfering with our work,' the voting official said. Wanja looked at the distance between them and wondered if she could cover it in one swift stride and fulfil her urge to punch her.

'*Wanjaa, chukua cardi yakooo*,' her colleague added, barely managing to keep a straight face.

'You are not above the law,' someone she could not see offered.

She bent down and picked up the card, then turned around and walked out without saying anything for fear that her rapid heartbeat would travel to her lips.

She swept past scores of people outside the primary school gates, acknowledging each other, showing off their inked fingers and joyfully taking pictures to archive their concluded obligation.

She got back home in half the time it took her to walk to the polling station; she was half walking and half sprinting in a frenzied rage, spewing out all the things she should have said. She made mental lists of all the people she would speak to so that the voting officer was never allowed back into public service. She regretted not taking down her name. Once she revealed her experience, the electoral commission would be breaking down doors to find the voting official and punish her for her foolishness. She hurled insults at her and made more mental lists of all the journalists she would call to report the voting official. But most of all she was pissed off that her father won.

As she locked the gate behind her, the absurdity of her situation hit her and enraged her even more. Inside the house, she tore at the offending card, ripping away the tape she carefully laid the night before, but this did nothing to quell her ravenous fury. She collected the now smaller pieces of paper and placed them on the electric plates of the kitchen stove when she couldn't find a box of matches. She watched the plastic give in to the hot surface, spreading itself further on the surface before the pieces of paper went up in tiny flames.

The television carried images of people voting all over the country, proudly flashing their purple pinkies in front of the cameras. Reporters spoke of a record turnout and prevailing peace at polling stations nationally. The picture switched to images of candidates casting their votes at their respective stations. Then totally unexpectedly, the image of her grandparents voting at the Machakos Primary School filled the screen. Muli smiled large and proud as he held the folded piece of pink paper above the ballot box. He paused for effect, looking into the camera before he released his vote. Everything about him was a performance. Mrs. Muli, an image of misplaced grace, cast her vote after him. She appeared startled by the applause which followed after she dropped her vote into the black box. Then they strode away hand in hand, acknowledging the presence of Muli's former constituents. This was the first time Wanja saw her grandparents make any kind of physical contact. Wairimu and Jommo followed her grandparents but the camera had already moved on, and Wanja sat up abruptly. Did the media completely snub her father? A part of her was mortified, another was thrilled.

'Interestingly enough, we've received news that Ngugi Mwangi, who has largely been viewed as Muli's protégé, opted to vote at another polling station altogether. Might this be a signal that things are already falling apart for this team?' the news reporter said, and the picture switched to a solo Ngugi casting his vote at what was obviously another location, with much fewer cameras. Wanja gasped.

When Ngugi cast his vote the reporter, an obvious supporter, got caught up in the moment. Ngugi paused briefly before he released the pink ballot paper into the box. A few people waved at him and shook his hand as the camera followed him out of the polling room. He acknowledged each one of them with a sincerity that must have been real. Wanja wondered when he became so good at this. She spotted familiar faces on the screen, relatives who travelled to Machakos so that Ngugi would have their vote and residents of Machakos who offered them something to eat during that first visit. She could also see that he was frazzled and tired and began to imagine all the things that might have gone wrong to warrant them voting at different locations. She was certain it wasn't the plan and the suspense would kill her. For the first time, she wished she went to Machakos with them after all.

On the other side of the screen, Ngugi was embarrassed

beyond belief. He wanted to run away and hide for a few minutes. He knew his voting experience would be different this time around, but he also didn't expect it to be such a production. He was up well before the sun and, when the walls of the house became too constricting, he decided to step outside for some crisp morning air, which did well to calm his nerves. He took what he thought was a short stroll around the village, and when he came back it was clear that he wasn't the only one who had trouble sleeping.

The house was awake and already monitoring the election. Hon. Muli sneered at Ngugi when he entered the living room in his sweatpants and sneakers.

'That seriously cannot be how you intend to go out,' he said.

'No, I went out for some air. We still have some time, yes?'

'Yes, but I prefer to be ready for anything.' Hon. Muli gave Ngugi's outfit a one last top to toe glance and turned his attention back to the television. Ngugi took his cue to go and get dressed.

Twenty minutes later, at seven-thirty am, there was another knock on Ngugi's bedroom door. Mrs. Muli called Ngugi down for breakfast. He was about to decline the offer—food would agitate his already jittery stomach, but decided to go down anyway. Everyone was already so on edge, it made little sense to stir things up. By then Mrs. Muli had completed her long winding prayer, and Hon. Muli was about to explode with irritation.

'Maybe we should all just go in and vote early? Or is that too radical an idea?' Wairimu offered. The sooner she voted, the sooner she could go back to Nairobi.

'Yes, that way we can all relax knowing that it is done.' Ngugi was so grateful to have his sister around.

'No, we have to wait until we know the rooms are ready and the media is there. Relax? *Heh*, my friend. This is when the work starts!' Hon. Muli said, and just then the phone rang, and Jane reported that they would be ready for them in thirty minutes. This sent Wairimu and Jommo upstairs to gather their things so that they could leave as soon as they voted. Mrs. Muli cleared the table, and Hon. Muli pulled Ngugi aside.

'You mustn't appear nervous; fear and doubt are read the exact same way.' Muli never sounded more on edge. 'Let me and mama vote first, then you can go followed by Wairimu and anyone else after that. Make sure you look straight into the cameras as you cast the vote. There are still people who have not made up their mind; seeing you on television might convince them to vote for you. Say as little as possible to anyone who isn't on the team, we don't want to be accused of campaigning. It would be a shame to get disqualified at this stage.' He rambled on and on and Ngugi ached to tell him to calm down and shut up. This was not his first time voting and of all the tasks ahead of him this would surely be the simplest.

'Shall we go?' Mrs. Muli and Wairimu were halfway out the door, followed closely by Jommo with their overnight bags in tow. Ngugi and Muli rushed around the house gathering this and checking that. Since he'd opted to arrive alone, Ngugi would need to drive himself and just as he settled behind the wheel to follow the car that everyone else was in, he realised that he didn't have his voter's card and bolted back into the house for it, trying to place the item mentally. It took a moment longer than it needed to, but he found it at the bottom of his bag, inside the wallet he barely touched now that the campaign met his every need.

He rushed back downstairs, jumped into the car and drove out of the compound when it hit him.

He didn't know where he was going. He checked both sides of the road for any trace of Muli's car. He reached for his phone on the dashboard but it wasn't there—he didn't think he'd need it today because the hills of Machakos made network access in some parts damn near impossible. He drove a few metres and stopped to ask an old man for directions. The man gave the most detailed instructions, but they were in *Kikamba* which Ngugi only understood marginally. He was too ashamed to admit this so he drove in the general direction of the man's instructions, hoping to find someone else to ask.

Ngugi drove around for thirty minutes. In the meantime, the Mulis, Wairimu and Jommo sat in the car at the polling station parking lot, hot, livid, panicked, and trying to find out where Ngugi could be.

'Maybe he got lost. Kavata never brings them here,' Mrs. Muli said, and Jane sent someone back to the house in search of Ngugi.

Inside the polling station, voting officials had no choice but to begin voting in all the rooms except the one reserved for the dignitaries. The thousands of people whose surnames also began with the letter M, and were therefore supposed to vote in the same room as him, were told that the electoral commission were yet to deliver the logs with their names on it. Disgruntled, they waited in the dust, under the hot Machakos sun. Journalists were growing weary of waiting for Ngugi and were threatening to cover the opposition's vote at Muthini Primary School. Muli insisted that a vote the media didn't capture was a wasted opportunity, so when they had waited forty minutes for Ngugi and couldn't reach him on phone, Hon. Muli decided to proceed without him.

Ngugi was mortified. When he eventually found the correct polling station, they would not allow him through the gate. He laughed at first, certain that Muli set this up to teach him a lesson on the perils of independent thought. But then, when the policeman at the gate explained why he would not be letting Ngugi in—he understood that this was no prank. Ngugi's voters card indicated that he was registered to vote at Muthini Primary School, not at Machakos Primary School. This was the first Ngugi was hearing of this. He hadn't even thought to check the card when he got it because he understood that this was just a formality. He explained who he was to the guard, looking desperately for a campaign poster that he could stand next to, but all the polling stations were stripped of campaign materials.

'And don't be clever, *kina* Muli *wameshaingia na watu wao*,' the policeman said, and respectfully asked Ngugi to stand aside. He did, awkwardly avoiding the gaze of people who thought they recognised him, but dismissed their suspicion because what kind of candidate would be standing around barred from their polling station on election day? Ngugi walked back to his car to think. It would do little good to try to force his way into this polling station, even if his ego really wanted him to. Polling stations were fortresses at the moment and his insistence would do little to help an already tense station. Essentially, it didn't matter where he voted. So he walked back to the policeman.

'Boss, Muthini Primary *iko pande gani?*' The guard offered him directions and Ngugi was on his way. He only realised that his opposition was voting at the same place when he saw all the cameras there. The policeman at this gate recognised him immediately and ushered him directly to the VIP room where his opponent was yet to arrive. He was eager to get this done as quickly as possible and before the press heard he was present, but by the time he finished getting his information verified there was already a gaggle of journalists waiting for him.

Ngugi now understood the cause for Muli's anxiety. This wasn't just about casting a vote. It was a grand performance. The room itself didn't bear the same dirty walls and potholed floors that he was sure were present in all the other classrooms. It smelled of fresh paint. An out of place maroon carpet lined the path from the door to the ballot box. By the lack of dusty footprints on it, no one was allowed to walk on it until the VIPs arrived. At least a dozen cameras sat angled towards the ballot boxes. The glare from the additional camera lights made the already warm room unbearable as the generator to which they were connected purred dutifully outside the open windows.

The energy in the room changed as soon as he stepped to the ballot box. Everybody swung into roles that they had rehearsed over and again—albeit for someone else. Cameras flicked on and newscasters updated their viewers. There was no ceremony or fanfare about it, not with hoards of people looking on in patient resentment, waiting for the VIP to vote so that they could.

When Ngugi took his position at the polling booth, cameras went off frantically and reporters competed to be heard over the ambient noise. He literally sprinted to his car after he voted. He didn't want to draw any more attention to himself and needed to go and prepare himself for Hon. Muli's wrath. Even if he botched it, he had done his part. He voted. The only thing left to do now was wait.

\*\*\*

As much as Wanja enjoyed the solitude of being home alone, by sunset on election day, she'd grown weary of the sound of her own footsteps moving through the house. She decided to go fetch her brother.

'Can I please stay at Aunty Wairimu's until Sunday? Please, Jaja?' Amani did little to hide the fact that Wanja's company was not as exciting as his cousins'.

'*Aish* Amani, today is Thursday. That's too long.' Wanja's attempts to lure him back home with bottomless tubs of ice-cream and endless TV hours proved futile. But in retrospect, she agreed it was best if he stayed with his aunt.

'Ok, you can stay until Monday, but let me ask Aunt Wairimu first. Have they come back from Machakos yet?' She could hear Amani and her cousins cheering as the phone switched hands.

'Hey you.'

'Hi, I saw you on TV!'

'Oh no. I was hoping that wasn't going to happen. So, was the thing you stayed behind to do worth it?' Aunty Wairimu's voice was deep with disapproval.

'Aunty, it's not like that.'

'What is it like then? I'm quite disappointed in you. Everyone, even those people who haven't spoken to us in years, came out to support your dad. You should have been there.'

'I know, it's just that he makes me so mad and he made it clear he didn't need my help.'

'I doubt those words ever left his mouth. I know how

much Ngugi adores you. You guys used to have such a great relationship. You mustn't let this thing with your mum ruin you and him. That's their drama and it has nothing to do with you. Remember that. You know your uncle doesn't even like Ngugi, but he showed up. If he could swallow his pride, who are you to hold on to yours?'

Wanja could do nothing but utter a misdirected apology.

'Save it for your father.'

'Do you know when he plans to come back?'

'No, I'm not sure how long he will last. Muli was so mad at him when we were leaving. He got lost trying to find the polling station. Ended up voting elsewhere. It was classic. Muli nearly exploded.' Wairimu chuckled and Wanja gasped.

'I was wondering why you weren't together on TV.'

'Yeah, anyway. You owe him an apology.'

'Yes, *Tata*. Can Amani stay longer? I can pick him on Monday.'

'No need to—I will bring him back so we can finish this conversation in person.' The line went dead before Wanja could respond.

Moments later she was bored and scrolling through her contacts, searching for friends likely to be in the city. While over four million people claimed to live in Nairobi, Nairobians almost always travelled upcountry to vote, so the only time the city got emptier than it did over Christmas was during an election. An election that happened two days after Christmas meant that the only people left in the city were journalists and vagabonds.

Tom answered his phone on the first ring, and she could tell by his cheerful tone that she found the company she needed. He shouted into the phone, his ambience bursting with the merriment she craved. To her surprise, he was at the ODM headquarters.

All the senior campaign team members travelled out of town to vote with various candidates. The only staff at the Nairobi office were the analysts and media liaisons required to be at work every minute until the results were announced. This didn't stop them from having a few liquor-bearing friends over at the office while they did so. To sweeten the fact that they had to work over an election holiday, the office arranged for Nando's to deliver grilled chicken, chips and beverages to the headquarters as often as needed. Simon, the human resources assistant, and Masese, the security guard, devised a plan to ensure they recorded at least three times as many people working than were actually there. The result was a steady and surplus supply of food. Masese was paid well for his efforts, as were Nandos' delivery guys and the taxis that chauffeured girlfriends, wives and significant others to the party headquarters. Wanja now understood the popular theory that only fools remained poor in an election year. Since politicians stole for four of the five years between the polls, the election year was the people's opportunity to earn as much as they could back. There was money in the air and everybody knew it. All anyone had to do was put themselves in a position to reach out and grab it.

Tom rushed towards Wanja, grinning as soon as she walked in.

'Wanja, *karibu karibu*. Did you bring ice? So glad you are here! The drinks are outside, help yourself. There are lots of options. Go crazy. Feel at home. *Karibu.'* His breath smelled of cigarettes and whatever elixir turned him into a sweeter, chattier version of himself. She smiled and handed over the ice and scanned the room.

The office that on a regular day sat about thirty people, now hosted at least a hundred. Tom, and whoever helped him set up the office, cleared the tops of workstations so no sensitive information was left accessible to wandering eyes. Computer monitors were disconnected and stowed away, and only those that were in use left in place. The TV screens beamed scenes from local and international news sources. Genge and reggae wafted into the office courtesy of the DJ who was set up on the lawn next to a plastic table that served as the bar. Wanja made her way through the crowd feeling awfully conspicuous—her uninked pinky fingers safely hidden from sight. Whenever she had a conversation with a tipsy, slurring workmate she realised how desperately she needed to catch up and took large sips of gin from her paper cup.

She spotted Tom sitting on the other side of the lawn, struggling to stay awake.

'You look exhausted—or is this your drunk face?' she asked.

'Both. This is my drunk, exhausted face. I've not been home in four days.' Tom sunk even deeper into his seat. Wanja sat next to him.

'What? Why? Who else?' She looked around and answered her own question. Now she noticed her colleagues asleep at different corners of the yard. Sally looked so inelegant splayed out on a blanket under a tree fast asleep. Before Tom could respond, his phone alarm went off and he stood.

'Arghh. This is why—back to work!' He whistled loud enough to make their colleagues stand and rush back to the office. Sally dragged herself to her desk with her eyes barely open—she looked like a completely different person in her stripped down look. She beckoned at the DJ to turn the music down. Omondi, one of the media analysts, stopped pouring himself a precious golden drink. Soila excused herself from the dark-skinned beauty who was perched on her lap. Anyone Wanja recognised as a workmate made a bee-line towards the office.

Wanja sat there wondering if the party was already over and why no one else looked worried. Guests still carried on with their conversations in lower tones without the blaring music to compete with.

She followed her colleagues to the office and had to collect her jaw off the ground.

Her colleagues, at least twelve of them huddled around Tom's workstation, were actually working. None of them looked either as drunk or as tired as they did less than a minute ago. You would think it was a Monday morning and the candidate was about to walk in at any moment and demand a status report. They watched the news on the six TV screens, all tuned to a different channel. They pounded away at their computers. Sheets of papers exchanged hands, a signature here and an endorsement there.

Wanja immediately thought there was some kind of crisis. She walked over to Tom's desk.

'What's going on?'

'We're working. Are you keen to make some more money while you are here?' he asked with his eyes on his screen. 'Sally has actually been covering for you, we weren't sure you'd come back with all the drama at your digz.'

'Also we imagined you would be in Machakos with your Daddy,' Sally chimed in with contempt.

Wanja rolled her eyes.

'Since you're here, *si* you just work? We pay

overtime—5k per hour, 7k if you work at night. There's food and booze.' His affection from moments ago vanished. 'And you can invite whomever you would like.' When Tom looked up, she was setting up her desk.

'On it.'

'Good. We need an article an hour. And please look into creating a Facebook page. We just realised that KPP has one,' Tom said and handed her a folder with their recent press releases. 'Keep the articles short. The news cycle is now down to four hours.'

'Ok, I'm on it.' She sat down and pleaded with her brain to wake up, wondering how on earth her colleagues were able to work the way they did. By the time she finished setting up the computer, the ten-minute silent interval in which she should have completed the work was over. Tom and the rest of the team transformed back into carefree frolickers. Glasses reconnected with their owners' lips like long lost lovers, and Soila's dark-skinned girl was re-installed on to her lap. All the while, Wanja sat struggling to decipher the tiny print on the too bright sheet of paper. After an hour of sitting in the deserted room alone, with guests staring curiously at her as they made their way across the office to the toilet, she was done. She stood, eager to connect with the newcomers who joined the party while she worked. Her hand was on the balcony door when Tom turned the music down and whistled for his workmates to get to work.

And so it went every hour on the hour. Each time the local media reported the number of votes counted from different polling stations, Simon would collate those numbers and verify them via telephone with the different ODM agents at each of the polling stations throughout the nation. If the tally was accurate, he would hand it over to Sally and her team. Each of them would record them in four separate logs, three of which they sealed and the fourth handed over to Tom who would compile a brief news story which would be shared with another team at the ODM election centre before it went to Wanja to be chopped up into short neat posts. The entire process—except Wanja's bit—was over before the actual news bulletin ended, and the team would be free to do as they pleased for the next fifty minutes.

Everyone devised their own system to get their part done in the shortest time possible and by the fourth hour Wanja mastered her task and managed to get it done in less than ten minutes as well. They were well oiled and it was exhilarating. *This* was an election! They worked all through the night—joking and drinking, counting and posting, as waves of friendly Nairobians passed through the office.

# 10
## LANDSLIDES
### 28 DECEMBER 2007

Kavata had grown from not wanting to hear about the Kenyan election at all, to following each minute of it via the Internet. She switched between different live news streams and refreshed her browser frequently to catch every single detail. When the results began to trickle in, it became evident that a win for Ngugi would not be as obvious as she assumed. She was beyond shocked. What happened? Losing this election would crush Ngugi. She thought back to those months after he'd been fired from the NHC. He was so distraught, but at least she was there for him. She wasn't sure that he could bare the loss of the election by himself. Convinced that it must have been some kind of error, she told herself to wait until the very end before she made any assumptions. She searched for ways to distract herself. She cleaned the house as much as she could without totally re-organising Mutheu's house. She sat down to watch TV, but found herself stuck on the news channels and irritated that they completely ignored the Kenyan election. When she found herself back at the computer, reading the same expired news, she decided it was time to venture out of the house.

***

In Nairobi, day broke and melted away the night's enchantment. Pockets of dazed people emerged from different corners of the ODM office in search of food, water, car keys and taxis. As soon as the team completed the 7 AM update, Tom pulled a thick wad of cash from his desk and walked around, dancing and dishing it out like the star of a bad music video. He paid Wanja last and stuffed the remaining cash into his wallet.

'Thanks. Do I need to sign anything?' Wanja's voice was hoarse, and the stench of stale alcohol oozed from her pores. She shoved the cash into her bag without counting it. Tom shook his head.

'You can go home for a few hours if you need to. Come back at two,' Tom offered, and Wanja almost shed a tear of joy. She was tired and transitioned back and forth from drunk to hungover so many times that she didn't think she could ever drink again.

'Yes please! Do you need me to bring you back anything? A T-shirt? Mouthwash?'

He laughed. 'Don't worry, I won't smell this bad when you get back. We found the key to the don's shower upstairs so Hazel is bringing me some clean clothes.'

Wanja was too tired to find the words to ask him who Hazel was and what she was doing with his clean clothes.

Wanja had managed to forget about Kavata and Ngugi and everything until she was by herself in the car heading home. She suddenly wished she could escape a little longer. All the events of the past few days seemed like they happened so long ago. She thought about Wairimu, and made a mental note to ask her to keep Amani for another day—but she needed to figure out what she would say to explain her sudden change of heart. She couldn't remember for how long Schola said that she would be away and made another note to call both her and Thuo.

Thuo! She still didn't know where he was. Pulling over to the side of the road, she dug through her purse for her cellphone and dialled his number, all the while recalling Schola's distress a few days ago when she told Wanja that Thuo had been taken. His phone was off. She would have liked to believe that her father would have arranged for his release, but it was very likely that if she had forgotten— Ngugi probably would have too.

Schola picked up almost immediately. She sounded tired. Wanja assumed she had woken her up and apologised before asking her if she heard from Thuo.

'*Sijui kwenye yuko.* I have not heard anything. Hasn't he come home?' Schola asked, and Wanja realised that she probably should have waited until she got home before she panicked.

There was no sign of him at the house and she reasoned that he, like Schola and the rest of the country, probably travelled upcountry to vote as soon as he was released. She considered going to the police station—she knew the OCS at the house that morning was from the Nyari Station. But she didn't consider this option for long. Wanja was terrified of policemen, and even more of police stations. She heard the stories about the stations and was lucky enough never to encounter them. Something about being so close to criminals unsettled her.

She called Schola again and asked for Cheptoo's number, but Thuo's wife didn't have a cellphone, Schola reported. So

Wanja settled on sending Thuo a text message: 'Hi Thuo, Happy Holidays. *Uko wapi*? Did you travel home well? Call when you see this.'

As she did this, she switched on the news to check how Ngugi was doing in the polls. The numbers were seesawing—it was too early to call but he gained a small lead since the last time she checked.

When Wanja returned to the office two hours later, all signs of the previous night's debauchery were gone. The office was fresh and clean; the alcohol bottles were gone and replaced with bottles of water and fresh coffee. Tom was napping at his desk, with a fresh face and clean, ugly shirt. *Hazel has horrible taste,* Wanja thought to herself as she put her bag in her desk drawer and settled in.

A few moments later, the rest of the team arrived and swiftly settled into their routine. In between news bulletins, each of them would walk over to the nearest couch or surface for a nap.

'You know your dad is losing this election, right? Most of the numbers from Machakos are in—there's no way he can make a comeback.' Soila joined Wanja on the couch at the reception later that afternoon after they all pieced together enough naps to spare some time for conversation.

'Is he? I checked the numbers an hour ago—it was quite close.' Wanja reached out for a TV remote so she could see for herself, but Soila showed her the numbers on her phone. She watched her closely.

*Hmm. I should call him,* Wanja thought and stood to make the call while glancing over at the huge blackboard at the back of the room where Sally's team entered all of the results in chalk before they took a photograph of them.

Ngugi was trailing by over twenty thousand votes and with over eighty percent of the votes counted he could still bounce back, but it was unlikely.

She stepped outside with every intention of calling him, but didn't know what she would say. She drafted and re-drafted a message to him and eventually just sent him a message asking if he heard from Thuo, and then she went back to her desk where Soila shifted and sat a little closer.

'Let me ask you, how did you end up working here— what did you tell your folks?' It was a question she had been waiting for the appropriate time to ask.

'They don't know.'

'*Ai*, how now? Where do you tell them you are going?' Wanja explained that there was never an opportunity for anyone to question her whereabouts, and this seemed even more shocking.

'Must be nice. I still have to explain exactly where I am every hour on the hour. You guys must live in one of those mansions. The ones where you only get to see each other when you sit down to mandatory supper. And you probably call it dinner.'

'Hmm...' Wanja was distracted when they got back to work.

The vote counting was progressing as well as could be expected, and there was a collective sense of relief that the election had been pretty humdrum. This was as good a reason as any to celebrate, albeit prematurely. People began to call their friends who were slowly trickling back into the city, eager to connect and share election stories from upcountry. Bottles in plastic bags clinked against each other as a new wave of guests walked through the office and to the balcony to recreate the makeshift bar. By 4 PM, the second day of the vote counting party was well underway and the atmosphere was electric. People showed up wearing the colours of the party they were supporting even if they were in enemy territory. Each time Sally wrote a new result on the board, the crowd of predominantly ODM supporters went wild. Drinking games were formulated out of the exercise; chairs were cleared to make way for a dance floor in the middle of the balcony. Tinsel was peeled off the Christmas tree and worn around the waists of girls who made it their business to go around ensuring that no one's glass was left to run dry. When Nando's called to inform Tom that they spent the budget allocated by the marketing department, he reached into his bottomless pocket and threw money at the problem.

With each passing hour, the mood grew more frenzied. The ODM candidate was winning, but calls to wait until the final result was announced were heeded publicly and ignored privately. They ate, drank, danced and celebrated their victory. The party went on all through the night, and in the morning there were still people at the office glued to the screen, afraid the announcement would be made in the time it took to get home from the headquarters. Ninety seven percent of the votes were in. The margin was too large to fill by any means possible.

They won.

\*\*\*

In Machakos, Ngugi was out gazing at the eastern province hills when he received the text from Wanja asking about Thuo. He got on the phone immediately and tried to reach the OCS. When this failed, he phoned the police station.

'There is no such person here.'

'*Tafadhali* then check for me when he was released. I am sure *alikuwa hapo*.'

'We don't have that information. Offices are closed.' The line went dead. He then called Hon. Muli who was still fuming at Ngugi making a complete arse of polling day.

'How can you even be thinking about that now? You are wasting your energy on things that can wait. Ngugi, you must prioritise. We have to go over your victory speech,' Hon. Muli snapped.

But Ngugi was not interested in watching the results trickle in, so he spent the day driving around Machakos, familiarising himself with the constituency that might soon become his responsibility. He called the police station again, this time asking the officer on the other line to look into the cell and check if there was a man who fit Thuo's description. The man on the other end said that he was alone at the station and wasn't allowed to open the cell without reinforcements. He promised to call Ngugi back once he could check. Ngugi gave his full names to the disinterested officer on the line, hoping that he would recognise the name and be motivated to help him. This didn't happen so Ngugi, who was still not accustomed to using the 'do you know who I am?' route decided to try other methods. He tried Thuo's cellphone, wondering what he would even say if he answered. He had no such luck.

He phoned the station one last time, this time channelling his best do-you-know-who-I-am voice. The officer responded to him in a similar self-important tone and informed him that in keeping with the law, all petty offenders were released on the eve of the election; the person he spoke of was not in custody.

Ngugi assured himself that all was well. Surely someone saw the news about Kavata and had been able to link the events to Thuo. *He's probably gone off home to vote,* Ngugi told himself. He must have found a way to talk himself out of custody—he would show up eventually. However, even as Ngugi gave himself an undeserved pep talk, a part of him knew that Thuo was never one to talk himself out of anything. Whenever Ngugi confronted him about finished shock absorbers or tyres that were too quickly worn out, Thuo would simply apologise and accept the responsibility, even if he was not to blame. His gut told him Thuo might still be in custody, but he could do nothing about it until he was back to Nairobi.

Ngugi stopped at the local market to eat some fresh pineapple and roasted cassavas. He thought he would be able to mill about anonymously.

'*Mkubwa usijali*, there is still time to bounce back,' was the sentiment he received from those who recognised him. Most of them were shocked to see him frolicking unaccompanied in public. To them it was a sign that he lost hope and was reacquainting himself with life as a civilian. He hadn't seen the results that came in overnight. When he last checked, ODM, his opponents, were winning by a small margin, but there was still a day or so in which he could catch up. His phone vibrated endlessly. He didn't need to check it to see that it was Hon. Muli calling to express disdain at Ngugi's refusal to watch numbers growing.

Those who didn't offer Ngugi encouragement as he walked passed them laughed as soon as his back was turned, exchanging comments in Kikamba assuming that he didn't speak the language.

'We can give him a stall here in the market since he will

need a job after the election. Then he can sell those dreams of his to his supporters.'

'Where are all his people now? They must be at ODM begging for jobs.'

More laughter.

'Hon. Muli is at home crying because he sent a boy to do his job—he should have just run again.'

He strolled past the different wares displayed on sacks laid on the ground or on carts, pretending to examine the produce as he peeled his ears to the words that floated around behind him. Ngugi stayed at the market long after he'd had enough fruit. The market commentary was informing him better than any opinion poll could. It wasn't the news that he was losing the election that intrigued him, it was the reasons why that he was interested in. The words 'cooking' and 'rigging' and 'stealing' were hot on the lips of anyone who called themselves his supporter. To the rest, he never stood a chance. Debates and heated arguments broke out as soon as people thought he was out of earshot. He was spreading discordance like a plume of dark smoke wafting behind him. Soon the apprehension that was spreading all over the country enveloped the market as well.

When he finally decided to leave and walked to his car, it was surrounded. Two men rushed over to him as soon as they spotted him.

'*Mheshimiwa*, you truly don't know this place. We're here to watch over your car. We thought there was a driver inside, but there's no one,' one of the men said.

Ngugi dismissed the young men as idlers posing as parking attendants for a small tip. Then he spotted a similar sized group of men standing a few metres away, watching them suspiciously.

'There are some people in this market who are not as happy to see you as we are. If it wasn't for us, your car would be ashes by now,' the second man added.

Ngugi saw real fear in the man's eyes as he spoke. He didn't imagine Machakos to be the kind of place where he needed to worry about his car getting stolen, but he quickly realised that this had nothing to do with his vehicle. It was about him. If there were allegations of rigging being made, they were probably coming from his camp and not the winning one. There were obviously lots of people who didn't appreciate being called thieves. He glanced in the direction of his unfriendly audience and then to his car. Several hate messages were written into the film of dust that coated its dark blue paint. Dominant among them was a warning for him to flee: *Kijana rudi nyumbani* alongside more mischievous ones like *please wash me*.

Ngugi didn't reveal the panic that was coursing through him. He walked around his car, greeting the men who stood guard and using the opportunity to check for deflated tyres. When he was inside the car, he pulled out four thousand shillings and gave it to one of the men who spoke to him, instructing him loudly to split it among all the people who helped him keep guard. As he drove off, he watched the other men surround the man like flies to a carcass. He abandoned his earlier plan to go to Ikuuni bar for a quick midday beer, and rushed back to Hon. Muli's house.

Hon. Muli was nowhere to be seen when he scanned the house a few moments later. Instead, a sea of worried faces met him the minute he climbed out of the car. He didn't know any of them, but that didn't stop them from rushing to him and sharing their opinions with him as he made his way to the threshold. He shuffled past them.

'What are you doing here? Didn't you get our messages?' Mrs. Muli was shocked to see him. She was sitting at the dining table with Jane who was speaking frantically into her phone.

Ngugi turned to Jane as she ended her call. 'What's the final tally?'

Jane handed him a sheet of paper. 'The last results came in five hours ago, but there has been a delay since then. They must be faking the numbers. The same thing happened in '97. There were delays in the results for many days then suddenly fake results were announced.'

'Thanks.' Ngugi scanned the numbers. Ninety percent of the votes counted. Jane was going on about all the reasons that they should be at the election centre. He always viewed her as Hon. Muli's longest serving minion, but he now realised that she was his most important asset. She witnessed and worked on three elections in over 20 years of service to Hon. Muli, and that made her Ngugi's most valuable resource right now.

'Where is *Mzee* now?' Ngugi asked.

'At the local election centre. He has gone to look for the agents we have been unable to reach.' Jane hesitated and her eyes fell on Mrs. Muli.

'Ngugi, did you eat?' Mrs. Muli rose and went into the kitchen before he could respond.

Jane didn't hold back. 'You need to go there. We all know that Hon. Muli's short temper will do no good at the election centre. He has no business being there and only went there because you don't seem interested in this whole thing. You agreed to do the work. The work started months ago.'

Ngugi nodded. She was right. Ngugi changed out of his *akalas* and linen trousers and five minutes after he arrived, he and Jane were on the way to the election centre in Machakos Town.

As predicted, Muli was working up a storm when Jane and Ngugi arrived at the election centre. Access was limited to candidates and their agents. Muli was neither of these and was forced to stand outside the perimetre gate, screaming at the guards to let him through. The volunteers who accompanied him were hovering around him like embarrassed children. As the crowd of spectators grew, Hon. Muli became more invisible to the guards.

Jane led the way and displayed a tag identifying herself as an agent, before she fished into her handbag and handed Ngugi a similar one.

She pulled Hon. Muli aside.

'Sir, there is a matter at the house that needs your urgent attention. There's a car waiting to take you. I will handle things over here.' She spoke in a loud whisper, in a bid to redeem whatever was left of his reputation. Ngugi couldn't tell if Hon. Muli could see through Jane's act or not, but it didn't matter. He nodded his head and asked vague questions before he dashed toward his waiting vehicle, shouting instructions to Jane over his shoulder and calling for his entourage to hurry up and get into the cars.

The scene inside the election centre was an elevated version of the one at the market. Tension hung in the air like a giant stretched catapult on the brink of releasing chaos. Every conversation was a shouting match, as if the person who could shout the loudest would be declared the winner of the election. Men were growling at each other like angry Rottweilers fighting over a piece of steak. Form 16s were exchanging hands faster than assets at the Nairobi Stock Exchange. Guards couldn't kick the people who were fighting out of the room fast enough to retain calm for more than a few minutes at a time.

Ngugi stood at the door taking it all in for a moment. An NTV reporter spotted him and rushed towards him. He stepped out of the way before he realised that she was approaching him and beckoning her cameraman to follow. Suddenly there were microphones, voice recorders and cell phones floating around him.

'What do you make of these allegations of rigging?'

'Do you think your opponents have stolen the election?'

'Can you confirm reports that you were attacked at a local market today?'

'What were you even doing at the market on the eve of the election announcement?'

'What are your plans if you lose the election?'

Ngugi looked around desperately for Jane and spotted her amongst the chaos. He had never given any kind of address without a script and he searched his memory for something relevant to say.

'*Mheshimiwa*, are you confident that this has been a free and fair election?' The question from a faceless journalist turned his attention to the large electronic screen that was the room's main attraction. He spotted his name, sitting third on the list of candidates. He imagined he was in second place all along, but part of him was relieved he was not at the bottom of the list. Another part of him was a little glad he wasn't at the top.

'All I can say is I am here to offer the electoral commission my support as they execute this delicate task. This is not the right time to air our grievances about the process. We must give them the space to do their jobs, and then proceed to the courts if we are dissatisfied with the result.' Ngugi gave himself a mental pat on the back. *That's what Obama would have said*, he thought to himself.

'Will you be filing a complaint when you lose the election?' another voice asked.

Ngugi's inner voice shouted a loud resounding no. '*If* we lose the election, and *if* there is reason to go to court, then we will do so. But I have no reason to suspect any foul play at the moment. In the meantime, we respect the process. And we will wait. Thank you all and keep up the good work.'

There was a collective moment of shocked silence amongst the reporters. They were so accustomed to being yelled at and pushed aside that his compliment stunned them to silence. Ngugi quickly stepped away before anyone else asked another question and walked away smiling—he found his voice in the midst of untold chaos, and he liked the sound of it.

As he made his way towards Jane, he thought about the comment Wanja made that he should have waited for five years. She was right.

Jane was in the middle of a conversation with an election official when Ngugi joined them. He was older than Ngugi, but was in good shape. The man looked displaced in the midst of all the chaos, like he would be better suited on the other side of a church confessional. She introduced him to Ngugi as Mr. Musyoka, one of the returning officers.

'Aaah. Mr. Mwangi. The man who brought my friend Jane out of retirement,' Musyoka greeted. Their chemistry was obvious. She laughed and touched his arm.

'Yes, and I didn't think I was coming back to work on a losing campaign. What's going on? Who's not doing their job? Are they cooking?' Jane asked and Musyoka looked around cautiously before he spoke, his gaze finally resting on Ngugi, as if to ask if it was safe to be honest around him. When Jane nodded, he revealed all.

'There's always rigging—you know that, Jane. There hasn't been a clean election since '92, not as far as I know at least.'

Jane nodded, and Ngugi fought to keep his face neutral.

'But this time, greed has made you guys careless,' Musyoka said and Ngugi's composure broke.

'What do you mean?' He spoke to Musyoka but his eyes were set on Jane whose face still relayed nothing. Musyoka chuckled.

'Now it makes sense,' he turned to Jane. 'He doesn't know anything?'

'He must know something, but *mwenye macho* can't be forced to use them.' She shrugged, Musyoka continued chuckling and Ngugi asked his question again, making it clear that he was comfortable being shamed for not knowing what was going on.

'Ok, I'm sure that you've recently had a gathering where a few of Muli's colleagues presented envelopes of cash to you?' Ngugi said nothing. Jane nodded. 'And maybe you heard that a few weeks ago the commission fired almost one hundred clerks and officers. I think the official story they gave was that the commission erroneously hired the officers well before voter registration was complete so they had too many.'

'Yes, I heard that.'

'Good, welcome to the classroom. Now the people who are paying for your campaign, and others like them who are paying for other campaigns, are not in the business of losing money. You might think they're paying for the cost of posters and t-shirts, but that's petty cash.'

'Ok...'

'What they are really paying for is to win the election. The only way to guarantee that you will win an election is if you can control it. The only way to control it, is to have foot soldiers on the inside doing what you need them to do. That, my dear friend, is what your people are investing in.'

'So, we replaced the fired clerks with our guys?' Ngugi was addressing Jane. 'How?'

Jane ignored his question. She was growing irritated.

'So what has happened now?' she asked her friend.

'You tell me! I'm hearing rumours of agents being planted as late as yesterday. Did you hire new people?'

'Yes. Muli panicked and asked for last minute additions.'

'And did you screen them?'

'Shit. There was no time. It was Christmas Day!'

'How many?'

'Not many, like sixteen guys.'

'Well, then Muli wasn't the only one who panicked last minute because I'm hearing that there are almost sixty rogue agents. The reason we can't release any more results is because each and every one of these new officials—who were planted at the electoral commission as informants, number changers and to create distractions as needed—have disappeared with the results from their polling stations. They left their polling stations with the official results, but they have not made it to Nairobi. No announcement can be made until the chairman has seen the original copies of all Form 16s and verified them with the numbers he received electronically. We have sent police to trace missing agents. One of them was found in her house. Her son was drawing on the Form 16s with crayons! Imagine that! Pure delay tactics!'

'Delay for what?'

'Everyone needs time to figure out the next move. I'm not sure anyone could have planned for things to go so wrong. And that's scary because they are growing reckless.'

Ngugi's mind was spinning with questions he needed to ask, but refrained from doing so. He sensed that Musyoka was not eager to divulge any more.

'That's crazy, but surely it's only a matter of time before someone finds out. They can't keep people waiting for ever.' Jane kept her voice low.

'That is why I am saying that you have been careless this time. At least in the past people knew to cover their tracks. When did these politicians become so brave and shameless?' A brief laugh escaped from Musyoka's lips as he said this—his expression loaded with nostalgia and regret.

'What now?' Ngugi asked. Musyoka and Jane glanced knowingly at each other.

'Look, Mr. Mwangi, what you said is right,' Musyoka gestured at a nearby screen which was broadcasting Ngugi's short interview from a few minutes ago. Nothing could be heard above the noise in the room but the words, '*N. Mwangi: I trust the process. Will go to court if need be.*' were displayed across the screen. 'The only thing to do is remain calm and wait and see what happens, then go to court later; if you want to. I wish your fellow politicians had the same sense as you. I am told that in some areas, people are already threatening to kill their neighbours if the wrong man is announced winner. Kenya is heading down a dangerous path. If things continue the way they are going...' Musyoka paused and thought for a while, as if the seriousness of the situation was dawning on him now as well. 'I just hope your passports are in order.' Musyoka excused himself, and advised them to go back to their base and watch things unfold.

Neither Jane nor Ngugi repeated what they heard when Muli shook them down for information the minute they walked in. 'What happened? Why is there so much silence coming from that damn election centre?'

'There's not much we can do. We have all the information that they have. We filed a formal complaint and came back. Now, we wait,' Jane lied. She knew that other than further agitate things, there was little Muli could do to help. Also, she couldn't tell him what she knew without revealing that she had messed up.

Ngugi didn't even bother chiming in. Muli would see through him. When Jane was sure that Muli was content, she asked that she and her team be excused. They had not slept in three days. She would continue to monitor the results from her hotel in town and would inform them of any developments. Mrs. Muli was quick to grant them permission to leave. She was eager for a break so that they could also rest.

That night, Jane lay in bed wide awake, her mind reeling with the information Musyoka shared. He was right. She'd been careless. If the slightest investigation was made into those mysterious appointments of returning officers, her name would come up for sure. It all happened so quickly that she had completely forgotten to clean up.

When Muli asked Jane to find a way to make sure that Ngugi won the election, Jane knew that planting agents was the only way to deliver a win while making some quick money. It had worked seamlessly in '97. Muli never questioned her methods—because she always delivered—and Ngugi, with his head so far up in the clouds, would not pay attention to the details. She phoned around and was happy to discover that she still had some friends in useful places. She found a contact a week before the clerks were to be sacked and asked to be included—but it never occurred to her to check who else was doing it. It was an expensive affair, they would need to contribute to the fund that would pay the sacked officers well enough to keep their mouths shut, not to mention the costs of hiring the new ones and making sure that key people at the commission would be discreet. Thirty million was the magic number. She drafted an inflated budget for forty million shillings and presented it to Hon. Muli.

Once Muli recovered from the shock of the price tag associated with the election victory, he asked Jane to call all his former politician friends to his house for a meeting. She didn't ask for details and she did as she was told. A week after this meeting, each of his friends sent their drivers to deliver envelopes of cash to Hon. Muli, trusting fully that they would get it back three-fold once Ngugi was in office. They insisted that they meet the young candidate before the election, and Hon. Muli happily obliged.

Hon. Muli's retirement had not been not kind to Jane. She stayed in the civil service for ten years after he left, but none of the ministers she worked for were as foolishly trusting as Hon. Muli. Once Transparency International placed Kenya on its corruption radar, it became harder for her to award government tenders to companies that she owned. Employing ghost workers became impossible because job openings now had to be posted on the new websites that every ministry was mandated to have, and were screened by external recruiters. Politics lost its lucrative lustre and she realised with sadness that it was no longer her time to eat. So she grabbed what she still could and handed in her resignation. She arranged for a hearty retirement package and bid civil service farewell.

A year after she resigned, she opened up a shop in the

city centre where she sold imported women's clothes from Turkey and Dubai. Her new business was an instant success. She rented a small stall close to all the government ministries and hired a cousin to run it. But most of her sales were made during her weekly courtesy calls to the offices she knew like the back of her hand. She even knew when the unofficial paydays were for each ministry, so she knew when her customers had undeclared incomes burning holes through their pockets. And nothing gave her more satisfaction than being that black African woman on shopping trips who could walk into a store in Turkey or China and spend thousands of dollars without even speaking the language.

Her husband retired two years after her but he lacked her business acumen so he promptly picked up a drinking habit. Months later he was a roaring, resentful alcoholic. He began to accuse her of hiding money and property from him, and suddenly had the time and the liquid courage to pursue any suspicions he held over the span of their twenty-one year marriage. Including the one that their second born child was not his. She denied it, swearing upon her dead parents' graves. He pulled the boy out of school, saying he would not be responsible for a bastard child, and Jane rose to defend her son. She cut her husband down to size. She was now the breadwinner and did not hesitate to remind her husband at every opportunity.

Her husband fought back. He took his clueless son for a paternity test and when it came back negative, he kicked the boy out of their house. He threatened to reveal that the great Hon. Muli had a long-term affair with his glorified secretary. Jane threw herself at her husband's feet; she begged and pleaded for his mercy. Jane and her band of middle-aged women derived great pleasure from chastising women who got caught cheating on their husbands. Having an affair was frowned upon but, for a woman of a certain age, getting caught was a cardinal sin for which there was no retribution. Her business would never survive the scandal.

Jane was not ashamed of her affair with Hon. Muli. It served her well. He turned a blind eye to all her corrupt dealings because it was his way of ensuring that she got what she needed to remain comfortable and quiet.

'I am a kind man; I cannot make a young boy suffer because his mother is a prostitute,' Jane's husband said one night after spending hours throwing her around the house like a sack of potatoes. His mercy had a price. He demanded a divorce and half of everything she owned. Her new properties, her stake in a few small businesses and all their life savings. He left her the house that they lived in and her clothes business, but with no money to run it, she was forced to close it within months.

Six gruelling years later, Jane rejoiced when she heard that her husband had a heart attack while driving his girlfriend, a former customer of hers, to Mombasa on holiday. He swerved into oncoming traffic and had a massive collision with a bus. He died on the spot. His girl survived the accident, but was traumatised by the gruesome accident that left her lover's body parts scattered across the highway. Weeks after the accident, she was MIA and unavailable for police statements. A year later, whatever was left of his assets were transferred back to Jane, but it still wasn't enough to revive her retail business and get her life back.

She received Muli's invitation to work on Ngugi's campaign in the same week that she decided to sell her house and downgrade her life once again. It was a blessing, but one she mismanaged and now, it was bad. She had to leave the country.

By the time she went to bed that night, she had done the math and convinced herself that her earnings from the campaign would be enough to start a modest life in Berlin.

# 11

# THE HAVOC OF CHOICE

## 29 DECEMBER 2007

Only two polling stations were yet to report their results to the ODM headquarters, so Tom and his team were unable to update the tally and confirm if they indeed won. He and Sally were on the phone frantically trying to reach the agents at the stations, but their phones were constantly engaged. The media was on standby and they had no choice but to wait. The late December heat, coupled with hangovers and lack of sleep, made the situation bleaker. The sooner they announced the winner, the sooner everyone would be able to take a break from celebrating and rest.

At 4 PM, they were certain that something was wrong. Results had been streaming in without the slightest glitch the past two days and suddenly there was no communication coming from the polling stations or from the election centre. In the absence of news, rumours of rigging, assassinated politicians, and vote tampering spread, and what was a wonderful and almost historic election began to appear massively flawed.

Wairimu called to check on Wanja.

'I don't like what I am hearing; a friend of your uncle's

just told him that the army are on standby. Are you at home?'

Wanja lied. She had every intention of leaving as soon as she hung up, but she didn't want to miss that moment when they won the election. She went into the toilet and phoned her father—the news coming in from Machakos wasn't great. Her phone beeped later with a message from him:

'Can't talk right now. Sorting out a huge mess.

Lots of rigging all over the place. It's appalling.'

She sat on the toilet seat for a moment, deciphering his message, trying to figure out if he was still upset with her. Whatever the case, this was much better than silence.

When the time came to announce the results, the chairman of the commission approached the podium as if it was a guillotine. He was sweating and his hands trembled as he put on his glasses and struggled to calm the crowd that had waited for over a day for their president to be declared.

Worry filled the faces of those who stood around Wanja. The house girls and *shamba boys* from the neighbouring houses with no access to televisions were invited into the headquarters.

'These *masaperes* had better not have stolen this election again, or they will see,' someone behind her said.

'Will we ever have a fair election in this country?' someone else said.

Wanja considered leaving for a second time.

Then he made the announcement.

There was no happiness, no hi-fives, no pats on backs or congratulatory messages. Dancers in colourful sisal skirts didn't show up out of thin air to punctuate the jubilant moment with their swashes of colour. Nor did the heavens open up to spread cheer in honour of what should have been a great democratic moment.

Instead, as soon as the announcement was made, computers and desks flew into the air—their punishment for getting in the way of fits of erupting emotions.

'Fuck this shit!' Tom kicked the CPU of his computer, causing the connected screen to fly out of its position as he swept the contents of his desk onto the floor. Those who could not find something to vent their frustrations at sat with their heads in their hands.

Sally and her team sat in the corner closest to their prized blackboard, releasing painful sobs. Whenever she wasn't weeping, Sally was searching for words to voice her pain, only finding the word 'No,' which she repeated for as long as it took for the tears to come back. They wept as if the thing they lost was a living, breathing, and loved human being. The pain of having the election stolen from them seemed unbearable to those around her. She wondered if it was all worth it.

It was the crying that shocked her the most. Wanja took her seat at her desk, unsure of what to do. It was mandatory that they release the report to the election centre, regardless of what it was, but no-one else was in the position to do so. Tom's phone was ringing from under his desk where it landed, strangely intact, after his rampage. She went after it on all fours and picked up while still under the desk, only realising moments later how ridiculous she must have looked.

The man on the line, one of the agents that they were trying to get a hold of, was speaking urgently. She was struggling to hear what he was saying, but here he was, refusing to confirm that the poll results that were just announced were correct. She scanned the room for Tom; this was not something she could, or wanted to deal with. The agent was screaming numbers into the phone and she asked him to wait while she looked for Tom, and a piece of paper to write down what he was saying.

'Who is this?'

'It's Wanja—just wait one minute, I need to find a pen!'

'There's no time to wait—these people are lying. They've stolen the election. Stop the announcement!'

'Yes, wait wait, I need a pen—'

'Where is Odenyo? I want to speak to him, get him on the line now.'

She spotted Tom standing by the bar at the balcony, pouring some whisky into a Styrofoam cup. She asked the agent to hold on while she called him.

'No, I can't wait—these guys are looking for us and taking our phones so that we don't say what's going on. Take this message or find someone who can! The only thing *you* people know how to do is steal!' She dropped the phone and rushed to get Tom.

While he and the agent spoke, she sat at her desk re-playing the conversation in her head, trying to figure out if she could recognise the voice of the person she spoke to. When Tom hung up she asked him who had been on the other side of the line. He responded without looking at her, and began to rearrange his desk. It was no one she knew, but that didn't ease the weight of his accusation.

Sally walked up to them, looking completely defeated. 'Do we have the numbers?'

'Yes, but they are different from the ones they just announced. They are quite useless.' Tom's voice was distant. He showed Sally the results.

'No, we should release the results as we have received them. Let those thieves come and tell us otherwise.' Sally looked in Wanja's direction for a split second and then looked away. Wanja considered leaving again, and this time she reached for her bag. Sally called the rest of the team together and for the last time they sat together, as they had every hour for the past two and a half days, and compiled their individual reports.

Then the gunshots started.

At first, Wanja was certain that they were hearing the fireworks. Although they were banned a few years ago, it was easy to get one's hands on a few packets without a license. Then Masese ran into the office and barred the doors, and everyone realised that things were thick.

\*\*\*

Thuo was joined in his cell by a man called Pato.

Pato was caught trying to vandalise an ATM machine at a nearby petrol station after beating the security guard who was stationed there to a pulp. The man was in a drunken stupor so deep that he didn't even stir when he was thrown onto the slimy floor of the cell. Thuo never saw anything like it.

Pato woke up a few hours later and looked around the cell with familiarity, as if he had been in there many times before. He glanced over at Thuo, nodded ever so slightly, then began to scream and shout that the devil took over his body, begging that a pastor be called in to cleanse him.

Thuo initially found Pato's antics hilarious, but quickly grew tired of them and warned him to shut up before he unleashed demons of his own on him.

Kiprop, the day guard with whom Thuo formed a friendship, was leaving. His shift was over and he was replaced by a police woman whose voice was unusually deep.

She preferred to keep the radio off and ran the police station as if it was a dormitory and she, the matron. She instructed people to be silent when they got in to the station, and told them not to stand too close to her because the smell of their rancid bodies was making her sick. Thuo's injured wrist was throbbing, but when he asked for some water to drink and a painkiller, she complained that he was being too demanding. She later brought him five litres of water and six painkillers, and told him not to bother her any longer. He took a few generous swigs and offered his cellmate some. When he declined, he decided to take a modest bath with the rest of the water and instantly felt better than he had in days.

A couple of hours later, the policewoman on duty hit the door with her *rungu*. She wanted to speak to one of them. Thuo remained seated, certain that it was not him she was interested in, and signalled to his cellmate to heed the call.

'*Ndio afande*,' Pato said meekly into the peephole.

'What is your name?'

'Patrick Moi.'

'No, it is not you I was calling. Call the other one.' Pato shrunk away from the door, leaving Thuo to take his place.

'What's your name?'

'Joseph Thuo Maliti.' There was silence on the other side of the door as the woman flipped through the pages of the thick book looking for Thuo's name.

'When were you brought in?' she asked when she couldn't find his name on the register.

'On Monday. *Asubuhi*.' Thuo was now curious. He realised that this was the first time anyone asked him his name. He wondered if it was at all possible that his name was not on the register and what that could mean for him. The woman flipped through the pages in the opposite direction.

'Are you sure you don't have other names? Give me your names as they appear on your ID.'

'Joseph Thuo Maliti.' Hope filled him faster than the water that now sat in his happy belly.

She started again at the bottom of the page and checked each name carefully, using a wooden ruler to guide her down the page.

'Who was on duty when you were brought in?'

'Kiprop.' The policewoman spun in her seat and looked Thuo straight in the eye.

'How dare you call him Kiprop as if you are the one who birthed him? Can you have some respect for officers!'

'Sorry, sorry madam. I was brought in by *Bwana* OCS and two other *afandes* but it is Officer Kiprop who was sitting at the desk when I came.' The policewoman looked through the massive log one last time, and then slammed it shut and reached for a newspaper. Thuo was still watching her several minutes later, his breath caught in his throat.

'Em, Madam, is there a problem?'

'Who has said that there is a problem? Stop looking for trouble.' Her voice vibrated through the room and Thuo stepped away from the door. His name was not on the booking log, of this he was certain. He was not supposed to be locked up. It hurt him that nobody cared.

At 6 PM, Kiprop strolled back into the station for his shift, beaming from a day off. Thuo confirmed his suspicions when he overhead the policewoman ask Kiprop about him. They spoke in their shared mother tongue and from his position just next to the peephole Thuo could only make out the mention of the OCS. Whatever Kiprop said didn't seem to satisfy the policewoman's curiosity, but her shift ended and she decided that this was no longer her problem. Before long, Kiprop was back in his seat, and the familiar sound of the static-filled radio transmission re-entered the room.

'*Ala*, they've locked you up without any charges?' Pato lay on his back on the bench opposite him.

'Is that what they said?'

'Yes! You didn't hear? Oh, you are a Kikuyu.' Pato raised his head slightly, lifting the arm that was shielding his eyes to look at Thuo, then replacing it and laying back down. 'You don't look like one.'

'What did they say?' Thuo wanted to shake the information out of this galling man.

'They said that when the OCS brought you in they couldn't charge you, so he told that Kiprop guy to lock you up until he decided what to do with you. But then the OCS got caught up in the election and only returned to the station yesterday. So Kiprop didn't write your name in the register. He is waiting to hear what the boss says.' Pato looked amused as he spoke. Thuo was stunned.

'*Ati* how long have you been in here?' Pato sat up.

'Since Monday.' Pato shot up to his feet and looked at Thuo in disbelief.

'*Ati* Monday! *Haiya* so you didn't vote? You were in here? The whole time?' Pato laughed hard, mocking Thuo for his stupidity. It took Thuo every speck of restraint to keep himself from showering his cellmate with curses and blows.

'Is this your first time inside?' When Thuo nodded in response, Pato looked at him as if having never been on the wrong side of the law was an indication that he was a lesser man.

'You don't know the *katiba*? Don't you know that they are not allowed to hold you during elections? You should have asked for bond. You would have been released and because there were no charges you would have been a free man. No court—nothing! But you stayed here, *heh*! You are really a fool.'

Thuo could not process the information that he received in animated bursts. Pato was looking at Thuo as if it were Thuo, not Pato himself, who was insane.

'Let me tell you about this police system. You have to know the tricks of it. I was in Gigiri Police the Friday before the election, but we were released on bond—only a thousand *bob*—and given court dates for next year. But, the courts will obviously be too busy dealing with rigging cases after the election to think about our small cases. So me, I am not going. You can get away with anything in this country over elections—even lusting over your *mkubwa's* wife.'

Pato paused and watched to see if he struck a nerve, but Thuo was stunned into silence. It is only later when Thuo re-capped the conversation that he realised that his cellmate must have heard from Kiprop that Thuo was allegedly having an affair with a big man's wife.

'If you are ever arrested, you must act like you are a mad man, or say that you are very sick, vomit and shit everywhere and make noise. Say you are dying or that you are possessed by demons. They don't like noisemakers, so they get rid of them quickly. The quiet ones, like you, you can rot here forever. Hehe! Monday! *Yaani* you missed the election. *Heh*! It was a hot one.' Pato continued rambling, but Thuo's mind was still processing the things he just heard.

Thuo stood up and began to call out for Kiprop, banging frantically on the door, and pressing his lips against the filthy peephole as if it would make his cries louder.

'Shut up! They are announcing the results!' Kiprop turned the radio to its highest volume and placed it on the corner of his desk closest to the cell. A few of the other officers at the station gathered around the desk. Suddenly, nothing else mattered and Thuo was swept up in the anticipation that engulfed the room, as if the outcome of this election would in some way change his current situation.

The chairman of the electoral commission was speaking frantically, his voice heavy with nerves. There were delays in releasing the results. The radio station reporter described the atmosphere as tense, but he didn't have to. It was clear even inside Thuo's cell that the nation was no longer at ease. When the chairman announced the name of the winning presidential candidate, there was a silence that lasted a few moments as Kenyans, who were mostly surprised by the results, processed the news.

Then followed an explosion of reactions.

The sound of the uproar at the election centre, which was carried through Kiprop's radio, was drowned out by the shouting inside the police station. Inside the holding cell, Thuo and Pato fought for a turn at the peephole so they could catch a glimpse of the action. They began to bang on the door, frustrated at the thought of being left out and desperate to contribute to the synchronised noise that engulfed the nation. The harder they slammed their fists against the metal door, the louder the chanting and shouting became. People ran out of their houses at the police quarters and filled the station lobby. Some of them were dancing and distributing beers, while others wailed. Eventually Pato and Thuo's consistent banging on the cell door provided a rhythm to the winners' songs, elevating their jubilation. The losers sat huddled close together at the station door, frozen in disbelief. One man held Kiprop's radio against his ear, certain that it was a mistake and that it would soon be rectified so that he could be one of the ones celebrating.

Moments later, a journalist was providing a frenzied report from the election centre. Thuo could hardly hear what the journalist was saying, but the words 'State House', 'rigging' and 'coup' punctuated his hurried report. The news spurred the losers inside the station to raise their voices, demanding that the celebrating be stopped because the winners were liars and thieves.

Long forgotten tribal stereotypes were now used as ammunition. A line was crossed. Men who worked alongside each other for years were blinded by murderous rage and could no longer stand one another.

Inside the cell, the two men stopped banging and listened as chaos brewed and seeped into the cell through the tiny hole that until this point was a welcome connection to the world outside. Thuo stepped away from the door and sat down on the bench, and when he looked up, he found his cellmate hovering over him.

'There's no way you people could have won the election. *Ni ukweli...* you have stolen it...' He spoke in intervals, as if in his mind anger was slowly arranging the information for him. Thuo was not looking forward to having to defend himself against his cellmate if Pato decided to mirror what was happening outside the cell. Even though the palms of his hands were twitchy and hot from banging against the metal door, he balled them into fists.

'*Lakini* you were sitting here during elections, so at least I know you didn't vote for that thieving idiot!' Pato laughed and the tension in the cell dissipated.
A distorted message coming in through the dispatch radio went unnoticed for several minutes while Kiprop disengaged

himself from the brawling. He stood on his desk and blew his whistle continuously until the room quieted down. All attention shifted to a message coming in from the Central Police Station.

'Switch off that radio!' Kiprop shouted, and a young boy scurried under a bench to retrieve the radio. No one noticed as he snuck out the door with it. After a few minutes of trying to decipher the static-filled message, Kiprop pulled out his cellphone and phoned the Central Station—the landline hadn't been operational for months, but he would apply for a refund for his airtime. The phone call only lasted a few seconds, but the message was loud and clear.

Pockets of violence, magnified versions of what was happening in the police station, broke out all over the country. Kiprop was instructed to get every available police officer ready for dispatch. As soon as he made the announcement, he expected his colleagues to spring into action, but they did not. They didn't hear the panicked urgency in the voice of the officer at Central. For them, the report of violence only further justified their anger, so the arguing and fighting continued. Kiprop, a junior officer, could do nothing to stop it.

It was only when the OCS' car swept into the station and he jumped out faster than anyone had ever seen him move, that the police men scurried out of the station's reception area to prepare for dispatch.

The OCS spoke quickly, pacing up and down the station, taking no notice of the furniture that was now scattered throughout the room. There were four trucks on the way to the station to collect those who were ready for the field.

'I want every single male officer armed and ready for battle. Female officers who have been on the force for over a year should also be prepared,' he shouted to no one in particular. The words 'Kenya is burning!' punctuated the OCS' sentences as he continued to issue instructions to anyone who was close enough to receive them.

Thuo's heart raced as soon as he heard the OCS' voice. Taking heed of his cellmate's advice, he rushed to the door in one swift move.

'*Bwana* OCS! *Bwana* OCS!' he shouted and slammed his hand on the door repeatedly as his cellmate egged him on, more for entertainment than for encouragement. The OCS registered not a flicker of recognition of Thuo's calls. He continued to pace across the station floor, talking into his cell phone and walkie-talkie almost simultaneously as policemen flitted past him in a frenzy.

Thuo kept at it, using his injured hand to bang on the door when the other one was tired. When the first police truck arrived to collect the policemen, the OCS practically threw anyone in uniform inside it regardless of how prepared they were. With each truck that came and went, the station grew quieter and calmer. Thuo found that the silence only made him more anxious that he would once again be forgotten. He kept hammering at the metal door long after his voice gave in and his cellmate found something else to entertain himself with.

An hour later he still refused to be silent. His body was exhausted. As he rested fully on the cool metal door, his hand was the only part of his body that still worked. Every bit of his energy was channelled into hitting the door consistently. The cell door swung open suddenly, and an unprepared Thuo fell to the ground in a clumsy mound, landing heavily on his already injured hand. It took a while for his eyes to adjust to the light, but they did just in time to catch a glimpse of the

OCS' boot before it struck him in the ribs.

'Are you mad?' the OCS roared, and lifted his foot to kick Thuo again. 'Do you think I have time for criminals when I have to protect the country from hooligans like you?' Another kick missed his groin by inches, and Thuo was just about to start begging for forgiveness when he felt himself being dragged back into the cell.

'*Pole Bwana* OCS. *Pole.*' Pato interceeded on his behalf. 'This one has been in here too long; he doesn't know what's going on. Just forgive him.' For the first time, Thuo heard fear in his cellmate's voice.

'Who are you?' The OCS's round form filled the entire door frame, blocking out all the light from the reception. His fly was undone. Thuo fought through the pain in his thighs and his ribs and his wrist. He stood up and faced the OCS, ignoring Pato's quiet warnings to stay down.

'*Bwana* OCS, my name is Joseph Thuo Maliti.' He watched the recognition spread on the OCS' face. There was no doubt that up until that moment, he had completely forgotten about Thuo and the fact that he was locked up by his orders. Thuo kept his gaze, loaded with questions and demanding explanation, on the OCS.

'*Bwana* OCS, I just want…,' before Thuo could complete his sentence, the OCS stepped back into the reception, slammed the cell door shut, and threw the keys on to the desk which was now manned by the same policewoman who, a few hours ago, questioned Thuo's confinement. She watched the entire episode in silent disbelief. A few minutes later, when she was sure that the OCS was tucked away in his office, she brought Thuo more water and asked if he was hungry.

\*\*\*

In Machakos, Jane reported to work as usual but avoided Ngugi's gaze as she walked past him on the veranda and into the house. Ngugi was certain that she could answer the questions that kept him awake all night, but he also knew he didn't want to hear the truth.

She and her team were packing up. Printers were going back into the boxes that ferried them here. Reams of papers were stuffed into bags and boxes. Mrs. Muli was walking around the house packing away anything of value. Hon. Muli pulled him into a corner and told him they would be leaving in a few hours.

Ngugi was shocked. This was the exact opposite of what they should have been doing, but it was completely like Hon. Muli to abandon ship at the slightest sign of trouble.

'We've organised a helicopter to pick us up at the Stadium at 2 PM. I think we should be able to leave without any trouble. From what I hear, it is not a good idea to take the roads. There is space for four on the aircraft, so pack your things.' Hon. Muli didn't look Ngugi in the eye as he spoke.

Ngugi looked over at Jane, wondering if she would be taking the 4th seat. 'We can't all leave. It will send the wrong message. You can go ahead, I will come tomorrow.'

Mrs. Muli was the first to object. 'Ngugi, let's go. It is best that you are in Nairobi for the announcement. What of the children?'

'Wairimu has Amani, and she will make sure Wanja is fine until I get there. It is just one more night. We can't all leave.' Ngugi was certain that he was doing the right thing and though he would never admit it, so was Hon. Muli. There was no more discussion on the matter.

An hour later, Jane put her team on the bus back to Nairobi, and then accompanied the Mulis to the stadium.

Ngugi was sitting on the sofa monitoring the news when he was startled by a bang on the door and the sound of several voices shouting. He remained seated for a moment, waiting for someone else to answer, before he remembered that there was no one else in the house with him. The shouting grew louder as he approached the threshold and peeked through the stained glass.

There were at least thirty agitated men and women staring back at him when he opened the door. The uproar heightened when the mob saw him, but a man who Ngugi assumed was their leader asked them to be silent and they shushed one another.

'*Habari, niwasaidie aje?*' Ngugi kept his voice as calm as he could muster. The mob leader stood up straight, and spoke in English, making it clear that this was not a friendly conversation. He looked past Ngugi into the house, searching for something, but Ngugi blocked his view. He stepped out of the house but kept his hand on the door handle.

'*Mheshimiwa* Mwangi, we are here to see Muli.' His eyes kept darting past Ngugi into the house.

'*Bwana* Muli *hayuko*. Can I help you?'

No sooner had the words come from Ngugi's mouth than the crowd flared up again. Hon. Muli's departure was in no way discreet. There was nothing subtle about a helicopter in Machakos, more so at a time like this when everyone was looking for any reason to panic.

'Let me assure you that we are still waiting to see what happens with the votes. I am here until the end,' Ngugi said.

'We want our money! We don't care if you win or lose,' someone from the back shouted. The mob leader shot a warning gaze to the back of the crowd, and they once again fell silent.

'Mr. Mwangi, whether you win or lose is not our concern at this time. Hon. Muli hired us to do a job and we have done it. Now he has run away, left us without talking to us about the work.' Ngugi let out a sigh of relief. This he could fix. Now that he looked at the faces in the crowd, he recognised some of them from rallies and events over the past few months. They handed out t-shirts and handled the on-ground logistics. Surely Jane would have made arrangements to pay them.

'Oh, that is what you want,' he smiled as he spoke, reassuring them that this was something he could take care of. He asked the leader for his name and asked the crowd to give him a few minutes while he called Jane to enquire. The crowd agreed and calmed down.

Ngugi locked the door behind him and scanned the room for any sign that Jane had the foresight that he sincerely hoped she did. When he could see no signs of money left behind, he rang Hon. Muli but his phone was switched off, as was Jane's. He continued to search in the most unlikely places. Mrs. Muli's wardrobe, the kitchen cabinets, under the bookshelf with volumes of books from the 1940s, but it was clear that he wasn't going to find anything. He could hear the crowd growing impatient and rushed outside with a paper and pen before he lost the delicate calm that he had just managed to establish.

He explained to the crowd that his assistant rushed to Nairobi owing to a family emergency and forgot to leave instructions for payment. Ngugi pleaded for calm and asked them to leave their invoices behind and come back in a few hours. He would have sorted it out by then. His side eye caught a glimpse of buses parking outside the gates. They were some of the ones that were in his convoy.

'Invoices *ni wewe*! Why did no one ask for *invoices* when we were busy working. Those are just tricks. Pay us now!' a short woman who stood next to the mob leader shouted, and the crowd agreed.

'Then how will I know how much you are owed?' Ngugi tried to reason as people alighted from the buses and joined the crowd. He wished he had left with Hon. Muli.

'Muli knows—ask Muli!' was the response.

'Listen to me now, I have heard you. But let me ask you something. When you were giving away T-shirts during the rallies, whose face did you see printed on the front of those shirts?'

'Yours!' came the unanimous response.

'And when you were out there telling people to vote, who were you telling them to vote for?'

'You!'

'And when you went to vote on Thursday who did you vote for?'

'You.' This question was answered hesitantly, and some people laughed nervously.

'Yes, so were you working for my campaign or Muli's?'

'Yours!' The crowd began to see where he was going with this.

'Yes, so it is my job to pay you, but we need to help each other.' Ngugi walked into the house and came back with several sheets of paper and a few pens and asked the mob leader and his assistant to go and write down the names and ID numbers of all the people who were owed money, as well as how much they were owed and for what. Those would serve as the invoices. Then he promised payment before the sun went down.

He almost dropped to his knees in relief when the last of the crowd was off his doorstep and he had closed the door behind him. He cursed Jane and Hon. Muli for leaving him in this position. Before long, another knock on the door.

He groaned and lifted himself off the ground and opened the door to one of the *kesha* coordinators who was wringing his hands. A few more familiar faces stood behind him watching.

'Sorry to disturb you sir, after those guys have just been here. It's just that the bus drivers won't leave until they have been paid.'

'Shit.' The words were out of his mouth before he could stop them, and the young Christian shrunk away from Ngugi as if the words would taint him. 'Sorry, it's been a long week.'

'No problem, the devil always tries to attack us when we are weakest.' Ngugi envied his simple thinking.

'How many?'

'How many devils?' He looked at Ngugi as if he was from another planet.

'How many buses?'

'Oh, sorry. Four. Four buses.'

'And the rest? I'm sure we came in with more buses than that.'

'Yes, the rest left in the morning. We stayed behind so we could attend the Sunday worship service with the locals.' Ngugi asked if the bus drivers had invoices, and was relieved that they did.

Ngugi was once again glad he carried around a wallet more out of habit than necessity. He told the drivers he was going into town to withdraw money to pay them, and he would be back in a few minutes.

He drove to the main street in town where all banks had ATMs and parked on the deserted street. The first three machines were out of service, no doubt because they were out of money. There was a war coming, and people were taking precautions. He tried a few more, frustrated when they wouldn't let him draw past his daily limit. There was no chance of any banks being open on the last Sunday of the year, especially during an election. He drove around the entire town, pausing at every ATM to try one bankcard or the other. He stopped trying when one of his cards got swallowed by the machine and resorted to looking for MPESA agents who could deposit money onto his mobile.

He got back two hours later than he expected, with cash in his pocket and a string of curses on his lips. There were several people milling about the house when he arrived. He tried Jane's phone once again before he got out of the car.

'I have the money with me, *pole sana*, we left in such a hurry I completely forgot,' Jane apologised.

Ngugi was unconvinced.

'I don't think there's anything I can do. Things are bad here. Everything is closed. I have some money on my MPESA; I will send that for now.' She hung up before Ngugi could put in another word. This was the last time he would hear from her.

As instructed, the mob leader and his assistant delivered a list of his debtors. His eyes almost rolled to the back of their sockets when he looked at the list. There were no more than thirty people at his door earlier that day. But the sheet of paper he held now held the names of a hundred and twenty seven people claiming they were owed a minimum of four thousand shillings each. He asked for the *kesha* coordinator to follow him into the house and paid him the money owed for the buses.

'Please be discreet with this cash. Make sure these people don't see you paying the drivers. I am waiting on some cash from Jane before I can pay them. Ok?'

The young man nodded. Ngugi insisted that the buses leave immediately and asked that everyone was dropped at the church as soon as they got to Nairobi. He insisted that they call him in case of any trouble.

When the buses were well on their way, he invited the mob leader and his assistant into the house and sat with them at the table.

'I see the number of people owed has grown.' Ngugi studied the list. The list was so long that some lines had two names written in them. The leader sniggered.

'You asked for an invoice, we gave you an invoice. We have done the work. We must be paid.' The fiery assistant crossed her short arms across her chest.

'That's true; you must get paid for your hard work. But as you know, today is Sunday and the banks are closed and there is no way I can get my hands on such money at this time. I have just tried to but all I could raise was this.' He pulled out a hundred thousand shillings and placed it on the table on top of the list and asked them to consider it a down payment. He would get them the rest before he left Machakos. His visitors' eyes lit up when they saw the money. Ngugi asked that they decide how the money would be distributed amongst the people on the list. He just wanted them off his property as soon as possible.

'We didn't do the work in bits. We didn't ask for a down payment before we started the work. Stop these stories of yours. If you didn't have money then how did you pay for Muli's helicopter to help him run away? We know you paid the bus drivers to get your people out of here. Was the work they did more important than ours? *Wacha siasa. Lipa pesa,*' the girl said.

Ngugi regretted his assumption that having her in the room would help solve the issues amicably. After long negotiations, and the crowd outside growing more impatient, they agreed to categorise the massive list in to those who needed to be paid in full and most urgently and that they would be back the following morning for the balance.

He settled down just before sunset and in time to catch the ECK's announcement of the presidential results. He navigated through the static filled reception, searching for the face of the ECK chairman. The tension reached boiling point when someone threw a plastic water bottle at the ECK chairman, and the police were called in to clear the room. No results could be announced in such an environment. Media and party agents were asked to cool off outside the building for an hour, after which they would be called back in for the final announcement.

While this was happening, another smaller room was set up for the announcement to be made. KBC, the national broadcaster, was the only media house present in the room with the chairman as well as a few foreign election observers. In that quiet orderly room, the commissioner announced the winner of the presidential election, and then he was escorted into a waiting car and whisked away to safety.

He flipped through channels hoping to catch the provincial results to confirm he actually lost, but all he found were scenes of unrest outside the commission headquarters, scenes of final preparations for a hurried inauguration and reports of violence and looting in Nairobi, Kisumu, and the

Rift Valley. He searched the house for a computer—but Jane took them all. He resigned himself to the fact that in the unlikely occasion that he won, people would be calling to congratulate him.

A president was declared, but only a third of the country supported him, the other third violently rejected him. And the rest were either fleeing from the resulting uproar, or watching intently, hoping that this argument didn't disrupt their lives too much. Every hour, another area was added to the list where violence erupted: Kibera, Narok, Naivasha, Molo, Limuru, Mlolongo. The fighting seemed to be creeping closer towards him. Unable to reach Wanja, he called Wairimu and insisted that she go and check on her, but Wairimu assured him that she had spoken to her when the violence began, and that she was safe and at home.

'She's probably just sleeping off a hangover,' Wairimu said, hoping to lighten the mood, but her voice was heavy with fret. 'You should make your way back, it could get worse and you don't want to get stuck in the *bundus*.'

'Yes, I will be back tomorrow... I have a few things to take care of first.' The small talk tired them and they promised to speak in the morning.

Ngugi sat in the dark room for several hours before deciding to listen to the voice in his head telling him things might get very ugly. He panicked. It was usually the thing Kavata did best, forecasting doom so she could prepare for it. So he channelled his wife and went up and threw all his things into his suitcase and put it in the boot of one of the cars that Hon. Muli left behind. Keeping watch for curious eyes, he got into the car and drove it a few metres away from the house, parking it at a distance he was sure he could run to if the need arose. He locked the car and walked back to the house; he switched on the security lights and sat in the glow of the television.

\*\*\*

Kavata looked down at the sleeves of the oversize grey sweatshirt and matching pants she bought from an outlet store a day ago. They were so warm and comfortable, and when she slid them on for the first time, she felt as if she was stepping into someone else's life. She couldn't remember ever owning a matching pair of sweats—she thought them lazy and unflattering. It was one of those American trends she gladly allowed to pass her by. She already missed her clothes. She spotted the bag of gifts she had almost unconsciously picked up for her kids. A baseball cap with a picture of two fingers holding up a peace sign for Amani, and pair of pyjamas for Wanja that she ended up wearing herself.

Mutheu called to check on her often. She sounded more American on the phone than she did in person. She had been following the news of the growing tension back home over the delay in releasing the results.

'That is why I left that place. Everything is so backward and primitive. They have no idea how a democracy works. It is no wonder that people like Obama want little to do with that place.'

Kavata was irked by her cousin's sweeping statements, but she said nothing. She just provided snippets of the information that she gathered. When Mutheu asked how Ngugi was doing, Kavata said she didn't know. She wasn't quite sure what to do with Ngugi's potential loss.

The results were due, but there was a strange silence online. Kavata refreshed pages over and over, but all she got was the same news that she could practically recite by now. The results were eventually announced with the chaos and disorganisation that she recognised, but something seemed different this time around. She couldn't quite figure it out. There were unconfirmed reports that a president was being sworn in, but no one explained who it was or why this was happening so soon. Reports of violence were not unheard of during elections, but the ones she was reading about now felt different. She was instantly worried about everyone at home. She sent Anne another email, although she hadn't responded to the first one letting her know that she arrived well. Then she waited.

For several hours all she received were short bursts of information from websites that required her to open accounts in order to access them. She recognised some of the names; Wanja often mentioned that she saw this on Facebook or read that on a blog. Unable to sleep in the wee hours of the morning, and when the lack of mainstream news drove her crazy, she opened a Twitter account and figured out how to use it.

Soon Kavata knew enough to understand that things back home were beyond bleak. Grainy cell-phone pictures of people protesting, looting, and killing, taken from inside cars and from bedroom windows, cropped up on her timeline every few seconds. They seemed to get more gruesome each time she refreshed her page. Foreign media was carrying reports of a war going on in Kenya, and Kavata couldn't watch any longer. When she couldn't get a hold of anyone on Mutheu's landline, she decided to go out to buy a sim card. As soon as she powered her phone, she called Wanja, Ngugi,

Anne, and then the landline. When none of them answered, she prayed it was because of the time difference. She decided to stroll around the mall for a while longer, stopping every few minutes to phone home again. When she walked past the food court, her belly reminded her that she had neglected it for the past few days. The meal options Mutheu left her were bland; she survived on a nibble here and there. Now she was ravenous. The girl at Wendy's asked her if she wanted to supersize her meal for an extra two dollars. *Why not*, she thought, and as she ploughed through her large meal she understood why relatives who moved to America always came back the size of a small house. She remained seated on the red plastic benches long after she could eat no more, staring at her cell phone and watching people milling about still buzzing with the holiday spirit. She spotted a man seated a few tables away from her. He was having a spirited conversation on the phone. Something about the way he spoke, his gestures and demeanour were familiar. Whatever he was hearing was obviously shocking because every so often the words 'Oh my God' would escape from his lips as he cupped the back of his head in his palm and shook his head.

Kavata watched the familiar stranger for a while before she decided to get closer to him. Her instinct was right. His dialogue was peppered with expressions from home. She hovered around his table, but he was so engrossed in his conversation that he didn't realise she was there until she tapped him on the shoulder.

'I'm off duty,' he said, his handset still connected to his ear.

Kavata only now noticed his security guard uniform. She took a napkin off a nearby table and tapped him on the shoulder again.

'I am off duty, Ma'am. Please go to the information desk for help,' he snapped and pointed into the distance.

Kavata shot him an apologetic look, at the same time wondering how he was able to switch on his American accent so swiftly. There was no trace of the accent when she'd been eavesdropping. She gestured to him that she needed to use his pen and he dislodged the ball-point from his shirt pocket and handed it to her.

'No, there's just some *mathe* here asking for a pen. *Endelea*,' he said as Kavata turned away to scribble on the napkin.

'Sorry, I just want to find out what's happening in Kenya. Will wait.' Kavata held the napkin up for him to read and waited for him to object to her pulling out a chair to join him.

He continued his conversation and she was happy to listen in, piecing together as much information as she could. It was a long phone call, and she was beginning to feel self-conscious, sitting there idly checking her phone, hoping someone would call her back. She looked back for her abandoned meal but it was gone. She asked him if he would like a drink and he scribbled 'diet Coke' onto the napkin. She walked to the counter, worried that he would run away, but he was still there when she got back and was thankfully winding up the call. He promised to send his caller some money and hung up.

'Thanks,' he took a long swig from his drink.

'I'm sorry to interrupt you. I have just been struggling to get any news from home, and it sounds like you might know more than I do.' Kavata only then realised how rude she must have seemed, but she was desperate.

'I'm Lawrence, by the way.' He reached over to greet her.

'Kavata. So what's going on back home?'

'It's shocking. Things have gone to the dogs. How much do you know?' His accent was back.

'Almost nothing. I was following the results, and then I read about a swearing in, and then something about a coup.'

Lawrence nodded. 'That's the long and short. My family lives in Nakuru. I was just talking to my brother. They have been begging me to send them airfare to come here for the past few weeks now. They somehow managed to organise the visas and everything. I don't even know how they pulled that off. I've been telling them to stay calm and hope for the best. Things over there have been tense for a while; rumours about things getting ugly if the wrong guy wins have been flying all over the place. And they have—things are thick.' Lawrence took another long swig from his drink and continued. 'Literally minutes after the winner was announced, thugs went to my home and told my family that they had a ten minute head start to flee. My mother thought they were just being dramatic and acting out. Then a family friend phoned her, from their house less than a kilometre up the road from us. They said the same group of men were at their house and they hadn't listened. When they came back, as promised, and found them in the house, they chopped up the father—to set an example.' Lawrence paused as the enormity of the words he'd just spoken coursed through him. When it passed, he was disoriented and looked around for a while before resting his gaze on Kavata. She reached across the table to steady his trembling hand. Tears returned to her eyes.

'This is unbelievable. How can this be happening in Kenya?'

Lawrence carried on speaking as if he hadn't heard her.

'Then, they carried pieces of his body around town,

shouting warnings that those who didn't leave would end up the same way. My mother's friend begged my family to leave.'

'Did they leave? Are they okay?' Kavata glanced at her phone, desperate for it to give her a sign that her people back home were well.

'They did, they just got into the car and drove. They left everything behind. My brother only carried their passports and whatever cash was in the house. They could only get as far as Limuru. They are staying with relatives there. My dad is a retired policeman, he insisted on going back to save the woman who warned them to leave. He's been gone for two days now, but he's alive and he calls home often. He says our house is a skeleton. They took everything, even the curtain hooks. He's been called back into the force to help. He says he has never seen such brutal mercilessness in all his days. He's calling it some kind of demon possession.' Lawrence smiled gently at his father's simple logic.

The napkin that they used to communicate was soaked with Kavata's tears for Lawrence's family. She got more tissues, and the two of them sat and talked for hours.

Lawrence didn't have the heart to tell his family that he didn't have the money to get them all out of the country. He complained of the perception that money was abundant in America. Every few months, a new cost was shoved his way: a sibling's tuition, his father's health insurance, a niece's school trip to Rwanda, textbooks, shoes, birthday presents. Each time he said that he couldn't afford it, his mother simply said that he was in America now, and God would provide for him. As if those in Kenya were not provided for as well. Eventually, even if he didn't have health insurance of his own, and hadn't been on holiday once since he moved to America, he stopped complaining, and picked up an extra shift at one of his three jobs every time the phone rang and the Kenya country code was displayed on the screen. He had recently paid for his family to holiday in Malindi. The cost of the trip broke his back and he just could not afford to send anything.

'It will be alright, the government will do something.' Kavata immediately felt stupid—she knew better.

Lawrence's response was visceral.

'The government? Ha! Who do you think is behind all of this? Who do you think is paying those guys to kill? This has very little to do with who did or didn't win. These kids are killing because someone is paying them more money than they have ever seen, to weed out all the *kiuks* in their villages and towns and slums. And it's just a matter of time before they start to fight back, and killing is not something that *Kikuyus* are unaccustomed to doing. They've been at it since Mau Mau. Did you know most if not all communities in Kenya have, at some point in history, fought with *kiuks*?'

Kavata shook her head and Lawrence carried on.

'The thing is, those guys, the ones that came to our home, I know them. I know their names, I went to school with them, we cheated off each other during exams and played football together. I fooled around with their sisters, and stole their parents' cars when they were away. Until a few weeks ago, they treated my siblings like their own. Do you actually want me to believe that they would carry my father's head on the end of a *panga* because of an election? That's bullshit!' His voice grew louder as he spoke, and the food court manager walked over to them to tell them that they were making the other customers uncomfortable, even if the only other person at the restaurant was sitting at the corner furthest away from them.

'So, what do we do? Do we just sit and wait?' Kavata asked when they were alone again. The things she was hearing still felt too brutal to be happening in Kenya. They sounded like exaggerated tales from a place that was vaguely familiar. But she saw the tweets, and heard the news, and could feel the pain of the man that sat before her.

'I guess so. Unless you have the money to get your family out of the country, there's nothing to do but wait.' Kavata thought about the envelope of money that was sitting at the bottom of her handbag. She asked a few more questions about Lawrence's family: if they had family or friends anywhere else outside of Kenya, and if they could go there instead. He answered her questions with his mind elsewhere, searching for other solutions.

It was his turn to ask questions when he realised that he knew nothing about Kavata. She gave him fragments of the truth, slipping in slices of the story that she and Anne scripted for her new life. Lawrence seemed unimpressed with her, and she was relieved.

They chatted on long enough for Kavata to get hungry again and for Lawrence to forget his problems. He shifted languages to Kiswahili often, grateful to have someone that he could share language with at a time when he was desperate to connect with home. Kavata indulged him. He was a charming man, much younger than Kavata but with an old soul. They realised that the short winter day was ending when the Wendy's staff began to pile chairs onto the tables and a voice on the intercom announced that the mall was closing in half an hour.

When Lawrence offered to drive Kavata the short distance to Mutheu's house, she made the decision that if it came to it, she would give him the money he needed to get his family to safety. She didn't tell him so just yet, partly because she hoped he wouldn't need it. She insisted that they exchange numbers, and she made him promise that he would keep her posted on how his family was doing.

There were messages on the answering machine when she got back home.

'I met this man at the mall. He was telling me what's going on at home,' Kavata offered before Mutheu could ask.

'It's all over the news. It is hell over there,' Zack said, and Kavata realised that she was on speaker phone. She turned on the television. 'Mo spoke to her family earlier in the day, they are safe. There has been a media blackout for a few hours, so no one's really sure how bad things are on the ground,' he added.

Kavata thought it was sweet that Zack was so concerned. She was happy that her cousin had found such a kind man.

'It's apparently only bad in the slum and rural areas, but you can trust the Western media to make it look like we are all savages. That's CNN for you,' Mutheu added, and Kavata ached for word from home.

'Have you heard from Ngu—from anyone back home?' Mutheu asked.

'No. I am getting worried now,' Kavata said, more to herself than to anyone else. The images on the screen matched the ones that Lawrence described. The places she saw were familiar, and she began to think about the people she knew who lived and worked in the buildings that now lay torched and naked.

*'Wanja, it's Mom. Please pick up.'*

Kavata sent different versions of the same text message to everyone. Then she settled back down in front of her computer screen. Each time the death toll went up a little higher, she prayed a little harder.

# 12
# ANYTHING BUT WAR

## 30 DECEMBER 2007

Kavata nearly burst into song when her cell phone beeped. It was Anne.

'My God, Anne, where have you been? Are you ok?'

'You've heard the news?' She sounded like she had gone without sleep for several days. 'I'm sure it will blow over in a few days but, Kavi, it is a mess. It got so bad so quickly, it's like everyone instantly developed an explosive temper. So many students have gotten caught up in the chaos and been locked up. So many have died. '

'Have you spoken to Ngugi or my kids?'

'Not yet. I can try them now. I just got home from the supermarket; I've been there for six hours trying to shop. Everyone is panicking and stocking up in case this madness lasts longer. Now we are hearing there might be a fuel shortage.'

'Please go check on my family, Anne. I can't reach them. I don't know where they are.' Kavata was crying.

'Be calm, Kavi, they are probably just dealing with the shock of everything. The violence hasn't spread to our side of town. I will go there as soon as I hang up, and call you back.'

Anne hesitated, wondering if it would do Kavata any good to hear the next piece of news. 'Thuo was arrested after you left.' It wasn't what she'd intended to share, but it was a start.

'Oh, no. No.' Kavata remembered his brief protest at her trip to the airport. 'Why would they do that, didn't he tell them where I was?'

'I don't have all the details. I called the police station that he was being held at, but they didn't have him so I assume he's been released.'

'Please call him as well to check. That's horrible.' Kavata gave Thuo's number to Anne.

'And Kavi...'

'Yes?'

'He lost the election. Ngugi didn't win.' Anne was just as surprised at the result.

'I know. It's funny how we didn't see this coming.' She told Anne about her cousin's suggestion that she should have waited until the results were out to leave him.

'Kavi, that's not all.' Anne's tone turned grave, and Kavata stopped breathing.

'What is it, Anne?' Lawrence popped into Kavata's mind, and she wondered if he would agree to drive her to the airport.

'Nothing has been confirmed yet, but there are rumours that the house that Ngugi and your parents were staying at was raided last night. Your parents weren't there, they had already left for Nairobi, but Ngugi insisted on staying until the announcement.' Anne spoke fast, as if she was breathing the words out of her system.

The violence was no longer a distant thing. It was knocking at her door, demanding to be let in to Kavata's life. She lowered herself onto her bed.

'Kavi, are you there?'

'How bad was it?' Her voice was barely audible. She repeated the question a few times for Anne to hear her over the delayed connection.

'The house is torched. Completely. That's all I know.'

'Is he… ok?' Kavata asked.

'We don't know.' A colleague from their school was in Machakos and phoned Anne to inform her when he couldn't get a hold of Kavata. 'It makes no sense, Kavi. There's been no other violence in Machakos yet. It looks like a random break-in that went sour. We have to believe that he is well…' Anne realised that she was rambling on to fill the loaded silence.

'Kavi, are you there?'

'Yes. Please find my children and let me know when you do. I'm coming back.'

\*\*\*

The images they were seeing on screen from the election centre were nothing as chaotic as what was erupting outside. Armed policemen shooting at protesters a few metres away from them invaded the TV screens. The newly elected president would be sworn in during an emergency ceremony to ensure that the army didn't take over as speculated. They all stared at the screens in disbelief, sounds from the battle-field outside reaching them a few seconds before they were transmitted to their screens as the war outside drew closer and closer.

Masese and Tom walked around the office, methodically closing windows, turning off lights and locking doors with the calmness of people trained for this eventuality. Tom walked over to his desk and retrieved what Wanja assumed was the last of the office's petty cash and stuffed it into the back of his trousers.

The screens showed ODM supporters making their way to the headquarters, to them, in a show of solidarity, and to personally deliver a message to their candidate that they would stand behind him until the presidency was rightfully restored to him. The police tried to get ahead of them, launching tear gas and rubber bullets to keep them away from the residential area they were approaching.

'Move your cars to the back now! That way they'll think no one is here,' Tom shouted as he jumped down from the desk he was stepping on so he could look through the only open window in the office. He ran out and those with cars followed him to the front parking lot, where they could hear the violence as clearly as they could smell it. Screams, sirens and gunshots pierced through the anxious neighbourhood. The brief milliseconds of silence in between gunshots were over-laden with hope that the last gunshot heard would be the final one. They kept coming, one after the other, random and regular like a clock losing time.

Tom navigated all the cars through the narrow passage that led to the balcony and they parked them in tightly. Wanja sat in her car, trying to decide if she should leave before the protesters made it to the headquarters. As if reading her mind, Tom hit the roof of her car, 'Move Wanja, we need to get back inside!' and she eased the car into the last of the spaces in the tiny yard. She and Tom then rushed back into the building where they all waited.

The commentary from the different news stations became bothersome as they remained silently huddled in the dark office, listening to the chanting and shouting that seemed to grow louder and more insistent with each shot fired.

The protesters held fort outside the gates. Whenever the shouting subsided, they would break into song. They sang dirges Wanja didn't recognise, but a few of the people in the room who did hummed along. In these moments of song, loss hung in the room as heavy as it had when the results were first announced and she got the sense, in spite of the metal gates and stone walls, that a subtle connection was made between the protesters and Wanja's hurting colleagues. And then, as suddenly as it stopped, the shooting and rioting, tear gas and shouting, started all over again.

Once the protesters were convinced that there was no sign of any ODM candidates in the building, they moved on, leaving their sadness behind. The headquarters remained frozen in silence, everyone unwilling to be the one to break the silence too soon.

Masese rose to un-mute the television and sat back down on a crate of untouched beers. Those sitting close to the other screens followed suit, and soon they were watching different sections of the country going up in flames.

An image of a road close to Wairimu's house stirred Wanja to her feet and in search of her phone. There were several calls from numbers that she didn't recognise. She grabbed her bag from under her desk and looked towards Tom, whose gaze was already fixed on her.

'You should probably wait it out,' he called behind her after she waved in his general direction.

'It could get worse. I need to be at home. I'll use *panya* routes,' Wanja called behind her.

Tom followed her out to the car and handed her the last of her payment. It was an absurd gesture at the time, but his message was loud and clear. It was, after all, just a job.

'Let her go. She'll probably be safer in her mansion,' Simon said to the last of her workmates who still insisted that she wait a few hours before leaving. One or two people took advantage of her departure to gather their things and leave. The workers from the neighbouring houses sprinted toward their homes when Masese peeked out of the gates before opening them fully. He flagged Wanja down before she drove out and instructed her on the routes to use and which ones to avoid, despite the fact that he didn't know which way she was headed.

It took at least an hour for her to navigate her way out of the maze created by roads rendered impassable by debris and police roadblocks. The policemen seemed clueless, unable to respond to the myriad of questions that frantic travellers posed every time they were redirected to yet another dead end. Each alternative route took Wanja farther and farther away from the highway that she needed to be on in order to get home. The radio stations were no help, with their warnings for people to stay home peppered with calm broadcasts from the inauguration ceremony at State House. It was getting dark and she was getting desperate. She decided to take the longest route possible home, past State House, assuming that it would be secure. This would mean driving parallel to Ngong Road, the busy street near Kibera where the violence erupted first.

*Things would have moved on by now*, she said to herself as she drove past burning tyres on the side of the road. The unknown number lit up her phone screen and for a moment, she imagined that it would be some miraculous guide. She was considering pulling over to pick up the call when her headlights fell on a group of protesters running towards her, chanting, shouting, breaking into cars parked on the side of the road with *pangas* and *rungus*. Her right hand reached for the door handle so that she could flee on foot. But it was not quicker than her left hand, which swung the car into reverse gear as her foot instinctively floored the gas pedal, reversing the car on to the very Ngong Road that she was warned to avoid. She looked ahead as she turned onto the road and sped down hoping for the best.

The amount of damage that was done in what felt like a few minutes, was unbelievable. Cars lay deserted with plumes of dark smoke leisurely rising to meet the already thick air. Shops sat exposed, with their display windows shattered and mannequins stripped. Wanja averted her eyes from the lumps on the road that looked like dead bodies, telling herself that they were sacks of vegetables that didn't make it to market, and that the liquid oozing from them wasn't blood.

This was not her Nairobi.

Near the city morgue, the police opened up the roadblocks to one-way traffic into the city and were quickly ushering motorists through. On the other lane, police and army trucks brimming with troops sped past to different areas of the city. She caught the panicked looks on the faces of the policemen as they were sent to meet their unknown fates and assured herself that was what bravery looked like.

She wondered if this was war but chased the thought out of her mind as soon as it was formed. This wasn't war. It was just violence. Violent unrest which appeared a little more war like, because her irrational hesitation to leave work when she should have placed her right in the middle of it.

'Go to your homes and stay there!' a policeman shouted as cars sped past the roadblock.

Her phone was still ringing. Her hand was still trembling when she reached for it so she placed it back on the steering wheel.

All the roads that led on to the highway were heavily policed so she began to calm down as she approached the suburbs closer to home, ignoring her relentless phone. She turned towards the Museum Hill roundabout and just as she joined Limuru Road, she heard the news seconds before she saw it.

'Avoid Limuru Road, Ngara and Parklands areas.'

Students from the University of Nairobi's law campus had joined in the violence. Cars behind her screeched to a halt and made rushed U-turns. She rolled up her windows but her eyes already began to sting from wisps of tear gas that negotiated their way into the car. She drove back towards the highway, this time turning towards Westlands, leaving the sounds of gunshots behind her and using only her instinct as a guide.

The roads on this side of town were as deserted as they were on Election Day. It was as if those who lived here had some prior warning to pack up their lives and stay indoors. The sky seemed a little brighter as the sun retreated happily into the horizon, proud to have done its job well. She rolled down the car window and welcomed the refreshing sensation the cool air brought to her eyes.

Past the Westgate mall, a few hawkers still sat, huddled around portable radios. When a car drove past they would rush to show their wares; overpriced puppies, pet rabbits, lampshades and flowers in bloom, to the potential buyers before they huddled back around the news.

Wanja had seen the hawkers countless times. On a good day, she would roll down her window and share a brief chat with them as they tried to pass the stray dogs off as purebreds. Other times she simply kept her eyes on the road and acted like they were invisible. Today, they seemed alien. It was as if they were performing a strange trade dance that didn't belong in the place her Nairobi was becoming.

The security lights flickered on with the last of the sun's rays, and the serenity of the suburbs caused her to slow down. It seemed impossible that just moments ago, she witnessed such severe carnage. She considered driving back towards the city just to confirm her hangover wasn't playing mind games with her. The voice on the radio was saying her country was at war, but this couldn't be what war looked like.

She reached into her bag for a tissue to dry her tear-gassed eyes and her fingers encountered the money scattered all over her bag. She was overcome with the urge to spend it all immediately. She made a sudden turn into the Indian-ran mini-mart that her mother shopped at since she was a little girl. The old man who greeted customers and handed out shopping baskets as they walked in was missing.

'We sent him home early because of all the *sabasaba* in town,' the shopkeeper explained, sensing Wanja's hesitation to enter the store without the usual welcome.

'Shop fast and go home. That's what they are saying,' the shopkeeper's wife pointed to the small TV set at the back of the shop, broadcasting images from a place that seemed too far away. She filled her basket with useless snacks and things that she knew Amani would enjoy when he eventually came back home.

She walked out of the brightly lit store, to the now all too familiar sound of shouting and chanting, and for a fractured second, she was relieved to not be surrounded by the sterile silence of the mini-mart.

'Don't worry, you can go home. They've been celebrating since the results were announced,' the intuitive shopkeeper said. Taking up the entire road was a mass of people as large as what Wanja imagined the ODM supporters outside the headquarters was. They were violating the eerie suburban silence with their joyous singing and gyrating. Tree branches and palm leaves danced in midair. Children hoisted on men's shoulders giggled and clapped their hands in excitement. Paths were created for oncoming traffic, and some motorists were even moved to the point of pulling over and joining in the festivities.

Transfixed, Wanja watched, waiting for the crowd to pass so that she could travel the few metres to her house. The shopkeeper's wife emerged from her shop and danced next to her. Her husband, who took over her position at the till, gave her a gentle smile. Twenty minutes later, the crowd was still snaking back and Wanja was weary of the ludicrousness of it all. She got back into the car and drove right through the crowd, feigning joy and happiness as she went through, unsure of what might happen if the crowd sensed any hesitation.

The crowd insisted that she roll down her window so they could really celebrate together, and Wanja obliged as soon as her bag full of money was tucked under her seat. Children who spotted her shopping bags as she inched through the crowd, asked her to share her groceries. At long last, with nearly empty shopping bags, she turned onto the road that would lead her home.

\*\*\*

'I'm going back,' Kavata said to Mutheu and Zack when they

got back in from Florida.

'Things look pretty uninviting over there. What good would it do for you to go back?' Zack shifted to face her and she noticed for the first time how handsome he was.

'None, probably. But at least I'll be there with my family.'

'Don't you want to give it a few days? Someone reported that the airports have been shut down,' Mutheu said, aware that there was no changing Kavata's mind. She would have done the same thing.

Kavata's rationale for needing to be back home wasn't completely clear to her until this moment. If things at home were as bad as everyone said they were, then Kenya would never be the same. She had to see it to believe it. She wanted to be there, with her family the moment their country changed.

'I doubt that it's as bad as we're being made to imagine it is, but if it is, then I need to be there.'

'I don't think all these guys are making this stuff up,' Zack said.

'Do you need anything? Do you have money?' Mutheu asked.

Kavata smiled and thanked them for their kindness. She was glad she waited for them to come back before she left, even if the waiting drove her mad.

At the Hartsfield-Jackson Airport, the man at the counter took an unusually long time to book Kavata's flight to Kenya. He was young and nervous and looked like this was his first day on the job. He kept apologising for the delay as Kavata stood by patiently and those behind her grumbled.

'I'm sorry ma'am, the system won't let me book your

flight. Would you like to fly to another destination?'

Kavata gave him a tight-lipped smile and shook her head. 'Maybe you should call someone to help you? These computers can be such a nuisance sometimes.' The man was relieved at her suggestion and pushed a button on the side of the desk that summoned a supervisor, who arrived promptly. The young man walked his supervisor through everything he'd done up to the point where he was unable to complete the booking.

'Curtis, what error number shows up on the screen?' The supervisor spoke to him as if he were a slow child and shot Kavata an apologetic look.

'Error number 4016,' Curtis responded.

'And what does that error mean?'

Curtis searched his memory for the answer, and when he couldn't find one he looked desperately at his supervisor as the complaints from the travellers behind Kavata grew louder.

'Well, check the handbook then. These folks have flights to catch,' suggested the supervisor.

Kavata was sure the supervisor didn't know either. Curtis flipped through a small thick book and his face lit up as soon as he found the answer. His supervisor walked over to the next counter and opened it up so she could serve the disgruntled people behind Kavata.

'I'm sorry miss, we are unable to book the final leg of your journey due to...' Curtis referred to the handbook again. '...temporary closure of airport at destination for security reasons.' He beamed with pride, as if he deserved a medal.

Kavata insisted that he try again, and Curtis obliged but got the same result.

'Can you tell how long the airport will be closed?' Kavata

asked, aware that she was asking too much from this sweet, clueless man. 'Can't I land in another airport? Try Wilson Airport. Or the other one, the Mombasa Airport. I really need to get to Kenya.' Kavata felt like she would jump over the counter and do it herself.

'I'm sorry ma'am; I do not have any information yet. What you could do is book a flight to Amsterdam. Things might have changed by the time you get there, and with your valid US visa you wouldn't need a transit visa. It's the best we can do, ma'am. ' Kavata agreed and reached into her bag to pay for the flight. As she did so, she realised that she forgot to tell Lawrence that she was leaving.

She phoned him as she waited to board the flight. He was shocked at the sudden decision and once she explained her reasons, he wished he too could go home. Kavata offered him the money he needed, and at first he didn't believe her, insisting that it was more money than anyone should loan to a person that they just met. Kavata insisted, saying that she would get in touch with Lawrence's brother as soon as she was back in Nairobi. She gave him the phone number and address to her house in case things got worse in Limuru and his family needed a place to stay and swore to be in touch as soon as she got home. Lawrence still seemed unconvinced by the time their call ended, but Kavata didn't blame him. Nothing about her actions over the past few days was logical.

She phoned Ngugi and Wanja, her entire being aching for one of them to answer. When they didn't, worry and anger began to wash over her again. Anne had not been in touch since they spoke the night before, so she found comfort in the fact that she would be home soon and everything would explain itself. Moments before she boarded the flight, Wairimu popped into her mind and she immediately scrolled through her contacts searching for her sister-in-law's number, scolding herself for not thinking of this sooner. It would not be unusual for Amani to be at her house if Ngugi was away.

Wairimu picked up on the second ring. Kavata had never been happier to speak to her, and she promised herself that once all of this was over, she would make an effort to build a relationship. Wairimu seemed calm, too calm, and Kavata began to doubt that she called the right person.

'Kavata?' She didn't conceal her shock at receiving the call. Kavata explained that she had been trying to reach everyone at home for the past two days.

'Where are you?' Wairimu asked. Her calmness was unsettling to Kavata.

'I am at the airport on the way back.' Kavata watched the boarding line grow shorter and shorter.

'Which airport?'

'Wairimu, I can't speak for long. I just need to find out if everyone is ok. Things on the news look horrible and I can't reach anyone from home. Have you heard from Ngugi? Is he safe? Do you know where my kids are?'

Wairimu reported that she talked to Wanja as well as Ngugi the previous day. He had a few things to wrap up before he went back to Nairobi. Kavata understood why she was being so calm. When Wairimu asked her if she would like to speak to Amani, Kavata glanced at the rapidly moving boarding queue and said yes.

Amani was overjoyed that she was coming back and asked if she brought him lots of gifts from America. He asked why she lied to him that she was going to the supermarket; didn't she know that people who lied went to hell? Her son's voice gifted her with a beautiful, unexpected peace. When all she saw and heard from home was unrecognisable chaos, Amani assured her that some pieces of home remained untainted by the anarchy.

When Wairimu got back on the line, Kavata shared the news that she received from Anne. As she suspected, Wairimu didn't know anything and was immediately plunged into worry.

'That can't be right. We spoke yesterday—a few hours ago! Who told you?'

'My friend Anne. A mutual friend from Machaa called her this morning. The attack happened last night.'

'Oh my God, Kavi. I have to call him. We have to go back!'

Everyone other than Kavata was on board and the stewards were looking at her curiously. She walked towards the boarding gate, as she tried to calm Wairimu down. 'No, please don't go back. They think he escaped, so he is probably on the way back to Nairobi. '

'Anything else?' Wairimu asked.

'No, that's all I know. I will call Anne again during my layover. In the meantime, please go to my house and stay there? I'm told things on that end of town are still calm.'

'Of course they are. We'll keep an eye out and leave when the roads are safe.'

Kavata wanted to speak to Amani again. She thought about how normal he sounded moments ago. She was sure that Wairimu was doing everything she could to distract him. 'Thanks for everything, Wairimu,' Kavata said as they hung up.

\*\*\*

At 3 AM, a media blackout began. Images of killing, burning

and looting were wiped off the screen and replaced with music videos, reruns of Spanish soap operas and Cartoon Network. Ngugi's eyes hurt from gazing into the white light so he finally turned off the television and lay on the couch to get a few hours sleep.

The media blackout saved his life because if the TV was on, he never would have heard the hushed voices on the other side of his wall. Nor would he have seen the amber glow of torches hovering outside the window. His hand reached out for his phone, plugged into the charger next to the television. He checked that his car keys were in his pocket and tip-toed into the kitchen moments before the living room window was smashed and thugs climbed into the house, declaring that they had come for their money.

Ngugi thought he recognised one of the voices but his fear made him uncertain. The man with the familiar voice led the rest up the stairs to where they imagined Ngugi was sleeping, and did so with the surety of someone who had been in the house before. Ngugi slipped out of the back door in the kitchen just as the men were breaking down the door to Hon. Muli's bedroom upstairs.

Ngugi ran into the darkness as fast as his unfit limbs could carry him. Save for the shouting and banging that was coming from the house, the rest of Machakos was still, bracing itself for the worst. He could hear the crash of glass breaking as he started the engine and drove off. By the time the thugs realised that Ngugi was not in the house, he was turning on to the main highway that led to Nairobi. The smaller Machakos grew in his rear-view mirror, the unsteadier his arms became, and soon Ngugi was trembling so hard that he could no longer drive. He pulled over to the side of the road just outside Athi River, jumped out of the car, and bent over to vomit, releasing the tension and fear that was threatening to choke him. When he was done, he sat on a rock at the side of the road and wept for all of his losses.

At sunrise, the sound of cars zooming past woke Ngugi up with a start. It took him a little while to figure out where he was, but within seconds memories of his close shave with death flooded his mind as he lay in the reclined car seat. He didn't recall getting back into the car or falling asleep, but he was glad he had. As the morning sun rolled over the now distant hills in Machakos, he felt refreshed, brave and invincible. He considered going back to face the cowards who attacked him, just so they knew he wasn't intimidated by them. Then he remembered what was happening around the country and took in his surroundings once more. Slower this time, so that he could really let it sink in. It dawned on him that he was completely alone. He couldn't remember the last time he had experienced such daunting solitude—or if he had ever experienced it at all. He thought about all the people who should have been sat beside him now, and his thoughts began and ended with Kavata. She'd always been there: when his friends fell away, when Wairimu slid into the background, when Wanja grew up—Kavata remained. And suddenly he began to wonder how he'd even made sense of the past two years without her.

He needed to get home. His cellphone was hot as if it had been in continuous use. The screen displayed forty two missed calls, more than half of which were from an undisclosed number. He went through the call log, Wairimu, Wanja and Hon. Muli tried to reach him as well as some colleagues who, he was sure, were calling about the election. He had several text messages as well, but before he could get to them, the phone beeped three times and the screen went blank. In his mind's eye, he could see his charger plugged into the wall at the house in Machakos.

He caught his reflection in the rearview mirror. The last few days had aged him. He stepped out of the car and bathed in the cool air and light warmth. He stretched and took several deep breaths, then changed out of his vomit-stained shirt. He was only an hour or so away from Nairobi and there were better chances of an uneventful trip back home if he continued his journey before those who fought the previous night woke up to continue.

He hadn't been driving very long when he got to a makeshift road block just outisde Mlolongo. Cars were parked on the side of the road, some of them torched and some stripped completely with parts of them being used to feed a hungry fire that burned through the night. On the left side of the road, a massive truck was derailed and used to block the weighbridge which would have been the only other way past the roadblock. There was no other way to get in to Nairobi. This must have been why the men picked this spot.

Some cars were being let through the road block, but only after rigorous interrogation. He considered waiting on the side of the road until the men eventually tired and left, but they had already seen Ngugi and they were beckoning him, waving sticks and *rungus* in the air as if they were welcoming him into their home to meet his fate. Ngugi decided to take his chances.

He was comforted that they didn't seem to have any real weapons. One of the road signs from the weighbridge that formerly read NO TRUCKS BEYOND THIS POINT was plucked off its pole and altered to read NO LUOS BEYOND THIS POINT.

Ngugi felt relief, then instant guilt. He rolled down his window as he approached the road block and tried to remain calm as the young men surrounded his car.

'Is there a problem?' Ngugi channelled his thickest Kikuyu accent.

The tension around the car dissolved almost instantly, although everyone stayed in place.

'No, not at all. We have no problems with people like you,' one of the men said in Kikuyu. 'You look like one of us, but you know some people are like chameleons so can we see your ID?' Ngugi reached into his wallet and pulled out his ID, catching a glimpse of his voter's card as he did so.

'Ngugi Mwangi, yes. No problem,' the man paused and recognition spread across his face. 'Aah, *Mheshimiwa*, it is you. You know we are not used to seeing big men driving themselves. Or have they already taken away your cars?' One of the other men said something from behind the car, sparking a brief conversation around him. Ngugi could only hear bits of the conversation through the closed windows. They were talking about the previous night's incident at Hon. Muli's house.

'*Mheshimiwa*, I hear you should be a dead man by now. *Pole sana, hawa Wakamba*, they are our friends but sometimes they don't always use their heads. You see, they are not like us; us, we are peaceful people. We cannot harm our own people. We are only angry because last night *Ajaluo* started calling us thieves and went around killing our people. *Ati* because they lost the election. Who told them they could ever win! Have they even won half an election before?' A heated debate broke out amongst the men. It seemed like they might have forgotten that Ngugi was still sitting here and he momentarily considered sneaking away.

The man tapped on the window, telling Ngugi to roll it all the way down. 'So now, we have taken it upon ourselves to guard Nairobi so that no more of them come here. They should go back to the lake and stay there.' He pointed towards the 'No Luos' sign as he spoke and leaned further and further into the car so that his face was now only a few inches away from Ngugi's. His breath was ripe with the sweet nauseating smell of *chang'aa*.

Another car approached the road block and the men's attention was diverted as they went after their new victim. The man who was speaking to Ngugi steered him towards a concealed opening at the weighbridge. He walked next to the car all the while, carrying on with his explanations about why he and his gang were better that the men who raided Hon. Muli's home.

'Now you have to pay some toll fees,' the man demanded when Ngugi was safely through the roadblock. 'This work we are doing is not easy.'

Ngugi handed him two hundred shillings. 'This is all I have, those hooligans took everything else,' Ngugi said, snapping his wallet shut before the man could see its contents.

From his rearview mirror, Ngugi could see the passengers in the car behind him being dragged out of their car. There were three men and a woman who, judging from their beachwear, had just come from Mombasa. The driver was arguing with one of the men, who hit him in the face. The driver fell to the ground. Ngugi hit the brakes, his car screeched to a noisy halt and some of the men turned back. Two men ran towards Ngugi, shouting at him to keep driving or else they would finish what the men in Machakos started. He drove away with the men ransacking the car then setting it ablaze. It happened quickly and methodically, as if they had performed the same routine several times before. He escaped with his life twice, and it dawned on him that his return home would not be as straightforward as he imagined it would be.

He had better luck with the ATMs in Mlolongo. It seemed that news of the violence had not affected the sleepy transit town in the way that it had Machakos. A few bars were still open with drunken residents staggering out of them, hissing in the mild morning sunlight like vampires. Mlolongo was celebrating a win, seemingly oblivious to what was going on a few kilometres on either side of the highway that cut through the town.

Ngugi stopped at the only petrol station that showed any sign of life. The woman at the pump was sleepy and uninterested in Ngugi's enquiries about news from Nairobi.

'*Watu wanauwawa*,' was all she said, as if widespread massacres were the most usual thing to talk about. When Ngugi realised that he would get no more from her, he asked if there was a television or radio somewhere he could use for a few minutes. She pointed to the poorly stocked convenience shop, 'Remove this car from here if you are not buying petrol.' She continued to nap while perched on an empty soda crate. The shop she directed him to was closed, despite the OPEN 24HRS sign that hung proudly on the door. He looked around the station for more signs of life and when he could find none, he walked over to the resting pump attendant and asked what time the shop would open. She didn't respond. Instead, with her eyes half shut, she pulled out her phone and dialled a number then put the cellphone back in her pocket. Seconds later, the door to the shop swung open and another man, looking just as disgruntled, walked back into the shop.

Ngugi walked around the scantily-stocked shop, suddenly realising how hungry he was. In the corner by the door, there was a charcoal *jiko* that was still simmering from whatever it roasted the night before. The metal grill dripped oil on the dying coals which sent a wonderful, fatty aroma into the store. Butcheries here served the best *mutura* in the country and Ngugi would have emptied his wallet for a six inch piece of the delicacy. As he looked around, he realised that his best bet at some nutrition would be the boiled eggs and *smokies* that were in the hotpot at the counter. When the shopkeeper offered him some *kachumbari* with his eggs, Ngugi declined, picked a few more things from the counter, and asked if the television behind him could be switched on.

The shopkeeper frowned at Ngugi's request. 'Does this look like a cinema?' He was obviously eager to get back to sleep.

'*Tafadhali* boss,' Ngugi pleaded. 'The radio in my car *haifanyi*, and I just want to make sure that things are calm in Nairobi before I continue with my journey.'

'*Kwani* what's happening in Nairobi?' the shopkeeper asked. Ngugi envied his ignorance.

'Turn on the TV, we find out—things were bad yesterday,' Ngugi said as the man flicked on the TV set, peeled an egg for himself and offered Ngugi a soda crate to sit on.

A female television anchor was interviewing the Commissioner of Police about the unrest. The man sat in studio in his elaborately decorated uniform. He was sweating so much in the studio lights you would think he was made of butter. He assured Kenyans that everything was under control and that policemen were dispatched to all parts of the country to maintain order. His words were contrasted by scenes from the streets and the violence of the previous night.

When the shopkeeper saw the extent of the violence, he opened the door and called out to his resting colleague, '*Haiya*, Carol come see. Nairobi is burning!'

Carol sprinted into the shop.

In some parts of the country, groups organised to retaliate and it looked like the bloodbath was far from over. The journalist asked him to explain the images, tilting her head to the side as if she was trying to flirt the truth out of him. Things looked far from under control, but the commissioner simply asked the media to be responsible in what they exposed the public to. She kept at it, asking him questions that he couldn't answer. His eyes darted around like a caged animal. Eventually he ripped the microphone off his lapel and said he had better things to do as the journalist shouted questions at his back and the camera followed him off the set.

The three of them sat for about half an hour, watching the news and eating boiled eggs. It was clear that no news channel had enough people on the ground yet to offer updates about the current situation—most of the images they were seeing were from the previous night.

He reached for his wallet.

'*Ni sawa*. The eggs are free. Merry Christmas. But you must pay for everything else,' the shopkeeper said, and wished him a safe journey as he walked out of the store. By the time he was back in his car, the door to the shop was also closed and his new friends were back asleep.

When he began to see stones and debris spewed on the side of the road as he approached the large airport interchange, he had to think fast. The roads were not as busy as they should have been at that time of the morning, but there was still a fair amount of traffic coming from the airport, going towards the city and to Mlolongo. Ngugi pulled over and stepped out of his car. The air smelled of burning tyres. He waved oncoming cars down and warned them about what lay ahead. He could see a long line of cars that couldn't get out of the airport because of the barricade that was erected on the road. Some of the cars looked abandoned, with ransacked suitcases sitting on the bonnets and beside the cars. Personal effects were strewn all over the place. Other drivers were also slowing down to a stop as they approached the road block, trying to figure out what to do.

Ngugi got back into his car and against his better judgement, drove towards the road block. The chants of 'NO ODM NO PEACE!' got clearer and louder as he approached the roaring vigilantes. Suddenly, he turned off the road, floored the gas and headed east before anyone had time to figure out what he was up to. Behind him, those standing by watching him jumped into their cars and followed suit. He drove over the uneven dirt terrain, raising crazy dust behind him as loose rocks hit the bottom of the car with loud knocking sounds. When the car got stuck in a shallow ditch, he reversed and manoeuvred his way out of it, making his way steadily towards the road. It was only when his choking car was safely on the tarmac that he turned back to see if the protesters were chasing them. They took no interest in his escape. Nor did they seem to care that several cars were following him. In fact, some of them looked amused that they had caused such fear. They were only there to seal off the airport but Ngugi wanted to be nowhere close to them if or when they changed their mind, so he floored the gas pedal and continued east towards Embakasi.

You didn't need to see the carnage to know that the people who lived in Embakasi were reeling from the events of a rough and unforgiving night. It was in the air, the smell of gasoline, the haze of smoke and the sound of shock as people emerged from their hiding places to assess the state of things. Embakasi was still. It was as if everyone was afraid to speak, or move, or breathe in case the violence, like a resting giant, might sense that there was still life there and come back.

Ngugi hadn't returned to Embakasi since his teenage years, when his father moved the family away from the city. He heard that the place had changed drastically, but this was not what he expected.

The Chinese were starting to lay the foundations for the famous highways that would finally make it easier for people to cut across the city without driving through its nucleus. This meant they had uprooted the existing roads. All of them. So, for months that turned into years, dust replaced the air in Embakasi as cars, *matatus* and pedestrians navigated the gullies the construction created. Frustrated tractors and mustard-coloured caterpillars squeezed their way through people's lives, trying to build them roads. This, coupled with the burning and looting and sporadic killing of the previous night, made Ngugi's old neighbourhood look like it had been through decades of war.

When he could proceed no further by car, he parked, got out of the car and walked in the direction of his childhood home. He walked past the caterpillars which were plastered with muddy footprints. It was clear that people tried to steal them, and when they couldn't, settled for siphoning the petrol out of the fuel tanks. Black hose pipes dripped remnants of fuel from the tanks onto the injured soil.

Ngugi walked around taking it all in, as if what he was

seeing would make sense to him if he stayed there a little longer. He walked past his old primary school. It stood untouched; there was nothing valuable to loot from a school. He continued towards Nyayo Estate, close to where he used to live. Things began to look more like he remembered. When he got to his old house, he hesitated for a while before he picked up a stone and hit against the metal bars of the gate a few times. There were signs of life inside the house, but no one came to the gate so he made his way back to his car.

There was a little more life when he got back to the spot where his car was parked. A small group of people were huddled outside a TV repair shop watching the news. The same anchor he watched a few hours ago was now reporting increasing death tolls in Kibera, Ngong, Umoja, Eastleigh, and Kasarani. Ngugi panicked. Kasarani was not far from where Wairimu lived, and those were all the places he needed to drive through to get home without driving through the city centre.

He spotted a few policemen guarding the Chinese contractors who came to assess the damage suffered to their equipment. He rushed towards them.

'*Habari zenu*, my name is Ngugi Mwangi.' He was tempted to add Honourable to his name, but then remembered that he'd lost the election. He waited for some kind of acknowledgement, but the policeman seemed tired and distracted. Ngugi explained his situation. That he was coming from Machakos trying to get north of the city. The policeman laughed.

'My friend, the only way to get across Nairobi right now is inside a body bag. You should have just stayed in Machakos, but now you can't go there because there is trouble at Athi River.' He wasn't saying anything Ngugi didn't already know, and he thought back to the police commissioner's statement that everything was under control.

'Is there no way to go across? I need to get to my family.' The policeman asked where Ngugi lived and snickered as soon as he responded.

'There's nothing to worry about, the suburbs are safe so your family must be ok. My advice to you is to stay here for a day or two. There are a lot of youth taking advantage of the situation so they can steal and loot. That is what happened here. They're coming from neighbouring areas to loot. Since they have already been here, they probably won't come back. So stay here. Then when they get tired you can take your chances. That's the best thing to do.'

Ngugi found a boarding house in Donholm and checked in for the day. The eager-to-please receptionist loaned him a battery charger and Ngugi spoke to Wairimu.

'My God! Ngugi, how dare you give us such a fright?' Wairimu sobbed when she heard his voice.

'I'm sorry, it wasn't my intention to have to flee Macha and spend the night in the car parked on the roadside.'

'When we heard that they burned the house down, we thought you were in it! Oh my God, Ngugi.' Wairimu whispered to someone that Ngugi was ok.

'Wait, what house?'

'Muli's. Kwani where are you?'

'They burned the house down? How do you know this?'

'Kavata called a few hours ago and told me. Apparently one of her colleagues was in Machakos and heard the news, then she called Anne. And Anne told Kavata. Kavata called me....'

Ngugi's mind was spinning. 'Kavata called you? From where? She's supposed to be in the States.'

'She is. Or rather she was. When she heard what happened she went straight to the airport. She's coming back.'

A smile spread across Ngugi's face before he realised it.

'She is sick with worry. She's been following *everything*.' Wairimu placed extra emphasis on that last word, and Ngugi understood that it meant that his wife heard of his loss. It didn't matter now.

'How are things over there?' Ngugi was reminded of his sister's fleeting safety, and that his son was there with her.

'Dicey. Kavata insisted that we go to your house, but it has been too risky to leave. It's better to travel in the night. Jommo is out getting petrol now so we can try tonight.'

'What route will you take?' Ngugi asked, and they talked about all the possible routes to Ngugi's, ruling out the ones that might be problematic.

'Where are you now?' Ngugi hadn't answered her the first time.

'In Donholm, at a random lodge. I've been through two roadblocks already. They were not interested in me. I bumped into a policeman who said it's best to stay here for a day or so. I will see what things are like later.'

Moments later, Ngugi was on the phone with Wanja who was just as relieved to hear from him. She was safe at home and confirmed that things were just as quiet as the policeman reported. In fact, they were borderline boring, she said.

'Your mother is coming home.'

'I heard, she sent me a text message.'

'Ok then, Aunt Wairimu will bring Amani home tomorrow. They might stay a few days until things calm down.'

'Ok.' Wanja was back to being aloof and Ngugi thought back to their last encounter. She was probably still angry at him, but it didn't matter. He was just happy to hear her voice.

\*\*\*

When Schola arrived in Kisumu four days ago and saw the large X painted on the stone wall of her one bedroom house from a distance, she approached it like it was a sleeping giant. This was not the first time she'd seen the ominous mark. When the new roads were coming a few years back, those who had built structures on road reserves found similar X's on their buildings and were given a year to demolish the structures. The second time she had seen the marks was during the constitutional referendum. Kisumu residents supported the new constitution, but there were a few people who had openly declared their allegiance to the old laws. These people were warned that if they voted for the old constitution, and it won, they would be forced to leave Kisumu, and their properties would be given to those who were more deserving. Their houses were marked with the X's to drive the point home. But, the new constitution won the referendum, and all threats were forgotten.

She had already heard that the famous X's were back in Kisumu, making appearances on the walls of Indian- and Kikuyu-owned businesses—but she was Luo and had worked and paid for all she owned. She convinced herself that it was a mistake but on her first night in Kisumu, when she'd grown weary of trying to fall asleep, she sprung out of bed and armed herself with bleach, soap and hot water and whatever else she could find in her house that would dissolve the oil based nuisance.

When the fighting started, Schola sat in her house, quietly listening through the thin walls to her neighbours' reactions to the news of their defeat. She didn't bother voting—elections never changed anything and from what she was seeing, this one was no different. She was angry and disappointed, but more than that she was afraid. Even if she erased the X on her door, there was no telling if those that drew it would remember that they had and she still didn't understand why. She sat silently in the dark, listening to each and every painful, frustrated scream that soared through the air. Kisumu was no small city, but somehow, sitting there in her dimly lit house with her eyes fixed on the door, she was certain that she could hear every emotion as it erupted.

When the gunshots and explosions started, the screaming became louder and she grew more nervous. Frozen with fear, she assured herself she would be safe, this was her home, she did nothing wrong and it was her right to be there.

In the morning, things quieted down as the violence swept past. She lay down on her bed, grateful to be able to rest her sore back and get some sleep.

She heard a loud bang just as she was fading away and dismissed it for more gunfire. But these gunshots were louder and more urgent than the previous ones. They were also much closer; it was almost as if they were right outside her door. Someone was banging furiously at her door.

Schola was not going to open the door and welcome her attackers into her home. If they wanted her out, they would have to carry her out themselves. She sat up in her bed, calmly waiting for them to break the door down, while hoping that they went away. The banging was relentless, and after a while she thought she heard a voice that she recognised. She got up off her bed and walked towards the door and the voice became clearer. It wasn't a gang of goons at her door, it was Helen, the young girl who had managed her shop for the last three years.

She collapsed into the house. Schola tried to catch her, but only managed to break Helen's fall. She was trembling so hard that Schola also shook when she tried to hold her. There was blood on her clothes, on her face—everywhere. She was crying, but there was no sound coming out of her lips.

'Helen? Helen? *Ni nini?*' What happened?' Schola screamed, searching the girl's body for the source of the blood, turning her over when she couldn't find any cuts on the front of her body. Helen just lay there, trembling and screaming those soundless screams. When she was sure that the blood wasn't coming from Helen's body, Schola tried to lift herself off the ground so that she could close and bolt the door, but Helen wouldn't let her. She clung to her with a vice-like grip.

'Shhh, shhh, *baas*, *baas*. You are safe, Helen. Let me just close the door,' Schola whispered. Some of her neighbours were already peeping into her house. Schola locked the door behind them, led Helen to the sofa, and knelt beside her.

'Are you hurt, Helen? What happened?'

'Mu-Mu—Mus.' Each time Helen tried to speak she would disintegrate.

'Musa? Did he hurt you?'

Helen wailed and shook her head frantically. It was a few minutes before Schola was able to calm her down. Then suddenly, she let go of Schola and was shoving her away.

'Mama, you must go. Go away. Run. They came looking for you in the shop. Go, run away now.' Helen spoke in between sobs, but she was barely audible.

'Wait, wait Helen. What happened? Musa *amefanya?*'

Helen shook her head as if she was re-arranging her memory so that she could speak.

Helen was at Schola's shop the previous night because they didn't have a TV at her parents' house and she wanted to watch the news. Musa, the building's watchman was there as well. When the shooting started, they were both afraid to go outside, so they locked the doors and decided to stay there until things subsided. At around midnight several men, about fifteen or twenty of them, broke into the shop. When Musa tried to stop them, they hit him on the head and then drove a *panga* through his stomach. Helen was hiding behind the counter, and she screamed when she saw him tumble to the ground. They dragged her out of her hiding place and put her on the ground next to the dying man. She didn't know what to do to save him. She wanted to cover the wound in his stomach to stop the bleeding, but she was afraid to touch the blood. The men laughed as they watched her fumbling and crying. Then they asked her where the shop owner was.

She lied that Schola was in Nairobi, and told them that she was a good Luo woman. They already knew this. They said that although she was Luo, she chose to work for a wealthy Kikuyu in Nairobi, so her business was funded by Kikuyu money. They were there to chase her away and claim the business. Helen sat still as the men looted the shop, stealing everything they could fit into their pockets and sacks and onto the *mkokoteni* that was parked outside. Life ebbed out of her friend who was still on the floor next to her, groaning and calling for his wife and children as he died.

'They killed Musa for nothing! They took everything.' Helen broke down once again.

This time, Schola didn't try to calm her down. She sat on the ground, looking at the blood that was now all over her hands.

Now she understood why her house was marked. The men said they would be back, they knew Schola was in Kisumu and they would be back to find her. If she had left the mark on her door, they would have done so already.

'Where is Musa? His body?' Schola asked.

Helen wailed at the mention of the man's name.

She had left him in the shop. She didn't know what else to do, so she had stayed there all night and came to find Schola as soon as the sun came up. The two women didn't move for hours. Helen stopped crying, but every time the slightest sound pierced through the silence she would begin to tremble again.

Schola heated some water and gave Helen a sponge bath where she sat, then put her in some clean clothes. Every few minutes, Helen would ask Schola why she was not getting ready to run away. Schola never responded; she didn't know what to say. Where would she go? This was her home. She thought about Thuo and Cheptoo. Maybe she could go to them in Nakuru but she didn't know if they were there, or in Nairobi, or if Thuo was still in jail. Panic and worry coursed through her, but for the sake of Helen, whose warning potentially saved her life, she remained calm.

That evening, Schola encouraged Helen to go home to her parents so she could then go take care of the man rotting in her shop. The violence moved on to a different part of Kisumu and after explaining what happened to a sympathetic neighbour, Schola was able to convince him to drive Helen home in his taxi. She walked the short distance to her shop and stopped dead in her tracks at the sight of it.

The wooden door hung open on its only remaining hinge and there was a trail of blood leading out of the door like a bleeding body was dragged out of the shop. She prayed that wasn't the case but when she stepped into the shop, Musa's body was nowhere to be found. She raced around the shop, searching behind boxes, around corners and under collapsed shelves, but there was no body. There was only the thick metallic smell of the pool of blood that was congealing on her Formica tiles. She let out a frustrated yell and leaned against the counter, trying to understand who would steal a dead body.

She nearly collapsed when the man who owned the shop next to her greeted her from the doorway. He heard everything from his house above the shops and called the police, but they never came. He sent word to Musa's wife that her husband was dead and the distraught woman came to the shop just minutes after Helen left. She insisted on taking her husband home and wouldn't accept anyone's help, but she couldn't lift him on her own, so she ended up dragging him out the door. Thankfully, Musa's brother arrived and helped her. He would be cremated by sunset.

Schola's neighbour looked around the shop and offered his sympathies before he walked into his untouched shop. Helen's continuous pleas for Schola to leave Kisumu came back into her mind. As she looked around the business she spent years building, she lost all desire to live in a place that so viscerally rejected her. She didn't know where she would go, but she was going to leave. She looked around the shop for things that she would take with her, but found nothing. She forced the broken door shut and locked it, and then she walked away.

When she got home, she packed a few things and went to speak to her neighbour. He was a Kisii man and, although his house wasn't marked, he was also afraid of being targeted.

He was making arrangements to go to Kisii that night. It was the longest possible route to Nairobi but it was her only option since buses were not running. He would drive her for a fee, and they agreed to leave at midnight. Schola locked up her house and climbed into her neighbour's old Toyota. She hoped that she would find her home as she left it, if she ever came back. And if she didn't, she prayed for the strength to build a new one elsewhere.

# 13
## AMANI
### 31 DECEMBER 2007

The violence subsided in most parts of the country as the year drew to a close that night. Murderers, thieves and protesters took some time off to rest, take stock of how much they had stolen, and cash in their body counts for payment from the politicians who had paid them to kill and to keep killing until the rightful president was declared. With wallets full of blood money, they went out on to the streets that they now claimed, to welcome a year that would be like no other. They tasted power and it was good, and things for them could never be the same. Those who suffered took advantage of the silence to dry their eyes and go out searching for bodies to bury, some envious that their departed ones found a strange and sudden peace. Those who could, fled to safety, and those unable to do so, could only hope the worst was over.

Jommo was stirred from his sleep by some noise downstairs. He shot out of bed and reached for the dagger he kept under the mattress. He crept downstairs and followed the sound of crashing buckets. He raised his arm to strike the figure in the darkness and stopped only seconds before he realised that the figure was a child. It was Amani. He flicked the light on and was just about to tear into the little boy when he noticed the tears on his face and the wet patch on his thighs.

'Amani, what's up? Did you have a little accident?'

Amani wailed with shame.

'Don't worry, even me I used to wet the bed. Everyone does it.' Jommo sat on the floor next to Amani and helped him climb out of his wet trousers. This only made him cry more. *'Aki*, it's true. Everyone wets the bed. Even your cousins.'

This worked. Amani's sobs dissipated enough to string together some words. He wiped his face with his hands.

'Has Mom come back? I want to go home.'

'*Ai*, you've only been here a few days! I thought I was your funnest uncle?'

'But you are my only uncle.'

Jommo laughed and wrapped a towel around Amani. 'I don't know if your mom is back, and I don't want to tell you a lie. So let's do this. You go take a shower and put on some fresh clothes. Then we wake everyone up and we can go continue the fun at your house. *Sawa*?'

Amani nodded enthusiastically.

'Eh, me, I only make deals with men. And men don't make deals with tears in their eyes.'

Amani wiped his eyes again, shot his hand out to shake on it, and marched to the shower, thrilled to be going home to his mom and his bed and his things. Here, Aunt Wairimu was obsessed with the news and was always saying that the country was going to shit and taking her with it.

'How can a country go to shit?' he asked one day and Wairimu jumped, unaware that he was there.

'You won't understand, go find your cousins, Amani,'

Wairimu said. Amani stormed off, tired of people pretending that everything was fine and telling him that he wouldn't understand. At least at home he could still understand some of what was happening when people pretended.

Later that morning, Jommo checked every news channel for updates on the violence before he packed his family into his car to head out to Ngugi's house. Wairimu phoned and texted everyone she knew who lived in the distance between the two houses and asked them to peek outside the window and check that all was clear. And the two of them discussed every possible route they could take in case there was chaos on the road. But it all didn't matter. They would never have been able to avoid the huge mob that was heading straight for them as they sat in their car, less than a kilometre away from their home.

'Shit.' Jommo slammed the brakes, put the car in reverse and drove right into the car he hadn't seen behind them. The force of the impact was so intense that Amani, who was standing in the foot-well in between his cousins, was flung into the gap between the two front seats.

He was stunned silent for a while as he lay wedged between the front seats, and then he let out a shrill cry. 'What's happening? Uncle Jommo, what's wrong? Who are those people, what do they want?' Amani was asking even though he knew that everyone would just pretend and tell him he didn't understand. He just wanted to go home. He wanted to see his mom. Would she be back yet? She would answer him.

His cousins pulled him back onto the seat. Wairimu looked back to check that he wasn't hurt, then told him to sit down and strap on his seatbelt. She tried to conceal the tremble in her voice when she spoke.

'Stop pretending!' he screamed at Wairimu, and turned to his cousins. At least they were listening to him, but seeing their fear only made him want to cry more. And the worry on Jommo's face was making Amani sure that he was not going to get home to his mom and his bed and his things. Jommo cursed again as he tried to manoeuvre his way around the crowd, which now closed in on them. They grew more frenzied each time the car inched back and forth. Wairimu was saying something to him, but he couldn't hear her over Amani's cries, his children arguing and the mad mob outside. Amani thought he recognised some of the men. These were the men his aunt had been watching on TV when she would say that the country was going to shit.

'Auntie Nimo—are these the men from the TV?' Amani asked, in between sobs and being shushed by his cousins whose eyes were also filled with terror.

'Be quiet, Amani—put on your seatbelt,' Wairimu said.

'Uncle Jommo, I want to go home,' Amani was tugging at Jommo's shirt, tears and snot running down his face.

'Amani, be silent and sit back. We are going home just now,' Wairimu said, before she turned to her husband.

At home, she tried to avoid watching news of the violence while the children were in the room, but at some point it became impossible to hide the truth of what was happening in the country from them.

'Uncle Jommo—please take us back,' Amani pleaded again.

'Are all your doors locked?' Jommo shouted as the crowd came round to his side of the car and demanded that he roll down the window. Wairimu was now shouting over the commotion, saying something about weapons, but

Jommo wasn't paying any attention to her as he inched the car further into the dense crowd. Most of them were on the right side of the car and were jostling and rocking it wildly. Wairimu looked out of her window and noticed the wide ditch that the tilting car was threatening to tip over into. All three children in the back seat were screaming and crying. Amani squeezed his eyes shut.

'Jommo, stop!' Wairimu shouted so loud that some of the men outside the car heard her and echoed her. They started calling Jommo by name and telling him to listen to his wise wife and stop the car. 'They don't have any weapons, Jommo, they're celebrating. Stop and let them pass!'

Jommo studied the crowd for the first time, feeling like a fool. Wairimu was right. There were no weapons in the air, only branches, tinsel and PNU banners. The crowd was only getting worked up because Jommo's refusal to stop and celebrate with them must have meant that he was for the opposition. He looked through the rear-view mirror at the car behind them. Their windows were rolled down and although there was terror on their faces, the people inside the car were waving and cheering with the crowd.

Jommo rolled down his window to speak to them.

Amani screamed, 'Don't do that! No!'

Wairimu shushed him and started to apologise to the crowd for the misunderstanding, explaining that their children were afraid, and they were eager to get them home. A man bent down and looked into the back of the car to speak to the children. His dark skin was covered in a light layer of red dust which almost matched his bloodshot eyes.

Amani squeezed his eyes shut, as if he saw a monster. When the man shouted into the car, Amani yelped, jumped out of his seat, and unlocked the door on the left side of the car.

Before his cousins could do a thing, Amani bolted out the door—he was going to get home if he had to run there himself.

Jommo looked back just in time to see Amani climbing over his cousin and out of the car. Jommo reached backward to try and grab him, but his seatbelt restricted him.

'Amani, stop!' Wairimu shouted, snapping hers off.

It was too late.

When Amani got out, there was hardly any ground for him to step on. If Jommo had kept trying to manoeuvre his way away from the crowd, the car would probably have landed in the wide drainage ditch that Amani now tumbled into head first.

The last thing Wairimu saw before she swung her door open was the shocked expression on her nephew's face as his head bounced heavily off the concrete.

'Jesus! Amani!' she screamed.

Jommo tried to pry his door open against the clueless crowd. The man he spoke to saw everything and tried to get the crowd to move, without much success. Jommo barked at his kids to stay in the car and lock the doors before he climbed over to the passenger side of the car and followed Wairimu out through her door.

Wairimu tumbled down the slope and landed feet first into the ditch, all the while listening desperately for Amani's cries. She was struggling to lift Amani's still body out of the narrow space at the bottom of the ditch. Jommo got to them and lifted him out. Wairimu shrieked when she saw how much of Amani's blood, which was gushing out of the cut on the top of his head, collected in the ditch. She kept calling him, praying for him to respond. Amani lay in Jommo's arms as he struggled to climb out of the ditch without his hands.

The man with the dusty face called out to Jommo from the front of the car. He beckoned at Jommo to hand the child to him. As soon as the man had Amani, he too seemed paralysed by the amount of blood that was pouring out of him. Jommo climbed out, pulled his wife out of the ditch and reclaimed his nephew. He shouted at his eldest son to jump in the front seat and stepped aside for Wairimu to get into the back and placed the still bleeding boy onto his wife's lap. He pushed the now apologetic crowd aside violently as he made his way to the driver's seat. The crowd scurried out of the way as Jommo sped off to the Aga Khan Hospital.

***

Jail cells all over the country were filling up fast and were getting dangerously close to becoming a crisis of their own; the police's strategy was to end the violence by making as many arrests as possible. When the Kenya Defence Forces stepped in to help, they instructed that the holding cells be emptied out as soon as possible. They were confident the violence would be under control before the end of the day, and they would need space for all the criminals they planned to apprehend.

That morning, the door to the cell Thuo sat in for one week swung open and Thuo and his cellmate Pato were informed they were getting moved to the prison in Rongai until further notice.

Thuo began to protest, but Pato hit him on the back of the head and warned him to be quiet. Kiprop was back at the station. Thuo hadn't seen or heard from him since the night the election ended. He searched Kiprop's eyes for clues as to what was happening, but the man's eyes were dark and exhausted. Kiprop led the two men to the back of the waiting police cruiser and sat opposite them. His gun was pointed at them as the truck sputtered to life.

'If you try anything, I will shoot,' he said, and Thuo didn't doubt he meant it. Then he rested his head and closed his eyes. The floor was sticky and littered with discarded clothes. The tinny smell was overwhelming, but it was nothing compared to what Thuo had endured. He took in the fresh air, happy to be out of the cell and reluctant about what lay at the other end of this journey.

Kiprop was fast asleep by the time the cruiser arrived at the next police station to pick up more people. Soon, there were several men tightly stacked into the back of the truck like beer bottles in a crate.

When Pato was sure that Kiprop couldn't hear him, he whispered to Thuo, 'You should go.'

'What?'

'They didn't enter you into the log, so no one is going to know if you make it to Rongai or not. You should run.'

Thuo glanced over at Kiprop, who was still sleeping soundly despite the increased activity around him. He was trying to hear his own thoughts over the sound of his increasingly rapid heartbeat.

'What are you thinking about? If I were you, I would have been at home by now ploughing my wife. *Heh*, I've surely never met a fool like you,' Pato added when he saw Thuo's hesitation.

It was exactly what Thuo needed to hear to make his decision. The worst that could happen was that he would get caught and thrown back onto the truck. Pato was still goading him to make a run for it, and even though Thuo knew that his cellmate was, as usual, looking for something to amuse himself with, he was somehow convinced he could do it.

He didn't know how much farther they had to go before they got to the prison, but the farther they were the better—he was running out of time. There was hardly any traffic so they were travelling quite fast, only slowing down to make turns or for the giant potholes on the road, and each time they slowed down a little, Thuo would prepare to jump, only to change his mind at the very last second. He was either afraid that the car behind them would run him over, or worse, alert Kiprop of his attempted escape. Or that the terrain on the side of the road didn't have enough vegetation for him to hide behind once he got off. One time he closed his eyes and prepared to jump. His mind was ready, but his body just would not move.

'You see now. That's why people like you end up rotting in prison,' Pato whispered to Thuo. 'You have a perfect chance to escape and here you are acting like a little girl with...'

Thuo shot up off his seat, swung his legs over the door and jumped off the moving vehicle. He felt Pato shove him off the cruiser, his final encouragement before he pulled one standing man down to take Thuo's seat so that no one noticed him missing.

Thuo's left foot landed on a sharp stone and pierced through his shoe. The pain caused him to lose balance and fall on his knees. He yelped and checked himself. Then he quickly got up and ran to the side of the road, listening behind him for the sound of Kiprop shouting at him or that of the cruiser screeching to a halt. He braced himself for a bullet to pierce through his back. When none of this happened, he kept running anyway, only slowing to look back when he was sure that he had created enough distance between them. From this distance, he could see Kiprop still fast asleep with his mouth hanging open, absorbing the raised dust. Some of the inmates were looking back at Thuo, their faces expressionless. And there was Pato, grinning widely. He waved back at Pato, turned around, and continued running.

Thuo only stopped running when his lungs cried out for dear mercy and his starved body threatened to collapse if he pushed it any further. The putrid stench from the police cell still followed him despite the fact that he was miles away from it. When he stopped to rest on a heap of abandoned car tyres, he realised the horrible smell was coming from his body. He had not bathed in the days spent wading in a shallow pond of human waste. The bottom of his trousers were caked in the foul mess, and his shirt was so stained and stiff with sweat and tears that it looked as if it was dipped in brown starch.

Thuo immediately became aware of his appearance. His phone, wallet, belt and shoelaces were not returned to him, so the only way he would get home would be at the mercy of good Samaritans whom he hoped would give him a lift, but there was no way anyone would give him a second glance looking the way he did. He scanned his surroundings, spotted a petrol station and cajoled his aching feet to carry him a few more metres to it. To his delight, there was a black hose pipe coiled around the air pressure pump at the station's entrance. He staggered towards it, anticipating the relief of cool water gliding down his parched throat and dehydrated body. He uncoiled the hosepipe and reached for the tap.

It was locked.

He looked around for someone to unlock it, realising

only now that the station was closed. He walked around the abandoned establishment, searching for a second, unlocked tap somewhere. When he couldn't find one, he resigned himself to drinking the water from the large plastic drum that sat in between the petrol pumps. The soap stung his tongue and his throat. He washed his face, took off his shirt and used it to mop his torso before he wrung it out and put it back on. He was about to do the same thing with his trousers when a guard emerged from the back of the station.

'*Wewe! Unafanya nini*? Does this look like your bathroom?' The guard picked an empty can from a nearby bin and hurled it at Thuo who was already running out of the station. His wet shirt clung to his body and the breeze as he ran was refreshing. He tried not to think about the shame of being treated like a stray.

At another gas station a few metres down the road, he tried a different approach. This station was open and there was a long line of cars waiting to fuel. Thuo recognised the look on the driver's faces. It's the same expression he himself wore when he hoped that the fuel pumps wouldn't dry out before he fuelled the Mwangis' car.

He approached one of the attendants and explained that he was caught up in the election violence and was trying to get back home. He just needed some water to drink and perhaps a place to freshen up.

The busy attendant barely looked at Thuo as he directed him to a room behind the convenience shop where there was a toilet and shower that he could use. Thuo locked himself in the small dark stall, removed his shoes and stood fully clothed in the tepid water. He relished the spray of the water as it washed away layers of dirt and he could finally feel his skin again. The anguish of the past few days slithered down the drain with his dirty bath water. He felt human again.

He thanked the attendant and continued his trek towards Nairobi, the weight of his wet clothes slowing him down as his wet feet slipped around in his shoes.

He almost forgot that he was a fugitive, and that if Kiprop got to the prison and reported him missing, the police would be out looking for him at any moment. The image of the sleeping policeman popped into his mind and though he doubted this would happen, he took precautions anyway. He kept himself concealed behind bushes and shrubs when he could, and ran across the sections of the roadsides that were bare.

It took him over two hours to get to the junction at the highway that led to the city. With almost clean, dry clothes, he was less conspicuous. He stood among a crowd of people waiting for buses and *matatus* that arrived infrequently and were often packed beyond capacity. A newspaper vendor was shouting at the waiting passengers.

'Buy the paper! Forty bob only. Or rent it for 10 bob, *ndio muone* the warzone that Kenya has become.'

Thuo stood behind a man with a newspaper and looked over his shoulder as he flipped through the pages, his face frozen in disbelief.

The headline read WE WILL NOT BE SILENCED.

It was the paper's response to a government directive that banned all media reports of the post election violence, now being referred to as PEV. Inside were pages upon pages of dead bodies, burnt homes and looted properties. Policemen were firing bullets and tear gas canisters at groups of unarmed protesters in one series of photos. In another, armed protesters were chasing policemen. And in another, old women and children were being trampled on by frenzied crowds.

'Dear God,' Thuo gasped as the man turned around to return the paper to the vendor.

A lorry stopped at the bus stop and everyone began to push and shove to climb on board. Thuo hesitated to get on, he didn't know where it was going and nobody around him seemed to know or care. Women lifted their children up for strangers to hoist them on board before they struggled to lift themselves on to the back of the four tonne truck.

Thuo's body was on the moving vehicle but his mind was busy etching the images he just saw into his memory. He tried not to worry himself with thoughts of his family, but there was now good reason to worry. Never in a thousand years would he ever have imagined that things were so bad.

From where he stood, he could see most of the city. It looked calm. Too calm to be the place where those pictures were taken. He thought about Ngugi and Kavata and their children, and wondered if they kept up with the news in their part of the city. Dense smoke rose into the air above one section of the city not too far away from them. It spread to the blue skies above the rest of the city and Thuo almost wished that he could blow it away. He looked towards Kangemi and willed this truck to head in that direction, but it didn't. In fact, it was heading north, towards the thick black smoke.

Thuo's fellow passengers began to shout at the driver to stop and let them off. He was driving further into Kibera towards the gunshots and into the thick smoke that, they now realised, was teargas. He kept on driving, insisting that he knew where he was going and that nobody forced anyone to get on the truck in the first place. He drove like a madman, driving on pavements and speeding down the wrong side of the road. Thuo wondered how the driver was able to keep his eyes open. Every time Thuo tried, the sting of the toxic gas would force them back shut. The next time he tried to squint his eyes open, it was just in time to see the truck heading straight for an electricity pole.

The sound of the collision and the alarmed screams from the passengers were mistaken for some kind of an attack by the police who were a few metres away. They responded with more tear gas and opened fire into the thick haze. People began to climb over each other to get off the vehicle that moments ago had been their chariot to safety. Thuo held on to the side rails for dear life as people pushed past him. The driver tumbled out of the vehicle and was running away when a bullet hit him in the back, sending him soaring a few feet into the air, before he plunged into the ground. Thuo had heard the sound of gunshots before. But never the thud of a bullet entering a body. It was a sound he didn't think he could ever forget.

Thuo forced his eyes open and looked in the direction that the gunfire was coming from. He saw the police heading cautiously in his direction. They looked like aliens with their gas masks and guns, shooting at any and everything that moved. Thuo knew he would never make it off that truck alive, so he climbed over the side and clambered into the front through the passenger window. Once he was inside, he folded himself into the tiniest ball he could manage and hid in the foot-well.

The police were close, and their gunshots even closer. Thuo kept his eyes shut; he didn't want to see his death coming.

Some pleaded with the police to stop shooting, 'Please, *kuna watoto hapa*. We have no weapons.'

The shooting continued for a few more moments and then he heard footsteps approach the truck. The footsteps shouted, instructing his colleagues to stop shooting. Then he hit the side of the truck with the butt of his gun and barked at whoever could still hear him.

'If you can hear me, you have five minutes to disappear from this place before we start shooting again.'

Thuo didn't believe the police man. He stayed where he was, eyes squeezed shut. He heard a few people jump off the truck and run, and when gunshots didn't follow, he regretted his decision. He stayed put until a fresh round of gunshots in the distance confirmed that the police were gone. He swung the door open and ran towards the tin shacks.

He knew he was on the wrong side of Kibera when every house he walked past was marked with the ODM colours. It was common knowledge that this slum was zoned based on tribal and political allegiance. Those who were caught on the wrong side never lived to tell the story. He abandoned his initial plan to find a friendly spot to hide out until his eyes stopped burning as that would lead to a certain death. He had no clue where the Kikuyu side of Kibera was, but he didn't think he would find out any time soon. He turned around and walked back towards the truck that brought him here.

The tear gas wafted away, revealing several bodies scattered like large rag dolls all over the place. It was worse than those images in the newspaper. The man whose shoulder Thuo looked over in order to look at the paper was dead, on the side of the road. His left shoe was missing and his leg looked broken. Thuo thought to drive the truck out of Kibera, but there were dead bodies in the back. He walked in the direction the police came from, reminding himself over and over again not to run because here, running could get you killed.

***

Cheptoo made every effort to make Nakuru feel like home. She taught herself the language so that she could teach it to her children so that their peers wouldn't make fun of them whenever they visited their father's home. When she would go to the market, women would gossip about her in Kikuyu, expecting her not to understand what they were saying. She enjoyed the shocked expressions on their faces when she responded to them in their language.

It was always easier when Thuo was there with her. Nobody whispered behind her back, and if they did, he would be quick to put them in their place. There were more whisperings and warnings this time around, and she was desperate for her husband to come home. When she could take it no more, she locked up her house and went to stay with Thuo's aunt who was more than happy to accommodate her and her children. It was clear that she was also worried about her nephew's non-Kikuyu wife.

There were all manner of rumours about things happening in Nakuru. The lake was filled with bodies of Luos and Kalenjins. Men were being forced to drop their pants and prove that they were circumcised, and if they hadn't been, then gangs would hold them down and perform forced circumcisions. Men who fought these circumcisions got their entire penises chopped off and stuffed into their mouths as the crowd taunted them for being both uncircumcised and homosexuals. If they eventually bled to death, their bodies were thrown into the lake. Kalenjin women were spared death. Instead they were ripped away from their homes and taken to the homes of Kikuyu men, where they were tied to beds and raped repeatedly for days until semen and blood oozed freely out of them and collected in pools around their bruised buttocks.

The only reason Cheptoo was hesitant to leave Nakuru was because she was waiting for Thuo.

'What good will you do him if you are dead, my child?' her husband's aunt asked. 'Leave the children with me and run. They will be safer here.'

Cheptoo could not argue with this logic. Her children had Kikuyu names and would be much safer with their aunt in Nakuru than on the road with Cheptoo. She often said that she wished they looked more like her; now she was grateful that they took after their father.

They cried painfully when she left the house in the dead of the night and rode the army truck that was ferrying non-Kikuyus to Eldoret. The ride was uneventful but she was surrounded by gloom and suffering. Some people cried during the entire journey. Men clutched their bandaged arms, heads and crotches as they slept; the pain of their injuries too severe to endure while awake.

The driver stopped when they were in Eldoret and asked those who could to stand up and lift the canvas sides of the truck so that they were able to get some fresh air. They were safe now.

Cheptoo was now able to see the people she travelled with more clearly. They looked more distraught in the light of day than they sounded in the dead of night, but were happy to have escaped Nakuru with their lives and whatever was left of their dignity. They continued towards the camp set up for the internally displaced at the Eldoret show grounds.

The streets were heavily policed and felt safer, and Cheptoo could finally stop holding her breath.

The truck came to an abrupt stop in front of a well-known Anglican church. The road was blocked and several people in the truck began to worry their safety was short-lived. A tall man holding a rifle walked up to the driver and calmly asked him to wait a few minutes. They were performing a cleansing ritual and several people gathered to watch. He was a Kalenjin man. The man asked the driver who the people at the back of the truck were. The driver explained that they were Kalenjins who were fleeing Nakuru, and went into a few details of what was going on there.

The man came to the back and apologised to them for their misfortune. 'I am told that you are refugees from Nakuru and have suffered greatly.' His Kalenjin accent was music to Cheptoo's ears but she was shocked that he was referring to her as a refugee. She only heard that word used to refer to people from Sudan, or Somalia, or Congo. Surely she was not a refugee. '*Poleni sana*—don't worry you are safe now,' the soldier continued before he called out to a few of his colleagues to bring them food and water.

Cheptoo watched as men in plain clothes, also holding guns, went into a small store and emerged with sodas, water, biscuits and corn chips, and placed them on the floor of the truck for them to devour. People came alive as they grabbed as much as they could. Cheptoo handed snacks to the men who were unable to move because of their injuries. She was horribly thirsty, but something about these men didn't feel right. She was uncomfortable accepting food from them.

There was some commotion in the distance, but Cheptoo hadn't been unable to tell where it was coming from until she stood up to distribute the snacks. She could see the church clearly. There were hundreds of people gathered around it. The men at the front of the crowd were nailing the doors of the church shut. There were people inside the church, screaming and crying and waving their hands out of the church windows, begging to be let out.

A man climbed out of a window at the back of the church, and froze when he saw the size of the crowd. He ran around like a decapitated chicken, looking for a gap in the throng of people through which he could escape, but nobody would let him through. They just pointed and laughed at him, a few of them kicking him and pushing him back towards the church.

The men who seemed to be in charge walked around, dousing the church in a fluid Cheptoo couldn't quite see. She assumed that it was holy water since this was a cleansing ritual, but she couldn't understand why they would be cleansing a church.

The man who escaped was exhausted, humiliated and injured, but he fought on. When he could walk no more, he crawled around on the ground heading back into the crowd, and each time he was kicked back towards the church. He was no longer amusing to watch, so two men carried him towards the church and bound his wrists to a wooden pole. They doused him in the same liquid they used on the church and set him on fire.

Cheptoo began to scream.

She rushed to the side of the truck and jumped out. She ran towards the church, and struggled to get through the crowd. Behind her, the men who fed them warned her to stay away, but they didn't bother to run after her. When she realised that she would never get through the dense crowd in time, she turned back, ran up to the driver and begged him to do something. He was a soldier, they would listen to him. He simply shrugged his shoulders and asked her how she could want to spare their lives when these were the same people who were throwing her people into Lake Nakuru.

She went back and fought her way through the thick crowd, her shouts for people to stop watching and do something earned her scratches and pinches from invisible attackers. She almost made her way through the crowd when the church went up in flames.

The crowd leaned back away from the flames and Cheptoo forged forward. The screams from the church were loud and guttural, and Cheptoo covered her ears for fear that her head might explode.

The crowd spat her out in front of the church. She watched the man burn. He was running on the spot so fervently that it was almost as if he wanted his soul to escape the pain that his body was feeling. When this didn't work, he just began to shake. He vibrated so hard that the beam he was bound to looked as if it would come apart. Cheptoo rushed to the men who were responsible for this and begged them to stop, pulling on their shirts as she screamed at them. A heavy blow sent her flying so close to the church that she could feel the heat of the flames licking her body and smell the porky scent of burning flesh. She looked up from the ground at the man. His eyes were fixed on her as he died.

She screamed again. She gathered soil with her bare hands and threw it towards the church, trying to put out the flames, when someone grabbed her by her braids and dragged her away from the church.

'We will throw you in there if you do not stop this stupidity,' said the man who held her by her hair. She didn't move anymore. She watched as the ravenous flames devoured the man's body, only relenting when he was reduced to a charred skeleton. She listened as the screaming and banging inside the church was replaced by coughing and garbled choking. She looked around her for a sign that this was just a bad dream. The faces around her were blank. Some people shook their heads; others were filled with satisfied hate. There was no sympathy, nobody tried to help, and nobody spoke a word. They simply stared at the burning church, with the flames glinting in their eyes, making them look possessed by an evil fiery spirit.

The crowd began to thin out when the only sounds coming from the church were those of sizzling wood and the building collapsing. The men responsible walked away proudly, their weapons slung over their shoulders like farmers coming home from a day of digging the earth. Cheptoo's eyeballs felt like there was a film of dust over them, protecting her from seeing anything further. She shut them for a moment, and when she opened them again, there were only a handful of people around the smoking church. The truck that brought her here from Nakuru was nowhere in sight. Her entire body ached, there was blood oozing from the gash on the side of her face and her clothes were so badly torn that all her underwear was visible.

She was kneeling on the ground at the same spot, eyes still on the church, when the Red Cross vans arrived at the scene. At first, the medics just stood and stared. Some of them broke down into tears while others bent over to vomit in the bushes. They stood around talking and staring. There was no need to hurry, it was clear that there was no one inside the church that they could save. One of them spotted Cheptoo and rushed towards her with a medical kit.

'Mama, are you in pain?'

Cheptoo said nothing. She couldn't speak.

'Did you see what happened here?'

Silence.

'Were you inside the church?'

'Are you in pain?'

Cheptoo turned to look at the medic, and then back at the church.

'Will you let me look at your wound?'

She looked at him again, and then back at the church. A fresh wave of tears consumed her.

The medic opened his kits and began to clean Cheptoo's wound. She didn't flinch as the antiseptic touched the wound. Or when the medic called his colleague to help carry her to the shade. She just sat there, with tears streaming down her face. By the time he was done with Cheptoo, there were bandages all over her body, and twelve stitches on her head. The medic sat with her until more people came to help them move the bodies to the morgue. Firemen arrived and reluctantly sprayed the church with water so that the medics could go inside. They pried the doors open and then drove away.

The medic tried to speak to her again. Then he said something about her being in shock as he injected a white fluid into her veins. She felt the prick of the needle and looked down at the medicine leaving the canister, wondering what good it would do.

The medic left her to assist extracting the bodies from their charcoal grave. She watched him work. He was putting tags on the bodies to help identify them once they were brought up. She stood up and walked towards him. The medic saw her approach him and told her that she should stay off her feet. When she got to him, she snatched the tags from him and began to help.

'No, mama. That is not allowed. Only trained personnel are allowed to handle dead bodies,' he said, but Cheptoo was already tagging her second body.

'We need all the help we can get, Kosgey, *muache asaidie*,' another colleague said.

Kosgey handed Cheptoo a pen. 'Don't think about it too hard. Just give them any name, or number,' he said, and walked into the church.

Cheptoo recoiled at the idea. These were people not numbers, but she had to get the job done. Eventually she settled on Kiambaa Church #1, Kiambaa Church #2 and so on. She tied their name tag onto the burnt toes that the medics left out of the zipped bag and then zipped the body bag shut.

Watching them lift the man's remains off the church steps was difficult for Cheptoo. He was still handcuffed to the church, so it took a while to cut through the wood and release him. He was the only person whom she actually saw alive. She clearly remembered what his face looked like as he ran around the crowd, fighting for his life. It was as if he accepted death already, but wouldn't give his aggressors the benefit of knowing so. He was strong and full of life, and now simply a charred mass. So light that it took one person to lift him and put him in the body bag.

There was no way of knowing how many people were in the church before it was set alight, and none of the Red Cross team knew what to expect when they arrived at the scene. They didn't have enough body bags and had to wait for others to be brought to them. The church massacre caused a fresh outbreak of violence in Eldoret, so there was no telling how long it would be until more bags got delivered to them. Most of the victims were children, so they decided that they would fit two small bodies in one bag. Eventually, the only choice was to transport the bodies on the back of a pickup, covered in linen sheets.

The team of ten volunteers looked at the church in complete disbelief as the last of the victims' bodies were taken to the morgue hours later. Cheptoo counted twenty eight bodies, fifteen of whom were children. The volunteers milled about the scene, collecting used gloves and pieces of human that fell off the victims as they were being moved. When they were ready to leave, Cheptoo was standing outside the vans. She had nowhere to go. One of the volunteers saw her and opened the van door. When Cheptoo explained how she got to Eldoret, the volunteer asked her to travel back to the Red Cross office with them.

They drove away from the church in silence. Cheptoo looked back and noticed for the first time that there was a crowd gathered around the church. She wondered how long they had been there, and if those people were part of the same crowd that stood by watching. She was suddenly able to feel again. In a flash, the pain in her body became real, as did the intense hatred she felt for the hundreds of people who stood by and watched twenty eight innocent people burn to death.

\*\*\*

Kavata shouted at the man at the information desk at Schiphol Airport who told her that no airline was flying into Kenya. She was irritated by the way he was referring to Kenya as if it was some kind of warzone and she was not holding back in giving him a large piece of her mind. When she was done with him, she spun on her heels and walked away. She went from airline to airline, stood in every line and tried to book a flight to Kenya. Each time getting the same response: JKIA was apparently closed.

'Taken over by bandits or something. We can issue a ticket, but we cannot guarantee a departure within the next forty-eight hours,' said the flight saleswoman with thick black hair and the longest eyelashes Kavata had ever seen. She was just about to launch into her fifth tirade of the day when she spotted a uniformed man watching her from a few feet away—an instant reminder that this was not her country.

Her feet were swollen and her lower back ached from standing for so long. She looked up at the information screen that she had been studying for hours and looked for a flight that would get her as close to home as possible. A flight was departing for Uganda in an hour, from a terminal at the other end of the massive airport. Kavata hobbled across and got there just in time. She purchased her ticket and made her way to the boarding gate, only realising when she was safely fastened into her aisle seat that the flight had a six hour layover in Dubai.

Once off the aircraft in Kampala, Kavata made her way directly to the Kenya Airways flight office. Here she got a more palatable version of the story.

'JKIA is open,' said Marcus, the flight salesman who she was pleased to discover was also Kenyan, 'but only for departures and connecting flights. No airline wants their aircraft to be sitting on that tarmac for long lest they get torched.' Marcus recommended that she stay in Kampala for a few days. 'Or you can take a bus in to Kenya,' Marcus said as a joke, but Kavata sprung at the idea.

'Yes, I will take a bus. Where's the station?'

'That's not wise either. Stay here a while,' Marcus backtracked, but Kavata was already scanning the airport for a Forex bureau. She exchanged some of her dollars for local currency, then went into the ladies room and changed clothes. Her mother always told her that she should look her best when she travelled internationally. This was why she opted to travel in the Sunday suit she left Nairobi in, but it would be ridiculous to board the Akamba bus in a tailored suit in the January heat, though she wasn't sure that her new sweat suit was any better.

The taxi driver who drove her to the bus station almost pulled over when Kavata told him she was heading to Kenya.

'My sister, have you not heard what is going on over there? I cannot take you there with a clean heart. Just stay here. Things are peaceful here.' He insisted on buying her a newspaper so that she could see just how bleak things were. Kenya was all over the front page of the Daily Monitor. Kavata thanked him for the paper and politely asked him to proceed with the trip. At the bus station, the driver gave it one last try as he parked next to the Akamba bus terminal. It was deserted.

'You see my sister, the buses will not travel empty. Going is like suicide. I can take you to a nice hotel. A not too expensive one. Or an expensive one if you like.' He reminded Kavata of Thuo, and this only fed her resolve to go home.

'No, thank you. I will be fine here.' She paid the man, got out of the car and made her way to the ticket office.

The next bus to Nairobi was due to leave that evening. However, the bus would only depart if it was more than half full.

'The last bus that went to Kenya has been stuck there for

three days. Taking an empty bus there isn't worth the risk,' said the ticket agent.

Kavata thought fast. 'I'd like to book 35 tickets,' she said, and the man smiled and flipped the sign on his desk over to indicate that bookings for the route were open.

No one asked any questions when it was time to leave and none of Kavata's fellow passengers arrived. The conductor simply asked her if they should depart and she nodded, eager to be on her way.

There was only one other passenger on the bus, an elderly man who ignored the fifty nine empty seats in the bus and chose to sit right next to Kavata. She froze when he secured his seat belt and looked at the conductor, her eyes pleading with him to step in. The conductor chuckled and settled down into his seat next to the door.

'Excuse me, the bus is empty. You can sit anywhere you like,' she offered. The man didn't move, and she wondered if he heard her. 'Sir?'

'This is the seat I have paid for,' he said, displaying his ticket. He was right. Kavata undid her seatbelt and asked her fellow passenger to let her pass by him. The old man's gaze remained fixed forward. When he didn't respond the second time she asked, she squeezed herself through the small space between his knees and the seat in front of him. He grumbled and sucked his teeth, and complained that she stepped on his toes when she hadn't. Once free, Kavata made her way to the front of the bus and sat down right next to the driver. She had a much better view of the road from here, and even if she was at risk of being thrown out of the window in the case of an accident, this was the only single seat on the bus.

There were no passengers to collect at the bus stops between Kampala and the Kenyan border so the bus flew past the stops, shaving minutes off the fourteen hour journey. However, since the border officials hadn't expected anyone to be crossing into Kenya, they had closed the border and gone to sleep.

The border was a slouching metal fence with sections missing from the Kenyan flag painted on it. There wasn't even a lock on the gate. Kavata thought they should have been able to simply swing it open and enter the country, but that was not the case. The bus driver hooted continuously as all the time they saved was lost waiting for the border to open. Two hours later, the bus driver pointed towards one of the guest houses and told Kavata she would have to spend the rest of the night there and find her own way across the border when it opened in the morning. This bus would go back to Kampala.

Kavata would have none of that. 'I paid to get to Nairobi. Let's go find whoever is in charge here.'

'Madam, I am not going through that gate. I can get arrested for illegal entry. If your border patrol is lazy, it's not my problem,' the conductor said at first. But when she offered to pay him for his help, he agreed.

She had never physically crossed a border, but Kavata always imagined country borders were fortresses with huge metal gates and tall manned towers, metal detectors, sniffer dogs, and underground tunnels. However, the border at Busia was far from that. The immigration office was a small dilapidated structure with a tin roof and wooden door. Behind it were the quarters where the immigration officials rested in between shifts. The conductor pointed towards the door she needed to knock on, promised that they would wait for her, and then scurried back to the bus.

When the immigration officer emerged from the dark

room, Kavata understood why her companion fled. The man was a giant. Everything about him was intimidating. The palm of his hands looked like they could flatten a small village when he held them out and asked why he was being woken up. His voice sounded like a thousand empty water drums tumbling down a steep tarmac hill. Kavata stuttered before she found her voice.

'We need to cross the border.' She felt silly for being intimidated by him. She was at least two decades older than him.

'The border is closed.'

'Isn't this is a twenty four hour border?' Her voice didn't betray her again. The man studied her as best as he could in the dark and asked how she got there.

'By bus, and we have been waiting for two hours. *Tafadhali* let us through now.'

'Where are you going?'

'To Nairobi.' The man laughed.

'You think anyone can get to Nairobi?' He laughed harder as he went in to the dark room, emerged with a flashlight and a set of keys, and led the way to the immigration office.

When he looked towards the bus and noticed that there were only two passengers on it, he sent insults into the air at being woken up to check two passports. He turned around and in a few giant steps he was at the flimsy gate, swinging it open and motioning for the bus to go through. Kavata rushed back towards the bus, her sleepy feet resisting her rapid movements. Within seconds, they were in Kenya.

An hour later, Kavata was stirred from her nap by an urgent tapping on her shoulder. The bus came to a halt in front of a roadblock built using tyres, stones, metal sheets, thorns and pieces of wood. The road block stretched out far across the sides of the road, and it was clear that whoever erected it didn't want anything or anyone slipping through. It was high enough for people to be standing completely concealed on the other side of it.

'*Tuko wapi?*' Kavata hoped that they were closer to Nairobi than she imagined.

'Webuye, just outside the town.' The driver was already putting the bus into gear so that he could reverse and turn back.

'Is there another way around it?'

'No, we are going back. We've told you no one is coming to Kenya, now see. When we get through this one, there will be many others on the way. I don't plan to die today.'

'No. No, don't go back. Just give me a moment to think,' she begged and the driver laughed.

'This is not the time for thinking,' he said.

'Is there somewhere I can find a taxi or a matatu?'

The conductor walked to the front of the bus and asked her why she was so desperate to get back to Nairobi. They seemed unconvinced by the simple reason that she was rushing back to family. The conductor and driver deliberated in Luhya for several minutes, during which the elderly man joined in on the conversation, happy to be part of something that excluded the woman who refused to sit next to him.

The driver was given strict instructions to turn around the minute there was any sign of trouble on the road. However, he was willing to help Kavata. He made a quick phone call, after which he confirmed that a cargo train from Malaba was scheduled at midnight. It would be passing through Webuye in about an hour and would go all the way to Mombasa via Nairobi. It was common for passengers to use the train; the conductor used it several times to get home. Although it was illegal, the bribe you would pay if you got caught was still cheaper than any bus ticket. The thought rattled Kavata.

'It's the only way madam,' the driver said, sensing her hesitation. 'Or I can take you back to Uganda and you can wait for the roads to be opened, but the way things are looking that could be months.'

'Is it safe?' she asked. She looked down at her throbbing feet. The conductor lowered his voice and leaned in to Kavata as if there were more people in the bus who could hear them.

'To be honest madam, these are very tricky days we are having. In fact it is very unsafe for a Kikuyu like you to be over here. But if you just keep to yourself, and not talk to anyone, you will be fine. Just keep your mouth closed.' Kavata thought to correct the man and tell him that she was actually a Kamba, but it made no difference. All her documents bore Ngugi's name anyway.

'Another thing. We are really risking our jobs by taking you to the station. These buses have trackers so if they check, this could get very costly for us.' Kavata expected this.

'How much?'

'Four thousand shillings.' The old passenger protested and the conductor corrected himself. 'Five thousand.'

Kavata insisted that she would only pay them once they were in Webuye and the train arrived.

'You won't be able to find it without me anyway,' the conductor said. The deal was struck, they drove back towards the border and turned off on to a *panya* route that led them to the station.

The conductor was totally right. The train only stopped for three minutes, and in that time passengers had to lift themselves on to the train that was designed to carry trucks and cars and construction materials. He had already warned her that she would need to be quick. She put her bag on her back and made sure that their payment was in her hand when the train arrived. It was made more problematic by the fact that rowdy youth took over the train and turned it into their own little country. The empty cargo cars towards the back of the train were reserved for Luos. The next few ones after that one were for Luhyas. All other tribes were free to find space on the other cars that were laden with cargo. The young men warned that those who were found in the wrong sections would be thrown off the moving train. Kavata and the conductor sprinted to the 'others' car and when they got to it, the conductor grabbed Kavata by the hips and hoisted her onto the train. She landed heavily on her chest just as the train began to move. The conductor ran alongside, holding out his hand for his payment. Kavata was just able to put the money in his hand before he tripped and fell down the slight slope on the side of the tracks. Kavata panicked for a while before she saw the man shoot up off the ground and wave her goodbye after he counted the money and stuffed it deep into his pocket.

Kavata swung her legs off the side of the train and looked around for the first time. There weren't very many people on the train with her, which was no surprise. There wasn't much room for passengers in the midst of the red building bricks tightly packed into the car. Those who could, climbed up to the top of the stacks and sat on them. Those were the most comfortable seats in the house if you were able to withstand the wind that attacked you as the train teetered on. Everyone else was forced to make do with whatever narrow floor space the cargo allowed. Most of the available space was taken so Kavata could only scoot back and rest her back against the bricks. Her bag provided cushion against the hard surface.

Her throbbing feet begged for her attention. They had almost doubled in size since she got off the plane in Amsterdam, and now looked like they would explode at the slightest prod. She thought about how far she had travelled and how far from comfort her entire trip was. The privilege that she unconsciously carried on her sleeve now clung to her tighter than the Aldos on her swollen feet.

Kavata looked around her again, taking in this version of her country that she knew was there but had managed to erase from her reality. Some people on the train didn't even know about the election violence. They were just trying to cross provincial borders the only way they knew how. She listened to one man a few feet from her explaining what was happening in the country to an older woman who could see that things were different but didn't know why. Kavata envied this woman and how untouched she was by the election.

'What foolishness,' the woman said when the man finished telling her why there were more people than usual on the cargo train. 'When are you going to understand that you are fighting for someone else's benefit? I fought for independence. Yes, don't look at me and assume me. I was there on the front line. With hundreds of other women. But see me now—too poor for the news. The men whose leadership we defended lived like kings and I am forced to sneak into Nairobi every month to beg for a pension which is never guaranteed. Until we all learn to live as stateless individuals, we will never be free. We will keep fighting to protect someone else's bank account. *Ati* how many people have died? Those are the real fools.'

All those around her considered her words silently as the train approached Eldoret.

\*\*\*

For the first time since she turned eighteen, Wanja spent New Year's Eve at home alone—it was depressing. Her grandparents dropped in briefly to check on her and tell her that they were planning a short trip. Her grandmother slipped her a few thousand shillings to stock up, so the next morning she woke up and drove to all the shops in her area. The supermarkets had never been so poorly stocked. There were more humans than products on the shelves. And by the looks of things, the liquor section was the first to be depleted. In the end, she settled for whatever she could find at the Sarit Centre and busied herself with Twitter as she stood in line for hours waiting to check out.

She noticed that someone else was posting for ODM and she wondered if the office was open. She assumed that everyone listened to the warnings to stay indoors and stayed away from the office, but it was clear that the work was going on. She considered calling Tom when her phone rang and her uncle's name was displayed on the screen. She cursed at the thought of having to leave her place in the queue because they were at her home and she wasn't. She crossed her fingers and answered the call. She heard crying in the background.

'Wanja, it's your uncle. There's been an accident. You need to come to the hospital. The Aga Khan. Come as soon as you can.'

She didn't completely understand the words she was hearing.

'What? Tell me more?'

Her uncle simply repeated what he said, 'We'll give you details when you get here. Drive safe.'

As she abandoned her shopping trolley and rushed out of the store, the shoppers around her descended on her groceries like hawks.

She grazed the car bumper on a potted plant as she drove into the hospital parking lot. She climbed out of the car and ran towards the emergency entrance, noticing the drops of blood at the entrance to the hospital. It took a moment for her eyes to adjust to the bright light at the emergency room reception, and when they did she took in all the people in bloodied clothes sitting in the lobby. She scanned the room for signs of her uncle and spotted her two cousins huddled together. She rushed towards them. They started to cry when they saw her.

'What happened?

Their sobs overpowered their words. She couldn't understand a thing they were saying. She looked around for Jommo.

'Where are your parents? Where's Amani?'

More sobs. She wanted to shake them and get them to talk as she tried to make sense of what happened. Her uncle called her and her cousins were here. So something must have happened to Amani or Wairimu. She sat next to the eldest of her cousins and held his hands.

'JJ, I need you to stop crying and please tell me what happened.' She spoke slowly, using the calmest voice she could muster. The boy narrated the story starting from the time when they had their New Year's Eve party, and Wanja listened, edging him on to the point where Amani or Aunt Wairimu, or worse, both of them, was injured. She began to look around for her uncle as her cousin rambled on about a crowd, and Amani being thrown to the front of the car. *Oh God, it's him* she thought as her brother's name brought her attention back to what her cousin was saying. She was slightly relieved when he didn't mention Amani getting hurt, but when he got to the part where her brother ran out of the car into the crowd, she knew it was him. She heard the words, 'he was bleeding from the head,' 'Mommy kept shaking him,' and 'he wouldn't wake up,' and she shot up from her chair and began to shout her brother's name as she ran through the emergency room.

She hadn't gotten very far when a nurse took hold of her.

'Where is he?' she screamed, and startled the doctors and nurses in the already hectic emergency room. 'Amani Mwangi, my little brother.'

The nurse led her to the cubicle. Jommo turned around as soon as she walked in. He was covered in so much blood Wanja recoiled. There were tears in his eyes as he held Wanja back and tried to explain to her what she was about to see, but she fought past him.

Aunt Wairimu broke down as soon as she saw Wanja. There was even more blood on her. It covered every inch of the front of her body. It dyed her skin and dripped from the hem of her skirt. She wondered if perhaps her cousin was mistaken and it was her aunt who was in the accident.

Then she saw him.

He was lying still on the bed. His eyes were closed and he looked so at ease that he had to be asleep.

'Wanja, there was an accident. He's gone.' Her uncle's voice broke and Aunt Wairimu stepped back and collapsed into a chair behind her.

Time stood still. The room was frozen and silent.

In that tiny space, death owned the room, and they all knew it. It engulfed Amani's still body wider and deeper with each loaded, passing moment. And none of them could move or breathe or speak. There was only space for stillness and to watch death take their sweet boy.

'No. He's my little brother,' Wanja whispered, as if she would wake him up if she spoke too loud. Then she changed her mind and decided to wake him up.

'He's my little brother,' Wanja said, looking at his swollen head and shifting it slightly so that it wouldn't sit at such a weird angle. 'Amani—wake up small bro.' She touched his shoulder. He was cold. Why was no one bringing him a blanket. She remembered how it irritated him when she called him bro.

'I'm not a bro, I'm your brother,' he would correct her as he rolled his eyes.

'Amani—wake up, little brother.' She didn't notice the nurse who was standing behind her in case she fainted, or that there were tears in her eyes as well.

'Amani—' she touched his face. It was colder than his shoulder. 'Please bring him a blanket. He's cold,' she said to her uncle. She looked up when he didn't move, but he only stood staring at her. She needed someone to explain why Amani was so cold and what they were going to do to make him warm again. When her mind started to make sense of what happened, her body began to tremble uncontrollably.

She thought she would die from the pain in her chest.

She wanted to die from the pain in her chest.

Her little brother was dead.

# 14

## AFTER '07

### 1 JANUARY 2008

When Ngugi's car choked and sputtered to a halt, he was glad it was outside the Gigiri police station adjacent to the American Embassy. He was tired, hungry and frustrated: he didn't think he would be able to deal with any more curve balls.

His journey home from Embakasi should have been pretty straight-forward, he knew the back routes well and was careful to avoid potential trouble. More often than not, this meant that he would be driving off the main roads on muram roads that bore all manner of sharp objects planted on the roads by car jackers and thieves. He had three flat tyres already. When the same tyre was flat the second time, he was convinced that the repair guys at the gas station were ripping him off so he called for roadside assistance. As expected, all services were suspended for security reasons. The operator laughed when Ngugi protested and asked to speak with her boss.

'He's not here and if he was he'd say the same thing,' the operator said before he asked if he needed anything else and then hung up.

He'd been hesitant to ask for directions. The violence turned parts of the city into dangerous territory for outsiders, but by the time he was ready to get back on the road he was willing to take his chances. A young woman, about Wanja's age, approached him. Her directions were sketchy and unhelpful.

'Drive until you see the man repairing bicycles and turn left then right at the maize roasters. If you ask anyone from there they will help you,' she said, and continued on her way.

'Are there any buildings I should look for? *Hakuna watu wengi kwa barabara* so the roasters might not be there,' Ngugi called after the woman. She stopped and turned around. She was desperate to get to her mother's house in Roysambu and would be happy to show him the way out of here if he would give her a lift.

Roysambu would get him to the right side of town but he was still hesitant. She noticed this and spun on her heels. '*Sawa buda—shauri yako.*'

'*Sawa*, let's go.' She looked harmless enough and it would not kill him to have some company. She wasn't very talkative, which Ngugi was grateful for, but she did share that the house she and her sister lived in was robbed two days ago. They'd taken absolutely everything. Thankfully both she and her sister were out when it happened, but none of them wanted to sleep in the house. So her sister went to her boyfriend's place, and she was headed to her mother's house until the storm passed.

She waited in the car at a gas station as Ngugi got his spare tyre repaired. He watched her from outside the car, expecting her to start snooping around the car for valuables, but she hardly moved and he felt like an idiot.

'We'll have to use some back routes,' she said when they

were moving again. 'To avoid the road blocks and police.' Ngugi was more than happy to oblige. She directed him past the sections of road where the tarmac ended, and she encouraged him to keep going when the road was so narrow people ducked into adjacent shacks and corridors so the car could pass through.

'Is this really a road?' He opened his window and folded the side mirror so that it didn't get knocked off as pedestrians squeezed past him.

'Yes, this is where I live. I know it,' she said with a defensive pride, and once again Ngugi felt foolish.

'Turn here,' she pointed to the left, and Ngugi executed the narrowest turn that led to a dead end at a massive garbage heap.

It happened really fast. The girl calmly climbed out of the car and Ngugi assumed that she was being proactive and helping him navigate out of the tight spot she'd put them in. Then she whistled and half a dozen men emerged and began to strip his car of its side mirrors, wheel caps, indicators and headlights. One of them managed to get the boot open and was off-loading the spare tyre Ngugi just repaired as well as the tyre kit. Another reached in, opened the passenger side door, and continued to rob him.

'*Leta simu tafadhali?*' Ngugi reached into his pocket and handed over his phone.

'*Asante mkubwa. Na* wallet?' Ngugi obliged and the man pulled out the last of his cash and handed the wallet back at Ngugi.

'I'll leave you these so you don't have to replace your documents.' The polite robber then sifted through the glove compartment and slammed it shut before he reached into the back seat and grabbed Ngugi's bag. He opened it and the smell of vomit made him pull the zipper immediately.

'Ahh. What's in here?' he twisted his face

*'Nguo chafu,'* Ngugi said, and the thief returned the bag and got out of the car.

'Happy New Year,' he leaned into the car and said before he disappeared into the maze behind him.

All in under a minute. Ngugi didn't know whether to laugh or cry. A now familiar feeling crept up his throat and he swung his door open and hurled out the watery contents of his already empty stomach. He started to worry he would have to abandon the car and get home on foot when he heard the sound of cars whizzing past. It sounded like it was coming from the other side of the garbage dump. He heard it again, and this time something caught his eye in his rearview mirror. The road was right behind him. He was at the end of a narrow road leading off the tarmac to the garbage dump. He inched forward to straighten the car and then reversed on to the paved main road and stayed on it until things began to look familiar.

Most of the roads were open, and those that were not had police and military officers diverting traffic. The sound of gunshots didn't startle Ngugi anymore. When he heard them, he simply turned around and drove away from the sound. He didn't plan to pass by Wairimu's house, but when he found himself in her neighbourhood he decided to check that they'd been able to get out. He was glad to see that things were relatively calm, and even happier when the security guard at the entrance to her estate confirmed that he saw them leave early the previous morning and they had not been back. The guard recognised Ngugi and lied that he had voted for him, and then he glanced at the car and asked if he had trouble on the way. Ngugi just smiled and thanked the man for his support.

Within minutes, guards from the hyper-securitised American embassy in Gigiri were standing at Ngugi's car, demanding that he move it as it was a potential threat.

'I've run out of petrol so if you want me gone, you will have to help me move.' Ngugi shrugged his shoulders knowing full well that they couldn't leave him there. They grumbled as they swung their rifles over their shoulders and pushed the stalled car into the gates of the Gigiri police station.

This station was familiar territory and Ngugi was promptly greeted by some of the policemen on duty. There was more activity than usual at the station. An old buddy of Hon. Muli's explained that they were now taking cases from Mathare because the stations could not keep up with the amount of work that was coming in.

'The media are reporting death tolls of up to eight hundred in just four days, but that might be for Nairobi only,' he said. 'This is not just violence—it was a full blown civil war, worse than the struggle for independence—if you ask me,' he said, and Ngugi listened in horror. What he'd been through seemed like child's play compared to what was happening in other parts of the city. 'Are all your people safe?'

'Yes, *wako salama*,' Ngugi answered, wanting to be home now more than ever. He couldn't bring himself to ask if there was anyone available to drive him home because he knew that this man would bend over backwards to help him. He was about ten kilometres away from his house and it would take at least another hour to walk home. He was exhausted, but it wouldn't kill him.

He bid the police at the station farewell and told them

he would be back for his car in a few days. He avoided the questioning gazes as he left without greasing the policemen's palms as was customary during visits such as these. As he walked home, he realised that while he'd used this route home countless times, he'd never been on foot. There were things he noticed for the first time, like the reason people were always getting knocked down on this road was because there were sections with absolutely no footpath between the end of the tarmac and the riverbed. He needed a new lens through which to view his country.

Ngugi arrived to an empty house. He walked around enjoying the feeling of the cool tiles against his burning feet. He recalled his final moments in this house before everything fell apart. His argument with Wanja, the hundreds of supporters who sat outside to see him, Amani walking around the house with his amusing stickers, Kavata leaving...

It all seemed like centuries ago and in light of what happened since, it felt like water under the bridge.

He reached for the landline to find out where Wanja was. She didn't pick up and he looked around the house for signs that she had been there. Wairimu didn't pick up her phone either so he decided to try again once he'd washed the last few days off his body.

He heard voices in the house while he was in the bathroom. Wanja was back. Keen to see that his daughter was safe, he dressed up and called out to her as he walked down the corridor to the living room where the voices were coming from. He glanced outside as he passed by the front door and saw Wairimu's car in the driveway and wondered why Amani wasn't running down the corridor to meet him as he usually did.

In the living room, Jommo was standing by the window gazing out onto the balcony. The blood on his shirt and trousers had dried up and now looked like brown paint. Wanja and Wairimu were holding each other, rolled up into a tight ball on the sofa. Wanja's eyes were swollen shut and Wairimu looked like she had lost weight. Ngugi's nephews were resting on the sofa. They didn't stir when he walked in. He assumed they were asleep.

'What's going on?' He scanned the room for his son. Jommo began to speak, but Wairimu stopped him. She stood up and turned to face him. She was dressed in a hospital gown and was still holding on to the bag with her bloody clothes. She looked as if it hurt to be on her feet.

'Ngugi, please sit down.'

Ngugi studied her. 'Are you hurt?' he asked, directing the question to Jommo as well.

'No, I'm not hurt.' Tears filled her eyes.

'Is Amani napping?'

No one said anything.

'Wairimu, where is my son?' He looked around the room again.

Jommo took a few steps towards Wairimu and held her to support her. She shrunk away from him and hissed at him not to touch her. Jommo didn't bother to hide the tears in his eyes as he went back to his spot by the window.

'Ngugi, there was an accident on the way here yesterday.'

'Wairimu, where is my son?' Silent, exhausted sobs emerged from Wanja as she lay spent on the sofa. Ngugi's eyes were fixed on her.

'Ngugi, he's gone. He died. I am so sorry Ngugi....'

'What are you saying? He can't be dead...'

'He is. I'm so, so...'

'What are you fucking saying?!'

Silence.

'No,' at first a whisper, and then a scream.

Everything vibrated. He punched the cabinet that he was leaning on. No one tried to stop him as he punched the wall and knocked vases off their pedestals. He overturned the chest of drawers filled with Kavata's china.

Wairimu stood in the way of his rampage. Numb to the shard of glass that sliced her foot. Ngugi tugged at the curtains until they snapped off their hooks and sent framed photos flying off the walls. The children huddled into an even tighter ball with their heads buried under their hands. Wanja stared at her father with tears streaming into her wide open mouth. Ngugi looked at her and paused for a splintered second; Jommo used the moment to step in.

'Kids, let's go to the bedroom,' he said as he lifted Wairimu out of the way and placed her on the couch. Then he opened the balcony door and took one step towards Ngugi. It would have been easy for Jommo to restrain Ngugi, but he didn't dare. His grief fuelled a strength that no muscle ever could.

Ngugi looked at Wanja and then at the rampage he caused. Amani's stickers were still all over the house where he left them.

His loss was not his alone. Wanja was still looking at him and for the first time in years, he saw the little girl he was once obsessed with protecting. He rushed across the room to his daughter and held her, and they sobbed together and shared a moment they would both remember as the worst of their lives.

\*\*\*

Cheptoo's dreams were filled with so many images of burnt bodies that sleep was pointless. She lay down on a mattress on the floor of the Red Cross office with three other volunteers from different parts of the country who were afraid to sleep at their hostels in case they were attacked. She went over the events over and over again, each time forcing herself to remember a new detail. Like the buttons on her blouse and how they popped when she was struggling to get through the crowd. And the man who nudged the man next to him to look at her exposed bra. Or that she initially thought that the men behind the burning of the church were policemen, because they used handcuffs to bind the one man to the church. And the shoes—so many shoes. And the way they melted and glued toes together so that she was forced to pry them apart in order to tag them.

The medic insisted that Cheptoo see a counsellor as soon as they got back to base. Cheptoo was reluctant at first, but eventually agreed, desperate to remove the images from her head.

The counsellor was a woman about the same age as Cheptoo, who explained what she could do for her.

'I am here to help you release and guide you towards healing. But you will need to do the healing yourself,' the counsellor said, going on to say things like 'embrace the pain' and 'surrender to the process' that made Cheptoo distrust her. Cheptoo didn't want to heal herself; she didn't ask to be chased away from Nakuru or to come to Eldoret and see the things she saw. She wanted the people responsible to undo everything or pay for it.

'Have they arrested anyone yet?' she asked. The counsellor shook her head. Cheptoo went back to the images in her mind. 'I can help. I saw all the men who did it. I can help the police find them.'

The counsellor spoke in hushed tones as if she was sure that someone was listening. 'That's not a good idea, you would be putting yourself in harm's way.'

'What do you mean? I was there. I saw them.'

The counsellor explained that it was more complicated than it looked. There was no telling if the police were involved in the massacre or not. How could they explain why none of them were there to stop them, or that they hadn't gone to the church even hours after the massacre? Cheptoo hissed when the counsellor told her that she should leave it to God to deliver justice to the people who did this.

'Don't even start with that God nonsense. How could God let all those children die? Were you even there? Are you mad?' Cheptoo began to cry again as new memories flooded her mind.

The counsellor could not stop Cheptoo from going to the police. It was the right thing to do after all. She only asked that she consider the repercussions carefully. If she hoped to see Thuo and her children again, then recording a statement was not the wisest thing to do.

Cheptoo considered the counsellor's words, but they did not deter her. The next morning, she went back to her and told her that she still wanted to record a statement, but she also wanted to leave Eldoret. She needed to get back to Nairobi and if the Red Cross could help her, she would record the statement and leave Eldoret immediately.

There were no Red Cross vans coming or going to Nairobi. Supplies were being transported by helicopter, and there was no way they could get her onto the helicopter unless she was in critical condition, and even then, the hospitals in Nairobi started turning away patients because they were beyond capacity. The best they could do was get her on the train which was due in Eldoret later that day.

Before she left for the police station, all the volunteers gathered to bid her farewell. Some of them hugged her tight and applauded her courage. She smiled back, thinking to herself that they must not know the meaning of bravery because she felt like a coward. A medic changed the dressing on her wound and gave her a bag with some painkillers and bandages.

At the police station, the counsellor insisted that a policeman take Cheptoo's statement inside the Red Cross van, away from any curious ears. He joined them in the van with a sheet of paper and reluctantly wrote down her statement.

Cheptoo relayed every detail she could remember. How many men she saw with jerry cans of petrol; what the man who handcuffed the incinerated man was wearing; what he looked like; how many men brought them snacks. She noticed the policeman stopped writing well before she was done speaking.

'What's wrong?'

'I have no more space,' he held up his sheet of paper.

'I can wait, go get more. Bring many—I have a lot to say.'

'You can continue, I will remember everything and write it down later.'

'I can wait,' Cheptoo said, and her counsellor shifted, uncomfortable in her seat. The policeman didn't move.

'Carry on Cheptoo—we don't have much time,' the counsellor offered.

When they were done, the policeman thanked her, folded his sheet of paper, put it in his shirt pocket and climbed out of the van. They then sped towards the train station, and on the way there, the counsellor encouraged her to go to a police station in Nairobi and record a second statement once things calmed down.

*** 

Kavata was desperate for a toilet. She'd spent the last hour trying to figure out if she would be able leap off the train at the next stop, run into the bushes to pee and then get back on. She convinced herself that she would be able to do it in three minutes, then she saw the number of people waiting to get on the train when it slowed to a stop in Eldoret. There were three maybe four times as many than there had been in Webuye and she was sure that if she got off the train, she would be stuck in Eldoret.

Most people rushed towards the 'others' cars and her fellow passengers kept gesturing for them to move on to other cars. There was no more space on this one—but they kept coming and clambering to climb on. Kavata stood up when someone grabbed her legs and tried to use them to climb on.

'There's no space—try the next one,' she said, but they continued to jump up, holding onto her hand, and eventually she and a handful of other passengers relented and helped as many people onto the car as they could. She pulled three women up when the train began to move again and the people on the cars were shouting at her that those were enough.

There was a woman with the entire right side of her face bandaged who was trying to get on. Kavata grabbed her arm and pulled her up. Kavata lost her footing for a moment and one of the men who was behind her had to help her get the bandaged woman on board. The woman thanked Kavata when she eventually caught her breath.

As there was now only standing room left on the train, they spent some time rearranging themselves. More people climbed onto the top of the bricks so that there was room for the rest to sit in two rows at the edge of the train. Kavata guarded the corner she sat in and refused to move when people tried to edge her out of the way, even if it meant having to sit with her knees hugged into her chest. Finally, when everyone had a space to sit or stand or lean, the man who appointed himself the prefect of the car made an announcement.

'*Sikilizeni*, especially you who are down there at the edge of the train. No one else can get on this train from now on. If you help someone up, you will need to give them your space!' He glanced over at Kavata as he spoke.

Four hours later, the train stopped in Nakuru and a few people hopped off, but no one got on and Kavata finally found space to stretch her legs. The woman with the bandaged face also shifted position and was now right next to her. Kavata studied her, wondering why a Red Cross volunteer was travelling on the train.

The bandages covered half of her face, but Kavata didn't need to see it to recognise that the woman was crying. It was evident by the sudden jerking of her shoulders. Kavata reached into her bag and pulled out a packet of Kleenex that she bought in Atlanta. The brilliant white of the tissue looked so out of place on the train. When the woman turned her face to thank Kavata, they both gasped.

'Mama Wanja! *Haiya*, what are you doing here?'

'Cheptoo, what happened to you?'

Their questions came fast and overlapping. Then relief at seeing a familiar face washed over them and they shared a heartfelt but awkward embrace that, like the Kleenex, felt misplaced. They spoke fast, trying languages on like new shoes, switching between English, Swahili and Kikamba before they realised that they had both learned to speak their husband's language, and whispered to each other in Kikuyu.

'Why are you here?' Cheptoo asked.

'*Heh*, Cheptoo... where do I even start?'

'Where did you go when you left?'

Kavata took a deep breath, allowing herself a moment to craft an iteration of this story that would suit Cheptoo, as well as her inevitable audience. She glazed over the reasons for her departure, dwelling more on her journey back from Atlanta.

'So that Sunday when you disappeared, *ulienda ng'ambo*?'

Kavata nodded. 'And you? Where are the children? And Thuo?'

Cheptoo held one finger up. 'Did Thuo drive you to the airport?'

Kavata nodded and braced herself. 'But I didn't tell him I was going. I didn't tell anyone. He just dropped me and left.'

'And why didn't he tell them?'

Kavata remained silent. Cheptoo's anger took over.

'He was arrested. He has been in jail for I don't know how long. Because he took you to the airport.'

'*Pole sana* Cheptoo. There must have been some mix up.'

'There was no mix up. You were reported missing and he was the last one to see you, so they put him in jail.' Her voice grew louder with each word. 'Why wouldn't he tell the police that?'

'Surely he must have.'

'Then why didn't they release him? Someone must have bribed the police.' They were both clear who this *someone* was.

'Of course,' said someone behind Kavata, and she turned around and gave them a death stare.

Cheptoo abandoned Kikuyu. The unfamiliar tongue could not carry the anger that she felt for the primary source of all her agony. Kavata was trying to calm her down but that only made her angrier.

'Don't tell me to be quiet; you don't know what my life has been like because of you. I have been to hell. I have seen devils. So many that I know they will be following me until the day I die. Don't tell me to be quiet!' The passengers on the train were now silent and listening, thankful to have something to entertain them during the journey.

'What did you tell him? Why wouldn't he say something? Thuo is always so ready to do anything for you, it's like you have him under some spell.' Cheptoo somehow found room to shift so that she could look at Kavata properly with her unbandaged eye. 'If Thuo was not in jail, I would never have to leave Nakuru and see those horrible things I saw in Eldoret. Look at me!' She held up her bandaged arm and pointed to her face.

'Cheptoo, I swear to you I didn't mean for any of that to happen. There must have been a mix up. I promise as soon as we get back I will find out exactly what went wrong.'

'What will that do now,' she sneered and tried to stand up. She winced and sat back down, but suddenly she couldn't bear to be seated next to Kavata. It felt like she was one of those people who were killing their neighbours.

Kavata begged Cheptoo to calm down. 'Please

understand, I told him to go right back home...' Cheptoo wouldn't hear it. She spat back at Kavata and someone shouted at her to be quiet, they were trying to sleep.

Cheptoo stood up again, using the passenger on her left as a crutch, but the woman shoved Cheptoo away, who fell back down, landing heavily on Kavata. There was peace on the train before she got on it and more people were getting irritated. '*Wewe*, some gratitude for the woman who almost fell off *akikupandisha*,' the prefect barked.

Cheptoo calmed down, but her face was so tightly twisted into a frown that a section of her bandage came off. She turned to the woman on her left.

'Please just exchange with me.'

'*Sawa*.' She stood and stepped over Cheptoo, then sat in between the two women.

Kavata started to speak but bit her tongue. She needed space to organise her mind and the train needed silence. She leaned over and glanced at Cheptoo, who was sobbing again. She reached over and squeezed her knee and placed her Kleenex in her hand.

'Chep, from the bottom of my heart, I am sorry,' she said and sat back, making sure to make eye contact with the woman next to her.

\*\*\*

The only reason Schola was able to leave Kisii for Narok was because she had money. Nairobi was the only place she could go to so she paid a policeman ten thousand shillings to get her as close to the city as possible. That place happened to be Narok. She pulled the money out of her brassiere and climbed into the police truck in between two policemen, who were young enough to be her sons. They kept trying to start a conversation with her but she remained silent. Each time they encountered a police check manned by the army and a soldier questioned why a civilian was travelling in the front of a police truck, Schola would have to reach into her blouse and pull out a bribe.

For the entire length of the journey, the driver rubbed his knuckles up and down Schola's thighs as he changed gears. She ignored it at first, not wanting to give him the benefit of knowing he was bothering her, but this only served to encourage him further. She had enough of it and began to protest, when a foul stench took over the fresh air and forced her mouth shut.

A humongous pig ran across the potholed road that cut through acres and acres of wheat. The policeman on Schola's left insisted he wanted to go after the swine. They could slaughter it when they arrived at Narok and have a feast. He jumped out of the van and ran toward the pig like a child chasing bubbles. His prey went towards some houses he assumed were the farm workers' quarters, and when he got there he called out to his colleague to come and help him. They hit the jackpot. There were at least a dozen pigs over there, he said, milling about feeding. They could sell them for a fortune.

Then he looked closely at what they were eating and began to shriek. His colleague ran after him.

The greedy pigs were happily feasting on decomposing human bodies. Their carcases were strewn all over the clearing at the front of the houses, limbs and disjointed torsos discarded further away by the indiscriminate pigs. Schola sat in the van listening to the two men screaming, but she didn't move from her spot in the car. She wished that she had taken the driving courses that Kavata used to insist on. Then she would have left the foolish men there. Instead she waited in the van. She knew what the men saw; she now knew the thick smell of stale death. It made her even more eager to get home.

The one who found the bodies was in shock; he trembled and mumbled incoherent things for the rest of the drive. The driver got tired of stopping every few metres so his colleague could vomit and insisted that he travel the rest of the way with his head hanging out of the window.

'That's what you get for always thinking with your stomach, you *jinga*,' he said, acting unfazed by the whole thing, but Schola could feel his body stiff and frozen next to her. He even stopped molesting her upper leg because he couldn't stop his hand from trembling as it travelled from the gearstick to the steering wheel and back.

The Narok police post was deserted, the only other vehicle there looked as if it hadn't moved in years. All she saw on the way to the police post were scattered tin shacks and mud houses along the road. She just needed to get to the town, but didn't know how far it was, and the quickly receding sun was telling her that it was not a good idea for her to go find out.

Her money was no good in Narok. No matter how much she offered them, the policemen were adamant that they would not go any further. They both had never been to Nairobi and they had no business going there. It was two days since she left Kisumu and now the sun was setting on the third day. She followed the police men into the converted four foot container that served as their police post. They were setting up their beds for the night, two thin mattresses in opposite corners of the room.

'How much do you want to take me to Narok town?' There was no response from the driver. His colleague was already fading into a stuttering sleep.

'*Afande*, please help me. What am I supposed to do in this bush?' The driver shot up from his mattress.

'Mama, you said you wanted to go to Narok. This is Narok and yes it is a bush. That is why people do not travel through it at night.' He pointed to a chair behind one of the two desks in the room. 'If you want to go to town, you will have to wait until morning.' He turned and faced the wall. 'And lock that door, unless you want us to be attacked.'

Schola had been unable to find sleep since her journey began, but somehow she found herself dozing off as she sat in the wooden chair with her head resting on the low table. The silence outside was a welcome and soothing break from the gunshots that punctuated the darkness of the past few nights.

She wasn't sure how long she was asleep, but it didn't feel like it was morning yet so she wondered why the driver was waking her up.

Before she knew it he grabbed her by the arm, lifted her off the seat, and threw her onto his mattress. Only then could she see that he wasn't wearing his trousers. She looked over to where his colleague was still fast asleep. She opened her mouth to scream but he held her by the neck and told her to be quiet unless she wanted to be fed to the pigs as well. He then pushed a disgusting cloth so far into her mouth she was sure she would swallow it. She gagged as her throat rejected the coarse fabric, but when he tore her blouse open and squeezed her breasts before he stole the last of the money from her, Schola understood that swallowing his dirty socks was the least of her problems.

Schola didn't make a sound the entire time. She willed her body to turn to stone so that she wouldn't feel a thing, but she felt each thrust slice through her like a thousand splinters lodged in the exact same place. The sound of the other policeman snoring and mumbling a few metres away from her as she got through her rape added to her torture. She hit the floor hoping that the sound would wake him up, but he grabbed her hands and pinned them to the side of her body and gave her a final warning before he went limp. She hoped he was dead. His grip around her wrist loosened and she pushed him off her. He looked at her, with eyes full of questions, when he dismounted her and there was blood on his penis and on her thighs. She made sure to hold his gaze. She wanted him to look at her, to see the woman that he defiled, even if the feeling of his eyes on her made her want to peel off her skin. He avoided her gaze and stood up, picking up the wet sock she spat out. He walked over to the waterless sink and wiped himself with the sock. He lingered there with his back to her as if he hoped her to be gone when he turned around.

Schola rose from the ground and looked at the wad of cash beside his boots. She picked it up just as he turned around and when he began to protest, she stood up straight and shot him a stern glance that dared him to steal anything else from her. She turned around and opened the door, grateful she didn't lock the padlock. It was a struggle, but she fought through the pain so she didn't limp when she left the police post in the dead of the night and walked down the road she hoped would lead her to Narok town.

She had not gone very far when she heard her attacker calling after her, warning her that there were bandits and wild animals on the way. She kept walking, step after painful step. There was nothing left to lose.

***

Thuo spent the night at his doorstep, hoping that Cheptoo would emerge. When his neighbour found him in the morning, she told him that Cheptoo left before the election and had not been back since. News of Thuo's arrest spread around Kangemi, so he was not surprised when people avoided his gaze as they walked past him. No one was quite sure why he'd been arrested, but it didn't matter. He soon noticed that people generally were not talking to one another. Certain parts of Kangemi experienced their own versions of hell and people were silently coming to terms with it.

Thuo's neighbour was happy to let him wait at her house for a few hours, but when it began to look like Cheptoo would not be home anytime soon, she suggested that he get a locksmith to let him in. Thuo had no money to pay him, but in these times, televisions and radios were precious possessions so the locksmith was happy to hold on to Thuo's radio until he paid his bill.

He paced around their home. It was unbearable without his wife's presence and the silence soon grew suffocating. Thuo walked around the neighbourhood asking if anyone had seen her lately. He received gruff responses; no one was interested in helping him find his wife. Everyone had lost something. Thuo fought to keep thoughts of his children out of his mind—that would certainly throw him overboard. He thought sitting in a jail cell was the worst thing that could have happened to him, but he was wrong. At least there he could assume that his family was safe and waiting for his return.

When he could take it no longer, he gathered whatever valuables he could find around the house. Their VCD player, a few disks, their clock off the wall and went back to the locksmith. He asked him to loan him some money and hold these items as well until he was able to pay him back.

When Thuo arrived at the Mwangi residence, the gate was unlocked but he wasn't sure if he should ring the bell or let himself in as he had done daily for over fifteen years. He walked up the driveway, uncertain of what he was doing or what to expect when he got to the front door.

The house showed no signs of life. It was past noon but the outdoor security lights were still on, a sign that Schola wasn't there. She was the only person who would have heard from Cheptoo. Memories of what happened the last time he was on this driveway caused him to hesitate. Fear gripped his limbs so that he was unable to move, and made him realise that he might be re-opening the door to his prison cell by being here. He looked up at the home of the people he thought he knew so well, and for so long, and marvelled at how suddenly everything had changed.

He noticed Ngugi's car missing from the driveway and that offered some relief. He remembered how stupid he was to imagine that his life would improve fundamentally when Ngugi won. Part of him wanted to confront him, to ask him why he treated him so badly and allowed him to be locked up for so long. But as he stood in Ngugi's driveway, he realised that it didn't matter. These people were not his family and an explanation from them would mean nothing because things, he realised now, had changed. There was nothing left for him here. He turned to walk away.

'Hello?' Thuo's first instinct was to run, but he turned

around instead. Jommo walked towards him. Thuo had never seen Jommo at Ngugi's house. He looked so out of place with his ill-fitting clothes and tired eyes.

'Oh, Thuo. *Ni wewe, habari.* Are you working today?' The news of his arrest hadn't spread as far as Thuo thought.

'No, I don't... I came to look for Schola.'

Jommo looked at him blankly.

'*Mama wa kazi.* Is she in?' Jommo shook his head.

'*Sawa.*' Thuo turned around to leave.

'*Ngoja* Thuo. Ngugi might need you today. I don't know if you have heard but we have some bad news.' Thuo turned around.

'*Ni* Amani. There was an accident. *Amefariki.*' As soon as Jommo said it, he realised that he didn't want to be the one to share this news with one more person.

'Ah ah. That can't be.' Thuo's voice was barely audible. His mind rushed to thoughts of his own children. 'Amani?' Shock forced him off his feet and he lowered himself onto the pavement, cradling his head in his hands. Jommo brought him a glass of water.

'*Poleni sana.* Where are they?' Thuo said when he found words, gesturing towards the house.

'Wanja is here. Kavata is on her way back from—' Jommo hesitated, '—her trip.'

'And *Mzee*?'

'He arrived yesterday. He is inside.'

'*Na watu wako?*' Jommo enquired about Thuo's family, if they were safe and if they were affected in any way by the violence. Thuo explained that he remained in Nairobi, leaving out the details of the reasons why, and that he had not heard from them in days.

'How can we help? *Uko na simu?*' Jommo asked and Thuo

thanked him but he was hesitant to involve any member of Ngugi's family in his problems. He didn't want to be here. He didn't know if he was still welcome. He couldn't find the words to explain this to Jommo, but he didn't need to. Jommo sensed it and decided to call Wairimu out to speak to him. Since the accident, she had busied herself doing chores around the house and Jommo knew that she was trying to keep her mind occupied. She would be happy to help Thuo. Wairimu came out of the house almost immediately, with eyes as drained as her husband's.

'Thuo, I'm so glad you are here.' Her voice was shallow and strained.

Thuo stood to greet her, and she threw her arms around him. Thuo remained still, unsure what to do with the gesture.

'Please, come in Thuo.' She led him to the house.

'*No, wacha* I come at a better time,' Thuo declined.

Wairimu held his hands. 'Thuo, I don't know the details of what you have been through and I can't begin to even imagine. But on behalf of my brother, I am very sorry. I know he will not say this to you today or any time soon because of what has happened, but know that I know that he regrets it. You don't have to forgive him, but please come inside and let us find a way to help you find your people. Please. We don't want to lose anyone else. So we're going to help, *upende usipende.*' Wairimu didn't even bother to conceal her tears.

Thuo sat tentatively at the dining table as Wairimu plied him with food and drink, then handed him a phone to call whoever he needed to. Schola's was the only number he could remember. Schola was now at a refugee camp in Naivasha trying to get to Nairobi but it was impossible. The highway was closed and no one would risk the journey. She told Thuo how she lost everything in Kisumu save for the clothes on her back and Thuo never heard her sound so desperate and defeated. There was no fight left in his friend's voice. They spoke for several minutes while Jommo and Wairimu stood by, waiting and hoping for the smallest morsel of good news.

Jommo was instantly on the phone and calling everyone he knew in Rift Valley and within a few minutes, they'd called Schola back with news that a friend of Jommo's, who owned a fleet of tour vans, would be at the camp to collect her before the end of the day. He would bring her home.

Ngugi walked into the living room and Thuo stood and looked straight at him. The pain in Ngugi's eyes was unbearable, so he lowered his own eyes.

Thuo's voice broke as he spoke; his mind was filled with thoughts of his own son. Ngugi stared at him as if he was looking at a ghost, his mouth gaping like a fish out of water. Thuo began to think that he was wrong to think that he could be here when Ngugi pulled him into an embrace and apologised over and over and over again. There were tears in both men's eyes when they disengaged.

# 15
## THE LONG WAY HOME
### 2 JANUARY 2008

Schola shed her first tears when she heard of Amani's passing. She pleaded with Thuo to tell her that he was lying, to take back his news—she didn't want it.

He took the long way home from the shopping centre where Jommo's friend dropped Schola off. He wanted to spend a few moments with her and give her a little more time to process her loss before she encountered everyone else's grief. Ngugi, Jommo and Wairimu already gave him more help trying to find his family than he expected but Thuo decided to go to Nakuru as soon as he got Schola home safely.

The stories he heard about the extent of the violence were beyond belief, and regardless of attempts to convince him that it was a bad idea to go to Nakuru, he could no longer sit back and hope that his family would appear.

Schola had not spoken with Cheptoo since the day Thuo was arrested. This was the final confirmation that Thuo needed before he set out for Nakuru. When he told Schola of his plans, her tears for Amani grew into sobs for Thuo. She begged him to stay, to give it a few more days.

'Thuo things are very bad over there. I was only able to come back safely because of Jommo's friend, and even then it was difficult. I've lost one of my sons, Thuo. Please, I cannot bear to lose another,' Schola begged.

He already left word with his neighbours to call him if Cheptoo arrived in Kangemi, and gave them the number of the phone Ngugi gave him to use, then delivered the same instructions to everyone in Kangemi who knew his family. He taped a note to the door of the house as well, just in case they arrived when Kangemi was sleeping.

When Thuo and Schola arrived at the Mwangis', she went straight to her quarters, grateful to have snuck in unnoticed. Everything in her room was just as she left it, and the familiarity of it brought her great comfort. She stripped, wrapped her clothes in a plastic bag, and slid them under her bed. She would burn them later. She was exhausted and her body was screaming out for rest, but she bathed, put on her pink chequered uniform and made her way to the kitchen.

Wanja was the first person she encountered, but there was no sign of the poised young woman Schola left behind a few days ago. Now she appeared lost and confused, just the way Amani looked when he woke up from his afternoon nap. When Schola wrapped her arms around her and shared condolences, Wanja didn't respond. She just stood there and shrugged when Schola released her and asked her if she wanted anything to eat. Wairimu came into the kitchen and told Schola that she didn't need to work right away, but Schola insisted that she wasn't tired.

'I slept for the entire journey from Naivasha,' she lied, but both women could see that she winced with each step.

She didn't ask what happened to Kavata's china cabinet, and the rest of the furniture, when she swept across the house trying to make it look as unchanged as possible. She suspected that nobody would eat, but decided to cook a meal anyway. There was hardly anything to eat in the house. She still had some money; she could picture it in the paper bag with the clothes she planned to burn. She decided to ask Thuo to drive her to whatever market was open, but when she looked for him and realised that he wasn't sitting on his stone in the garden like he usually did, she knew he decided to go ahead and chase death in search of his family.

Her voice shook as she told Wairimu what she suspected.

'Schola thinks Thuo has gone to Naks. Can you call your guy and see what things are like over there?' Wairimu woke Jommo up from his nap.

Jommo wasn't sure he could convince Thuo not to go to all lengths to find his family, or whether he wanted to. However, he was able to convince Thuo, who hadn't gotten very far due to the limited public transport, to come back and allow them to at least organise his transport.

'He can take my car; he needs to. He won't get far on foot,' Ngugi offered. None of them noticed him standing by the door.

By the time Thuo returned to the house, Jommo and Ngugi were sitting together and Jommo had made a series of calls. His sources in Nakuru confirmed that the violence prevailed, but because of the high police presence in the town, the damage was confined to the more rural sections of Nakuru. A curfew was in effect and many people were against it which he feared would cause more protests. The situation in the areas around Thuo's home was dire in the beginning, but the fighting moved on and things were calmer now. The only vehicles getting in and out of Nakuru were army trucks and relief vehicles. Jommo's contact would try and get to

Thuo's Aunt's home and check on his family. Thuo gave the man directions. Later that day, Jommo's contact reported that he visited Thuo's aunt. She was unharmed and was looking after Thuo's children, but they had not heard from the wife since she left for Eldoret. He would only be able to extract Thuo's family in a few days after tensions around the curfew subsided. Thuo's respite was short-lived. Why Eldoret? How did she get there? Where was she sleeping? Did she even have money still and, how could he ever live if anything had happened to her?

The airport was reopened a day ago, but it was still not fully operational. Flights took off filled with fleeing foreign nationals but hardly any flights were landing. The Americans issued a travel advisory against Kenya and the Brits, who claimed to be keeping an eye on things before they made any decisions, were discreetly extracting their citizens. There was still no sign of Kavata, and Ngugi was beyond worried. Hon. Muli would probably be able to locate her quicker than he could, but each time he thought about calling her parents, the grief and apprehension about having to share the news with Kavata stopped him. It didn't matter how many times he closed his eyes and tried to form the words he would speak to her in his head. It was too difficult. He could never be the one to speak the words he knew could break her for good. Yet he knew no one else should.

Hon. Muli answered the phone with his voice full of the sun; he was basking in Zanzibar.

'Ngugi, great to hear from you! We were so worried when we heard what happened in Machakos. But then we also heard that you were unharmed so we relaxed. Don't worry about the house. Mama insisted that we insure it years ago.'

Ngugi took a deep breath. 'Amani died,' he said, and his tears came suddenly and uncontrollably. It was the first time he uttered the words, and it felt like the first time hearing them as well. Hon. Muli was speaking, but Ngugi couldn't hear his words. He didn't even realise that Wairimu took the phone from him and put it on speaker phone. Or that the unrecognisable sound he was hearing was that of Mrs. Muli screaming in the background.

There was silence for a few moments before Hon. Muli ended the call. He would be back in Nairobi the following day to find Kavata. As Ngugi listened to Mrs. Muli wailing on the other end of the line, he could swear he was hearing Kavata.

\*\*\*

The train hadn't moved for over an hour and nobody seemed to know why. Kavata hopped off to finally pee and scurried back on to wait with the patient crowd. It occurred to her that they might be sitting there for days, waiting for some kind of explanation as to why their journey had come to a premature end. If there was something wrong, nobody would tell them because there weren't supposed to be any people on a cargo train in the first place.

Kavata stood up to look over the edge of the train. One by one, passengers were hesitantly disembarking, careful not to go too far in case the locomotive sprung back to life. Kavata asked the train prefect if he could see anything from the top of the bricks. He shook his head and said that these trains were known to break down for days. There was probably something wrong with the engine. That wasn't good enough for Kavata. She didn't know exactly where, but she knew they were stuck somewhere in Thika—less than an hour away from Nairobi. She was sure that they would be able to get home if they could just find their way to the highway.

She turned back to the train prefect and asked him if he could see the highway.

'*Si* it's just over here.' His bottom lip pointed westward.

Kavata looked over at Cheptoo—the woman who sat beside them had hopped off as soon as the train stopped as Thika was as far as she needed to go anyway. Cheptoo was dozing off. Kavata nudged her. 'I think we should get off here,' she said.

'Do what you like. I'm not going to just follow you blindly. I'm not Thuo,' Cheptoo spat. Kavata was starting to grow weary of her. She slipped her shoes back on to her now slightly less swollen feet.

'I am getting off here. This train might be stuck here for days and I need to get home,' Kavata said. '*Ata wewe* you can do whatever you like.'

'What if there is fighting here as well?' Cheptoo asked.

'We have to have faith that there isn't. We've come all this way.' Kavata didn't wait for Cheptoo to respond before she strapped her bag to her back and leapt off the train.

'Just over here' ended up being about eight kilometres away and the two women were exhausted by the time they saw any sign of the Thika-Nairobi highway. By this time, Cheptoo was beyond furious at Kavata; she wouldn't so much as glance in her direction. But all was forgotten when they saw that beautiful stretch of grey tarred road.

With no landmarks or signs to guide them, it took a while to figure out which side of the highway led to Nairobi and which one went back to Thika. When a *matatu* with a Thika sign on it whizzed past them, the two women ran across the highway and stood on the other side of the road, sticking out their arms at every passing car.

After a while they came up with a hitch-hiking system of sorts. They saved their energy and enthusiasm for cars that they could see had space for them.

'Look out for cars with two passengers. One passenger won't stop for strangers—it's too risky. And three passengers are too many,' Kavata instructed.

They waved and jumped and pleaded for these cars to slow down but the drivers did everything they could to avoid looking at them. They adjusted rear view mirrors that were already perfectly aligned, fidgeted with their radios, checked phones or simply looked dead ahead. Kavata recognised the gestures. She had often been the one speeding past strangers in need, convinced that they were robbers posing as hitch-hikers. It would be a miracle if anyone stopped.

Cheptoo was resting on the side of the road peeling off the bandages on the side of her face. They were moist and unsightly and did nothing for their cause. Kavata gasped when she saw how badly injured Cheptoo's face was. She went over to help her with the clean bandages.

'What happened, Chep?' Kavata tried one last time, this time in Kikuyu. There was a long silence before Cheptoo spoke, starting with the day after Kavata left.

She begged Thuo to tell the police what he knew about Kavata's disappearance and he refused to speak, even when he was being called a criminal. She told her about the days and nights she spent looking around the house for clues of where Kavata might have been so that she could take them to the police and have her husband released. Knowing that if it was up to him, Thuo would remain locked up for months, unable to speak up for himself. She explained that she only left for Nakuru at the very last minute, because she didn't want to leave her husband rotting in a jail cell. Then, she talked about the violence and killing in Nakuru. About the church in Eldoret.

Everything that Kavata wanted to say felt inadequate, because it was. Cheptoo's rage was justified. Everything Cheptoo's family suffered over the course of the past week was linked to Kavata's choice. She put Thuo in that cell and Cheptoo would never have been in Eldoret and by herself if Thuo was with her. She would never have seen all those things.

'I'm sorry. I'm sorry. I'm so so sorry. I don't know what else I can say, Cheptoo. I am sorry.' She continued chanting her apology and Cheptoo just looked at her. 'It was never my intention.'

'Of course you can say that. It wasn't your intention but it is your fault. And for me there is no difference between those two.'

'I understand your anger, Chept...'

'Don't say that. You never will. You know Mama Wanja, I have always admired you. Even before we met, when Thuo was working for your parents. You were always determined not to take after your father. I was happy when Thuo told me you took a job teaching. I thought that it must be so nice to work because you want to, not because you must. I can tell you today that you are nothing like your father.'

The words brought Kavata some respite.

'You are not like him, but you are not better than him either. Muli is aware of his power and he knows how to use it. He knows its danger, but you don't. You don't understand that every little thing you do affects *sisi watu wadog*o.'

'Please don't call yourself small. There's noth...'

Cheptoo rolled her eyes. 'But we are. We are small people because we are always the ones shifting our lives so that yours can stay the same. When you tell Thuo to work late, it means that we don't get to eat on time, or at all, because he always brings home our supper. When you tell him to lie to your husband, and I'm sorry but I don't care why you did it, Thuo will do it even if it means that he sits in jail for a few days. And you don't know it because you never have to live with the consequences of your choices. Just like these politicians who will never suffer a day because of this election. *Kuna watu na viatu*—stop denying that to yourself.'

Cheptoo waited for a response but Kavata didn't have one. It was a truth she never considered. She hung her head.

Cheptoo softened her voice. 'I know you didn't think of these things. And I know you are a good person. *Lakini* you must open your eyes. You and I are not the same, and to think that we are is stupid. Kenya *ina wenyewe* and you are one of them.' Cheptoo wished that Kavata could experience, even a fraction of, the turmoil that she had been through. But being there now, in the midst of all her sobs and sorries, she admitted to herself that she didn't wish suffering on Kavata; Thuo was as much to blame for her situation as Kavata was, and in her heart of hearts that is what irked her the most. Cheptoo reached into her bag and pulled out the same pack of Kleenex Kavata gave her and held her hand until the tears passed.

'So, *kwani* what happened to make you go away like that? Without saying anything?' Cheptoo asked.

Once again, Kavata found herself editing her thoughts

for a Cheptoo-appropriate version. The reasons for her departure which felt so fundamental a few days ago, now seemed so foolish and childish that she couldn't bring herself to speak of them.

'Things became difficult because of the whole election thing.'

'Why did you allow Ngugi to work with your father. *Si kwa vbaya* but you know that Muli is just using him. He looked so foolish *na vile* he can be a good leader.'

Kavata smiled, of course Cheptoo would get it. 'I didn't allow him. I was never asked.'

'*Ai, kwani* he just went and did all of this without you knowing.'

Kavata nodded.

'As in behind your back?'

'Basically. By the time he told me, his paperwork had already been accepted.'

'*Ngai*, Me, I would have killed him.'

'I wanted to. That's why I left.'

'And why did you come back?'

'*Si* he lost,' Kavata said. Both women giggled and it felt wonderful for a moment.

'*Heh, Kazi kwetu.* We need to chop those horns of theirs,' Cheptoo said. '*Twende.*' She stood and helped Kavata up.

They contemplated walking the rest of the distance home, then an idea snuck into Kavata's mind and she walked towards the pineapple farms and found a bush to hide behind. Cheptoo assumed that Kavata went off to pee again and continued trying to flag down cars. Moments later, when Kavata emerged fully dressed in the Sunday suit she shrugged off in order to fit in, Cheptoo saw what she was doing. She let Kavata take over the hitch-hiking, and a few minutes later they were sitting in a young woman's air conditioned car. The three women listened to the radio on the way home. The man on the radio reported that protesters had uprooted the train tracks in Kibera and therefore no trains were able to pass through Nairobi.

# 16

## THE DARKNESS

### 3 JANUARY 2008

The woman was going to Westlands and was happy to get both Kavata and Cheptoo as close to home as she could.

'This is just fine. I am so grateful.' Kavata held the woman's hand for a moment and looked in her eyes. 'Now you know where I am, please come for tea whenever,' she said.

'No worries, I've been driving alone for so long it was nice to have some company.'

Kavata turned to Cheptoo.

'Are you sure you don't want to come out here. We can try and find him from here.

'No. If you find him you can bring him home. You know where we live,' Cheptoo said. 'And if he is not home. I will find him,' she added and ended that conversation.

'Please hoot,' Kavata asked the driver when she saw the padlock on the gate. She climbed out of the passenger seat and Cheptoo got out to take her place just as Schola emerged from the house. She spotted Kavata and rushed back into the house for the keys to the gate. Cheptoo paused when she saw Schola, finding it odd that she was there. She stood, one foot in the car.

Schola rushed back out towards the gate, keys trembling in her grasp. Avoiding Kavata's gaze, she was close enough to confirm that it was indeed Cheptoo she saw in the car. Cheptoo got out of the car as Kavata waved the woman away.

'*Habari* Schola.'

'Ehh.' She couldn't look her in her eye and Kavata recoiled, sure that Schola was also furious with her.

'Ngugi *yuko*?'

Schola hesitated, 'Ehh.'

Kavata walked past her and Schola waved Cheptoo towards her. Kavata didn't see the two women melt into each other, but she heard Schola mention to Cheptoo that Thuo was out of jail and had been sick with worry for her.

Kavata saw Ngugi's face first. She saw the pain there and it was unbearable. She looked away, to his body which was frail. She could tell that he was forcing it to stand strong for her. She was drawn back to his face, finding more courage each time to hold his painful gaze for a moment longer before she looked away to her daughter and Wairimu. Jommo was there, and their children, and her parents. It was there in their faces as well. She searched for Amani. And looked back at Ngugi and stopped walking. And watched as Ngugi broke down. Wordlessly. Piece by piece.

*Where is Amani?* She was screaming at Ngugi and he was shattering. And Wanja was sobbing and her mother was wailing and Schola was running but no one was telling her.

*Where is Amani?* Her eyes were locked on Ngugi—his on her. He was walking towards her and she didn't want him to.

'Don't do it.'

He kept coming.

'Don't come here.' Her hands covered her face. They felt cold on her skin.

He kept coming. He held her.

She couldn't breathe. Her eyes were elsewhere. Everywhere, looking for her son.

'I can't breathe.'

Her eyes were everywhere when she found her breath and screamed so loud only darkness remained.

# 17

# SUNDAY LUNCH

## 4 JAN 2008

A ny pastor you asked would tell you they never saw their churches as full as they were that Sunday, a week after the violence hit the country. After days spent watching the country burn, hearing gruesome stories of hurt, loss and heartbreak, Kenyans drew back the curtains of their homes and unlocked their doors. They left their radios tuned, televisions on and internet connections streaming while they dusted off their hats and polished their cars, listening for the news just in case the fragile calm they were experiencing ruptured once again and forced them to abandon their Sunday plans. When they were sure all was well, they packed their families into their cars and did what they were taught to do in the face of a crisis. They went to church.

'Let us pray.' Pastor Simon's solemn call lifted those around him to their feet. They shuffled into a circle and held hands. The Mwangi balcony was too small to accommodate the hordes of people who arrived to offer their condolences after Pastor Simon informed the congregation of Amani's passing during the service. He encouraged his followers to keep the family in prayer as they dealt with the loss of not only the election but their son as well.

The tents that were sent away after the meeting with Ngugi's advisors were brought back to accommodate the hordes of mourners who gathered to pray for the family and plan the funeral. Kavata refused to stand for prayers, but the pastor didn't protest. Next to her, the pastor's wife wrapped her arm around her shoulders and pulled Kavata towards her. There was so much to pray for, Pastor Simon didn't know where he should start. He prayed in long, drawn-out sentences with gaping silences that left the room unsure of whether or not it was time to say Amen.

Kavata didn't pay much attention until the pastor mentioned her dead son's name. She stopped bothering to hide the tears that now flowed relentlessly from her eyes. Her tears watered the grief which grew inside her like yeast and she didn't want it to end. She listened to the pastor's prayer carefully and wanted to stop him and tell him he was praying for the wrong thing. He didn't need to curse the evil spirit that caused boys to disobey their parents and rush out to an angry mob. Nor did he need to ask God to grant her family peace and understanding so they may come to terms with their tragic loss. The only thing Kavata wanted the pastor to pray for was that Ngugi and Wanja and everyone else was freed of their sadness. She wanted the pastor to pray for her family's grief to somehow be transferred to her so she could carry it until it killed her. These thoughts occupied her often. She would spend hours trying to work out ways to heal her family, how she would feel all their pain for them. She wanted to. She grew obsessed with her pain. She embraced it. She allowed it to wash over her and force her to stay in bed for days on end. But she hated to see everyone else feel sadness as if they too lost a son. Other people's sadness irritated her.

So she eventually stayed away from everyone, but couldn't escape Ngugi.

Amani's short life filled her Betapyn-induced sleep every night. She remembered the pain of his birth and the overwhelming silence that filled the delivery room the minute her body released him. And that strange warmth of his body fresh out of her womb that was both familiar and unlike anything else. How his face began to form expressions only she could understand, and utter words only she could hear. His first steps when he tumbled and fell and then burst out into the most enchanting giggles. She dreamed about how jealous she felt of Amani's friendship with his sister, and how curious and in awe he was of his father. How he would lift them all out of the darkest day when he laughed that beautiful, forced laughter that would grow and swell and infect them all.

She knew her dream was close to the end when images of those final days would come to her. Those days when she would force herself not to think about what it meant to be leaving him behind when he was so young. When he would say something that would make her want to tear up her passport and stay home. That angry and disappointed look he gave her that spoke of how he didn't understand why she just wouldn't let him go to the supermarket with her, even if he promised not to throw a tantrum at the chocolate displays near the lines at the check-out counters. She would sob and sob at this point of her dreams, and then be filled with a quiet, empty silence that was only broken by the dawn of a new damn day.

The first few seconds of her day were happy. If she was with Ngugi, in their bed, at home, then everything must have worked out. Then something would remind her that

Amani was gone and that she wanted to die. It was a different thing everyday: her tear soaked pillow and the sound of Ngugi sobbing; Wairimu sitting beside them on their bed, begging them to sit up and eat something.

Kavata and Ngugi hadn't uttered a word to each other since she returned. What could they say? She would often catch Ngugi staring at her in that lost way he did when he needed her to point him in the right direction. It was a look she had not seen in ages and for the months before she left, it was all she wanted to see when she looked at him. Now, she didn't know what to do when their eyes met or when they both lay in bed with their backs to each other, trying to stifle their sobbing.

Wanja refused to be involved in any of the funeral arrangements and banished herself to her bedroom every time the steady stream of guests arrived at their home.

People milled around Kavata at the end of the prayers, muttering inaudible words and placing clammy hands on her shoulders. They spoke in hushed tones, regretting that they were visiting the Mwangis under such circumstances but relieved to be in the company of people other than those that they had been holed up with for days. Anne, Wairimu, Cheptoo and Schola busied themselves with making sure that there was always food and drink for the steady stream of mourners. Anne hadn't left the family's side since the moment she heard about Amani from the nurse at the hospital who eventually answered Wanja's phone. She had been there in the background everyday, but she wasn't even sure Kavata had seen her, or anyone around her for that matter. She saw Kavata's grief, everyone did. It was the largest thing in the room and it only seemed to grow bigger each time Kavata moved, or tried to speak, or looked at her daughter. Anne was helpless against it—she couldn't reach her friend. So instead, she poured tea into a dozen cups a minute, and tried to anticipate the family's every need.

Later that Sunday afternoon, once the crowd thinned, Wairimu called the family in to the living room for an update on the funeral plans. All the city mortuaries were full so his body was still at the hospital morgue, but they were insisting that the boy's body be moved immediately. Hon. Muli had pulled whatever strings he could to get him a space at a prestigious funeral home, but this would only happen in three days. They would need a place to keep him until then.

'Bring him here,' Kavata said. The sound of her voice startled them all. She sounded three times her age.

'We can't do that,' Jommo began to say, but quickly backed down when all the women shot him a stern glance that instructed him to stick to his lane. Hon. Muli took over to explain why this was not a good idea.

'Bring my son home!' Kavata insisted. 'I don't want him there by himself. He must be terrified.' No one was going to treat her son as if he didn't have a home, she said. Kavata would bring Amani home if it meant buying a freezer to put him in.

Ngugi was the first to realise that his wife had every intention of bringing their son's corpse home. He knelt down on the floor before her, and cupped her face in the palm of his hands and kissed her tears as they fell from her eyes.

'Will you drive me to the hospital?' Kavata asked when her sobs offered her a moment to speak.

Ngugi nodded. 'Let's go see our son.'

# EPILOGUE

There was no record of the statement she gave in Eldoret when Cheptoo went to the Criminal Investigation Office in Nairobi, and volunteered herself as a witness to the church massacre. Although there were about four thousand people standing around the church on the day that it was burned down, only four people were arrested in connection to the burning. They were acquitted for lack of evidence despite Cheptoo's testimony. The handcuffs that were used during the massacre bore a police serial number attached to a policeman in Eldoret. He claimed that they were stolen the week before the church massacre.

Mrs. Muli blamed Hon. Muli and all his politics for the loss of her only grandson. She held it over his head for months, and eventually banned Hon. Muli from ever touching politics. Further, she wanted to move back to Machakos and insisted that he build her a well that actually worked, so that she could finally explore farming.

Thuo worked for the Mwangis for two years before he quit

his job to open a tour and travel company with Jommo. Today they have over sixty buses across the country. They named the company Amani Tours and Travel.

Lawrence's entire family died during the violence. Kavata offered to pay for his ticket home for the funerals. He came home but never went back to Atlanta. He now lives in Nairobi, where he runs a successful online service through which Kenyans abroad can buy their families back home goats, chicken and other livestock to slaughter during family celebrations and public holidays.

Jane now lives in Germany, where she works as a caregiver at an old people's home.

Wanja got used to seeing her name in the newspaper once she decided to stay in politics. She became the party's Communication Manager and was at the forefront of their campaign for the next election, which ODM lost, again. Rigging was alleged. Hon. Muli still refuses to speak to her, and so does Sally. The void left by Amani's death was too severe to endure so she eventually moved out of her parents' home, but visits often to help nurse her mother out of her unrelenting sadness.

Ngugi never ran in another election. However, an old drinking buddy from his university days ran for office and was elected as the youngest president in the country's history. The new president appointed Ngugi the Cabinet Secretary for Land, Housing and Urban Development. The first thing Ngugi did was make sure that the houses that he built for the National Housing Council were re-allocated to the people for whom they were intended.

Kavata spent the next two years of her life saying no. At first she refused to climb out of her bed, or bedroom or house. She said no to any kind of comfort or anything that promised to offer any kind of relief from her pain. When the darkness eventually lifted, she found the voice to say no to all the things she'd hated and had been tolerating and saying yes to. Like garments made from brightly printed fabrics, unexpected house guests, carrots. Her darkness lifted some more when she decided to say no to any kind of contact with her father. The first time she even allowed herself to consider saying yes to anything was on a Saturday morning three years after Amani's death when she woke up to two dozen men in brown overalls packing up all their belongings to move them into the modest apartment Ngugi had rented for the both of them. It was located as far away from Nyari as he could find.

A few years after the violence, Schola stumbled upon a newspaper article that focused on the sexual abuse that was inflicted during the violence. She read that at minimum, 40,500 women and children were raped between December 2007 and June 2008. The article shocked her. After years of keeping her secret and feeling incredibly lonely about this, she discovered that there were 40,500 people just like her. It was comforting and heartbreaking all at the same time. Some people in Kisumu tried to find her when they discovered her vandalised shop. They said that it must have been a mistake that her business was attacked. That the attackers must have had a personal problem with Musa. That it was probably a robbery gone wrong. A year later, she heard that someone had taken over her shop—they just walked in and took it.

She didn't care. She was never going back. Schola passed away in her sleep four years after she was raped. In a letter to Cheptoo, she explained everything that had happened to her in 2007 and slipped the title deed to her shop into the envelope. 'It is yours if you want it,' she wrote.

The post-election violence carried on for the first few weeks of 2008 and only ended when an image of the leaders of the opposing parties shaking hands was beamed onto any working screen across the country on February 28th 2008. They signed an agreement for shared power, but by this point an estimated 1500 people had died as a result of the violence, though it is suspected the number is much higher. Many of those killed were shot in the back. The police continue to deny that they were the cause of these deaths, even if most of the armed protesters fought with machetes and *pangas*. According to the Ministry of State for Special Programmes, 663,921 people were displaced by the violence. Many of them were resettled elsewhere and, to date, have yet to reclaim their homes and businesses. Many still live in camps set up for the internally displaced, waiting to be resettled. No one is sure when this will happen. An estimated 78,000 houses were burnt in the country. Each time there is an election in Kenya, more people die and more people are displaced. The Electoral Commission of Kenya was disbanded soon after the 2007 election. The chairman of the commission was widely blamed for the violence. Four years after the election, he spoke to the media and said that he still did not know if Kibaki won the election fairly. He also said that he had no regrets over the 2007 polls. He never lived to see the next election.

# ACKNOWLEDGEMENTS

This was never the book I set out to write when I moved to Cape Town in 2012. Often, as soon as I would reveal to a new acquaintance that I was from Kenya, the next question from them would almost always be, 'How are you guys doing after that election?' Each time I'd say, 'We're fine, I guess,' and each time I questioned if we truly were. This questioning led me to revisit the post-election violence that we'd been unofficially told to accept & move on from. So, thank you to all those who asked if we were okay—I am still uncertain that we are.

Many hands and hearts have touched this book over the course of the seven years it has taken to create it and I am grateful to everyone who has guided and supported this long, precious process.

I am grateful to all the women who have come before me.

To my mother, Joyce Njeri Njunu, the hardest working, the most selfless woman I know, and the inspiration for everything I do; and my father, the late Isaac Njunu Koinange, who loved hard and dreamed big. Thank you for the never-ending faith and sacrifice. I owe everything to you!

Thank you to Imraan Coovadia, my grad school supervisor—you nurtured the physical and intellectual space for this work to emerge. To Peggy Jean-Louis, Maia Lekow and Chris

King, for opening up your spaces in Lamu and London when I needed to escape it all and write. Brittani Smit saw the potential in this book when I didn't and graciously reads everything I write before it goes into the world—I do not take this for granted.

Gratitude to Dina Segal and Christine Jacobsen, my dear friends and the unfortunate proofreaders of the first draft of this book. This version is much better—I promise! My literary agent, Jayaprirya Vasudevan, signed me before she read the manuscript—if that's not a show of faith then I don't know what is. Thank you!

I am grateful to Professor Chege Waruinge for a generous and truly inspiring conversation on the top of that hill that we all love, and to Sandra Chege for lending me her father for a few hours and for being my most stable and consistent sounding board. Gratitude to Tanner Methvin at Africa Centre and Angela Wachuka, my business partner, surprise copy editor and friend for trusting me to build a world where my art and my work can co-exist in an (almost) perfect harmony. To my editor, Cherise Lopes-Baker, the entire team at Jacaranda Books and Bunk Books and to Otieno Owino whose notes truly elevated my work, I thank you.

I have an incredible network of friends who are consistently guiding me to greatness; Atemi Oyungu, Kwame Amoafo, Porgie, Sofia Rajab, Kaz, Janet Thuo, June Gachui, Fikile Mthwalo, Wambui & Wanja Kibue and all the others that I cannot list here—may we be great together!

And finally, to my siblings Barbs, B, Mbiyu and Shee, and

my seven nieces and nephews, above all these things is the love and gratitude I have for you. May we always find each other.

# ABOUT THE AUTHOR

Wanjiru Koinange is a Kenyan writer, born and raised on a farm on the outskirts of Nairobi with her four siblings. Her articles and essays have been published in print and online platforms, including Chimurenga and Commonwealth Writers. She holds a degree in Journalism and Literature from Nairobi's United States International University (USIU) and a Masters in Creative Writing from the University of Cape Town, the product of which is her debut novel, *The Havoc of Choice*. When she isn't writing, Wanjiru is restoring Nairobi's iconic public libraries through Book Bunk—a social impact firm working to convert neglected public libraries into inclusive spaces of art, learning and community. Find her at wanjirukoinange.com